AWAKEN

An Amarah Rey, Fey Warrior Novel

Harmony A. Haun

ISBN: 978-1-7363432-0-3 Paperback
ISBN: 978-1-7363432-1-0 e-book
ISBN: 978-1-7363432-4-1 Hardback

First edition January 2021
Second edition March 2021
Third edition March 2022

Author Contact: harmonyhaunauthor@gmail.com

An Amarah Rey, Fey Warrior Books

AWAKEN

FEY BLOOD

DARK TEMPTATIONS

DEDICATION

This book is dedicated to my loving husband, Luis. He is the one who encouraged me to write this book and bring my characters and this new world to life. He encourages me in all my endeavours, is my number one supporter and biggest fan. Thank you for always believing in me, even when I don't believe in myself.

AWAKEN

An Amarah Rey, Fey Warrior Novel

Word Definitions

All "The Unseen" words are English words translated into Estonian. Click on each hyperlinked (ebook) word to listen to the pronunciation from Google.

Alfa: Alpha

Beeta: Beta

Esimene: First

Kaitsja: Protector

Konsiilium: Council

Libahunt: Werewolf

Maa Family: Earth Fey

Müstik Family: Mystic, First Fey

Õhk Family: Air Fey

Täiskuu: Full Moon

Täitjad: Enforcers

Tulekahju Family: Fire Fey

Valvur: Guardian

Vanemad: Elders

Vesi Family: Water Fey

Võitleja: Warrior

Võltsimatu: Pure

Amarah Rey Series Playlist

Listen to the entire series playlist here: Spotify

There's Got to Be More

Rock You Like A Hurricane by Scorpions

Everything around me is fuzzy. All around me, people are running, screaming, scared. I can feel their fear like it's a live wire sending electricity loose in the air. I can hear them, sense them, but for some reason, I can't see them. Why can't I see them?

I don't run.

I don't scream.

I'm not scared.

I imagine myself standing in the middle of a bright glowing white light. A Heavenly light that is so pure nothing evil can stand against it and it will protect me. I know the Devil is coming, pure evil is headed straight for me, but I will stand and fight. He's coming. I could feel it. This is it. It is time to fight!

"Our Father, who art in Heaven, hallowed be thy name…"

I open my eyes and let out a shaky sigh. The parking lot of BBVA Bank, where I work, is now empty. I slipped into a familiar and frustrating daydream while waiting for my car to cool off. The heat of the late July weather has sweat forming between my boobs. You

---

know, good ole humidititties. girl problems. I thank what lucky stars I have left that its dry heat and I don't have to also feel sticky along with my sweaty cleavage. Small victories, I guess.

I had this dream a few months back, but my mind keeps replaying it as if it's some kind of message but I can't for the life of me decipher it. I can never make out the details. Most dreams are vague like that. No matter how hard I try, I can only remember the intent of the dream.

To fight.

And oddly, the feeling of being at peace.

I had literally awoken from the dream saying the Lord's Prayer out loud. Even awake, in my darkened bedroom, I still hadn't been afraid. It should have scared me, right? I lower the air conditioner and immediately feel the heat slowly starting to push its way back into the car. I had just been sweating not a second ago, but now I have a chill and welcome the heat pressing against my skin.

A shiver runs through me that has nothing to do with the temperature as I finally pull out of the parking lot and start my twenty-minute drive home. I decide to call one of my best friends, so I can vent. I rarely enjoy talking on the phone, but with Cristi, it's always easy. Besides, this is our only way to communicate nowadays since she moved out of town and we can no longer get together for girl time. I don't have many friends and I miss her and our time together so much. Especially after days like today. It's true what they say about not appreciating what you have until it's gone.

"Hey, friend," Cristi answers excitedly. "How are you?"

I know she sincerely wants to know how I am because she is by far the most genuine, caring person I have ever met. She's a little on the sensitive and emotional side, which is the complete opposite of me, but she has a big heart and she uses every inch of it.

"Ugh. Not great," I say. "It has already been a hell of a week and it's only Tuesday! How are you?"

"I'm doing ok, just getting ready to make dinner. What's going on at work?"

"What's not going on at work is more like it," I sigh. "My boss has been on everyone's ass and people have just been so rude lately. I seriously don't know how I can hate and love people all at the same time," I laugh. "And I have just been feeling so lost, friend."

"I know what you mean about work, it has been rough for me too, and I've never understood why some people have to be so rude. What do you mean you're feeling lost?"

"Like, is this it? Is this all there is to life? Wake up, go to a job that doesn't satisfy you, go home, relax for a bit, go to bed, and do the same thing again the next day. Over and over. I'm so tired of it. I just feel so exhausted and unfulfilled," I sigh again. "There has to be more to life than this. Right?"

Cristi echoes my sigh with one of her own, "I wish I knew. I wish I had an answer because I am in the same boat as you. It would be nice if there were physical flashing signs in life directing us along the way," she laughs.

"Exactly! Why does life have to be so damn hard to figure out? I knew you would understand. I can't wait to see you this weekend. I can use a night out and a lot of drinks!"

"I understand completely. I wish I could do more to help but I cannot wait for this weekend, too! It can't get here fast enough. We'll both put this week behind us and let lose."

"Amen to that! Well, I'll let you get dinner started and I should pay attention to these awful drivers. I hate this traffic."

To be fair, Albuquerque traffic isn't that bad compared to places like Phoenix or Los Angeles but that doesn't stop me from complaining about it. Besides, yelling at people in the privacy of my car brings me great joy and is just the release I need from not being able to tell people how I honestly feel at work. They would fire me in 2.5 seconds flat if I said what was on my mind most of the time.

"Yea, I need to get up and stop being lazy, ugh," Cristi groans. "Drive safe, friend, and I'll talk to you later."

"I will. Ok, talk to you later. Bye." I hang up the phone and turn up the radio.

Burnin' It Down by Jason Aldean is playing. Jason Aldean is my absolute favorite artist but there's no way I'm listening to this song right now. I'm still hurting over a recent-ish breakup and every song seems to hit a nerve. I love how physical music is. It can trigger memories and all of the emotions and feelings a person has. Music is magic, but when you're hurting, it's dark magic. I change the station and *Rock You Like A Hurricane* by Scorpions comes on. Oh yeah, I can jam out to this one. I was born in 1985, but I love 80's music thanks to an older sister. I turn the volume up louder, drum my fingers on the steering wheel, and start belting out the lyrics. The car is always my very own concert stage.

I drive the rest of the way home trying to ignore the aching, empty hole in my chest as I let the music and lyrics consume me. I welcome the temporary distraction because I know that once I lay my head down to sleep tonight, I'll be haunted by the thoughts and questions that I have absolutely no answers to.

Who am I?

What am I doing with my life?

Awaken

Clubbin' by Marques Houston

It's finally Saturday night. Even when the sun is long gone, it's still warm outside. Inside the club is even hotter. We're dancing on the outside edge of a packed dance floor. I never enjoy being in the center and surrounded by so many drunk ass people. For one, I don't like being pushed, shoved, and stepped on. It brings out my inner bitch, which recently seems to always be just below the surface, pacing back and forth, ready to break through the surface at the first opportunity. Two, it's always too claustrophobic. I need to be on the outside of the crowd where I can breathe and escape easily if I need to. I hate feeling trapped.

We have to shout to hear each other over the thundering music, so we don't do much talking. It's almost too dark but the neon strobe lights placed literally everywhere keep it *just* light enough. Add in the alcohol and it's the perfect place to let loose and pretend that the people here are more attractive than they are in the broad, sobering daylight.

The thing I love most about coming out with Paula and Cristi is the fact that we never come out with the intent to pick up guys or to be hit on. We genuinely come out to dance out our demons. Besides, I've had enough of guys and their lying, cheating ass ways. They can *all* rot in Hell for all I care.

Yes, I'm jaded and yes, I hold grudges. It's one of my faults and no, I haven't tried working on it. I embrace it and hug it around me like a cozy blanket and sleep just fine at night. Well, I haven't been sleeping that great, but I swear it has nothing to do with the breakup. Ok, maybe just a little, but I shouldn't be thinking about that right now. I'm here to have fun I keep reminding myself.

We came out tonight because Cristi is in town for the weekend and I jumped at the opportunity to do *anything* to avoid being alone. Lately, I have just been feeling so out of place. I try to chalk it up to the break-up but it's so much more than that. It's a strange feeling in my chest that I can't explain. It's overwhelming and all I can focus on lately. Since I don't know what the Hell it is or what the Hell to do with myself, I distract myself as often as possible, but even my distractions are starting to need distractions. Something is wrong with me.

It's 1:00 a.m., we have been dancing all night, and my feet are starting to kill me in my high heels. Did I mention it's hot in the club? Not just hot, I can feel and touch the moist heat in the air from too many bodies in such a small space. The fog machines go off again adding more haze and mystery to the room full of strangers. I'm sweating, tired, and I can feel a headache coming on.

"I need a break and some fresh air," I yell to be heard over the booming base.

"Yeah, I could use some fresh air too," Cristi nods in agreement and fans her face with her hands.

"All right. Let's go to the roof," Paula says as she grabs my hand to lead us to the stairs that lead up to the rooftop patio.

I reach back for Cristi as we push past sweating bodies that smell like too much cologne and perfume, and underneath that, body odor.

Cristi is 5'5 which is one inch taller than me. We're all wearing heels, so we look taller than we are. Cristi is wearing black high heels, black leggings that cut off mid-calf, and a white shirt that has a low v-cut neckline that leaves her amazing chest in full view. It doesn't matter what Cristi wears, she can't hide the fact that she has big breasts, so why not show them off? I would if I had them. She locks eyes with me as I look over my shoulder, she smiles and her big green eyes are sparkling with happiness, and I can't help but smile back at her.

I grip her hand tighter as I return my focus to the body in front of me. Paula is 5'6 and athletic. She's wearing beige ankle booties and a dark navy-blue romper that has beige flowers on it. Her outfit is also very low cut in the front, but she doesn't have the chest Cristi does. No, she's all legs and ass. I could squat a million pounds for the rest of my life and never have an ass like hers but that doesn't stop me from trying.

Then there's me. I'm wearing black heels, black shorts, and a black crop top. Yup, black like my heart. The only color on me, besides my colorful vocabulary, is my fire red hair down to my ass, matching red lipstick, and some tattoos. I work out five to six days a week, so I have a nice body and decent muscle tone. I have some curves too, but nothing like Cristi or Paula. I'm just your ordinary, average girl. Most days I'm fine with who I am but lately I've been craving to be something more.

I shake my head and focus back to the amazing ass in front of me. Paula is now leading us up the stairs toward the rooftop patio. She sways her ass to the music as she pulls me up, and I hold solidly on to Cristi's hand behind me. Holding hands keeps us together and seems to be a deterrent to the single, drunk, fuck boy that likes to target a girl when she's by herself. Cowards.

Speak of the Devil and He shall appear. I roll my eyes at the two guys coming down the stairs, already anticipating their fuckery. As we pass them, one of them reaches out and grabs my arm. There's an electrical shock as his hand meets my arm. I feel something inside me open up and it feels like there's a gush of warm wind that comes from inside of me and explodes outwards. It feels like a dam breaking inside of my chest and I'm suddenly flooded with an intense warm and tingly feeling across my skin. It sends chills down my spine and my heart is suddenly in my throat. I hear the guy make a small gasp and I see Cristi shudder, but Paula seems unaffected.

I look at his hand on my arm, and in the blink of an eye, I swear his hands were almost skeletal with claws instead of fingernails. It scares the shit out of me and I'm frozen staring at his hand on my arm. When I can finally think again, I push those scared and ridiculous thoughts out of the way and make room for the anger that's always bubbling just below the surface. As I said, it's easy for guys to piss me off nowadays. The poor guy has no idea what he's gotten himself into.

"What the Hell?!" I yell as I yank my arm out of his hand. "What gives you the right to think you can lay a hand on me? Who the fuck do you think you are?" Great, Amarah, that was nice and subtle.

He puts his hands up as if to show he's harmless. Yeah right. I don't believe that for a second. I stare way too hard at his hands held up in the air but they're just hands.

"Whoa! What are you?" He asks.

What am I? What kind of question is that? Maybe he means, *who* are you? I'm not sure and I sure as Hell don't care. I'm pissed.

"You should learn some damn manners! Try approaching a woman with respect instead of putting your hands on her like you own her!" I yell in his face. "Fucking asshole. Come on, let's go," I start back up the stairs, not waiting for Paula or Cristi. Normally, I wouldn't have responded this way. At least I don't think so. I'm acting like every man is the one who broke my heart. I know it isn't fair, but I just can't bring myself to care. Men are disgusting.

"Damn, Rey! You let that poor guy have it!" Paula says, laughing.

Paula is always my hype man and backs me up and supports me, hands down, no matter what. I'm surprised that Paula and I have never been in a fight at a club. We aren't bitches, and we hate drama, but we sure as Hell didn't back down or take anyone's shit either. Case in point.

"Yeah, she did!" Cristi is laughing too, which in turn, makes me laugh. Her laugh is one of those laughs that is contagious. It always brakes through my moods and makes me feel better. "But he shouldn't have grabbed you like that. It would have pissed me off too. Are you ok, friend?" She touches my shoulder as she asks.

I smile even though I'm still feeling uneasy. I can't shake the feeling that something just felt...*off*. Had I seen claws? No way.

That's just the Fireball shots talking. Has to be the alcohol. So, why am I not convinced?

"Right?! He got what he deserved. Yeah, I'll be fine. He just pissed me off," I say as I rub my arm where he had grabbed me. I have a chill that has nothing to do with being cold. It's too hot outside to be cold, even dressed half-naked.

"I'm gonna run over to the bar and grab some water. Do you guys want anything?" Cristi asks. The rooftop patio has a bar, seating areas, and speakers so you can still hear what the DJ is playing inside but, thankfully, not nearly as loud.

"I'll go with you. I could use some water," Paula agrees. "You coming?" She looks at me and tosses her head in the direction of the bar.

I look across the patio and see the crowd at the bar and I'm just not up for it. I shake my head, "you guys go ahead. I'm gonna stay here and get some fresh air but grab me some water too, please. I'm getting a small headache." They nod in agreement and say they'll be right back, and I watch them walk off towards the bar and the buzzing crowd.

When I lose sight of them, I turn around and lean out over the rail, closing my eyes and take a deep breath of fresh air in through my nose and slowly blow it out through my mouth. I need to get a hold of myself. I stay standing with my eyes closed and focus on how the night air feels against my skin. The slight breeze stirs strands of my hair against my face. The crowd and the buzzing noise slowly fade away as I focus on myself, trying to clear my head.

The breeze turns cooler, pushing away the heat of the night and I welcome it. My skin has felt flushed since the encounter on the stairwell and the coolness of the breeze gives me welcomed chills and goosebumps erupt down my arms. This breeze feels…different. It feels physical. As if it had hands and those hands are caressing my skin. My heart beat increases and butterflies take flight in my stomach.

I suddenly have the feeling that someone is staring at me and standing way too close. I jerk my eyes open and began to yell at the person who decided to invade my space.

"Seriously?! What the…" but no one is there. I let out a shaky breath, "get a hold of yourself, Amarah. What is wrong with you tonight?" I ask myself out loud. Next time, not so much Fireball.

I lean back out onto the rail and watch the people and cars on the street below. People are in groups together, laughing and enjoying the night or walking to and from this club and the next. I can hear laughter, music, car exhaust, horns, and all the boisterous, joyful noise of a busy night. Everyone is out to have a good time and let go of reality for a few hours and the normality of it all allows me to finally start to relax.

Then I notice someone on the opposite side of the street. He's just standing there, alone and utterly still, leaning against the building. His arms are crossed over his chest and his feet are crossed at the ankles. He looks relaxed but his energy is anything but. It looks like he's trying to hide in the shadows but I see him. Boy, do I see him. I'm not sure why but I feel drawn to him. Out of all the people coming and going, I found him. It's like my eyes knew exactly where to look.

Wait, is he staring at me? I glance around to see if there is someone else he may be looking at, but no, I'm by myself. Everyone else is over by the bar. I look back at him, and although I can't see his eyes hidden underneath the ballcap, I know he's watching me. He holds his weighted gaze on me, and I can feel it as if fingertips are touching my skin.

He looks to be about 6' tall but at this angle and this far away it's hard to be sure. I can't help but appreciate how his black v-cut t-shirt fits him like a second skin. Even this far away, I can see how the shirt pulls tight across his massive chest and strains to contain his arms. His black jeans sit low on his waist and tuck into black boots. I realize he's wearing all black like I am and can't help but wonder if he's mourning a broken heart too? As magnetic as he is, even this far away, I doubt any girl has ever broken his heart. My eyes slowly make their way back up his body and I admire his strong, defined jaw and beautiful, full lips. I desperately want to remove his ballcap and reveal the rest of his face.

My heart starts to race, my skin feels hot and the new swarm of butterflies are going insane inside my stomach. Everything else around me fades. The world narrows and it's just him and I, staring at each other. My heart is pounding too loud in my ears and banging too hard against my chest. It feels like a caged animal fighting to break free. I have the urge to go to him. To touch him. To feel his muscles bulge under his skin. To press my lips to his. Just the thought of kissing him has me feeling things I've never felt. I swallow hard.

Who is he and why is he just standing there, alone, staring at me? Why am I reacting this way? I'm being ridiculous but my eyes keep getting drawn to those beautiful lips. I want...no, I *need* to taste him. I close my eyes as I imagine what he feels like. An involuntary groan escapes my lips and helps snap me out of my fantasy.

I open my eyes and desperately wish I could see his. I want to see what emotions are lurking in them but they're hidden in the shadows of the cap. It's been nine months since I broke up with my ex, and I haven't reacted this way to anyone. I realize I've been holding my breath, so I let it out slowly. Something touches my arm, I jump and give a high pitch, girly scream. Paula and Cristi are back from the bar.

"Holy shit! You scared the shit out of me!" I say with a nervous laugh.

"My bad! Here's your water," Paula says. "Why are you all jumpy?"

"You ok? What are you looking at," Cristi asks?

"There is this guy that is just standing there staring at me. Creeped me out! Look," I turn around to point to where he had been, but he isn't there. "What the hell? Where did he go? I swear he was just there!" I scan up and down the street, but there's no sign of him anywhere. Had I imagined it? Just like I had imagined the claws on the guy in the stairway? Seriously, what is wrong with me tonight?

"That is so strange," Cristi says as she looks over the rail with me, but there's no sign of him. It's like he just vanished.

"It's all good, girl. We believe you," Paula says, but she doesn't concern herself with searching for him. She sits down on the bench next to us. "My feet are killing me! I don't think I'm up for any more dancing tonight."

"Yeah, me either," I say. "I'm feeling really out of it. Next time, not so many shots of Fireball...Paula!" I smile because we both know I'm not serious.

She throws her head back and laughs, "Yeah, ok. Whatever you say, Rey!"

"Well, let's call it a night and head home," Cristi suggests. We agree and head out of the club and request an Uber.

We're dropped off at my house at almost 2:00 a.m. It feels good to be home. As soon as I lock the door behind me, I immediately feel better.

Safe.

A tightness that I didn't even realize I had in my shoulders since my encounter with the guy on the stairs finally eases. It's strange and not logical at all that we feel safe in our homes when all it takes is an eager person to break a window or door to get to you. Silly or not, I feel better.

I sigh in relief, kick off my shoes and scoop up the 15-pound ball of fur begging for my attention. My dog, Griffin, is the cutest Dachshund mix ever! He's black with brown paws and brown mustache and the biggest, floppiest ears. I dare anyone to change my mind. He excitedly kisses me and wiggles his entire body to let me know how happy is that I'm home. And he's right. The rest of the world and all tonight's craziness is locked outside. I'm home.

Paula and Cristi are sitting at the kitchen island talking about the night. I have an open concept so you could see the kitchen and living room both when you walk in.

The kitchen is spacious with a large island that seats five people. It has a corner sink surrounded by white cabinets, black granite countertops, and stainless-steel appliances. It's a recent remodel and I love it, but the real fireplace is still my favorite thing about this house. Something about snuggling up with a good book and a glass of wine next to a fire just does it for me.

I walk into the kitchen with Griffin in my arms and open a cabinet, searching for the ibuprofen. "Well, girls, another successful night out in the books! I had a blast, but this headache has got to go. Anyone need any?" I shake the bottle.

"I'll take a couple for my poor feet," Paula says.

"I'm ok," Cristi shakes her head.

I grab a glass from the cabinet by the sink and fill it up with water. I take my pills and then hand the glass to Paula. "My old ass is going to bed."

I hug them both and we all say goodnight. I can't put an end to this strange night fast enough.

3

The Handsome Stranger

I Knew I Loved You by Savage Garden

I'm so tired and so ready for my comfy bed. I want the ibuprofen to kick in soon. Griffin jumps onto the bed and waits patiently for me. I walk around the left side of my king-size bed to my closet. My closet takes up the entire wall with big, sliding glass mirrored doors. It isn't a walk-in, but it's still too much space for little 'ole me. I don't have a lot of clothes or shoes and the space is half empty. Just another glaring reminder of how single I am. I put my heels away and throw my clothes in the hamper. I pick up a tank top from my folded pajama pile and slip it on. I step over to the nightstand and pull out some boy short style underwear. Nothing fancy to see here, boys and girls.

Griffin's eyes follow me as I walk around the bed and into the bathroom. I brush my teeth and finish getting ready for bed. I can barely keep my eyes open as I slip under the comforter. Griffin cuddles up and I wait for him to settle before I place his little blanket over him. I grab the ceiling fan remote, hit high, and then click off the light. My ears are ringing from the noise of the club but I barely register it as sleep quickly pulls me under and I start dreaming.

The dream starts off with an insatiable thirst. I get up from bed and walk sleepily into the kitchen. I hit the light switch that turns on the lights under the cabinets and the kitchen illuminates in a warm, soft glow. I reach for one of the Snoopy mugs that are hanging on hooks above the coffeemaker and pour some water from my filtered faucet into the mug. It isn't cold but it tastes amazing as it quenches my parched mouth.

A sudden movement to my left draws my attention. I walk over to the sliding glass doors that leads to the back yard and peer out. It's dark outside and I can't see anything but my own reflection in the glass. That must have been what I saw out of the corner of my eye. My own reflection.

Something in my gut is telling me to go outside. No, not telling me, pulling me. It feels like there's a string tied to my ribs and it's being tugged. I unluck the door and it makes a quiet swish as I slide it open. As soon as I step out, the motion sensor light floods the patio with blinding light. Good thing this is just a dream or I'd have been wide awake by now. Come to think of it, I would be scared, too, if this wasn't a dream.

I walk to the far end of the patio where it meets the edge of the lawn. This is where I feel drawn to but all I can see beyond the patio are shadows. "Who's there?" I ask. My voice even sounds calm, kudos to me.

I sense him before I see him. He steps out from the shadows and into the edge of the light. I gasp and instinctively take a step back but I immediately want to move forward and close the distance between us. It's the same man from the street outside of the club but he's no longer wearing the baseball cap. Did he follow me home? Now, my heart is racing and I'm not sure if it's from fear or attractions and I have to remind myself that this isn't real. We dream about what's on our minds. This makes perfect sense. I'm obviously attracted to him so there's no hidden meaning here.

He's barely standing in the light, but God, he's gorgeous. I knew he'd be attractive but seeing him this close definitely proves it. And here come the damn butterflies again.

"Who are you?" I ask. "What do you want?"

His voice is deep and smooth and sends a shot of desire low in my stomach. "Please don't be afraid. I'm not going to hurt you. My name is Logan," he introduces himself, "What's your name?"

"Forgive me for not just believing you. You followed me home and most people just don't do that unless they're bad guys. My name is Amarah Rey, but since you're standing in my backyard, I thought you'd know more about me," I'm acting unimpressed when I really want to tell him anything he wants to hear. "What do you want?"

"I didn't follow you home...*exactly*. I seem to be drawn to you and your power," he says as he takes a few tentative steps forward.

I stay where I am and wait for him to say more but he seems to think what he said explains everything.

"Ummmm, ok. What power?" I ask.

"Your power," he shrugs and slides his hands into the pockets of his jeans, and damn, why is that the sexiest thing I've ever seen? "I don't know how else to explain it. It's just a part of who you are. It's inside of you. It *is* you."

"Ok, well, that's great. Extremely insightful thanks," I mock. "I'm pretty sure I would know if I had power and I sure as Hell would have used it a time or two if I had any, but...I don't. Looks like you've got the wrong girl."

Logan shakes his head and his eyes pierce me, "I have the right girl."

Why is my heart racing? His words and his gaze make me feel things I shouldn't be feeling towards a perfect stranger. I'm suddenly aware that I'm only wearing a tank top, no bra, and underwear, and I feel way too vulnerable and exposed. Heat slowly creeps up my face, and I hate that I'm blushing. This is a dream. I am in control and I refuse to be embarrassed! Besides, confidence is way sexier than embarrassment.

I tip my chin up in forced confidence, "ok, well then, what do you want with it?"

"I don't want anything with it. I am Kaitsja, Protector. I have been protecting your people for centuries. You don't need to be afraid of me," he says with a cocky smirk and an air of confidence as if everything he's saying isn't the craziest shit I've ever heard. Hell, as attractive as he is, I'm tempted to stand here and let him talk crazy to me all night!

"All right, Logan," I draw out his name for emphasis. "I hate to break it to you, because you seem to be enjoying this, but you're not making any sense at all. I have no idea who *my people* are. Do you mean humans? Or us poor females that need a man to protect us?" I say sarcastically as I cross my arms and rolled my eyes.

"Your people, your ancestors, are Fey," he's studying me now as if he's trying to decide if I'm being serious or not. "You really don't know who you are, do you?"

"Fey? You mean like Fairies?" I chuckle.

Logan sighs and runs his right hand through his chocolate brown hair. It immediately falls back over his brow but it's not quite long enough to get in his eyes. The muscles in his arm flex with the motion and I'm not at all unhappy with my magnificent view. The dim light still manages to illuminate his creamy caramel skin. It doesn't escape me that he's made out of two of my favorite things.

Chocolate.

Caramel.

He looks good enough to eat but how does he taste? My mouth is watering and it takes me a second to realize he's still explaining things to me.

"There are several Families of Fey, and yes, Fairies is a word that has been used to describe them. The Fey are vital to the survival of humans, and right now they are losing the war against the demons." Logan genuinely seems worried and thankful didn't notice my little drool fest.

"Your power is…potent and strong. It's like nothing I've ever felt before. I had to find it. I had to find *you*. You could help us win the war." He walks closer to me, "your power called to me. *You* called to me, Amarah. Don't you feel it?"

He's so close to me now, invading my space with his large body and his intoxicating energy. He's taking my oxygen and making it hard to breathe. One more big step and I can reach out and touch him. I want to. I want to run my hands up his arms and over his chest. I want to feel his muscles under my hands. My eyes are doing what my hands want to do, roam over his body. My gaze lingers on his lips again, but now I can see the rest of his face.

I look up into his eyes and gasp. My heart skips a few beats as I'm frozen, entranced in the most beautiful green eyes and darkest lashes I've ever seen. They're green with hints of yellow like a rolling, wild field with the sun shining down on it and I'm lost. I'm utterly lost and I never want to be found ever again. He's the most perfect man

I've ever seen, and if I thought it was hard to breathe before, now it's impossible. I should be terrified of this strange man in my backyard but I'm not. I want nothing more than to throw myself at him, give him everything I have and learn everything about him. Discover every inch of his skin. This man is all-consuming and that scares me in a whole other way.

I somehow manage to compose myself. Crossing my arms, I hold them tight to my body so they can't betray me, but they're itching to reach for him.

"I'm sorry, but you don't seriously expect me to believe all of this, do you? You're talking about power and Fairies and war! I mean, what war? None of this makes any sense."

"Then you'll need to convince yourself." He reaches his arm out and puts his hand up, palm facing towards me, "put your hand out and mirror mine."

Humoring him, I do as he instructs. We're still far enough away that my outstretched hand, and his hand, have about an inch between them. Even his hand dwarfs mine. I imagine him wrapping those strong hands around my waist and lifting me easily. The sheer size of this man has my heart racing and desire pulling low in my stomach.

I pull my eyes away from our hands and my mind out of the gutter. I have to clear my throat before I can speak, "ok. Now what," I ask, skeptically.

"Let go of your fear and doubt, Amarah, and concentrate on yourself. Feel the power inside of you. You can't run from it or ignore it. You *are* the power. Concentrate."

I'm thoroughly confused and starting to think he's certifiably insane, but I listen and give it a try. What else do I have to do? I close my eyes and focus on myself. At first, I can't really feel anything. I don't have a single clue as to what I'm doing or how to do whatever it is I'm supposed to do. Then I feel a cool breeze against the palm of my hand and travel up my arm. It feels like wind but also so much more...alive. It's like it can actually touch me, like it's caressing me. This breeze surrounds me completely and then seems to travel inside of my body, touching me in places no hand can ever reach.

Something stirs inside of my chest. My mind flashes back to that spark I felt when the guy at the club grabbed my arm. I feel that spark again and hold onto it with my mind. It sits like a comfortable weight in my chest. I imagine blowing on the spark and watching it grow brighter, stronger. I imagine pulling this spark out of my chest and I feel the warmth tingle down my arms. It's foreign but it's...me. It's inside of me but it's alive and I intuitively know that, as a part of me, I can control it and use it as an extension of myself.

I send my warm power down my arm and out of my hand and into Logan's. I feel it mingle with the cool breeze from whatever Logan is doing. I feel it as solidly as if I'm touching him physically but it's just this strange power.

Mine exploring him.

His exploring me.

And it feels right.

It feels new and familiar at the same time.

Logan's hand finally makes contact with mine and the instant his skin touches mine, something inside of me clicks into place. It feels like my heart explodes in my chest and there's a flood of blood in my chest. It fills up every lonely nook and cranny.

Every missing piece made whole.

Every broken piece healed.

Two halves of one whole.

Complete.

Then he intertwines our fingers and the firmness and strength of his grip sets my skin on fire and I sigh in bliss. I want to feel his strength laid out on top of me. Dominating me. Claiming me. I'm hyper aware of every inch of my skin and how close I'm standing to Logan but I'm also completely relaxed.

My eyes are still closed but I feel when Logan take the final step towards me bringing our bodies almost flush against each other. He overwhelms my senses. One man shouldn't take up so much space and air. I can feel the heat coming off his skin as if he's a furnace, and if I get too close, I'm bound to get burned. I finally open my eyes and see that there's a faint white glow coming from me and a faint blue glow coming from Logan.

Logan smiles and his words come out a bit strangled, "your eyes are like honey fire. I've never seen anything like it." His free hand caresses my cheek and I automatically lean into his touch, his glowing green eyes hold mine like there's nothing else in the world to see. His eyes are my new gravity and he's the world. Everything else slips away except for him.

His eyes are devouring me, his thumb gently strokes my cheek, "beautiful," he says softly as his eyes fall to my lips.

"Logan," I barely breathe his name and my lips stay parted in anticipation.

I can feel the hard rise and fall of my chest as I wait for him to kiss me. It's an urge like I've never felt before. How can I crave him already when I haven't even had a hit yet? My need is desperate. I feel it clawing at my chest. He licks his lips and slowly, so agonizingly slowly, lowers his head towards mine. His lips are full and inviting, calling me to them without saying a word. My free hand gently touches his chest to steady myself as I tiptoe to meet him. I can feel his heart beating rapidly in his chest, matching the frantic speed of mine. His eyes finally close as he turns his head slightly closing the last of the distance between us.

His scent invades my senses, clean and woodsy and utterly masculine. My heart feels like it's going to explode, my skin is tingling all over, and it feels like an eternity before I feel his lips fall on mine. It's a soft, tentative touch, barely a brush of lips. My body is trembling with the balance of being on my toes and the need for him to take my mouth with his. I want to scream at him…*please!* I want to beg him to kiss me but I have no breath to speak.

With one hand still on my face, he lets go of the hand that's holding mine and places it on my lower back. As he pulls me tightly against him, his mouth finally claims mine. His lips are soft full, and sweet. It's still a tentative kiss. Almost like he's making sure it's alright. His lips say one thing but his body says another. His hands hold me with a possessiveness he has no right to claim and I have no right to want. I'm aware of every inch where our bodies touch and it still isn't enough. Both of my hands are on his chest now and I can feel the heavy rise and fall of his chest. Still the kiss doesn't progress or deepen but has me reeling nonetheless.

He reluctantly pulls away and it makes me feel good to know he's just as affected by it. By *me*. He takes a small step away from me and the power around us slowly fades. My teeth sink into my bottom lip as I swallow down a frustrated groan. I'm not ready for the kiss to end.

"Amarah, I'm so sorry, I didn't mean…" he runs his hand through his hair. "I don't know what came over me."

I feel a little shaky from the power, and a lot giddy from the kiss, even though it had been a simple touch of lips.

"Whoa!" I laugh shakily. "That was…don't be sorry."

"Yeah, that was…*intense*," he agrees but I can already see the gears in his mind turning. His recovery is a Hell of a lot better than mine.

"I didn't realize you don't know who you are, and your power is…." He shakes his head, "I'm sure you have a ton of questions and I would be happy to answer any I can, but not tonight. I have to go."

That makes my heart ache and my chest tighten around it. I don't want him to go, and that's just silly. "When can I see you again?"

That sounds way too needy. I silently chide myself and try to act more nonchalant, "you know, so you can answer my questions and explain all this weird shit to me." Yeah, that's better. Act like you don't care, Amarah.

"I'm not sure. I need to go see someone." He runs his hand through his hair again. He doesn't even seem aware that he's doing it and I wonder if it's his nervous habit?

"But I promise I will be back soon," he says as he gives me a sly half-smile and then disappears into the darkness, leaving me standing alone in my backyard with the lingering feeling of his lips on mine.

Friends

This Is The Hunt by Ruelle

There's a faint noise getting louder and louder, pulling me out of sleep. As my mind starts to wake, I recognize the noise as Ruelle's song, *This Is The Hunt*. In my haste to go to bed last night, I forgot to turn off my damn alarm. I groan as I reach for my phone on the nightstand and dismiss the alarm. I squint my eyes against the light illuminating my face and make out the time. 5:50 am. I groan even louder as I realize I only slept for three and a half hours. Griffin is still cuddled up next to me and doesn't move a muscle. He's obviously not ready to get out of bed either.

The blackout curtains keep the creeping sunrise at bay and the darkness and the warmth of Griffin and my blankets envelope me. I immediately playback last night's dream and smile to myself. Hot damn! The things I would let that man do to me.

"It was just a dream, Amarah, calm down. You know guys like that don't exist in real life." I remind myself.

Now that my body is awake, the urge to pee drives me out of bed. My body is a bit tight and sore from all the dancing we did last night, so I take a few seconds to stretch and get the blood flowing. I make my way into the bathroom and give myself a once over in the mirror and shake my head. No way last night's dream was real because there's no way a guy like Logan would want to be all up in this hot mess. Maybe I should invest in some sexier pajamas? Who am I kidding?

After taking care of business, I tiptoe down the hallway and proceed to make as little noise as possible so I don't wake up Cristi and Paula. The soft dawn light is streaming in through the kitchen windows but it's not quite enough to allow me to see what I'm doing, so I hit the light switch that turns on the lights under the cabinets.

The deja vu is instant.

I reach for one of my Snoopy mugs and freeze. There's a Snoopy mug sitting on the counter exactly where I had left it in my dream. My heart is in my throat and I just stand here staring at, waiting for it to grow feet and move so I can justify it being here.

Surprise, surprise. It doesn't.

No way, I shake my head and run my hands down my face, pacing in front of the mug. I'm still staring at it as if it's somehow alive and is going to jump at me any second. Last night had *not* been real. It had all just been a dream. Paula or Cristi must have left the mug here before they went to bed. Yup, that has to be the *only* logical explanation.

I walk over to the sliding glass door that leads out to the backyard, open the blinds, and check the lock. I sigh with relief as I unlock it and walk onto the patio. I scan the backyard but there's nothing out of the ordinary. I shiver suddenly and goosebumps rise up along my arms. I rub them as I head inside and lock the door behind me.

Grabbing the Snoopy mug, I down two cups of water and immediately start to feel better. My mind is clearer and my body is more alert but it's just not morning without coffee. Summertime or Wintertime, doesn't matter, coffee comforts my soul. I busy myself at the coffee station and allow myself to daydream as I wait for the coffee to brew.

Everything that happened last night is so strange. The things I think I saw when that guy grabbed me. Imagining Logan on the street, staring at me. Or was that part real? Was he really there and therefore, caused the dream I had about him? That seems logical. How else could I dream of him? I don't even want to get into the details of the dream. Everything he said about the world. As If this is a damn fantasy book instead of real life.

The strong smell of coffee and the sudden silence of the now brewed pot call for my attention. I cuddle up on the couch with a blanket draped over me and my Snoopy mug seeping glorious warmth into my hands. I inhale the unmistakable aroma of coffee and when that first hot sip hits my tongue, I let out a content sigh, close my eyes and lean my head back on the couch.

The dream makes its way back into my thoughts. I allow myself to relish in the possibility that a man like Logan does exist out there somewhere, but the likelihood of me being the one to find him, In Albuquerque of all places, not likely to happen at all. And a demon war? And power? Fairies? I snort, I just can't wrap my brain around any of that being real. Which sucks because that means I will never feel those muscles under my hands or feel those lips on mine. Just thinking about it I can feel his lips pressed to mine. I reach up and touch them, trying to ease the ache they have to kissed for real. Just the memory of his hands possessively holding my body has my heart rate increasing. I felt something stirring in my chest, a spark that feels ready to ignite.

"Morning friend," Cristi says with a yawn as she ambles out of the hallway with a yawning Griffin trailing behind her.

I jump and almost spill coffee on me. I push all the crazy thoughts in my head out the window.

"Morning sunshine. You scared me." I laugh nervously. "I didn't even hear you get up. I was too busy daydreaming about the perfect man that doesn't exist."

"I didn't mean to scare you. I heard you out here, so thought I'd join you. Mind if I get some coffee and then we can daydream together?" She asks.

"Help yourself. That's why I made more." I smile at her from the couch. "Hey, did you or Paula use one of the Snoopy mugs last night?"

"Mmmm, not that I remember. Paula used the glass you gave her for water, but she left it in the sink. We went to bed like 10 minutes after you did. Did something happen?" She asks as she pours herself a cup of coffee.

I turn sideways on the couch so I can see her. "I had a weird dream last night. In the dream, I used a mug and placed it on the counter. When I woke up this morning, the same mug was sitting where I had left it in my dream." Damn, I sound crazy even to myself.

She sits down next to me and pulls some blanket over her. "That is weird, friend. But you probably got up last night and used it, and you just think it was a dream."

That's what I'm afraid of, I think to myself.

"Yeah, you're probably right. I get thirsty after drinking like that. I remember being thirsty last night, so that's probably what happened."

But I can't shake the fact that last night had seemed so real. I'm having a hard time believing that I got up, used the mug and went back to bed. I'm having a hard time believing *that* part had been real, but the rest had only been a dream. It was either all real or none of it was but one thing I do know is real. I can't get Logan out of my head.

"How did you sleep?" I ask to distract myself.

"I slept great but I don't want to think about everything I have to get done today before I head back home," she says.

"Ugh, I know. I wish you could stay longer. No, scratch that, I wish you still lived here! I miss you and one night out is just not enough Cristi time." I stick my bottom lip out and pout obnoxiously. I have a feeling that I'm going to need someone to talk to. I have Paula, but she's always busy with her own life too. Man, it sucks being an adult. Why was I in such a hurry to grow up when I was younger? Damn this hindsight shit.

"I know. I miss you, too, and I miss living in the city where I can go out and get what I want when I want. Small town living is *not* fun," she laughs.

"Oh, I know. Been there, done that. Well, at least we got some time together. I guess we need to count our Blessings." Griffin comes strolling in through the doggy door, jumps on the couch, and waits expectantly. I lift the blanket and he climbs into my lap and curls up. He's such a cuddle bug in the mornings.

I sip my coffee, and I *do* feel Blessed. My life is far from perfect, I don't have a Logan, but I have more than I need and amazing friends. Sometimes we have to stop living in the chaos and negativity, slow down and remember to be grateful. Easier said than done on most days, especially days like today when something just feels off.

We hear a loud and exaggerated yawn coming from the spare bedroom. "Aaahhhhhhhh! It's too early!" Paula yells from the room and Cristi and I both giggle.

"Get your grumpy ass up and come and get some coffee!" I yell back.

A few minutes later, Paula walks out of the hallway and stops when she sees us. She throws her arms up and stretches, "mmmm, good morning. Where is this coffee at?"

"Everything is right there," I point to the coffeemaker. "Get some and come join us."

I hear her getting her cup of coffee ready and then I hear a loud sip followed by, "yassss! Just what I needed."

She makes her way into the living room and I lift the blanket so she can join us. Griffin blinks up at us, she rubs his head, "oh, hi Griffin," and then she pulls the blanket back over herself, me, and Griffin. We all laugh at the simple silliness of it all and I am grateful. I love these girls!

Way too soon, we are hugging and saying our goodbyes. I don't want them to leave, but both Paula and Cristi have to get on with their day. We all have lives and shit to do. I have to do the laundry, clean the house, get ready for a new work week, and then, most importantly, relax. It's my typical Sunday routine. It's boring and it's lonely. I wish I had something else to do, mainly in the shape of a six foot, gorgeous and muscled man with green eyes.

I sigh, "guess I better get to it."

5

Back to Reality

Bump, Bump, Bump by B2K

Turning on my TV, I select the Spotify app, and hit shuffle on my liked songs playlist. I have everything from country, to pop, to rap, to rock almost a little of everything. Music, like coffee, is food for my soul. There's a song for every emotion and everything you want to say or express. It's beautiful.

I keep hitting the next button until something with a beat comes on. *Bump, Bump, Bump* by B2K comes on and I turn it up loud and start my wonderful adulthood chores. Man, I wish I could be a kid again where the only thing I had to worry about was keeping my room clean, doing the occasional dishes, and taking out the trash. Now I have an entire house to clean.

I'm going about my chores absentmindedly. The movements and tasks are so common they've become second nature. My body knows what it needs to do but my mind is repeatedly being pulled to thoughts of Logan no matter how many times I try to focus on something, *anything* else.

I can't stop thinking about the way I felt in the dream. It was so real, so vivid, unlike any dream I've ever had. It feels more like a memory than a dream, but I know that can't be true. Still, I can't shake the feeling of his hand clasping mine.

His lips pressed against mine.

The warm tingling of power along my skin only to be cooled by his power mixing with mine. Just thinking about it causes my heart to race and my chest to restrict, making it hard to breathe. I feel that stirring spark in my chest again and my fear snaps me back to reality.

I'm standing in the middle of my living room, paralyzed, with the vacuum in my hand. The vacuum is whirring loudly but all I hear is my own heartbeat pounding in my ears.

I turn the vacuum off and shake my head, "nope. No way. This is not happening. It wasn't real, it *isn't* real. It's just my body reacting to the dream."

After I've calmed down, I turn the vacuum back on and concentrate hard on vacuuming the rug. I'm staring at it like it's a calculus problem I'm trying to solve but vacuuming is a mindless task and my mind wanders too easily. I need a bigger distraction.

I need a workout.

Yes, a workout will take a lot of concentration and energy. It will be a nice release of all this pent-up tension in my body. Within minutes I've down my pre-workout, changed into my workout clothes and am walking to my gym in the backyard. From the outside it looks like a storage room but inside is a decent-sized area covered in mats, a rack of dumbbells, a bench, a pull-up bar, some small things like loops and jump ropes, and a TV hanging in the corner so I can follow along to my workout program. Can't forget the Bluetooth speaker to blast workout music too.

One wall is taken up entirely with mirrors so I can watch my form and make sure I'm lifting correctly. No sense in throwing weights around if you aren't going to do it right. It feels hotter than usual and I'm ignoring the fact that I'm the one over-heating and it has nothing to do with the actual weather, as I turn on the A/C and begin my warm up.

An hour later I'm sweaty and exhausted but I feel great. The upside? The workout was exactly what I needed and thoroughly distracted me and drained me. The downside? I have no energy left to finish my chores and I'm totally fine with being a procrastinator for the rest of the day.

After a shower, I finished the laundry and then had a late lunch, and now Griffin and I have been cuddled on the couch binging the Harry Potter movies as if we haven't seen them a million times before. I can't help thinking there has to be more to life than this. What am I actually doing with my life? I'll be getting up to go to a job that I absolutely despise in about twelve hours. How do people actually find their passions and do what they love? What do I even love? Do I have a passion? Do I have a purpose in this life? Or is my purpose to be absolutely miserable and mundane?

My phone chimes on the side table next to me breaking through my depressed thoughts. It's a text from Cristi.

Cristi: hi, friend. I just wanted to let you know
that I made it home!
Me: Ok, good! It was so good to spend time with you,
but I miss you already!

Cristi: I miss you too! Hopeful I can come back to visit soon. I've got to unload all this stuff and get ready for work tomorrow. I'll text you tomorrow.
Me: Sounds good. Have a good night 😊
Cristi: You too! Goodnight 😊

I glance at the time and it's already 7:00 p.m. I sigh and get up and walk into the kitchen. "I need some wine," I say to Griffin.

I decide on making some popcorn too since I had a late lunch and I'm not in the mood to cook dinner. One upside to being single, I guess. Popcorn and wine for dinner and no one to judge you.

I sit back down on the couch with my wine and popcorn and continued to watch The Prisoner of Azkaban. Griffin comes and cuddles up next to me, and it makes me smile despite my melancholy mood. He warms my heart and it makes me feel good to not be completely alone.

I imagine what it would be like to have Logan sitting next to me watching Harry Potter. His arm slung across the back of the couch. His big, gorgeous body pressed against mine. I could almost smell him. Like a crisp, woodsy morning. My breath catches at the scent I swear I can remember. I can't believe a dream has affected me like this. Keep dreaming, Amarah, a guy like Logan doesn't live a boring life like you do. He would not be ok with wine and popcorn for dinner. Hell, a guy like Logan simply doesn't exist.

Monsters in the Dark

Heart Of The Darkness by Tommee Profitt

Deep into my third glass of wine I hear a noise in the backyard. My heart is in my throat instantly. Am I hearing things? Again! This is happening too much this weekend. After the weird shit at the club and then the dream I can't help but be paranoid. Griffin sits up and growls looking towards the window and the doggy door underneath. Ok, if Griffin hears it too, I I'm not imagining it. The curtain is closed so I can't see out of the window. I place my wineglass down on the side table and walk to the window. I pull the curtain back, but I can't see anything. It's dark out.

Too dark.

I look at my phone and it displays 10:23 p.m. Holy shit! It's way past my bedtime and I'll be paying for it at work tomorrow. Alright, Amarah, you're just being paranoid. Just go check outside and make sure everything is ok so we can go to bed.

"It's ok, Griffin, it's probably just the wind or a cat or something." I don't know who I'm trying to convince more? The dog who can't understand me or myself? Definitely myself.

I approach the sliding glass door and unlocked it. Wait, I should grab a knife or something, right? Just in case. I pull out the drawer by the stove and grab a decent size knife. It's thin and about nine inches long. Yeah, this will work. I take a deep steadying breath and push my fear aside. I'm just being paranoid I remind myself again.

I step outside and the patio light blazes to life. Once again, I'm standing outside in my pajamas aka underwear. I really should start wearing more clothes to bed but that's a problem for another time. The patio light is usually very bright but tonight it seems to be having a hard time penetrating the thick darkness. The night feels heavy. I can almost feel it pressing in all around the light trying to snuff it out. It feels...*alive.* Unlike my dream last night, I'm scared and my heart is pounding wildly in my chest.

"Who's out there?" I yell out into the darkness. My voice shakes showcasing my fear.

There's no answer and I can't see shit. I walk out to the edge of the patio and take a step onto the lawn. I stand as still as I can, trying not to make a sound, and just listen. My body is on high alert and I'm straining to hear something, *anything*, but there's nothing except the pounding of my blood coursing through my veins. I realize I've been holding my breath and reminded myself to breathe. My eyes have adjusted better but I still can't see through the unnatural blackness. I can't hear anything, but I feel it. I feel it deep in my gut. Something or someone is out there. I feel a pull on that gut feeling drawing me to the left side of the lawn. I turn and take another step deeper into the darkness.

I have a split second to register two red, glowing eyes and a vicious growl before something very large and very heavy ploughs into me. My hand lifts the knife in front of my body out of sheer survival instinct. I hear someone scream and then there's a sharp pain radiating through my body as the darkness finally consumes me. White dots appear before me and I blink rapidly trying to clear my vision. Things come into focus in bits and pieces and my throbbing head seems to be struggling to process what I'm seeing.

A monster.

I'm staring up into a snarling face that isn't human. I'm flat on my back and my throat is on fire because I'm the one screaming. I see a clawed hand rear back to strike and there's nothing I can do. I'm trapped underneath its massive body and the knife is no longer in my hand. The claws come racing down towards my face and then the darkness finally wins, maliciously dragging me into the abyss. There's no more screaming. There's no more pain.

I come to lying on the grass, staring up at the night sky and the twinkling above me. They're beautiful and I should spend more time appreciating them. The peaceful moment is quickly yanked away from me as the pain in my head reminds me that I'm hurt. My thoughts are fuzzy but the memory of my attack is coming back to me. Then I hear it. Growling. Only this time there's more than one source. Fuck. Are there two of them now?

The fear and adrenaline rush through my body at the thought that I'm not alone. I'm still in danger. I sit up quickly and the backyard starts to spin instantly. I make my way onto my hands and knees and fight to keep my head up and focus. I'm starting to see white spots again but I can just make out two…*things* fighting. I say things because neither one is anything close to human but all I can see are flashes of the scene in front of me.

Chocolate brown fur.

Claws.

Teeth.

Red eyes.

Claws.

A spiked tail.

Red blood.

My kitchen knife sticking out of the stomach of a walking skeleton.

I shake my head trying to focus but I only send my mind spinning, delirious with pain. The nausea rushes up from my stomach and before I know it, I'm puking up my guts onto the grass. I collapse onto my side as the darkness pulls me under again. Before I lose consciousness, I swear I hear a wolf howling.

Is This Real

Nothing Is As It Seems by Hidden Citizens, Ruelle

I wake up to something warm and wet on my face and heaviness on my chest. Griffin is sitting on my chest and vigorously licking my face. "Griffin," I mumble, remembering how to talk. His little body wiggles at the sound of my voice and he lets out a tiny howl. He's happy that I'm awake. Hell, so am I. I'm lying on my back on the couch in my living room and I can't for the life of me remember how I got here. Did I pass out watching TV? My head is pounding with a headache deep in my brain and my throat feels sore. I groan as the pain shoots through my head with the tiniest movements. Ugh, I must have had too much wine.

A noise in my kitchen sets my heart racing and the pounding in my head intensifies. All this adrenaline and heart pounding can't be good for my health. I raise up on my elbows as slowly and quietly as I can and peek over the back of the couch.

A man is standing at my sink.

And not just standing at my sink, he's *dominating* the space. His presence is like a vacuum, sucking the oxygen right out of the room and out of my chest.

His back is towards me and he doesn't seem to be aware that I'm awake, so I take a moment to examine him.

He's shirtless and his back is ripped with muscle. His shoulders are broad and powerful then his physique tapers down to a narrow waist. I admire the hard lines of muscle that frame his spine as my eyes travel down. His jeans are sitting dangerously low on his hips, revealing the band of his underwear and my mouth waters. I gulp it down as I notice how his jeans fit tightly over a firm ass and thick, muscular thighs. I'm close to drooling at this point when he turns around almost giving me a heart attack with the new view.

Logan.

Great. Just great. I've passed out on the couch and am having another dream about my handsome stranger. But damn, the vividity of these dreams is insane because my head is splitting! Still, Logan is shirtless this time so I'm not going to complain. My damaged brain is doing alright. And damn is he impressive without a shirt.

His chest is smooth, no hair. Hallelujah! His skin is smooth caramel except for a scar I can't quite make out over his heart. His chest is impressive and my eyes travel down to an even more impressive stomach. His abs resemble a washboard and the infamous V is begging me to explore where it leads. The only thing standing in the way of this man being perfect are the gashes in his chest, stomach, and arms. Still, perfect is the only word I can think of to describe him.

Perfect.

Damn, those arms. I want to feel them wrapped around my body, possessively.

His voice forces me out of my saucy daydream, "Good, you're awake. How are you feeling?" He asks as he puts the towel he was using to clean his wounds down and starts walking towards me

I'm all but drooling watching his magnificent body in motion. I can't even form a cohesive thought much less string together an entire sentence.

I managed to close my mouth and say, "ummmm...I feel like I was run over by a bus but I'm sure I'll feel better once I wake up."

"What do you mean? You *are* awake," he looks puzzled. Ha! Join the club. "I'll feel better once I wake up from this crazy dream because there's no way all of this is real," I say as I sit up and curl my legs under me.

He joins me on the couch and the space is suddenly way too small. I want to reach out and touch him. I want to feel the warmth of his skin and taste the sweetness of his mouth. I realize I'm staring at his lips when I see them quirk up into a knowing smirk. I quickly glance down and my hands fuss with a loose string on my shirt.

Griffin is now climbing into his lap, smelling him intently. He's not afraid of Logan or growling so I take that as a good sign. Dogs can always sense bad people.

"This is not a dream, Amarah."

Why does my heart race when he says my mind? And why does his voice have to be so damn sexy? I can't look at him without thinking inappropriate thoughts. I can't listen to him without thinking inappropriate thoughts. I'm doomed.

"This is all very *real* and you need to understand that because what happened tonight is not a coincidence. The demon was here for a reason. For you. Thank fuck I was here," he runs his hand through his hair and as I finally meet his eyes, I see the worry in them.

"So, you're telling me that, that…*thing*, that thing that attacked me was real?! *You're* real?" My voice comes out a little shaky.

"Yes," he says confidently. "Why would you think this is a dream?" He cocks his head to the side and smirks at me again, "do you have dreams of monsters and shirtless men you don't know often?"

I can't help my glance at his naked chest and stomach and I feel the blush heat my neck and face immediately.

"No!" I exclaim. "I just…" I shake my head as I try and take in everything he just said. "Just…how can all of this be real? What does it mean? I don't understand! Why is this happening to me?" I hug my knees to my chest and rest my aching head against them. I can feel the panic starting to rise up and I have to remind myself just to breathe. I'm safe. Right now, I'm safe.

I mean, there is a stranger in my house. A fucking sexy stranger that I want to bang but a stranger nonetheless. I don't know him or his intentions. Oh shit, Oh shit. I start rocking back and forth as my chest is dragging in big gulps of air. I feel his heavy body as he sits next to me. He brushes my hair away from my face and tucks it behind me ear. Just that light brush of his skin against mine has me shuddering and losing my breath for a whole new reason.

"Hey, it's gonna be ok," he says sweetly.

He gently places his hand on my back and starts to rub in soothing circles. His touch is like Heaven. If Heaven could touch you. His energy seems to penetrate through my shirt, through my skin, directly to the heart of me. It eases my panic but also stirs that fire inside of me. That spark of…something I have been feeling.

I finally turn my head to look at him. His peridot eyes capture mine in an instant. My lips part on a sigh as I stare up into his beautiful face just inches away. I want to move into his lap, cradle his face in my hands and claim his mouth. I want to claim him as mine. I've never felt such need to have someone before. Why does he affect me like this?   I swear I see him glance at my lips, too, before he swallows and meet my eyes firmly again.

"I know it's a lot to take in but I'm here. I'll be here every step of the way and we'll figure all of this out together, ok?"
I can't even think of anything to say, so I just nod my head. I look into his handsome face, into his drowning green eyes, and I believe him. I don't know anything more than this strange man's name and yet, he's sitting next to me on my couch with my dog in his lap, and I trust him.

Since I don't make the best choices in men, insert my dick of an ex here, my judgment should be in question, but it just isn't. I feel it down to my core that he's telling the truth, and that he's one of the good guys. He's here to help me. Lord, help me if I'm wrong.

8

So Many Questions

Whomp! There It Is by Tag Team

I get up to get water and ibuprofen for my pounding head for the second night in a row. I definitely can't keep this up because consistent ibuprofen is *not* healthy. I lean my back against the counter and try to wrap my brain around everything that's happened but my thoughts are all over the place.

"I have so many questions but I don't even know where to begin," I say shaking my head.

"Alright. Well…" Logan gets up from the couch and comes to sit in one of the barstools at the island. My eyes follow his body greedily, admiring how lean and agile his body is. I grip my glass harder and drag my eyes up to his trying to focus. Now is not that time to be distracted, no matter how nice the view is.

"I'm here to answer anything I can. How can I help?" He asks, clasping his hands together and leaning onto the island.

He's more focused than I am, obviously, but that damn smirk gives him away. He knows how nervous he makes me and he's enjoying it. His teasing, half-smile doesn't help the heat crawling up

---

my cheeks. Fucking Hell, how many times am I going to blush in front of this man?

I clear my throat, "ok, well, since you're here, a strange man sitting in my kitchen and I know absolutely nothing about you, and yet...oh, God," I remember the kiss. I thought that it had all been a dream but now I know it had been real. That sent the heat right back up my cheeks as I continue, "I *kissed* you."

He chuckles, "yes, you did." His eyes meet mine with such intensity and heat that I have to look away.

"Just for the record, I don't normally go around kissing strangers. I thought it was a dream. But ummmm, well, clearly that's not the case so let's just move on. Who are you?"

His eyes are sparkling with humor and I know he wants to say something but he dips his chin and says, "ok, I suppose we can start there. I'm Logan Lewis and I'm Kaitsja, which means Protector, of the Fey, which you already know. I'm the only one of my kind. What you don't know is that I'm also a Werewolf." He says it as if it was the most common thing in the world. Like if he had just said, *I'm a teacher*. Not the same thing!

I just stare at him. I scratch my head and that brings my attention back to the throbbing that's still there. It's making it hard to think. Well, I mean that and that fact that my entire world is being turned upside down and inside out... *Whomp, there it is*, me and Tag Team.

"So, Werewolves are *real* and... you *are* one?" I ask it as a question, more to make sure I heard and understood what he said the first time.

"Yes. I am," he says as his eyes turn from green to amber and then back again. His eyes never leave my face as he monitors my reaction.

"Sweet Jesus!" I gasp as I place my hand at my chest as if I can stop my heart from climbing into my throat.

"And I'm single, in case you were wondering," he smirks again and I swear he's going to stop my damn heart.

I purposefully ignore his last statement and try to focus on the fact that he's a damn Werewolf!

"So, the scratches, which already look like they are healing by the way, are from...that thing...that attacked me. That was you I saw then? Fighting it." I'm talking out loud more to myself than expecting an answer as I try to piece it all together. "What was that thing that attacked me and did you kill it?" I flash back to the monstrous face inches above mine and I shiver.

His smirk disappears and his lips set into a hard line. They're not any less inviting this way either. "That was a soldier demon that attacked you. I mentioned a war to you last night. The Fey are guardians of humans, so to speak. They keep the demons from overrunning both The Unseen world and the human world but... recently, they have slowly been losing the war and we're all worried about what the future looks like. Your power seems to...*attract*. It's like a beacon. Even I felt it. I think that's how the demon found you tonight."

"And what do they want with me? To kill me?" I ask, my voice hollow.

"That's my best guess," he shrugs. "But honestly, I don't know. We're at war with them, Amarah. It's safe to say they want to eliminate any threat, especially one as strong as you. If they can track you when you use your power, it's going to be extremely important for you to learn to control it. As far as killing it," he shakes his head. "I destroyed the demon's physical form and sent it back to Hell but he's not dead. They just keep coming back."

"So…" I rub my forehead that is still throbbing and I have no idea if it's from the attack or this conversation. "Demons and Hell are real and demons are trying to kill me. Yeah, that's not frightening at all," I say sarcastically.

"Why me? What is this power I have and why is it just now that this is happening? I mean, I'm thirty-four and have lived this long with nothing crazy happening to me."

"Your power was unlocked somehow last night. It's always been there, hidden just under the surface, waiting until you were ready to accept it. Something must have happened last night to activate it." I remember the guy from the club. "Last night a guy grabbed my arm and I felt a physical shock from it, and then I felt something inside of me explode outwards. I don't know how else to describe it. I also could have sworn that the guy who touched me had claws instead of hands. Does that make any sense to you?" I ask.

"Yes, I think so. Demons can possess so, it must have been a General demon that touched you and when your power reacted to it, you saw his true form. For whatever reason your power has decided you are ready, and the touch from a demon was all it took for your power to unleash. That's also when I sensed your power and found you at the club. Last night, when I said I had to talk to someone, I went to see the Müstik Queen, Anaxo, about you. She explained who you are."

My head is spinning, "so who am I?"

"You are what we call, Võitleja, Warrior of the Fey. You, like me, are the first of your kind, so we're in unfamiliar territory. The Queen says that you were created in our greatest time of need. I told you the war has been going on for centuries but the demons have been getting stronger and the Fey have not been as successful at sending them back to Hell. I will leave the details for the Queen to explain because I don't know much more than that."

"Wow. This is probably going to sound insane, but I had a dream, not that long ago that I was fighting the devil. In my dream, I wasn't scared. I felt like I *was* a warrior. I woke myself up saying the Lord's Prayer. That's why I got this tattoo of Archangel Michael," I point to the side of my right thigh. "That dream has stuck with me unlike any other, but still... if I hadn't seen that demon for real..." I shake my head, "I wouldn't believe any of it."

"I understand. I imagine it must be difficult to believe something that has only ever existed to you in stories. Believe me, I'm keeping the information as simple for you as I can for now. You will learn so much more throughout your training and I don't think your dream was a coincidence at all."

I sit down at the island catty-corner to Logan so we can be face to face and continue our conversation. It's extremely difficult not to reach out and touch him and I have no idea why I'm reacting this way to him. I haven't even glanced at a man since my ex and yet I want to throw myself at Logan. I have no idea what in the Hell is going on and all I can do is shake my head and grip my glass tighter to keep my hands off of him.

"I just can't believe there is this whole other hidden world. What did you call it? The Unseen? How is it that no one knows about it? I mean, like the...humans?"

"For the most part, we preternatural creatures can pass as humans. Some have to use glamour, or magic if that makes more sense to you, for their appearance, but not all. We also learn to keep our power in check. Usually, humans can't sense our power, our auras, but some humans that are sensitive can. So, we learn to control the power and only use it when necessary. Also, humans are blissfully ignorant and oblivious," he explains as if it's all very simple.

"Now that, I believe!" I say laughing.

He smiles a big, genuinely, radiant smile, and my entire body melts onto the floor. Fuck, he's gorgeous and that smile is my new favorite addiction. We make eye contact and the look in his eyes is heated and intense. My eyes dropped to his lips wanting to feel them on mine again. It's suddenly way too hot in this damn kitchen and I feel that familiar heat creep up into my cheeks. Damn it! I look down at my hands holding my glass of water.

Logan chuckles again and reaches over to gently lift my chin up with his finger. My stomach flips at his touch, sending desire pooling low in my gut and the butterflies take flight.

"You don't need to be embarrassed around me, Amarah. I'm drawn to you as well. I feel it too."

I look up and meet his eyes, "well, you're doing a hell of a better job at hiding it than I am!" I exclaim.

"Only because I've had centuries tied to my powers and emotions and have learned a lot of control in that time. I have solid control over many things, but I have to admit, you're definitely pushing me to my limits of control," he says as his thump gently brushes across my bottom lip. I'm staring at him staring at my mouth and I start to lean forward just as he drops his hand and pulls away. I feel the loss of his touch deep in my soul.

I shake my head and once again try and focus on what he said. "Centuries! Jesus, that is just so hard to comprehend."

I slowly meet his gaze again, "but seriously, I've never been attracted to anyone the way I am to you. It's physical, I mean look at you." I wave my hand up and down gesturing at his body, "but it's deeper than that too and that scares me," I admit.

He smiles, "I can control my emotions and body so they do not betray me at the wrong time, but...I will admit that I have never felt a connection like this either. I have the strongest need to touch you and to protect you," he closes his eyes as if concentrating on pushing those feelings down. "One thing you should know about your power now being activated is that you will no longer age from this point on."

"I'll do what?! Are you saying I am immortal?" I ask in disbelief.

"No, not immortal, as far as I know. However, you are the first of your kind and I have never been around a greater power than yours. You have the power to do so much good, but with that also comes the power to do terrible things. People with power always have the choice to be good or bad."

"I'm far from perfect but I'd like to think I'm a genuinely *good* person."

"I hope so." He seems to contemplate his thoughts before he speaks again, "few things can hurt me because I'm a Werewolf and I was given a Fey life-force which makes me more powerful and very hard to kill. You..." he closes his eyes and shakes his head, "you have the power to undo me, to destroy me. I felt it last night when we touched each other's power." He reaches out to me then and brushes my hair behind me ear. That one small touch, sends my heart racing and throbbing between my legs. "It scares me too."

He's looking at me now, his hand cupping my face gently, giving me his peridot eyes, raw with need. I can feel his need as if it's my own. I'm being pulled into him like gravity and I have no control over it. And I desperately want to collide with him. He finally breaks the stare and it takes me a minute before I find my voice.

"Well, shit," I say with a lot of feeling. I sit back in my stool and don't know what to think or what to say.

This is all too much to take in. I need to be led by the hand from the shallow end of the pool into the deep end. I know if I get too much all at once, I'll drown. I have so much to think about and try to wrap my brain around, so why do I keep going back to the fact that Logan said he was attracted to me too? That he's single. Really, Amarah? That's what you want to linger on? Yeah, I'm in deep shit.

9

Are You Listening?

Levitating by Dua Lipa

Logan and I talk for a long time. It's now 2:00 a.m. and I'll be useless at work tomorrow, or rather, today. At least my head doesn't hurt anymore. Logan said when I learn to use and control my power that I'll be very hard to hurt and can use it to heal not only myself but others. At least there are perks to the job.

We're sitting on the couch because it's more comfortable than the bar stools. "My mind is still racing but I need to try and get some sleep before I have to wake up and go to work in a few hours," I say, smothering a yawn.

Logan looks at me with something like *are you serious* and *I'm disappointed* written across his features. "Really, Amarah? Have you not been paying attention to anything we've talked about tonight?" His tone is flat and scolding.

Why is he upset? I'm the one who's had my life turned upside down over a weekend. Pretty sure I remember that, considering I'm the one at the center of it all. "Of course, I have," I say, defensively.

"No, you haven't," he shakes his head, "if you think you can still go to work at that human job."

"What do you mean? I *have* to work. I don't know how things work in The Unseen but bills don't exactly pay themselves, Logan," I say sarcastically.

"You don't have to worry about that anymore. The Fey Queen will take care of all of that now. Plus, did you forget that you will no longer age? It would take a few years before people realized it, but how would you explain that? Oh, and the fact that you would now endanger them because demons would most definitely show up and try to kill you. Or did you forget that too?" He sounds upset.

"Well, shit!" I say with feeling. "Of course, I didn't forget, Logan. I just hadn't thought about all of that and just how much my life will change. My life is changing overnight and apparently, I have this enormous responsibility to help the Fey and to protect the world and yet I have no fucking clue how to do any of that! Hell, I don't even know who I am anymore! So, forgive me if I'm not perfect and don't know what I'm supposed to do!"

"You're right. I'm sorry. I know this is a lot for you to take in. I'll do my best to be more patient and understanding," His voice is softer now and his eyes seem sincere as he watches me.

"Thank you," I say, and mean it. "So, now what?"

"Well, you can take care of your work situation. Tell them you have a... I don't know, family emergency or something, and that you can no longer work there. Then, I will take you to meet the Müstik Queen, Anaxo, later tonight. She has already contacted the other Leaders from the other Fey Families. They are on their way here and we will have a meeting to discuss all the recent events, to discuss your training, and to meet you."

"I still can't believe all of this. It's crazy and yet, it also makes sense. Just last week I was telling my friend that something was missing from my life. It felt like I had this hole in my chest and I don't feel like that anymore. It is insane but strangely also feels…" I shrug, "right."

"That's good. It will feel better and better as you go through your training and learn who you are and what your power is and how to control it. The more you use it, the more you should feel like your true self. Now, until you've started your training, you need to have someone with you in case a demon find you. I'll stay with you for now. I parked my truck down the street, I'm gonna go get it and park it in the driveway. I have a change of clothes in there and would love a shower if you don't mind?" He asks.

Wait, what?! Logan is staying with me? *Here.* In *my* house. And he'll be naked in my shower! The image sends another heatwave up my cheeks but my voice comes out normal. Thank God.

"Ummmm… yeah," I clear my throat. "Of course, that's fine. You can use the spare shower and sleep in the guest room. I just cleaned it today, actually," I say nonchalantly, but I know he saw me blush. Again.

He pulls in a lifted, black Chevy Silverado 1500 into my driveway. He jumps out of the driver's side, opens up the back door, and comes back into view holding a duffle bag. The truck suits him. He's still not wearing a shirt or shoes and it doesn't seem to bother him. He looks one hundred percent comfortable and confident walking around with just his jeans on.

God, his body is sculpted like a damn Greek God statue. All rippling muscles and easy masculinity. Yeah, this is going to be a problem for me. I mean, as far as problems go, it's a good one to have! He's gorgeous, has good taste, and I'm ready to take Beyonce's advice and put a ring on it. What in the Hell is wrong with me?

I make sure he has some clean towels in the bathroom and I wait in the living room while he showers. Griffin is curled under the blanket, asleep. He doesn't seem very phased by Logan being here or demons attacking me or our lives changing *forever*. It must be a pleasant life, being a spoiled dog.

I hear the shower turn off and a few minutes later Logan emerged from the hallway wearing nothing but a towel wrapped very low around his waist. I mean, very, *very* low. Like sweet baby Jesus I'm going to have a heart attack low. I swallow hard and am instantly burning up. He is in fact, perfect. The cuts that had been there just hours ago are now gone. His arms ware big and muscular even without him flexing. His chest and stomach are smooth and perfect, except for the scar over his heart. And those obliques are begging to be explored with my hands, mouth and tongue. His body is like a mystery I need to solve in order to survive.

I can see beads of water on his skin. My eyes catch one and follow it as it trails a line down, down, down towards the towel and stops in the line of hair that starts below his belly button. I've never wanted to be a bead of water so badly in my life.

My heart is pounding and I can't think of anything else except the man standing, almost naked, in my living room. I want to get up and stand in front of him. I want to feel the heat of the shower coming off his skin and onto mine. I want to trail my lips and tongue down his chest towards the towel too. I want to yank the towel free and see every stunning inch of him. I want him to grab me and pick me up in those muscular arms. I want...

"Amarah!" Logan almost screams my name. "Did you hear what I said?"

I blink and look up at him. What he said? Shit, he was talking to me and I was too busy fantasizing to hear him. Oh, this is bad.

"Are you alright?" He asks with that cocky half-smile as he moves further into the living room and stands directly in front of me.

I'm blushing for the millionth time and it takes me a couple of times to find my voice. "Ummmm… yeah, yes," I say with more confidence. "I'm fine. Do you need anything?" I force myself to look at him. His body is massive and I feel like it takes forever to drag my eyes up his body until I meet his heated eyes.

He smooths his hand through his hair, "no, I have everything I need." His voice is husky and slithers across my skin. I swallow again and know I have to get out of the living room before I embarrass myself further.   "Ok, great," I stand up to leave but all I do is manage to put our bodies *very* close together and Logan doesn't budge. I can feel the warmth from the shower coming off of him just like I knew I would but I want to feel it on my naked skin.

"Well, I'm going to get some sleep," I mutter. My mind tells me to move my damn feet but they won't listen. I feel rooted to the floor, standing inches in front of Logan.

"Ok," he whispers.

He reaches out and moves my hair behind my ear again. I close my eyes and shiver from his simple touch. Then, he slowly trails his fingertips down my neck and I let out a heavy sigh that shatters the silence and brings my back to myself. Did I really just sigh like that? Out loud? From his *fingertips* brushing my skin? I'm blushing again, beyond embarrassed and moving into mortified territory.

I finally get my feet to move and step away from him. "Make yourself at home. I'll see you in a couple of hours. Goodnight." The words spew out of my mouth like a run on sentence. I'm so nervous and afraid to make a complete fool of myself that I can't get away fast enough.

"Griffin, come on!" I yell as I'm already in the hallway, not waiting for him to follow me. I do *not* trust myself around Logan and his amazing, almost naked, wet body, and I'm not going to sleep with a stranger. A sex personified stranger but a stranger nonetheless.

I wait for Griffin in my bedroom and then I shut the door. I contemplate locking it but it's not like Logan is going to come in here and ravish me. Even if I do want him to. I walk into the bathroom and turn on the light. I look at myself in the mirror and I look flushed. Flustered. How embarrassing! He must get a kick and a huge confidence boost out of me.

My hair is uncombed and had just dried naturally from my shower earlier. I also have zero makeup on. Great, Amarah, way to make an impression. I get ready for bed and join Griffin. As soon as I lay my head on the pillow, the mental exhaustion hits me and know I'm about to sleep great.

I fall asleep to the image of Logan standing in front of me, dripping wet from the shower with just the towel on. His fingertips leaving trails of fire on my skin. If I have things my way, this is going to be one Hell of a dream!

Time To Quit

Never Be The Same by Camila Cabello

Amarah. Amarah, hey, wake up."

I feel the hair being moved from my face and a brush of lips on my cheek. I blink my eyes open and Logan is sitting next to me on the edge of the bed, in my darkened bedroom, looking scrumptious. His hair tousled from sleep and he's wearing nothing but basketball shorts. My heart immediately wakes up in my chest. Oh, I could get used to waking up to him.

I can't keep the cheesy smile off my face. "How long have you been sitting there?" I mumble in a sleepy voice.

He smiles back and shrugs, "sorry to wake you but you've got a job to quit, remember?" He intentionally ignores my question and I'm praying I didn't do anything embarrassing in my sleep. Like fart!

"Ugh, don't remind me," I say as I sit up, yawning. "This is not going to be fun. Well, maybe it will be. It's not like I actually *like* the job. I'll just miss a few people I work with...and some customers."

"Well, either way, coffee should make it better, right? I figured you're a coffee drinker since you have space dedicated to it in your kitchen." He starts walking out of the bedroom, "c'mon, I just made some for us, I hope you don't mind."

He made us coffee? This gorgeous man walking around half-naked in my house made us coffee!? Son of a bitch! He *is* perfect. The signs just kept coming. I could seriously get used to this. I uncover Griffin and he yawns too.

"C'mon Angel, time to get up."

I walk out of the hallway and there's already a lot of light in the kitchen coming in through the windows. The clock on the stove says it's 8:06 a.m. Great, I have to at least call my boss, or former boss I guess, and tell him I won't be going in today...or ever again. I definitely could use coffee for this.

The sliding glass door to the backyard is open letting a cool, fresh breeze waft into the kitchen. Logan must be outside because he's not in the kitchen but I don't see him sitting on the patio either. I grab one of my Snoopy mugs and noticed one is already missing. I add my hazelnut creamer and poured the coffee on top. Voila! That's all I need for an amazing cup of coffee. I love coffee but I'm far from being a coffee snob.

I walk outside and Logan has a Snoopy mug in his left hand and is playing fetch with Griffin. It makes me smile and warms me up inside from my head down to my toes. I sit down at the patio table, kick my feet up, sip my coffee, and watch Logan throwing the ball repeatedly for Griffin. His muscles bunch and flex every time he stoops to pick up the ball and again when he throws it. His smooth caramel skin looks flawless in the morning sun. I could seriously watch this all day. Hell, I could watch Logan do anything… or nothing at all, literally all damn day.

"You're screwed now," I yell from the patio. "Ball is life for him and he can play for as long as you can throw!" I laugh.

He smiles that big genuine, body melting smile, "oh, I don't mind! He's a cute dog. Speaking of, you have a thing for cute dogs, huh?" He says as he holds the Snoopy mug up.

"Don't judge me!" I laugh. "Dogs are sweet souls! They just love you and never talk back. Unlike men," I shrug. "It's a no brainer."

"You know, I'm... kind of, a version of a cute dog once in a while," he winks and gives me his cocky teasing half-smile.

I bust out laughing, "I don't know if *cute* is the right word to describe you in Wolf...well, *any* form, but I think I'll have to determine that one for myself. Last time I glimpsed you in Wolf form you weren't exactly pet friendly."

"Ha! Yeah, I guess I wasn't, was I? Well, I'm sure you'll have plenty of chances to see...*all* of me," his teasing smile is back, "and decide. Did you call into work?" He asks as he starts walking towards the patio.

Just the thought of seeing all of him makes my heart pound and other things throb. I'm not thinking of seeing the Wolf form either. God! Why does he make me react this way?! And why do all of his clothes sit so damn low on his hips? Focus on the task at hand, Amarah. You can do this.

I stare into my cup so I can pull my thoughts out of the gutter, "ugh no, not yet. I'm not sure there will be enough coffee for this. Don't get me wrong, I hate that job and I dread going to work every single morning but," I sigh, "I don't know why this is so hard for me. It just feels wrong to leave people hanging. I know it's not logical because they will replace me in a heartbeat but it's still hard for me to do. If that makes sense," I shrug.

He pulls up a chair next to me. "It makes sense, and it speaks to who you are. It's kinda sweet," he says teasing again. "But you're right. You're just another employee they will replace. You don't owe them anything, Amarah." He leans towards me, reaches out, and touches my arm, causing me to look at him finally. "You have a higher calling and people who need you."

I let out a breath that has nothing to do with being overwhelmed about what I have to do and everything to do with this sexy stranger sitting next to me. I look into his dazzling green eyes from two feet away and for a minute I forget about everything. My old life, everything I thought I knew, and a silly job I have to quit. This new exciting and terrifying world I'm apparently a big part of. All the responsibility and change that's about to happen. I forget about demons and war. I just want to fall into his arms and get lost in him.

I feel myself leaning towards him automatically. I don't even realize what I'm doing until his eyes are suddenly closer and his hand is on my cheek again. His eyes dropped to my lips and his thumb trails across my bottom lip. I suck in a breath and hold it like I forgot how to breath.

"I want to kiss you again," his eyes move back to mine but I can't speak. I want to scream, *yes! Kiss me please you sexy fool!* But all I manage is to let out a heavy sigh. He has to be able to hear how hard my heart is pounding in my chest.

I don't know what he sees in my eyes but he moves even closer. His lips are almost on mine. I can feel his warm breath on my lips. I can smell the coffee on his breath.

"You can tell me to stop," he whispers.

I don't want him to stop and I swear I can *feel* his need too. I bring my hand up to his face and close the distance between us. It's still a gentle, soft kiss. Still tentative and cautious. Just his lips on mine, nothing else. Nothing more. I feel a spark in my chest and gasp, pulling back from the kiss and kicking myself for it.

He swallows hard and pulls away. "I sure hope being around you gets easier," he says. "Then again, a part of me hopes it doesn't," he smiles and runs his hand through his hair as he settles in his chair.

"I agree," I smile and shake my head, trying to refocus. "Ok, where were we? Oh yeah, quitting a job. I'll need to text a friend from work too and let her know I won't be going back." I gather myself, let out a big breath, "I'm ready. Let's do this!"

Nothing else seems to matter anymore. Everything seems inconsequential. The only thing I can think about is the feeling of Logan's lips on mine. The way his green eyes look at me. The way he makes me feel. All of the unspoken promises of kisses, touches and pleasure to come. He consumes me. And I know that no matter what happens now, as long as Logan is by my side, I'll be ok. I feel this deep connection to him in my soul. I know this is exactly where I'm meant to be and what I'm meant to do. I'm a little scared but a lot excited. I can do this.

I grab my phone, find my boss in my contacts, and hit the call button.

You Have Got to be Fucking Kidding

Break A Sweat by Becky G

I did it. I feel like an enormous weight has been lifted off of my shoulders. Crazy, right? Considering the fate of the entire world seems to be in my hands. Strangely, I feel at peace. Like I'm on the right path. I take it as a sign to let go of the past and continue moving forward. It doesn't hurt that moving forward includes Logan. As long as I have him by my side I'm up for anything. Hell, he's lived over three hundred years, so he *must* be doing something right. Right? May the odds be forever in my favor.

"So, what's next?" I ask.

"We need to get ready for the meeting tonight. The other Leaders from the different Fey Families are traveling in and will arrive today. You'll meet them along with the Queen. I'm sure everyone is very excited to meet you and to get you started in your training. The sooner that happens, the better for all of us."

"What should I expect? Is it just a casual meeting? Will they be able to answer more questions and give me more details about everything? I don't like surprises, and I don't like being unprepared. I may have some slight control issues," I say with a light grimace. "It's something I'm working on, but so far, no bueno."

"Well, until you're trained, you'll have to let go of those issues because you won't be in control. So, maybe this is a test. As far as the meeting goes..." he smiles a very devious smile, "it's a *formal* meeting which means you will need to formally represent the Fey as, Võitleja, our Warrior."

I cross my arms and scowl, "I do *not* like that smile. What does that mean, exactly?"

His smile widens. He's having way too much fun at my expense. "You'll need to dress the part," he gives me an idea of what that means and what it looks like.

"What?!" I exclaim. "I need to wear what?!" I shake my head, "I have nothing close to that in my closet."

"Oh, not to worry, the Queen sent me back with some goodies," he wiggles his eyebrows and smiles. Yeah, he's having way too much fun with this.

It's hard for me to stay scowling and defiant with Logan utterly amused. His smile cuts through my weak attempt at being tough. I can't help but smile back.

"You are unbelievable," I say laughing. "Fine. If that is what they want and how I have to *officially* showcase myself as the Fey Warrior, I guess I have no choice. But that doesn't mean I don't get a say in it. Deal?"

"Deal," he agrees. "We have plenty of time for you to get an outfit together, shower, and get ready for the meeting. It is at 5:00 p.m. and should take us about thirty minutes to get there from here. There will be food, drinks, and mingling after the formal meeting is concluded. So, I hope you're ready to be social."

"Great," I say sarcastically. "Since we have time, I'm going to get a workout in, and then you can show me the...*costumes*, I get to choose from," I say as I head back into the house.

I take my pre-workout and go to the bedroom to change. Coffee alone never affects me much, so the pre-workout is still needed. I put on my best pair of workout shorts. You know, the ones that sit just right on your hips and hug and accentuate the booty. Yup. Those are the ones. I'm about to sweat my ass off and shouldn't care about how I look but Logan is here. I know he's already seen me in a tank and underwear with no makeup on but I still want to try and look good. It's absolutely ridiculous, I know, but I do it anyway. The shorts are black, spandex type material, and I pair them with a black sports bra, throw my hair in a ponytail, grab my shoes, and walk out of the bedroom, heart racing and I haven't even started my workout.

Logan is sitting at the island. He doesn't say a word but men don't have to. A woman can always sense when a man's eyes are on her. 99.9% of the time I hate feeling like a piece of meat, but this is the 0.1% that I don't mind at all. In fact, I want it! I want his eyes on me. Even more, I want his hands on me. Jesus, Amarah, I scold myself at my inappropriate thoughts.

I don't say or do anything differently. I walk into the kitchen and fill up a glass with water for my workout and head out the sliding glass door to the gym in the backyard.

"I'll make chicken, veggies, and rice for lunch after my workout, but if you want something different, you'll have to go get it or order a delivery."

"That sounds perfect," he says as his eyes follow me out the door.

"Great," I reply without looking back.

Once inside the gym, I shut the door, and lean against it. I giggle and shake my head, "get a hold of your damn self, Amarah. You're acting like an inexperienced schoolgirl." But I can't help it. Logan makes me feel like I've never felt before and I'm legit, giddy. I walk over to the air conditioner and turned it on. It's already starting to get hot, and it's only late morning. Then again, the blood boiling in my veins probably has nothing to do with the weather.

I manage to focus and workout hard for a solid hour. I'm exhausted, but I feel great. It's one of those things that shouldn't make sense, ya know? Like, how can I feel great by exhausting myself? But working out is therapy for me. Something my body and mind need for a release. I'm also, suddenly, starving!

I walk out of the gym at the same time Logan walks out of the house. He's breathing hard and his chest is dripping in sweat. My heart is racing again and it has nothing to do with the workout I just did. I'm starring at a gorgeous, muscular man who is wearing only basketball shorts, is breathing hard, and has sweat dripping down his chest. My mouth is open and I'm sure I have a look of pure desire on my face. Since when is sweat sexy?

"I went for a run while you worked out," he says as if he knew I would ask what the hell he'd been doing.

"Eeewww. You like to run," I say it as a statement. "I guess you're not perfect after all."

"I can't say I enjoy running but in our line of work, you need endurance too, not just strength, so you better get used to running too," he says pointedly.

I shake my head, "I can think of another activity that's more enjoyable for endurance," I bite my bottom lip as I brazenly rake my eyes slowly down his body and back up again. The look on his face is priceless.

"Amarah," his voice comes out husky and deep and I don't think it has anything to do with being out of breath from the run. "You look at me like that and…"

"I'm starving!" I interrupt him before he can finish that line of thought. I'm not sure I have willpower if he voices what we're both feeling. "I'll get lunch ready and then we can figure out this meeting dress code." I head into the house before I can change my mind.

I make enough chicken, rice, and veggies for both of us. Logan shares a couple pieces of his chicken with Griffin. He seriously is making a good impression on me. I'm not sure if it's on purpose or if that's just him being his genuine self. I guess time will tell.

We finish lunch, and he goes outside to his truck and walks back in with a large suitcase. He lifts it onto the island and unzips it.

"It's all yours."

I walk over to the suitcase eyeing it as if it's a snake ready to strike. I look at Logan for any signs of what he's thinking but his face in frustratingly blank. His eyes are on me waiting to see my reaction. I toss open the top of the suitcase and my face falls. I open my mouth, then shut and open it again. I pull out a piece of clothing, if that's what you can call it, and look at Logan. He has that big, devious smile on his face again.

"You have got to be fucking kidding me!"

Warrior or Dominatrix

Back In Black by AC/DC

The inside of the suitcase smells like a new car. It's full of what looks to be black leather outfits, but all I can make out are pieces, straps, and buckles. What I pull out doesn't even seem to have a shape. I'm picturing the white bandage looking outfit from the movie, The Fifth Element.

"What on earth is this? How am I going to find something to wear if I can't even picture what the hell it is supposed to be?" I ask angrily. "I thought you said we were going to a meeting, not a damn S&M party!" I'm scowling.

Logan is laughing hysterically. "The look on your face!" He points with one hand and grabs his stomach with the other and doubles over.

"Well, I'm happy you're getting a kick out of this but seriously, I am *not* putting something like this on. They are just going to have to deal with it and accept me however the hell I show up."

Logan is gaining control of himself but still has that ridiculous smile on his face. "Oh, Amarah, you're so stubborn. I'm sure we can find something that you will be more comfortable in, but you might have to compromise just a little. The good news is, it doesn't have to be as extreme as that," he points to what I'm still holding. "C'mon, let's see what else is in here."

We start digging things out of the suitcase and there's a *lot* in there. Thankfully, not all of it was terrible. It takes a very long time, but I finally settle for what I think I can be comfortable wearing and moving in while also displaying the strength of a fierce Fey Warrior. Although, since I'm not a fierce warrior yet, that last part will be harder to pull off.

"Alright, well, I guess I better go shower and get this over with. I don't know what we're gonna do if this outfit doesn't work out because the rest of it..." I just shake my head.

"I'm sure it will be fine. I saw what you were wearing at the club. This seems to be fairly similar," he says matter-of-factly. "I'll shower after you."

I sigh, "fine." This task of finding an outfit has slowly drained the fight out of me. I just want to get this over and done with. I gather my little pile of leather and head off to the bedroom to get ready.

I'm standing in the bedroom staring at myself in the closet door mirror. I have to admit that I do look good in the outfit. I workout and have muscle tone, which makes the outfit work better for toughness. I don't have a lot of curves, but I have enough for it to also be a bit sexy.

I decided on a halter top that crisscrossed at the chest and again around the stomach. The halter top is designed with a low v-cut and shows off my cleavage. They're average but the halter top definitely perks them up. I'm wearing black shorts that have no pockets and hug my ass right under the cheeks. The zipper is in the back with a small hook inside to secure them. Can't have them unzipping in the middle of a fight!

I finish the outfit with a pair of ankle-high black boots that have a small heel but not enough to hinder my walking or make me twist my ankle. It's just too hot for longer boots or pants. I'm already going to be uncomfortable as it is much less sweating my ass off in all this leather, but surprisingly, it is comfortable. It moves well with me and I don't feel restricted.

My long, red hair is pulled up in a very high ponytail. Even so, my hair falls down almost to the top of the shorts. With my hair pulled back, it leaves my face exposed. I added some black eyeliner to my normal mascara only makeup routine, finishing it with a touch of blush and bright red lipstick. I'm ready to go but I've been standing here, staring at myself, for what feels like forever. I'm stalling.

Meeting Logan is one thing, but once I leave my house, it will all be more real. In my home, I'm still safe in my bubble and can tell myself that everything is fine. Nothing has changed. I'm still on my turf where I'm comfortable and in control. Once I go to this meeting, everything will change. I'm suddenly not ready for any of it.

There's a knock on my door from Logan, "Amarah, are you ready? We need to get going soon."

I let out a very heavy sigh, "yeah, I'm ready." I give myself one last look in the mirror. I stand up straight and lift my head. I need to be fierce and confident. "You can do this," I whisper to myself and then I walk out of the bedroom into the living room where Logan and Griffin are waiting.

"Jesus," Logan says as his eyes slowly rake over my body and take in my outfit. It makes me blush yet again, but looking at him, that's all I can think to say too.

"I didn't realize you have to dress up too."

He's wearing a pair of skin-tight, black leather pants that have a darker, thicker stripe of leather that comes from the outside of the thighs and down across to the inside of the knees. His black combat boots are tied up to the bottom of his calves. He has some leather straps tied around his upper arms, but other than that he's not wearing anything on his upper body.

"I'm a Protector and you're a Warrior. We are in the same line of work basically, and we showcase that. Everyone has their role, but we exaggerate it for these formal meetings. You'll get used to it and damn, this look suits you *very* well," he says with that half-smile and his eyes on my chest.

If I wanted to be his piece of meat earlier, I have no doubt in my mind I am at this moment. I shift in my stance, nervous at his attention. "It's not as uncomfortable as I thought it would be," I shrug.

He closes his eyes and then they meet mine. He seems to be struggling to keep his eyes on my face and not on my exposed body. Hell, I was having a hard time not staring at his body too.

"That's good because once you add on weapons it will be until you get used to them, but that will come later, with your training," he says hurriedly, like he knows I'm about to argue. Does he already know me so well?

All I can do is sigh again, "fine. Let me make sure Griffin has food and water and lock up and we can go."

I have to use the oh-shit handle inside his truck to help me jump up onto the seat. It isn't an enormous truck lift, but I'm not very tall. I buckle in and Logan starts the truck up. The air conditioner blasts to life, and the radio is on and set to a country station. I swear, this man is after my heart. I shake my head and focus on the important things. I'm about to be thrown into a whole new world that I only ever believed was stories and fantasy. I have no idea what to expect, and I'm getting extremely nervous. This is it. This is happening. The Fugees song comes to mind. Ready or not, here I come.

Fey Headquarters

Ready Or Not by Fugees

We head south on Tramway and hop on I-40 going West. Logan changes lanes until we're in the fast lane. He drives like he is. Confident. Not crazy and reckless but also not like a grandpa. We stay in the fast-lane for quite a while and neither of us speaks. I'm staring out the window, too lost in my thoughts to have a conversation anyway.

We finally make our way over to the right side of the freeway which means we'll be exiting soon. My heart starts to race, again. All this increased heart rate can't be good for me, I think. We exit on Rio Grande and get into the left-hand turn lane. Maybe now would be a good time to ask where we're headed?

"Where exactly are we going?" I break the silence.

"To the Fey Headquarters."

I scoff, "yeah, I figured that much, Captain Obvious, but where exactly is that?" I sound irritated, even to myself.

"I won't take that personally because I can only imagine how you must be feeling right now. Headquarters is in Historic Old Town.

It's the very first building built here in Albuquerque," he says as if it should have been common knowledge. It isn't.

"Wow. A history lesson on top of my world being turned upside down," I say sarcastically.

"I thought you wanted to know more. I thought you wanted more answers and explanations."

I sigh, "I do. I'm just nervous and that makes me cranky. Sorry."

We circle the small area that's considered Historic Old Town, twice, before we snag a parking spot. You can hardly ever find parking here. It's made up of mostly small, one-way, side roads, and a handful of merchandise shops and restaurants. It's a very popular destination for tourists. Albuquerque isn't a large city, and there might not be much to do as far as activities compared to large cities, but there is a lot of culture here. There are things here that you just can't find in other places, like red and green chile, for example. And no, I'm not talking about pickled jalapenos.

Logan parks the truck and turns off the engine, "are you ready?"

"Ready or not."

We hop out of the truck and I follow Logan's lead. He threw on a t-shirt so he isn't walking around Old Town half-naked. Even though I'm fully dressed, I still feel way too exposed. The outfits aren't exactly your everyday wear, and we're getting some weird glances. Logan doesn't seem the least bit phased but it makes me unbelievably uncomfortable.

We walk into the center of the Old Town Plaza and head towards the San Felipe de Neri Church. It's a single-story church built in Beige Adobe with an Adobe wall surrounding it. We walk through the wall entrance and we're standing directly in front of the church. There's beautiful red brick laid from the wall all the way to the steps leading up to the entrance. The door is a double, grey entryway door that's arched on top, very medieval. The roof is steepled in the middle with a cross standing solidly in the center. On each side of the main building stand two towers that have what look like windows facing forward. The towers also have smaller towers on top of them that are also adorned with crosses on top. I count six crosses just from where I'm standing. There are more buildings to each side of the Church that have been added on over time and I can't help but admire all this building has been through and still remains standing solid and strong.

"Well, I guess it makes sense for the Headquarters of the Fey to be a Church. They are, after all, fighting demons. The symbolism is spot on," I say and I'm not being sarcastic this time. "But it is smack dab in the middle of a tourist spot. Aren't you guys worried that you'll be discovered? That someone will see something they can't explain?"

"Not really. The Queen pays the Pastor and Church staff to keep the actual Church legit. All the Church staff and maintenance workers know about The Fey, the demons, and the war. They are on our side, obviously. The families that work in the Church have been doing so for generations, and they get paid handsomely for their discretion. The actual Fey Headquarters is underground," he explains.

"I see. That oddly makes a lot of sense."

"C'mon. Let's get you inside. We don't want to be late," he leads the way through the front doors. The room inside is lined with pews on each side. There's a raised stage upfront with a podium and the walls are lined with stained glass art. In the center of the stage, towards the ceiling, hangs a statue of Jesus on the cross. Yup, everything looks and feels just like a Church should.

We walk down the aisle between the pews and then head off towards the right. Logan pulls aside a drape that hides a door. No one comes to stop us as we make our way through the door. We're in a small hallway and we walk past what look like offices. We pass a few people in robes either in their office or walking in the opposite direction down the hallway. Everyone just nods at Logan, not saying a word.

We finally came to the last door at the end of the hallway. It's a regular-sized door and has a sign that says *staff only* on it. Of course, we go through this one. I don't know what I was expecting but I definitely wasn't expecting a regular storage room. The walls are lined with shelves full of binders, Bibles, extra robes, and all sorts of supplies and random Church decor. Logan walks to the opposite end of the room and moves a shelf forward on one end, creating a gap to squeeze through.

"C'mon, it's through here."

I walk over and through the passage. Logan follows me and moves the shelf back into place. He then reaches out to the empty wall, pushes on it, and it opens. Voila! A hidden door.

"Well, that's nifty," I say thoroughly entertained by all of this.

"Hidden in plain sight," he smiles. "Well, sort of. We can't have just anyone walking in and discovering The Unseen. The entrance is hidden well enough, and the staff knows everyone who is allowed to go and come. They will stop and question anyone they don't know. It's worked for us this far," he shrugs. "Well, this is it. Are you ready?"

"You asked me that already, remember?" I shake my head, "no, not really, but do I have a choice?"

"Not really," Logan sounds sad. "I'm sorry for that, but I promise you, it's not as bad as you think." He gently grabs my shoulder and gives me his sincere eyes. "These are *your* people. This is where you belong. I *feel* it. Trust me," he says with a gentle, reassuring squeeze.

"I know," I whisper. Because I feel it too. "And I do trust you. Let's go."

A Whole New World

A Whole New World by ZAYN, Zhavia

Logan gestures for me to enter the hidden passageway. There's a small landing before stairs decent into the unknown. There are light fixtures spaced far apart along the wall lighting the stairs just enough to see where I'm stepping but dark enough that I can't see the bottom. I definitely hadn't been expecting to see electricity running down here. What I had been expecting was dark, ominous stairs, covered in spiderwebs and medieval torches lining the wall. Shadows that moved and swayed and rats scurrying along the floor. Yeah, my imagination was definitely getting the best of me.

The quiet bang, as Logan pulls the wall-door closed behind us, makes me jump a bit and pull me back to reality.

"You ok?"

"Yeah, just super nervous," I say as I wring my hands in front of me.

Logan takes my hand in his with another gentle squeeze that says, *I got you*, as he leads me down the stairs. The stairs seem to go on forever and forever. I shiver as we continue descending into the Earth and I feel the temperature change. I can feel the Earth all around me. I feel like the Earth is alive and I feel the weight of it all around me. It's a bit terrifying to think about how much dirt is above me and all around me. What if something caused it to collapse while we're inside? There would be no surviving. I shiver again, this time, from the thoughts of being buried alive.

As if he can sense my dread, Logan stops and addresses my thoughts out loud, "we've been using this underground Headquarters for almost as long as I've been alive. I assure you it's safe and constantly inspected by a member of the Maa Family, to ensure its structure is sound."

I have no idea what that even means, so I just nod, still gripping his hand in mine, desperate not to lose our connection.

He's standing a few steps below me which puts our eyes level. His eyes appear darker green in the dim light, but if I look hard enough, I can still make out the streaks of yellow. Logan firmly grabs my chin and makes sure my attention is on him as he continues.

"I wouldn't have brought you here if it wasn't safe, Amarah. I would never do anything to put you in danger. Do you understand?"

His words are comforting but even more so are the *feelings* I can somehow feel him projecting. I have no idea why I feel this connected to him. To a complete stranger. It's mind-boggling and disorienting to feel so much from another person.

Again, all I can do is nod in response.

"Amarah, I need to hear you say it. I will never let anything hurt you. Do you understand?"

"I understand."

He dips his chin, satisfied, and continues to lead me down into the abyss. We finally get to the bottom landing and walk through another short hallway before we come to yet another closed door.

Logan opens the door and keeps a hold of my hand as I follow him through. I'm suddenly standing in a huge, open room. More than a room, a grand hall or something you would see in movies. Perhaps a huge theatre but even that thought doesn't do this grand room justice. It's very well lit, with enormous chandeliers hanging from the vaulted ceiling. The room is massive and makes me feel *tiny*. I imagine this is what Z from the movie Antz felt like when he left the colony and saw just how big the world is.

My eyes slowly take in the room. There's a raised dais on the opposite side of the room, a few stairs lead up to a…throne. There's no other word for it. A beautiful, throne that looks like it was carved out of one gigantic piece of marble. It's a sparkling pearl white with streaks and swirls of gold throughout. There are two smaller chairs on each side of the throne that seem to have been carved from stone as well, except they're a dark slate grey and half the size of the throne.

There's one gigantic table that runs vertically off to the right of the elevated dais. I count ten chairs on each side plus one end chair. There's no chair at the end closest to the dais. My guess is that no one would sit with their back to the Queen. Other than the dais and the banquet sized table, the room is completely empty, yet it feels full. I feel the energy in the space as if it's alive and filling the space with life. I'm not sure why, but I feel comfortable in it.

I take it all in, spinning around and around, wide-eyed, "wow! I was not expecting this to be down here! And there's a *throne*. An actual legit *throne*. For a *Queen*," I giggle. "So, I guess the movies get some things right after all!" I can't help but sound like an awestruck child.

Logan is smiling at me, "I've seen this hall a million times. It's easy to forget the magnitude of things when it becomes normal. Thank you for reminding me to appreciate what we have. It's easy to lose sight of simple things when you have lived as long as I have. I look forward to your reminders."

"You're welcome!" I say joyfully with a smile, my nervousness temporarily eclipsed by my awe.

Logan steps into my space, hand reaching for my face. His fingers slide into my hair at the nape of my neck as his palm cups my jaw. He caresses my cheek with his thumb as his eyes dart back and forth between mine.

"Beautiful." He holds my gaze longer than is normally comfortable but I can look into his eyes for hours.

Days.

Months.

Years.

Until the end of time.

Hope ignites in my chest along with need. The memory of his lips on mine seared into my soul. *Kiss me, please,* I think to myself but the thoughts are so loud I feel like I'm screaming them at the top of my lungs.

His Adam's apple bobs harshly as he steps back, his hand dropping from my face. "Make yourself at home. I'll go tell the Queen that we're ready and see if the others have arrived," he walks towards the dais, around it and then disappears.

He left me alone, and suddenly, I feel it. I feel very alone in this enormous and unfamiliar space but I don't think it has anything to do with my surrounding and everything to do with the man whose presence enthrals me. I walk towards the dais to get a better view of the throne and to be closer to where Logan disappeared. Chasing his energy.

The only sound to be heard are my footsteps on the hard-packed ground. I'm suddenly very aware of myself. I hear my breathing, which sounds normal, but I hear my heart beating a little too quickly. I'm sure nothing bad is going to happen to me. Why would Logan protect me from a demon and then bring me here to get hurt? He wouldn't. I mean, I don't know him. I don't know his motives. Maybe this is all a trick. Maybe he isn't one of the good guys. Maybe his goal has been to distract and disarm me this whole time.

"Amarah, calm down. Get control of your damn self. You're acting like a scared child and being ridiculous for no reason," I chastise myself.

I'm standing at the bottom of the stairs leading up to the dais. Seven stairs lead up to the massive throne. The throne is beautiful and magnificent in its simplicity. Very much like most things in nature are but there's no denying the respect it commands. I can see that it has been worn down through time but that does nothing to dissuade its authoritativeness.

How does a river cut through stone? With persistence and time. I wonder how many people have sat on this throne through the centuries? How old is the Fey Queen? Who will be next in line if she dies? Can she die? Who are the other two chairs for? Bodyguards? Advisors? The other Leaders? Is there a Princess or King? I have so many questions and don't even know where to begin.

Approaching footsteps bring my attention back to the present. They're coming from the same direction that Logan had gone. I back away from the dais to get a better view around it. I see Logan, back to being shirtless, towering behind a woman whom I assume is the Queen because she's wearing a crown. My heart is pounding again and my hands are sweaty. This is it. This is real. Oh shit!

15

Queen Anaxo

Kings and Queens by Ava Max

My first thought is how can this be the Queen? She looks like she can't be much older than me. Then again, Logan is three hundred years old and looks just as young. Once I move past the shock of her age and my preconceived ideas, I admire her beauty.

She's one of the most beautiful women I've ever seen and my eyes sweep across her taking it all in. Her pale skin is alite from a glow that seems to come from inside of her. It illuminates her sunflower yellow hair that moves like a real sunflower dancing in the breeze as it reaches for the sun. The front pieces are pulled back, leaving her face and neck unconcealed, but the rest flows freely around her shoulders and down her back.

Her gold dress shimmers and glints with every move. The dress is strapless and hugs her tight, pushing up her small breasts. Delicate and somewhat see-through lace in the design of flowers and leaves covers her midsection. The dress pleats and flows loosely around her lower half. A thin cape is slipped on, over her head, rests across her collarbone, and rests like a soft caress against her bare arms and flutters behind her. Diamonds are sewn into the veil catching the light and reflecting it back to the world in eye-catching winks at every angle.

Her crown.

A beacon.

A halo.

Gold and steepled in the front with an enormous diamond in the center, surrounded by three spikes on each side, it should have been menacing but it's anything but. It radiates light, just like the rest of her. Her crown is a golden sun sending golden rays of light across the room. It's so palpable that I want to close my eyes and feel the warm energy against my skin. I want to bask in her presence like a cream-drunk cat. I manage to keep my eyes open and jaw shut but I'm certain I have a look on my face exactly like I feel. Awe.

She stops a few feet in front of me, "hello, Amarah," she inclines her head slightly. "I'm Anaxo Andrews, Queen of Fey. It is my absolute honor to finally meet you."

Her voice is soft and eloquent but strong and firm at the same time. She smiles and it's absolutely radiant. It's one of those contagious, genuine smiles that makes you smile in return. Her eyes are the palest grey I've ever seen. Like a winter's day, but not cold. No, like a warm winter's day when you want to be outside playing in the snow. Her entire presence is warm and comforting like a bright summer day.

"The honor is mine, Queen Anaxo," I sound as nervous and unsure as I feel. "Although, I'm not sure if I should bow...or would that be curtsey? Or..." I'm fidgeting, wringing my hands and not portraying a fierce warrior *at all*.

She laughs sweetly and her voice reminds me of a bird singing a lovely Spring song. "I will not hold you to the customs you have not been trained in. It is quite alright, I assure you. I'll take no offense. At least not yet," she says smiling. "I appreciate the outfit. It will help remind the others of who you are. Although, it has less of a... punch... without any weapons. It will have to do for now. The others will arrive shortly. Please," she gestures towards the big table, "have a seat."

I walk over to the large table and take the seat at the end of the table closest to the dais. The dais is now on my right and the door we had come in through is to my left. I want to see as much of the room as possible, but there's still a whole lot of the open room behind me, and that makes me nervous.

Logan escorts the Queen up the dais steps and she takes her place on her throne looking completely comfortable and regal. Logan comes back down and takes the seat to my immediate left. He smiles winks. "See, nothing to be scared of. You're doing great," he encourages me.

"I feel utterly ridiculous and out of place. I'm going to make a fool out of myself in front of everyone and the Queen! I cannot believe I'm doing this," I spew in a frantic whisper. I feel panic stirring inside of my chest. What was I thinking coming here?

Logan reaches for me. I feel his strong, steady hand in mine. His comforting cool breeze washes over me for just a second but it's enough. He seems to know how to always comfort me and calm me down. He somehow provides me balance and confidence through himself.

I take a deep breath and blow it out slowly. "Thank you," I say quietly, and smile at him.

He smiles back, "the Queen likes you. I can sense it. She's the only one that truly matters at the end of this all. As I said, this is a formal meeting, and yes, you'll meet all the Leaders, but the Queen is the one with the ultimate power and decides everything regarding the Fey. Remember that as we go through the night. Don't try to please everyone because that's impossible. Don't take anything anyone says or does tonight personally. Remember, a lot is going on in a world that you know almost nothing about. Take tonight in stride and then take the rest one day at a time. Treat this situation like everything else you have ever learned and done in life. You never start off perfect, but practice and hard work can make you an expert. This is no different."

"Well, gee, thanks for that pep talk, Tony Robbins," I laugh. "Ok, all jokes aside, seriously...thank you, Logan," I look into his eyes and squeeze his hand trying to show him how much his support means to me. "Thank you for being here with me and thank you for believing in me. I'll do my best not to let you or anyone else down." I glance up at the Queen, "who are the other two chairs for?"

"I know you will, Amarah, and I have zero doubts. I've felt your power and that's with you not even knowing how to use it. You'll do great things, of that, I'm certain. As far as everything else, it will all be explained in due time. I'm not worried and you shouldn't be either."

Well, that makes one of us, I think to myslef. I *am* worried. How can I not be? I don't want to ruin the moment by expressing my doubts though, so I keep them to myself. Now is not the time to be showing any type of weakness, physically, mentally, or emotionally. I know that. So, I just give him a small smile, nod my head, and pray to God that I'm not in as much deep shit as I think I am. I don't have time to dwell on the thought because, just then, a door I hadn't even seen at the back of the room opens. Here goes nothing.

Take Your Place

Let's Get It Started by Black Eyed Peas

The door that opens is at the end of the room next to the door that we had come through. I had no idea the door was there and realize all of my attention had been focused on the dais, throne and tables. I take the time to glance around the outer walls of the hall and I had definitely missed a few things.

Also, towards the back of the room where the doors are, two identical archways opposite each other lead off each side of the main hall. I have no idea what's behind the new door or what's beyond the arches, and I have no clue what's behind the dais either. Man, I am really not starting off this new venture with my whits about me, that's for sure. I'm mentally chastising myself for my lack of awareness but my attention is quickly centered on the man walking toward us.

He's taller than Logan, but not by much. I'm putting his height at about six feet three inches tall give or take. His long legs make quick work of the distance between us as he strides right up the middle of the room with unwavering confidence. He has a nice tan to his skin, darker than Logan's creamy caramel shade, black hair shaved short to his head, and a very clean-cut beard and mustache that's little more than a five o'clock shadow. His expression is stern but not unfriendly.

I can't help but compare him to a sophisticated gangster with his all-black suit, black dress shirt, black vest, black tie, and black dress shoes that I know I'll be able to see my reflection in if I look. The suit looks expensive, and even though it's tailored to perfection, it looks like he'll bust a seam with any sudden, wrong movement. But what really makes me think *gangster* instead of *Wallstreet* are the muscles straining against the confines of the fabric. He could drape a sheet over his body and there would still be no hiding his massive frame. He obviously lives in the gym, and as much as I'm a fan of a man in shape, there is such a thing as too big.

He is.

And yet, he moves lightly and quietly on his feet.

Gangster.

Predator.

I asses him as much as I can as he passes the table without so much as a glance in my direction. I failed to take in my surrounding earlier but I'm proud of my seating decision. I'd be squirming right now if I had my back to this new stranger. He stops at the bottom of the stairs that lead up to the Queen. He bends down to one knee, one arm to his chest and the other behind his back. I'm now thoroughly impressed with his suit as it remains intact.

He bows his head, "Your Highness."

"Ethan, thank you for joining us tonight. Please, rise. You're the first of the Leaders to arrive. Take a seat and we will begin all introductions when everyone is present."

He bows again, this time at the waist, before he finally gives the table where Logan and I are sitting his attention. He takes the seat opposite of me.

"Logan," he reaches his hand out to Logan who takes it instantly. "Always good to see you," his voice is deep and little gravely, fitting him perfectly.

"Likewise," Logan replies. "Ethan, this is Amarah Rey."

"Pleasure to meet you, Amarah Rey" he offers his hand. I take it, and it's a little awkward because his hand is so big compared to mine, but we manage.

"Nice to meet you. Please, call me Amarah," I reply with a small, nervous smile.

Ethan's attention is now fully on me, like he's sizing me up, and I want to slouch in my chair and hide. Instead, I make myself sit up straighter and meet his gaze. His eyes are a deep, chocolate brown, and although his stare is intense and hard, I also see something else. Sadness. His eyes look sad. Like they don't see much joy. It makes me ease my posture and give him a warmer smile.

"Ethan Wright is the leader of the Werewolf pack in this region. In formal terms, his title is, Alfa Libahunt, which translates to Alpha Werewolf."

My eyes bounce between Ethan and Logan. Wait...if Ethan is the pack Leader...what is Logan? I guess I just assumed that he was the Leader. I mean, I know he's powerful. He even said he was more powerful than a regular Werewolf because of his connection to the Fey. I also know he's Kaitsja for the Fey. So why is he not the Leader? Is Ethan even more powerful than Logan? I'll have to remember to ask him later. I don't think now would be the best time to bring it up. You know, guys tending to want to measure body parts and all that.

I know the confusion is already displayed on my face, but hopefully Ethan perceives it as confusion in general since that's not too far off either. I am confused about everything.

What I finally manage to say, "seems easy enough, but I still hope there's not a test later tonight."

Ethan chuckles, "I imagine this is all pretty strange to you but it'll become the new normal before you know it."

"I sure hope you're right," I sigh.

Just then, the same door that Ethan came through, opens again. This time three people are walking up the aisle towards the dais. There are two guys, one girl, and to say they're all beautiful is an understatement.

They're stunning.

They glide instead of walk.

Their postures are absolute perfection.

They all hold their heads high. You can tell they're important even though they wear no crowns of their own.

They form a single-file line, and one by one, they bow and curtsy to the Queen. She nods her head at each of them and thanks them for coming. They all take seats at the same table we're sitting at and I feel like the red-headed step-child. Literally. This could be one of those picture tests, *which one doesn't match?* And the glaringly obvious answer is...*me.*

Once everyone is settled, the Queen speaks for all of us to hear. "Thank you all for being on time however, one is late. Where is Princess Hallana?" She asks no one in particular.

Everyone at the table looks blankly at each other. It;'s the other girl who finally speaks, "I'm sorry my Queen, but we do not know. No one has spoken to her or seen her today."

"Very well," the Queen replies. "I'll deal with her later. We will begin without her." Her voice is still the soft tone it had been since I met her, but I can see a tightness around her eyes and mouth. She is definitely not happy with this Princess Hallana. I don't know anyone here but I do know I don't want to end up on anyone's bad side, especially the Queen.

The Queen continues from her seat on the throne, "Logan, it's time to begin all formalities for introductions. Please escort Amarah to her official seat and then you may take yours."

I look at Logan, wide-eyed and confused. He doesn't say anything. He just stands up and reaches his hand out to me. I hesitate, but only for a second, before I take his offered hand. He places my hand around his arm and escorts me towards the dais. We start to climb the stairs and I'm beyond confused as he leads me to the chair that sits to the right of the Queen. I just stand there, in front of the chair, and look at Logan with pleading eyes as my hand tightens around his arm. *Don't leave me here!*

He leans in and whispers in my ear, "this is your seat, Amarah. Please sit." My eyes are wide, heart hammering in my chest, but I manage to remove my death-grip from Logan's arm and do as I'm told. Logan walks across the dais and takes the other seat to the left of the Queen.

I'm sitting at the right hand of the Queen!

I'm on a raised dais.

Four pairs of expectant and curious eyes are on me.

They must be able to see the fear and uncertainty written plainly on my face. I slide a glance to the Queen but her attention is on the guests at the table.

When I woke up this morning, I was just a regular girl, with a regular job and a regular life. Now I'm wrapped in leather, sitting next to a Queen and getting introduced to Fey Leaders and Alpha Werewolves.

What in the actual Hell is going on?!

Leaders of The Unseen

Savage by Megan Thee Stallion

"Thank you all for being here on such short notice. As I'm sure you have heard, the rumours are in fact, true. We have our very first Võitleja, our Warrior, who is going to be the key to ending this war. This is a glorious day and one that requires celebration!"

"However, we need to all be mindful of the fact that our Võitleja, Amarah," she glances at me, "comes to us unknowing of our world. She is raw and untrained in our ways. She will require vigorous training from each of you before she can truly become our Warrior. Our greatest weapon in this war."

"Despite being untrained, Logan has reported that her power is unlike anything he has felt before. She is powerful and this gives me great hope for our future."

She looks at me again and we make eye contact, "I expect great things from you, Amarah, and I look forward to watching you grow in yourself and in your power."

I feel myself starting to hunch, so I straightened in my seat. I pick my head up and met the Queen's heavy gaze, "I won't let you down, my Queen." My words are solid and strong, but my conviction, not so much. Do I believe all of this? I had only accessed my power once, with Logan's help, and I'm not convinced or nearly as confident as Logan and the Queen are in me. Talk about a lot of fucking pressure!

"I know," The Queen smiles. "Now, let's start with the introductions, shall we?" She motions at the table and the woman stands up and comes to stand in front of the dais.

She is petite. There's no way she's taller than five feet flat but that doesn't stop her from being confident and exuding authority. Her skin is fairer than the Queen's, almost white, and her hair is such an odd shade, I can't pinpoint a color for it. In the shade it looks grey but, in the light, the grey shines more like silver with purple highlights. I'm not sure any salon would be able to replicate it no matter how many times they tried.

It's styled in a kind of messy, yet sophisticated, and effortless look with free-flowing pieces framing her face. A look I've tried to master on several occasions and always failed miserably. As I finally move my attention to her face, her eyes make me gasp. Now I know she must take advantage of human inventions because there's no way her eye color is natural. They're a deep, brilliant purple, like I'm looking at a cut and polished amethyst stone.

She's wrapped in the most elegant satin gown I've only ever seen on TV and magazines from the red carpet. It's white and silver, hugging her petite curves possessively before flowing more loosely around her legs. Her bare shoulders are also lightly covered with a sheer, silver cape that clasps around her dainty neck. A huge teardrop amethyst hangs from the clasp and rests solidly in the middle of her chest.

"This is Princess Aaralyn Armada, of the Õhk Family. They are Masters of Air." The Queen's voice grabs my attention.

"It's an honor to meet you, Võitleja," Aralyn bows her head in my direction but she doesn't curtsey. "I look forward to hosting you at our home and training you on the Mastery of Air," she smiles sweetly.

I don't know what to do or if I'm supposed to speak. I have no clue how any of this works! I'm a fish out of water, literally gaping at the beauty surrounding me. I glance at the Queen, but she's facing forward, attention on Aralyn and providing me no clues.

I decide to reply because it's the polite thing to do, "thank you, Princess Aaralyn. I look forward to all of your teachings."

My words seem to be sufficient because she walks back to the table and takes her seat again. One of the men stands up next and approaches the dais.

He looks a little shorter than Logan and his navy-blue suit, minus the suit jacket, hugs his slender frame. His suit vest immediately catches my attention. It's a beautiful cerulean with darker blue waves embroider from top to bottom, and it's held together by five buttons. Except the buttons are not buttons at all but stones. Round, polished sapphires.

His skin tone is more normal than Aralyn's and the Queens, but still fair. I meet his crystal blue eyes and they're already on me, assessing me just as much as I'm assessing him. His gaze is curious and not unfriendly, but I'm not exactly getting the warm and fuzzies from him either.

"This is Prince Vadin Williams, of the Vesi Family. They are Masters of Water." The Queen repeats her introduction.

He nods his head in my direction and his wavy brown hair seems to move and flow fluidly with the movement. Like water.

We exchange our pleasantries and he doesn't smile or scowl. His sharp features are frustratingly blank leaving me with no perception of his thoughts about me. He seems utterly indifferent to me and to the entire affair.

He returns to the table and the last gentleman is about to get up for his turn when the door at the other end of the room slams open again.

A woman is stalking towards us with determination and fire in every step and she does *not* look friendly. Her skin is like coffee with three creams, as if she spends a lot of time in the sun or a tanning bed. Her jet-black hair is as straight as an arrow flowing down to the middle of her back. She's tall for a woman but she's also wearing high heels that add at least four inches to her height. The heels have straps that resemble flames wrapping up her long legs and disappear beneath the skin-tight, red leather dress. The dress has ¾ sleeves, sits high on her chest, and covers every inch of skin from her neck to her knees but leaves very little to the imagination. She fierce and gorgeous and...*angry*.

She stops in front of the dais and I see her eyes move to Logan before she looks right at me, hands on her hips and sneers. Her eyes are black pits with a glimmer of fire behind them.

"So, *this* is her," she motions in my direction. "Great, just great. Look at her. She looks terrified. *She* is going to be our Warrior?" She laughs harshly, "we're doomed."

The Queen sits still and silent on her throne but I can see her jaw clenching tightly. She's *not* happy. When she speaks, her voice comes out just as it has always been, soft and pleasant. I don't know how she did it. I would have lost my shit at the disrespect this new woman is blatantly showing.

"This is Princess Hallana Chavez, of the Tulekahju Family. They are Masters of Fire." Her voice hardens a tad bit more, "they tend to be hot-headed and struggle to hold their temper. You will apologize to Amarah, our Võitleja, and the rest of the Family for your tardiness, lack of manners, and complete disrespect."

"This is insane!" She yells. "Look at her! She is a nobody. Even if she has power, it will take her a lifetime to Master it! We don't have that kind of time!"

The Queen is on her feet so fast I didn't even see her move. A powerful burst of wind comes off of her but it isn't aimed at me. It's aimed at Princess Hallana. She drops to a knee and seems to struggle against the Queen's power. Her head is bowed down, her hands gripping the Earth beneath her, as she holds her ground against the wind assaulting her.

This time when the Queen speaks, it's not friendly, "I will not allow this disrespect in my court!" Her voice booms and seems to come from everywhere. "You will apologize and you will take your seat at the table. NOW!" The Queen raises her arm, palm up, and Princess Hallana follows as if being pulled up by strings like a marionette doll and the Queen is controlling her.

The Queen's power is still in full force. I can feel it in the air around me making it thick and hard to breathe. I can't imagine being the one it's directed at. I kind of feel bad for the Princess even though she's no fan of mine.

Princess Hallana squares her shoulders and lifts her head in stubbornness but she accepts her place. Reluctantly, but she does.

"Forgive me, Võitleja," her voice is low and strangled, either from the force of the Queen's power or from her hatred and humiliation. Probably all three.

The Queen drops her arm and returns to her seat. The power is just suddenly gone and the Princess stumbles as it's pulled away. The look in her eyes is scorching and I know her apology is far from sincere. I have a feeling that I need to watch my back with her. She's shown her hand and her distaste for me is clearly received. She makes it the table, yanks out a chair and takes seat as her eyes once again travel to Logan.

"Now, let's pick up where we left off before we were so rudely interrupted," The Queen gathers her composure effortlessly.

The last gentleman from the table gets up and comes to the dais. His stature is similar to Logan but he doesn't match the muscle. Then again, I'm not sure anyone besides Ethan stands a chance at matching Logan's Greek God-like physique.

His skin is even darker than Princess Hallana's and his black hair hangs almost to his shoulders in unruly tight curls. He's wearing a chocolate brown dress shirt similarly embroidered to Vadin's vest, except instead of waves, his shirt is adorned with vines and leaves in all shades of green. His shirt is also held together by polished and stunning emeralds. The shirt is tucked into brown leather pants that hug his muscular thighs and disappear into tan combat boots.

"Well, I don't know if I can top that last introduction. Hallana kind of stole my...*fire*," he winks in my direction, his forest green eyes sparkling with humor. His eyes are true green, no hints of any other mix of colors and they stand out in great contrast to his dark skin.

"This is Prince Emrick Marshall, of the Maa Family. They are Masters of Earth." The Queen says one last time.

Prince Emrick places a hand on his chest as he bows in my direction. His smile is brilliant and warm, "it is my honor to meet you, Võitleja. I look forward to our training together and teaching you all about Earth Magic." His voice is deep and comforting and I appreciate his attempt to lighten the situation. His energy is calm and positive and I like him instantly.

I can't help but smile in return, "the honor is mine, Prince Emrick. I look forward to our training as well. Thank you." I give a small nod, hoping he understands my gratitude.

The Queen moves things along, "I believe you've already been introduced to Ethan Wright. He is Alfa Libahunt, the Leader of the Los Lobos Pack." Ethan stands and bows his head in our direction from the table. "Now that we're all acquainted, let's move forward, shall we?"

I wish I could see Logan from where I'm siting. I wish I could touch him for comfort. I wish I could ask him what else we have to do in this formal meeting. Not everyone here is in my corner, obviously, and just because the others have not spoken out, doesn't mean they don't feel the same way as Princess Hallana. I'm feeling insecure and honestly, just want to run screaming from this hall and never look back.

Show Us Your Power

Sex On Fire by Kings of Leon

"The war has always been challenging." For the first time, the Queen sounds tired. "We have succeeded in keeping Earth and humanity safe thus far, but, as you all know, we have been struggling recently." The Queen stands and paces across the dais, "we have fought, and we have sacrificed more than *anyone* else. We have lost more people than the Werewolves and those cowardly bastards, the Vampires, who still refuse to join the fight." She sounds disgusted as she mentions the Vampires.

Vampires.

Of course, there are Vampires!

Of course.

I mean, this *is* a magical world filled with all sorts of preternatural creatures so why wouldn't there be Vampires? My thoughts get stuck on this fact and I have a million more questions. Are there Vampires here, in Albuquerque? Are they hidden or out in plain sight? Do they burn in daylight? Are they repelled by garlic and Holy objects? Can they hypnotize with their eyes? Which facts are true and which are myths? Are they dangerous? Do I need to fear them?

I glance over at Logan. I can see him now that the Queen is not sitting in the middle of us. He turns my way as if he can feel my eyes on him. We make eye contact, and I'm not sure what my face shows, but he mouths the words, *it's ok.*

It's ok? How is *any* of this ok? I'm starting to agree with Princess Hallana more and more. I'm *way* out of my league!

The Queen continues, "therefore, we must start Amarah's training, immediately. We have no time to lose, and I'm completely aware of that," she glares at Hallana as she makes the statement.

"Yes, Amarah is naïve in our ways and completely untrained but she was born for *this* reason. We cannot ignore the miracle that we have been given. We need to believe in this path. We need to believe in Amarah. I know that some of you doubt the truth of Amarah's background, and that she was made for this, but I'm asking you all to trust me."

She's pleading her case to the table of Leaders. They all turn their attention to me and I have to physically steady myself under their scrutinizing gazes. I want to squirm. I want to duck my head and shrink away. I don't blame them for their doubt and hesitation. Hell, I'm doubting myself right along with them!

Of course, it's Princess Hallana who speaks, "my Queen, perhaps we can see a display of her power? If we can see what you already see," she shrugs as if it's no big deal, "then maybe that would ease our uncertainty." The others at the table nod and voice their agreement.

The Queen sighs, "very well. I believe that's a fair request." She turns to me, "Amarah, are you up for showing us some of your power?"

I look at her and then at Logan. Logan nods in encouragement. I look at the Leaders of the Fey Families, and Ethan on behalf of the Werewolves, and their expectant gazes. They need to see my power. They need to know that they're not wasting their time but investing it into something, *someone*, who cand help them. It's a reasonable request, and I understand it completely, but I honestly don't know if I can do it.

I look at the Queen and all I can do is be honest, "I understand the request and I would be happy to oblige, it's just…" I look at Logan again, "I don't know how," it pains me to admit.

I hear a loud, *humph*, and immediately look in Hallanah's direction as she crosses her arms in an, *I told you so gesture.*

"Well, how can we help?" This from the sweet, angelic-looking Princess Aaralyn.

"I'm not sure. I've only accessed it once. The night that it was… *activated.*"

"How did you access it then? Maybe we could do something similar to help you now?" Gee, little miss helpful.

"I seem to have a…" I clear my throat, "a… *connection* to Logan," I glance at him shyly and feel a slight blush rushing into my cheeks. Really, Amarah? Not here! I sit up straighter in my chair. "He helped me call my power that night."

"Very well," the Queen says. "Logan, will you assist Amarah in calling her power?"

"Of course, my Queen. I will do whatever I can to help," He stands up from his chair and comes to kneel in front of me. The

Queen sits back down on her throne, waiting patiently. I look at the table below us and everyone is watching. They're practically jumping out of their seats waiting to be wowed…or disappointed.

Logan cradles my face in his hands, forcing my attention back to him. That one simple touch calms me down and comforts me. Why does he have such a strong effect on me?

"Hey, are you alright?" He whispers.

"I don't think I can do this. I'm not ready! What if I'm not what the Queen thinks I am? What if I can't call my power. What if I prove Princess Hallana right?" I'm shaking my head.

"You won't. I know you're powerful. I've *felt* it. You need to believe in yourself, Amarah. You can do this and I'll be here, right beside you. I'll support you in any way you need. What do you need from me?" He moves his hands to mine and holds them softly, but firmly, letting me know I don't have to do this alone.

"I don't know! They're all staring at us. At me! I can't do this with everyone watching and waiting for me to do something…*spectacular*."

"Forget about them, Amarah. Look at me. Focus on me. Let the rest of the room just fade away. It's just you and me. I won't let anything or anyone hurt you. You're safe. Now, I want you to close your eyes so you can focus."

I nod and swallow down my nerves and insecurity. I close my eyes.

"Good, now take a deep breath."

I do.

"Relax and just listen to my voice. Feel my hands in yours."
As he says that last part, he lets go of his cool power and it blows across my skin, giving me goosebumps.

I shiver but it's not cold. Just the opposite, it's perfect. Comforting. I let his cool breeze caress and surround me. My body reacts to it, to *him*, and I feel that new weight stirring in my chest. I open my eyes and Logan's eyes are already on mine. He looks at me with such desire in his eyes it takes the breath right out of my lungs. My body reacts to that look, to Logan, like I knew I would. I stand, bringing Logan to his feet with me, but we never break eye contact.

Just like he said, there's no one else in the entire world much less anyone in this room. It's just Logan.

I'm the moth.

He's the flame.

And I'm trusting him not to burn me.

His lime-green eyes revealing everything he's feeling as clear as if he inked it right into my skin for all to see. This time, I don't stop my hands. I let them roam their way up his naked arms, feeling the muscles tense underneath my touch.

My hands end up on each side of his chest and my eyes are lost in his. This stranger is my new gravity. My truth North. And nothing and no one else matters. Not the Queen, not Hallana, not the war. Nothing.

My right hand is placed over his heart and I can feel it beating fast and hard. So alive. The mark on his chest that I thought was a scar is more like a birthmark with only a small scar near it.

I explore it with the barest touch of my fingertips. The large circle is nothing more than a slight discoloration and just as smooth as the rest of his perfect skin. I touch the smaller scar and trace it lightly. The skin is thick and damaged, and as I examine it, I make out the design. A star. He shivers under my hands and I feel goosebumps erupt on his flesh.

I close my eyes and concentrate on the spark in my chest. There it is. There's my power. Now that I have a hold of it, it seems so easy to do. Like breathing.

I hold onto my power and slowly pull it around me. I extend it and wrap Logan in my power with me. I can feel his chest rising and falling with his heavy breathing. His heart is a steady and deep beat under my hand. A beat that travels through my veins and resonates in my chest. My heart matching his cadence like a beautiful duet.

You and me.

Me and you.

I finally open my eyes to look at him but his eyes are the ones closed now. His lips slightly parted as he's lost to our power. Our connection. I want to stay in this place forever. Our private world. And just explore Logan on every level. But I know I need to do something. I need to focus on the reality of our situation and not just hide away in our special place in the world. In each other.

"Now what do I do?" I ask.

He opens his eyes and his voice is heavy with heat, "show them, Amarah. Show them your power." He leans down and kisses me.

I immediately meet him for the kiss, rising on my tiptoes to make the kiss easier. My hands are steady on his chest and his hands are gripping my sides. He pulls me flush against his hard body and my power ignites around us. His tongue slides across my lips, asking for more this time, and I don't deny him. I don't ever want to dent him.

I follow his lead and open my mouth to his. The moment his tongue finds mine it sends a shock wave of pleasure through my body, straight down to settle between my legs, and I can't contain the moan that races up through my body and into his.

He claims my mouth like he's kissed it a million times before. His hands clutch at me and he crush me harder to his body. Everything about it is hungry, aggressive, possessive, passion and fire.

Jesus Christ.

I feel like I'm burning up from the inside.

His tongue, his touch, is gasoline pouring on me.

I can feel the heat from me and the cool breeze from him mingling around us like a cocoon. A cocoon of passion and power. Safety. My heart is pounding in my chest and my skin is vibrating with power. When it feels like I'm about to drown in his kiss, in our power, I pull away with a groan and send that drowning power out into the hall with force.

Logan and I both stagger. I end up sitting back on the chair with Logan on his knees in front of me, head bowed. His shoulders are rising and falling with deep breaths as if he's just run a marathon. A sudden jolt of fear runs through me. What did I do? What did my power do? Did I hurt him? It takes me some time to find my voice, but when I finally manage to speak, it's low and hoarse as if I've been screaming.

"Logan, are you alright? Are you hurt?" I reach for his face.

He looks up at me with heavy-lidded, sparkling peridot eyes, and gives me his cocky half-smile. I let out a relieved sigh.

He runs his hand through his hair. "Sweet Jesus, you are something else," he chuckles.

I'm holding his face in my hands, searching his eyes for any sign of pain, "did I hurt you?"

"Not even a little bit," his smile widens. He grabs my hands and brings them to his lips, giving each one a kiss. "Don't be afraid of your power, Amarah. The more you try to hold it back and ignore it the more dangerous it will be. Accept it and will be able to control it better. Stop fighting it."

"I'm trying. I promise, I *am* trying."

"Ahem!" The Queen is standing over us and I'm suddenly mortified.

I made out with Logan in front of the Queen! Hell, I was practically climbing his body like he was a jungle gym. Not to mention the other Leaders. I'm ok with a little PDA but that didn't feel like the type of kiss to be shared in public. Son of a bitch. I feel my cheeks flaming. How am I going to face everyone after that?

"I don't mean to interrupt but, Amarah, why don't you have a look at what your power has done."

Uh oh. That doesn't sound good. My heart is in my throat and I swallow hard. What had I done? I squeeze my eyes tightly wanting to disappear. Wanting to wake up and realize this is all a dream.

"Aamrah," Logan's voice is comforting. Maybe I don't want this to be a dream after all. "It's ok, Amarah. Look."

I blow out a heavy breath, peel open my eyes and Logan. He nods, encouraging me. I finally look past him, towards the table where the Leaders are seated, and I can't believe my eyes.

19

What Lies Underneath

Underneath by Adam Lambert

I sit in my chair, eyes-wide and mouth agape. If I felt like a fish out of water before, now the feeling is even more pronounced. I no longer see the human beauty that had been sitting at the table. Every single person has been entirely transformed. I mean, they're still themselves but...wow! If I thought they were beautiful before, they're breathtakingly stunning now. The word that comes to mind is *mystical*.

Princess Aralyn's skin is shimmering, like an opal, or like someone has thrown pixie dust on her, and she has wings. They're almost translucent but as they move, they reflect the light in a rainbow of colors. They're impossibly dainty, just like her, and look like they will rip at the slightest touch. I know that can't possibly be true though. They have to be strong to carry her through the air.

Prince Vadin's skin is also shimmering, but not like Aralyn. No, his skin is shinier and has a wet look to it. When I look closely, I notice his skin is made up of iridescent scales in different shades of blue.

Prince Emrick's skin looks rough, like it has texture to it. It reminds me of the bark of a tree. He has small horns protruding out of his head. They remind me of an antelope's horns, about five inches, straight, with no curl or shape to them. His emerald eyes, which have stayed the same, are sparkling and he gives me a small smile as I assess his new form. He doesn't seem to be upset about what I've done. I can't say the same for the next person my eyes roam over.

Princess Hallana's skin is covered in scales, shades of red and orange. The spark of fire is even more noticeable behind her eyes. I'm sure if she could shoot fire from her eyes, she would be doing it right now. At me!

Their bodies all represent their Families. It makes sense but I can't help the shock that's taken over my system. They're no longer the perfect, elegant *people* they had shown me. No, they're so much more. They're mystical and stunning *Fey*.

I had almost forgotten about Ethan. As I take him in, I'm not seeing any difference. His body looks the same as it always has. I'm about to turn my attention away when he lifts his head and makes eye contact with me. His eyes are no longer the sad, brown eyes I saw before. They're straight amber, exactly like the stone. Wolf eyes. I can't help the small gasp that escapes me.

Just like when Logan changed his eyes for an instant, it's a bit unsettling to see animal eyes staring at me in Ethan's human face. The eyes are animal eyes but the look behind them is still human. Still intelligent. He looks...*dangerous*.

I turn back to the Queen still standing by us. She's still the same exquisite perfection that she has been all night. "What exactly did I do and how come my power didn't affect you?" I manage to ask through my shock.

"Your power has stripped away all glamour. You are now seeing their true Fey forms. Ethan is strong and has held on to his body, but a lesser Wolf would have probably been forced to transition into his Wolf form."

I glance at Logan, and he doesn't have Wolf eyes. The Queen notices my confusion and answers before I ask. "Logan is very powerful and also has Fey power in him as well as being a Werewolf. He won't be as easily affected by your power," she explains.

I hear him scoff quietly.

"Your power did not affect me because I'm not using any glamour. This is my true Fey form. You and I are from the Müstik Family. We were the First Fey Bloodline and the only ones who can pass for humans without using magic."

"Oh," I say, as if it all makes sense. Which it doesn't! I'm still in shock and don't even know if I'm absorbing any information the Queen is giving me. She doesn't use glamour, which means she's always this beautiful. How is anyone so flawless?

"I know it's a lot to take in, Amarah, but you *will* and it will all be ok," she smiles.

"Ok." Again, I feel like I'm hearing her words. They're entering my ears but I don't really feel them resonating yet. I feel like I'm in a daze, in a dream, trying to grasp onto something solid. Something that makes sense. But this is a whole new world and the only thing I'm missing is a magic carpet ride.

"Did I show enough power to help you convince them to believe in me? Just taking glamour away doesn't seem like much of a show," I whisper, not wanting the others to hear me

The Queen laughs and returns to her throne. "Oh, on the contrary, Amarah, that was quite the show," she looks at me and then Logan. She's teasing us and I blush again, hard.

"Leaders, Amarah asked if her show of power is enough to help you all believe in her. Would anyone like to explain to Amarah what's just happened? The Queen asks.

I look over to the table and they all look a bit taken aback at what's happened but also pleasantly surprised. Maybe I've made a friend or two in this process. Well, with one fire-breathing exception. Hallana glares at me and I swear she's trying to burn a hole straight through my heart with that stare. I don't understand her complete detestation of me. She doesn't even know me but it doesn't seem like she wants to give me a chance.

I'm surprised when Prince Vadin is the one to stand up. "Our glamour is the most basic of our magic. It's something that we learn to wield at an early age so we blend into the human world. It's one of the easiest things to do and to hold on to. It's like breathing for us. We can hold on to our glamour when other, stronger magic and strength fail us. We can hold on to our glamour through just about anything. We all fought your power and tried to hold on to our glamour. We all failed. None of us were strong enough to fight your power on this one simple task," he says this all matter-of-factly and like it doesn't bother him one way or another.

His words resonate with me and I don't know what to say. I forced them into their authentic forms against their will. Now I know why a certain Princess is even angrier at me.

"I'm so sorry. I didn't mean to strip you of your glamour. I honestly had no idea what my power would do. I just willed it not to hurt anyone," I shrug.

The Queen speaks again, "I believe, that subconsciously, you want answers and you want the truth. Your power stripped away the glamour to give you the truth. Your power *is you*. It will do your bidding regardless if you're thinking about it in your mind or your subconscious. Therefore, you need to become one with your power and control it. It can be very dangerous if you're scared or emotional. You don't want to lash out and hurt anyone by accident."

"No, I don't! Will you help me?"

"We will help you," she smiles at me before returning her attention to the Leaders. "Now, I take it that was enough proof for you all?"

They all nod their heads and agree that what I did is enough for them to give me a chance. For now.

"Good. Now, we will get this hall prepared for the celebration! You are all dismissed."

The Queen walks over to us. Logan has stayed kneeling in front of my chair the entire time, his hand resting on my knee, like a steady companion. A Protector.

The Queen addresses Logan, "I would like some time alone with Amarah, please. I'll show her to her room," she turns to me with a genuine, warm smile, "and I imagine there are still more questions in that brain of yours."

I feel the absence of Logan as soon as his hand leaves my knee and he stands to face the Queen, "of course, my Queen. I'll get ready for dinner and see what the others are discussing." He reaches his hand out and caresses my cheek, "you'll be safe with the Queen."

He bows his head and heads off in the same direction the others had gone before I can argue.

The Queen offers me her arm, "shall we?"

Home Away From Home

Home by Phillip Phillips

We walk arm in arm to the back of the hall and enter the same hallway the others disappeared through. I'm not sure what I had been expecting, but not just a...hallway. Well, more like a tunnel.

"I can't believe all this is down here," I say out loud.

"Kind of crazy, isn't it?" the Queen replies. "There are underground tunnels that connect all over the city. We control them all. Only a handful of people know these tunnels inside and out. Not even the Werewolves know all the entrances and tunnels."

We approach a split in the tunnel where we can either go straight, left, or right. The Queen steers us right.

"It took us a very long time to create what you see now. Some of these tunnels and rooms were man-made, while others are all nature's work. We have had centuries here to make it our home and become experts in the passageways."

"Well, it's amazing! I would have never believed this existed if I wasn't seeing it for myself. To be honest, I'm still having trouble wrapping my mind around it all."

"I know. It will take time. I understand this, but I must ask you to try harder. We need you sooner rather than later."

"I don't mean to be rude or disrespectful my Queen but that is a lot of fucking pressure!"

The Queen chuckles, "you may call me Ana. The title is for formal occasions and gatherings. And, yes, I know it's a lot of pressure however, you were *made* for this. Ah, here we are."

We had walked quite a way down the tunnel hallway and finally stop in front of a door. The Queen, Anaxo or Ana, smiles at me and opens the door. She leads the way through the door and then stand to the side so I can fully enter the room. It's very large, which I hadn't expected, and beautiful!

We stood in the entryway, which has a small bench and round table to the right, a coat hanger to the left, and then opens up into an oval room. A large king-size, four-poster bed sits in the middle of the room against the left wall. It looks like a bed fit for the Queen, not for me. The bed is covered in a grey comforter, a white throw folded across a corner, and topped with grey and white pillows. The posts of the bed are adorned with white, almost sheer curtains that are currently tied back.

As I take in more of the room, I notice an enormous chest at the foot of the bed, an extra-large, fluffy black rug that covers the ground from under the bed out to meet the vanity opposite the bed. I have the urge to kick off my shoes and see if the rug is as soft as it looks, but I manage to keep them on along with my composure.

On the wall opposite to where I'm standing, is a huge fireplace carved into the wall but I can't see where there's an outlet for the smoke.

"How is there a fireplace down here? There's no place for the smoke to exit?" I ask confused.

"We control the elements, Amarah. We can make a fire without the smoke," she answers. I just stare at her, still so confused by it all, and she just smiles back at me. My questions must be so amusing to everyone.

I pass the bed and fireplace and head towards an arched doorway on the right side of the room. I can suddenly hear the trickling of water. As I enter the next room, it becomes clear that it's the bathroom, but the word *bathroom* just didn't cut it.

I notice a smaller arched doorway immediately off to my right. I peek around the small corner and find a large, walk-in closet. It has a matching black rug and a cushioned bench seat right in the middle of the room. The closet takes up three of the four walls with an oversized mirror on the last wall.

I focus back on the bathroom in front of me. There's a long countertop with double sinks and another long, oversized mirror on the right-side wall that separates the bathroom and closet. The countertops are natural stone that has been sanded down to a smooth surface with sinks carved into them. On the left side, where there should have been a bathtub or shower, was an actual natural spring. It's round and larger than any hot tub I've ever seen. It could accommodate fifteen people, easily. There's water cascading down the far side in a small waterfall that came from the ceiling.

Walking further into the room I notice two smaller doors opposite each other. The one on the right, at the end of the countertop, is a linen closet, and the door opposite is the toilet. It's obvious the plumbing additions are manmade but everything is natural. It's stunning and impossible and blowing my freaking mind!

I walk over towards the spring and test the water with my fingertips. It's hot. A natural hot spring.

"Oh, my God! This is amazing! It's like a dream!" I exclaim.

"I'm so happy you like it, Amarah. This is your room to come and go here as you please."

She allows me a few moments to explore, see and touch everything. She's watching me with a soft, genuine look that I just don't quite understand. She's looking at me like I'm someone special to her. Maybe I am. Maybe I am this special warrior meant to fight with the Fey but the look she's giving me feels like...*more*. It feels like love and I don't understand it.

I follow the Queen into the bedroom and she picks up a picture from the bedside table and sits down on the bed. "Amarah, come sit with me," she pats a spot on the bed next to her. "I think it's time that I told you about your family. You need to know about your mother, grandmother, and how you were born." Her words are normal but her tone is sad.

All my joy and awe slip away as I reel at the thought of hearing about my family. My *true* Family. All this talk about power and demons and war distracted me from the biggest truth of all. Who I am. It hadn't hit me yet that the people I know as my family, my mom, and my two sisters are, in fact, not my family at all. My heart aches at the thought but I can't help the curiosity tugging at me too. I want to know who my actual family is. I want to know where I come from and my history. My true Bloodline. I want to know it all but I'm suddenly terrified to hear the truth.

My truth.

My Family History

"I suppose I need to start at the beginning. Our people have been on Earth since the beginning of time. We were created just as all the other beings and things on this earth were. We had our place in the world just as everything else did. We lived in peace and harmony for a very long time, in fact, we were often sought after for our medicine and healing. We've always been one with nature and could harness the elements. As time progressed, and men became more and more power-hungry, they started to fear that which was different. They started to fear that which they didn't understand, people who had power they so desperately wanted, and those whom they could not control. The Fey."

"Those ignorant and fearful people, who did not understand that we were just connected to nature, a part of it, started to call us Witches. They said we were unnatural, evil, when in fact, we are the most natural creatures on Earth. Nevertheless, they hunted us. Their fear made them hate us for no reason. Are you familiar with the Salem Witch trials that happened in 1692?" The Queen asks.

"I am, yes. Just what they teach us in school."

"I was there and so was your mother, my little sister, Alexandria, but we were just children at the time. My mother, your grandmother, Analise, was a midwife in Salem. In addition to helping women through their pregnancies, Analise was also known for her healing. Her connection to nature was quickly turned into something evil by mindless, fearful men. She was deemed to be a Witch and was sentenced to death by being burned at the stake."

I sit on the bed and listen to her tell me this unbelievable story about my grandmother. It's so hard to believe, but watching her tell the story, I know it's true. I watch her, and I know she's not longer seeing anything in this room. Ana has gone back in time and is reliving her time in Salem. I can see the raw sorrow and pain reflected in her eyes.

"We tried to run, all of us, but only some of us got away. My mother was caught and taken. They tied her up in the center of town, on a stake surrounded by dry straw. I stopped running and turned back. I couldn't leave her. I couldn't run away not knowing what happened. So I stayed and I saw it. I saw it all." Her eyes are staring into space, her voice is hollow and I know she's back in that day. Back in the horror of what she witnessed. I want to reach out to her but I don't want to distract her either. I need to hear this story. My history.

"I saw her when they lit it. My mother could somewhat manipulate the flames but she was not a Master of Fire. She couldn't extinguish them and they slowly started to burn her. Her lover at the time was a Werewolf, but he had kept that secret hidden like the rest of us. He tried to free her but he was held back by a crowd of men. Still, he fought. He couldn't change into his Wolf form without the help of the full moon so he was forced to try and fight as no more than a man. Even with his Werewolf strength there were too many to fight," she pauses to gather herself.

I don't rush her. I don't move. I don't make a sound. When she's ready, she continues, "my mother was slowly burning alive and she also had to watch her lover being killed because he was trying to save her, to free her. I cannot imagine what she felt at that moment but it must have been extreme pain both physically and emotionally. I heard her ragged screams, one after another after another. Until they stopped," her eyes are haunted by the memory.

"I thought she was dead but she was gathering all her strength. She gathered all of her power, everything she had inside of her, and in one last raging scream, she released it. It was like a sonic boom. I remember the echo of it in my head and the Earth shook and split. It was like the force of a tornado wind and an earthquake all in one. All of the humans were cut down. Dead. The fire had been extinguished and her bonds broken, but it was too late. She crawled to where her lover lay, unmoving. She was badly burnt and had no power left to heal herself. She was dying. She laid one last kiss on her lover's lips and collapsed against him. I ran to her but I was too late. She was gone."

"I'm so sorry, Ana. I know that no words can ever be enough to comfort you. No one should ever have to see their parents die. Especially a child and especially in such a horrific way. I can't imagine what that must have been like for you. What that still must be like for you."

"It was over three hundred years ago and I can still see it in my mind like it was yesterday. I'm thankful that it was me who saw it and not your mother. She was way too young at the time and I don't think she could have gotten past it."

"So, you are my aunt," I say with a small smile. Finally understanding the look of love I saw in her eyes. "Where is my mother?"

"Yes, I'm your aunt and we're family. I'm so happy to finally have you here with us. With me. I've watched over you, from afar, since you were born. I placed you with a family I knew could protect you and keep you safe. However, they did not know just how special you are. No one could know. I promised your mother I would watch over you and make sure you were safe. It is a promise I intend to keep still," she says with determination in her eyes. "You look so much like your mother, Amarah," she says as she hands me the photo she's been holding.

It's a picture of Ana with another girl. They are hugging and laughing in the photo. It's very candid and it makes me smile, "is this her? Is this my mother?" I ask as I caress the photo.

"Yes," Ana whispers.

My mother, like her sister, is beautiful, but completely different. Where Ana is fair skin and seems to be light itself, my mother is darker. Darker skin, dark brown hair, and hazel eyes. "I have my mother's eyes," I say out loud.

The realization bringing tears to my eyes. Even with the darker tones, my mother also has a light about her. It's like a light illuminated from within both of them. They're complete opposites and yet, absolutely the same. I want to look at this photo forever. I want to know everything there is to know about my mother, but Ana continues with the story before I can ask any mor questions. I listen eagerly.

"It wasn't until years later after your mother and I both Mastered our power that we found out what your grandmother had done. When she released her power with such force and with such anger, she caused a rip in the atmosphere. It took some time until anyone noticed what had happened but when they did, is when the war started. Since one of ours, a Fey, had caused the rip, we became the protectors of it. It was our duty and responsibility to keep humans and Earth safe. The rip was one between our world here on Earth and the demon realm. Once the demons discovered it, they started to use it. They climbed through it and walked on Earth amongst us." She pauses and I can see that more terrifying memories are flitting across her mind.

"The more powerful demons can possess human bodies and use them as their own for as long as they want. As long as the host body is healthy. The rip is located in what is now known as Roswell, New Mexico. Once we found out about the rip we travelled from Salem and settled here in Albuquerque, so that we could be close by and try and slow down the spread of demons throughout the country."

I just stare at her and don't know what to say. I have absolutely nothing to add, nothing to ask. I'm in shock trying to wrap my head around all of this information that can't possibly real but is.

She continues, "for centuries we have been fighting this war. For centuries we have been keeping the demons back, but something happened. We think the rip has gotten larger, allowing more demons through, and not just soldier demons. We started to see General demons coming through. They're stronger and more powerful than soldier demons. They report directly to the devil himself. This is when we started to see a power shift. We were no longer the ones winning the war and we needed something, a miracle, to change our odds."

She smiles and reaches for my hand, "that is where your mother comes into play. We were visited by Archangel Michael. He had been sent to us to deliver the good news. We would have a Warrior, but this Warrior had to be of Fey blood. Not just any Fey blood, but the Müstik Bloodline, your grandmother's Bloodline. I was the eldest sister, so I had become the Leader of the war. The Queen. I could not be the one to accept and offer this miracle. That left your mother. She understood the cost and she knew what was at stake. She accepted the honor without hesitation. Archangel Michael Blessed your mother, Alexandria, with you," she smiles brightly.

"I don't understand," I say, shaking my head. "What do you mean he Blessed her with me?"

"Oh, come now, Amarah. You know exactly what I mean. You are a miracle sent from Heaven! Your mother was *Blessed* with you. You have no mortal father. You are half Angel."

I stand up quickly. "I'm what?! No. There's no way. This is *not* true. This isn't possible," I pace in front of the bed. "I mean, how...why...I don't...I don't understand. You said my mother knew the cost. What did you mean?" I stop and stand in front of her.

"You cannot just create a life out of nothing, Amarah. Part of you is Angel and the other part came from your mother. She gave you her life-force. When you were born, she died."

My face falls at her admission.

"Do not be sad! Your mother is in Heaven and you are a miracle! Please believe that there was no other choice. Your mother was happy to give you her life-force. It was an honor and her greatest gift in this life."

She moves to stand in front of me, grabbing my hands to hold them in hers, "no one but me, and now you, know the truth about you, Amarah, and no one can find out. I cannot stress this to you enough but you have to protect this secret at all costs. No one is to know you are an Angel. As far as anyone knows, no one but your mother knew your father."

I feel the tears building up in my eyes, "I didn't ask for any of this. It's not fair! The people who I thought were my family, aren't, and the family I thought I would gain, I don't have either! Now there is this deadly secret and basically, I can't trust anyone but you. I can't do this, Ana. I can't!" My voice trembles as my legs give out from under me and I fall to the floor.

Ana joins me on the floor with tears in her eyes too, "Amarah, you must! You must believe and you must fight! Or else your mother has died in vain. She sacrificed everything because she believed in you! I believe in you!" She wipes a tear from my cheek, "please don't cry. Your mother's choice was her own. She loved you so much and I know that she is here with us now. She will always be with you. Honor her."

We sit on the floor for what feels like hours. She holds me while I cry. I don't think I've ever cried this much before in my entire life. Not even with my recent heartbreak that felt like the end of the world, which now, seems extremely trivial and childish. I'm crying because the life I knew is a lie. The life I gained is already one filled with pain. A mother I will never know. A father I never had. I'm supposed to be what, a Savior? I'm not a Savior. I'm not a Warrior. I'm not anybody!

How am I supposed to do this on my own?

Divine Assistance

Like A Prayer by Madonna

I only stop crying when there are no tears left. I'm lying utterly still, empty and numb in my aunt's arms, and it's as if she read my mind, she whispers softly, "Amarah Rey Andrews, you are *not* alone."

She helps me sit up and she caresses my cheek, wiping away the last wet traces of the tears, "you have me and I have you. You have Logan. You have a family of Fey. Not all of them are as…*difficult*, as Hallana. You are not alone," she repeats.

I cup her hand and lean into her comforting touch, letting is sooth what it can, "I know, thank you. But I can't help it. I do feel alone. It will take time. I just need time to process this all and to become a part of this new family."

"I understand and I'll be here every step of the way to give you anything you need," she smiles. "Now, we must get to the party or people may start to gossip. Hell, who am I kidding? They probably already are." She climbs to her feet and pulls me up with her, "however, there is one last thing to show you."

She walks over to the chest at the foot of the bed, opens it, reaches in, and comes up with a bundle in her arms. She shuts the chest and walks over to the bed where she lays it down. She gently unrolls the bundle, "these belong to you. Archangel Michael brought them and left them here with us on the day you were born," she steps aside.

I walk up to the bed and see two identical daggers and a sword in a scabbard. I pick up one of the daggers to examine it more closely. It resembled a Japanese Tanto, but not quite identical. It's beautiful. It's all black, black blade and black handle. I gauge the blade to be about a foot long. I hold onto the handle and it feels good in my hand, it feels comfortable, as if I've held it a hundred times before. I set it back down and pick up the scabbard.

It has an adjustable carrying strap and is solid black as well. I hold onto the scabbard with my left hand and grab a hold of the sword handle with my right. I slowly draw it out, and once it's free in my hand, it sends a powerful shock up my arm and into my body. I gasp and feel that power in my chest come to life, reacting to it.

There's suddenly an intense, white light filling up the room but it doesn't blind me. I can see through it and realize it's coming from the sword and…from *me*. It's my power, amplified. I look at the sword and notice crosses engraved all down the blade. Crosses that can only been seen with my power running through the blade. Again, this one resembles a Japanese Katana, but it's straight and just a little different. Not quite like anything I've ever seen. Like everything else in The Unseen, it's stunning. It's powerful. It's mine. I know it as surely as I know I need air to breathe.

The light slowly fades and I'm left holding the all-black sword in my hand. All traces of power and divinity hidden. I weigh it in my hand. It's the perfect length for me and not too heavy. Again, it feels *right*. Like it's meant to be in my hand.

"These are the most beautiful weapons I've ever seen. Well, I guess I haven't seen many weapons outside of movies, but still...these are unlike anything I've ever seen," I say, staring at the blades in front of me.

"They are Divine, literally. They have been handcrafted to fit you, Amarah. Now that you are paired with your weapons, you're ready to begin your journey. You *are* our Warrior," Ana says proudly.

And I can't argue it anymore. Whatever is inside me is real. It connected to the sword and showed its truth. I gently slide the sword back into its scabbard.

"Shall I help you put them on?" Ana asks.

"Yes," I smile brightly. "Yes, I think so!"

The daggers came with two thigh holsters. I put on the right and Ana helps me with the one on the left. They'll take some getting used to but they fit me perfectly. I slip the scabbard strap over my head and adjusted the buckle in front of my chest. I notice the buckle is black too. Nothing metal or chrome. Nothing to catch any light. It's all very stark and very black. I love it. I head into the walk-in closet so I can see the entire outfit from top to bottom.

"Now *that* is the punch I was talking about earlier! You look fierce. Like a Warrior," Ana says from behind me.

I practice taking out the daggers and putting them back. It's a foreign feeling and I need practice, especially with my left hand. I also practice with the sword. It's short enough to not give me too much trouble, but again, I need practice. Just like the leather outfit, the weapons aren't as uncomfortable as I thought they would be.

I'm determined to do this. I'll throw myself into The Unseen, into my training. I'll work tirelessly to Master my power and to help my family win this war. I'll take my place as Warrior and protect the humans, the ones I grew up with. The only family I've known and the friends I still have. I don't know what this means for me and the relationships I have with the humans but I *will* make it work. I will figure this out and I will honor my mother, Alexandria, and my Fey family.

I'm staring into the face of a new version of me. I have a long way to go but this is the start.

Right here.

Right now.

This is who I've always been meant to be.

This is my truth.

I give myself one more up and down in the mirror, square my shoulders, and take a deep breath. I turn around to face the Queen, "I'm ready."

23

The Other Woman

I See Red by Everybody Loves An Outlaw

We headed back down the tunnels the way we had come. This time, the Queen walks a few steps in front of me, and the personal side she had just shown me in private is gone. Her demeanor is the same as it was when I first met her, focused and elegant, but firm. It's in the way she holds her head, the way she holds her posture, the way she walks, and the confidence she exudes. Ana is gone. Queen Anaxo of the Fey is here.

We walk back into the massive hall and I almost don't recognize it. It has been completely transformed. There are long banquet-like tables against the walls that are overflowing with food and desserts. The lighting has been dimmed, and the room is full of people. I suddenly feel nervous and don't want to be in the middle of all these strangers.

A hush comes over the room as we enter. The bodies all move out of the way and make a clear path for the Queen. Everyone is bowing their heads and muttering acknowledgments to the Queen along the way but their eyes are all focused on me. I have no idea what to do so I just follow behind the Queen like a lost puppy as we make our way back to the dais. I find Logan standing close by and our eyes connect as if they're lasers trained on each other. Something passes over his expression but I can't decipher it, and before I know it, we're climb the stairs of the dais and there's no time to figure it out.

Logan is still dressed the same except now there's a skin-tight black t-shirt covering his upper body. Pity. I quite liked the muscle show.

The Queen motions for me to take my seat, and Logan takes his. It appears we're not done with formal introductions just yet. Everyone in the room shuffles closer to the dais and I feel every single set of eyes on me. It feels like the weight of the world and it's crushing.

They're all whispering and pointing making me feel like an animal on show at a zoo. It's agonizing and uncomfortable but I remind myself that I was made for this and I manage not to squirm. I sit on the edge of the chair, as straight as I can, because the sword strapped across my back doesn't allow for anything else.

Once there is absolute silence, the Queen voice pierces loud and clear, "thank you all for coming tonight. This is a truly special night and one that needs celebrating. I know you have all heard the rumors and the gossip, but for once, they are indeed, true. We have our miracle. Our leverage to win the war." She stands up and walks to the middle of the dais, "it is my honor to introduce to you all..." she looks back and extends her hand out to me, requesting that I join her. I hesitate for only a second before I join her and take her hand, "Our Võitleja, our Warrior, Amarah Rey Andrews!" She pulls me a little in front of her and takes a step back. I'm front and center, staring out into a crowd of people I don't know, and I have no clue what to do.

Everyone in the crowd bow their heads, and someone yells, "to our Võitleja!" The crowd echoes this statement and then the room falls silent again. They're all staring at me, patiently waiting for me to do or say something. I know I look like a scared deer in headlights as I stand on the dais, frozen, looking out at a crown of expectant strangers. I glance over my left shoulder to where Logan is sitting. He smiles at me and dips his chin in an encouraging nod. I desperately wish I could have him next to me right now. His hand in mine, settling my nervous and giving me his quiet, calm strength, but I'm on my own.

What do I do?

Do I pull my sword out and give a Warriors yell?

Do I pull my power out in a blazing white light around me?

What can I do to win these people over?

I take a deep breath and let it out slowly.

Honesty.

I just have to speak my truth and speak from the heart. That's all that I have. That's all I can give them.

"Thank you, all of you, for being here and for welcoming me into your world. I know you do not know me but this is my world too. I may not know much right now but what I do know is this."

I moved my gaze over the crowd, willing them to believe me. "I belong here. This is my home. I can feel it in the deepest part of me, where once I was empty, now I'm whole. I will work tirelessly to learn and understand the ways of the The Unseen. To understand *you*. I will work tirelessly on my training and join you in the fight as quickly as possible. I will fight to protect The Unseen, my home, my family. I know you expect a lot from me but please remember that I'm not perfect. I ask that you please have patience with me."

I place both of my hands on my chest, "I'm taken aback by the beauty that I see before me and I cannot wait to get to know each and every one of you and become a true part of this family. To earn my place alongside you. To earn your respect and your trust."

Looking out over the crowd I see a mix of feelings but mainly curiosity and...*hope*.

"Now, let's enjoy tonight and celebrate like we should! What do you say?" I ask as I put my hands up towards the crowd.

The crowd erupts in yells and clapping hands. I smile then, a genuine smile, and turn back to the Queen. She walks over to me and grabs my hands in hers, "well done, Amarah! You are a born leader. Let's join in the celebration, shall we?"

Logan asks to speak to the Queen, privately. I wonder what it's about but I can ask him later. Now that the night's responsibilities have been addressed, I realize that I'm starving. I walk down the dais and make my way to the back of the room where the tables with delicious food are. There are still a lot of curious eyes on me but no one stops me. I grab a small plate and napkin from one table and filled it up with finger food. I grab some shrimp, crackers, what looks like fancy deli meat and cheese, and pile it onto my plate. This is a good start.

I stand off to one side and survey the room. Logan and the Queen have already finished their talk and are both mingling with the crowd. I find Logan in the crowd easily. His energy is like a flame in the dead of night. He's talking to Ethan and Prince Emrick. A streak of red catches my attention as Princess Hallana makes her way towards them, exaggerating the sway in her hips as she moves. When she reaches the group of men, she circles behind Logan and trails her hand up his arm, and brushes her breasts against his back. I would say she leans in, but she's already way too close, as she whispers in his ear. There's a familiarity in the way she touches him so freely and openly that has my mind reeling and my heart sinking in my chest. When she looks up, I swear she looks right at me and smiles maliciously.

My heart sinks into my stomach, my chest tightens, and I'm instantly jealous. I have absolutely no reason to be. Logan and I aren't an item. I've known him for literally *two* days. Hallana has known him for how long? Centuries? She touches him like she knows his body. Like she has the right to. My mind races with questions and I hate it. Are they lovers? Something more? It's none of my business, so why do I feel this way? Why do I feel like I just got sucker punched in the gut?

"Get a hold of yourself, Amarah," I say out loud and turn away from the scene abruptly.

I'm not paying attention and bump into someone in my haste to look away, sending some of my shrimp falling to the floor. "Oh my God, I'm so sorry!" I exclaim. I bend down to pick up the shrimp from the floor. I stand back up to face my embarrassment.

"It's quite alright," Princess Aaralyn laughs sweetly. "Accidents happen and there was no harm done. See?" She spread her hands out to show that both her and her dress are unharmed.

"Thank goodness! I would have felt so awful if I had ruined your beautiful dress. Again, I'm so sorry. I was in my head and wasn't paying attention," I glance back to where Logan is. Hallana is still there, still standing too close, but at least she isn't touching him anymore.

Aaralyn follows my gaze, "ah, I see. He is handsome, isn't he?"

I can't help the heat that crawls up my cheeks. She caught me red-handed and I realize I need to do a better job of hiding my thoughts and emotions. I need to do a better job of controlling myself. Especially here, in this new world full of new people with new abilities. I don't know who will be on my side and who won't. I don't know who I can trust outside of Logan and the Queen. Even then, this soon, I'm putting a lot of trust in them.

"Yes, he is, but I'm not interested. I just got out of a relationship," I blurt out in defense.

Aralyn raises her eyebrows and tries to hide a little smirk, "hmmm, well, that's good. Hallana and Logan have been...*friendly*, for quite a while. I suppose the little display you and Logan had earlier will be a topic of conversation. Honestly, I don't know why Logan would have put you in a situation like that knowing how...*fiesty*, Hallana is." She's looking toward the group and sighs, "men are all the same. Human or preternatural, it doesn't seem to make a bit of difference." She looks at me then, "you're new here, Amarah. Most of us want the same thing. We want to win the war and we want peace and safety for our people. I do believe that you will have a lot of allies amongst us but do be careful. Especially with Hallana and her family. She is hot-headed, literally. They all are. You must promise me that you will be careful," she reaches out and gently touches my arm.

The look in her exotic, purple eyes is sincere. She genuinely seems to care and is giving me a warning. Maybe I found my first friend after all.

I smile, "I promise, I will. Thank you for the heads up, and for being so nice to me. It means more than you know."

"Anytime, I believe us women have to stick together! Now, if you would please excuse me? I'm going to be a dutiful Leader and make some rounds."

"Of course." We smile at each other, and then I'm left standing alone once again.

Alone.

Alone to try and defuse the bomb that was just dropped about Logan and Hallana. How could I not think about it? I find Logan in the crowd again. He's talking to someone else now, and Hallana is nowhere in sight. Just staring at him from across the room my heart pounds in my chest as if it's trying to hammer through my chest and run to him. It's like my heart can find him anywhere without even looking for him. I just know where he is.

I'm drawn to him.

I hate it.

I hate this familiar, constricting feeling in my chest. The one where you feel one way about someone and know they don't share the same feeling. The one I felt when I found out my ex was cheating on me. The one that leaves you wondering why? Why don't they love me too? What is wrong with me? What does she have that I don't? The feeling that literally breaks your heart inside of your chest into a million cutting pieces.

My throat is getting tight and my vision is getting blurry. I *will not* cry here in front of literally everyone. I blink rapidly, trying to fight back the tears. I turn and quickly walked towards the hallway where my room is. I have the urge to run full out, but I stand up straight and control myself. I walk, calmly, through the archway and down the hall to the door that leads to my room.

Once the door is closed behind me, the tears are unleashed. I cry quietly, my throat too constricted with emotion to let any sound escape. The only evidence of my pain are the tears that flow like waterfalls down my cheeks. I pull the sword over my head and lay the scabbard on the bed. I sit down at the vanity and look at myself in the mirror. I'm pathetic. Why am I crying? Am I seriously crying over a man that I've known for two days? I don't want to believe it. No, I'm crying because my life is a mess! Everything has changed in the blink of an eye. There's just too much to deal with and I don't even have time to cope with it all.

There's a knock on my door, "Amarah? It's me, Logan. Can I come in?"

I look at myself in the mirror and wipe at my face, trying to hide the fact that I'm crying. "Ummmm, yeah, you can come in," I yell back as I head towards the bathroom. I grab some tissue to clean my face and blow my nose. I look at myself in the bathroom mirror and puffy, slightly red eyes look back at me. There's no way I can hide the fact that had been crying. Great. At least he won't know *why* I was crying.

I walk to the edge of the bathroom and Logan is sitting on the side of the bed, facing the bathroom. I stay where I am and lean against the wall, trying to act like everything is ok.

"What's up?"

"Are you ok? I felt you leave the party and wanted to make sure you were ok." His eyes show his concern and I wonder how sincere it is. Is he checking on me because he wants to? Or is it his duty because of who I am?

"Yeah, I'm fine. It's just a lot to take in. I needed some space to think and breathe," I half lie.

He looks at me and doesn't seem convinced but he doesn't push the issue. Part of me is happy about that, and part of me isn't.

Do I want to talk about him and Hallana? No.

Do I want him to tell me that he doesn't want Hallana? Yes.

That it had meant nothing. Yes.

Do I want him to tell me that he wants me? Yes.

"Well, you don't have to go back out there if you don't want to. The Queen introduced you, and that was the goal of tonight. You don't need to be involved in all the Fey politics and gossip right away. That would be enough to send most people running away" he jokes, trying to lighten the mood.

I give him a weak smile, "ok, good. I'd rather not deal with any more crowds or expectations tonight. I need time to process everything. When can I go home? I just realized I'm kind of stuck here waiting on you since you brought me here. I can't just leave."

"I can take you home whenever you'd like. The Queen just needs to talk to you about what's next. You need to start your training."

I sigh, "fine. Can we talk to her now so I can get home to Griffin?"

I want so much to just go back home to my old world, to all my human problems that now seem so small and trivial. I just want to lie on the couch, cuddling Griffin, where the only thing on my mind is dreading the weekend being over. I don't want to think about Angels and demons. My human family and my Fey family. I don't want to think about Logan and why I feel the way I do. I definitely do not want to think about the way Hallana touched him or even worse, him touching her. I just want to forget about it all.

Logan stands up and starts to walk towards me. My chest tightens immediately, and I feel the tears just behind my eyes, ready to come cascading down again. I hold up my hand and shake my head, "please don't." My voice comes out as a shaky whisper.

Logan stops and we just stare at each other. I can't read his expression, but I'm a hundred percent sure he knows the one on mine. But does he understand it? Probably not. He doesn't know that I know about him and Hallana.

His body is tense and it looks like he's fighting the urge to take the last steps to reach me. Or maybe that's what I want to see.

"I'll go tell the Queen you're ready to leave."

I just nod my head in agreement, not trusting my voice. Logan turns and walks towards the door. He opens it and hesitates before he walks through, but he doesn't look back. He walks out the door and closes it with a solid click behind him. My knees buckle under me and I slide down the wall to sit on the floor. I hold myself and let my heart pour down my cheeks for the second time. This time ragged, gasping breaths accompany the waterfalls. Some Warrior I'm turning out to be.

24

Better Off Alone

Take A Bow by Rihanna

We're back on I-40 heading East this time. It's 10:21 p.m. and there isn't much traffic to deal with. I hadn't realized how much time had passed since I'd left home. Everything happened so fast tonight. I haven't said a word to Logan since we left. I have too many emotions and thoughts running through my mind. I don't know what to say? What can I say? He doesn't owe me any explanations. He isn't mine. I'm confused and tired, but mostly just tired.

I had spoken to the Queen one last time before leaving. It turns out that the Leaders had all discussed where I should train first, and I'm *not* happy about it. If it wasn't for bad luck, I'd have no luck at all. I'm going to be training with Princess Hallana and the Tulekahju Family. The Fire Fey.

I can't help but wonder whose idea it was for me to start there? I don't trust Princess Hallana as far as I could throw her. Logan will escort me to their home and stay with me through the training, however long it takes. I bet Hallana is the one who offered to host me first because she knew it would mean Logan would be there too. Yes, she'll have to put up with me, but she'll also get more time with Logan. The way she acted tonight, I have a feeling she's going to make it as blatantly obvious as possible that he's with her, and I just don't want to see it.

Before the party, I would have cherished the thought of being alone with him on this journey. Just getting to be with him always makes me feel happy and safe. Now? Ok, I still feel safe, but I can't help but see Hallana brushing her body against his. I can't help but feel jealous and I hate it. Just thinking about it makes my chest tight and brings my emotions bubbling up to the surface. Again, I tell myself that I have to do better than this. I have to learn to control myself and my emotions. I refuse to let anyone play on them or manipulate me by using them against me.

We're pulling up in front of my house, finally. Some tension slips away and more of the exhaustion takes its place. I had only gotten a couple of hours of sleep the night before and I'm feeling it now. Not only the lack of sleep and lack of food, but the overload of information that had been thrown on me tonight is almost too much to handle. I feel its weight, and I don't know where to even start trying to process it all. Normally, I would talk things out with Cristi, but how can I even explain any of this to...well, anyone?

Logan puts the truck in park and turns off the engine. I finally look at him and that's a mistake. Why does he have to be so damn gorgeous? Even in the dim light from my driveway, there's no hiding his contoured features and the smell of him in his truck surrounds me and messes with my senses. Control your emotions, Amarah.

"Thank you for bringing me home but you don't need to stay."

"Yes, I do, Amarah. It's not safe," I hate that just the way he says my name makes my body weak.

I want him to stay. My eyes find his lips, and I want to kiss him again and feel his hands on my body. I want to feel his muscles under my hands like I had earlier tonight. I flash back to Hallana caressing his arm just like I had, but with more experience, and that's enough to pull me back to reality.

I refuse to be the other woman.

My mind is strong but my damn romantic heart betrays me. When will it ever learn? We're supposed to learn from the pain but my heart doesn't seem to get the memo. It wants to throw itself at Logan and to hell with the outcome. It's pounding in my chest as if yelling at me to see things its way, but I focus my mind on the pain of seeing him with Hallana, and that helps me stay on track.

"You said that the demons track me when I use my power, right? Well, I have no intention of using my power. Hell, I don't even really know how. So, you don't have to worry about anything happening. Ok?"

"Amarah, I have to protect you. I can't do that if you don't let me. I know you want me to stay. I can *feel* it," he has a point.

Now that he mentioned it, I realize I can feel his emotions too. He wants to stay with me but just because he wants to stay with me, doesn't mean that he's not with Hallana. Men cheat. Men want to have their cake and eat it too.

I can feel that he doesn't like that I'm upset, I can feel his urge to protect me, but most of all, I feel his confusion. He really doesn't know why I'm hurt. Ugh, men and their completely oblivious nature.

I look away and shake my head, "I don't need you to protect me in my own home, Logan. Last time I was caught off guard. It won't happen again."

"But..." he tries to argue.

"No, Logan. I'm not asking you. I need to be alone tonight. I need time to think all of this through. I can't do that with you here," I'm still purposefully not looking at him. It makes it easier to stand my ground when I'm not drooling over him. "Thank you for all that you've done for me. I do appreciate it, but as I said, I need time to sort through all of this."

"Ok," he sighs, reluctantly, and runs his hand through his hair. "Whatever you need. You have my number. If you need anything at all, just call and I'll be here."

"I will. Thank you," I grab my house keys from the center console, open the truck door, hold onto my sword, and climb out of his truck. "Goodnight," I say and close the door before I can hear a response.

I walk to my front door, unlock it, and walk in without a backward glance. I shut the door and lock it behind me. I heard the truck engine come back to life, and I watch the glow of the headlights through the window as they backed away and fade.

I slide down against the door, pull my knees to my chest and cry some more. I cry at the feeling of my heart being stabbed. I cry at the thought of Logan and Hallana together. The fact that not letting him stay with me probably just drove him into her arms. I cry at my own stupidity for being so naïve and weak. I cry until there's nothing left to cry.

Griffin is barking and trying to get my attention. I scoop him up in my arms, grab my sword and head into the living room.

I sit down on the couch and lay the sword near my feet. I don't know why, but I want it close by, just in case. I hadn't lied to Logan. I don't plan on using my power and have no reason to believe that the demons will find me, but better safe than sorry. I give Griffin all of my attention until he calms down. I take off the boots and unclip the daggers from my thighs. I set them off to the side and then throw my feet up on the couch and let my body sink into the soft cushions.

Sleep takes me almost instantly. The darkness swallows me up, and I don't fight it. I don't even dream. I think I'm too tired and too overwhelmed to have any sort of cohesive thoughts. My mind is overflowing with information and even the dream realm can't make anything out of the jumbled mess that is my thoughts. So, I sleep like the dead and for a few hours…for a few hours, I'm at peace.

One Last Day

The Show Must Go On by Queen

I wake up at 7:00 a.m. I had a solid eight hours of sleep, and physically, I feel great. Mentally, however, is another matter. Part of me doesn't want to get up because that means my mind will start racing again, with a million questions. Another part of me wants to attack everything head-on and figure it all out. I have a feeling the latter part will be triumphant. There's just no world, the old one I know, or the new one I don't, where I can run away and hide. I sigh out loud and sit up on the couch.

Griffin gets up beside me with a yawn and stretches out his little body. I'm so thankful I have a low maintenance baby boy. He has water and food to access whenever he wants and he never overeats. He has the doggy door to go and come as he pleases, plus, a plethora of toys to choose from. He's a spoiled, happy boy. I mean, at least I think he is.

I realize I'm still in my leather get up and my hair hurts. I pull my hair free of the tight ponytail and run my fingers through it to loosen it up. Ouch! It's going to take a few minutes for my hair to relax and feel better. I need to take a shower and desperately want comfy clothes, but first, coffee. I walk into the kitchen and start the coffee pot. While the coffee pot produces my magic potion, I decide to shower, so I can relax and enjoy the coffee.

I double-checked that the doors are all still locked. I'm not sure what to do with the sword and the daggers, so I leave them where they are. I don't think I'm going to need them this early in the morning. I start walking down the hall and then turn around and walk back to the living room. On second thought, better to take them into the bathroom with me. If I don't need them, no harm done. If I need them, I'll kick myself in the ass for leaving the, literally Divine, weapons just lying around. I prop the sword up against the wall next to the opening of my walk-in shower, and that's as good as it's going to get.

What is it about showers being so calming? It's like the warm water washes away all your worries and uncertainties. At least for a while, anyway. A shower usually brings new ideas to light and frees your creative mind. I'm feeling better, calmer, but I have no new ideas. No new answers. No magical epiphany on what to do with...well, any of it!

I want to call my sisters and mom, and tell them everything but, how can I? How will I ever explain this to anyone? Who would believe me? Would telling them put them in danger? There are too many things I just don't know. I can't risk it. Not yet. Maybe when I learn to control my power, I can tell them. Until then, until I know more, I'm on my own.

I throw on my typical lounging clothes, a tank top and boy short style underwear, and head back into the kitchen to have my coffee. The first sip hits my soul, and I close my eyes, savouring the quiet, still moment. My cell phone rings next to me and disrupts my cherished peaceful moment. I don't recognize the number, so I hesitate on answering it. I don't enjoy talking on the phone for one, and two, I rarely answer numbers I don't know. If it's important, they'll leave a message or text me, like a normal person. I let it ring again, and I almost ignore it, but considering all the changes that have happened, I decide to answer it.

"Hello?"

"Good morning, Amarah. I hope I didn't wake you," Queen Anaxo's soft voice floats through the phone. Even over the phone, she seems to have this...*energy*. She's soft-spoken, yet she commands attention. It's amazing how she does it.

"No, not at all. I was already awake."

"Good. I hope you got some rest. I know yesterday was a lot for you. I thought I would call and see if you had any questions I could answer for you," she sounds genuinely concerned.

"Ummmm... yeah, I mean I know I have a ton of questions," I laugh nervously. "But honestly, I really can't think of any at the moment. I guess I just want to know when I'm going to travel to Princess Hallana's territory to start my training?"

"I know this has been a lot to take in. Take your time and just know that I'm here whenever you're ready. Now, as far as your training, I would love for you to start as soon as possible, but ultimately, you are in control. All of this needs to be on your time, when *you're* ready. I don't want to push you too hard or too fast, but just know that time is of the essence. The urgency is real. It takes Fey years and years to Master their power. You are different, Amarah. You are unique and I honestly have no idea how you will adapt to your training. I don't know how long it will take you to Master your power. So, it's important to start as soon as possible, so we can understand what we are working with. You are just as new to the Fey as the Fey are to you. We have never had a Võitleja before, so we're all in the same boat, figuring it out as we go. I wish I had a better answer for you."

"Thank you for your honesty. I appreciate you being transparent and trusting me," I sigh. "As much as I would like to take this slower, I know that the Fey are counting on me. I know how important it is that I face everything head-on and not get caught up in my head and doubts. I told the Fey last night that I would work tirelessly to join the fight as soon as possible. I can't go back on my word. I can't let them down and I can't afford to lose their confidence in me. What little there is anyway. I need to build on it and I can start by jumping into the deep end."

"You are capable of so much more than you know, Amarah. I know that you're strong and I think you will surprise even yourself on this journey."

"I wish I had your confidence," I laugh again.

"I have *Faith*. You are part Angel after all, and God doesn't make mistakes. You are also your mother's daughter, and she was the most fearless person I've ever known. Greatness is in your blood, it's who you are, and you will come to believe that, eventually."

"Thank you, Ana, for your support. For welcoming me so graciously. For everything."

"You're my family. It was never a question and never will be."

"Thank you," I don't know what else. "Well, since I have no job and nothing keeping me here, I can leave for Hallana's tomorrow, if that works?" I ask.

"That would be perfect! I'll tell Logan to pick you up around 8:00 a.m. tomorrow then. How does that sound?"

Just the mention of Logan's name and my heart skipped a beat. "Yes, that will be fine," I say calmly. "Oh, and one more thing, Ana. I have a dog and he is my *everything*. I need someone to stay here with him. He can't stay here alone."

"Not a problem at all. I'll make sure that someone stays there with him and he's loved and cared for. Is there anything else?"

I'm relieved and feel better about going now that I know Griffin would be taken care of. Although, my heart breaks just thinking about leaving him. I have to remind myself that it's just temporary.

"No, I think that's all for now. If I think of anything, I'll ask."

"Wonderful! This is my personal number. Call me anytime, day or night. I mean it," she insists.

"I will, I will. I promise," I say, smiling.

"Then I'll tell Logan about tomorrow and I'll talk with you again soon."

"Ok, sounds great. Goodbye."

"Goodbye for now," she hangs up the phone.

Well, I have one day to myself. I decide to call everyone after all. My mom, my two sisters, and my friends. I know I can't tell them anything yet. I wouldn't know what to say anyway, and honestly, I don't want to talk about anything mystical. I just want to have normal conversations. I'll enjoy this day, my last day as simple Rey before I truly accept who I am.

I'm the daughter of Alexandria Andrews of the Müstik Family.

I'm half Angel, Blessed by Archangel Michael.

I'm the one and only Võitleja, Fey Warrior. I have power that has unknown limits. What I'm truly capable of is a question everyone is waiting anxiously to find out, including me. I'll learn how to use my power and control it. I'll protect my people, my family in both worlds, from the demons, and I *will* become the woman I'm meant to be.

I am Amarah Rey Andrews, Fey Warrior.

No Looking Back

Leaving, On A Jet Plane by John Denver

My bags are packed, and I'm ready to go, when Logan pulls into my driveway. Although I'm not leaving on a jet plane, one thing is true, I don't know when I'll be back again.

I'm out the door before Logan can get out of the truck. I walk up to the passenger side back door and hear it unlock. I open the door and tossed my bag up onto the seat. It isn't very heavy. What do you pack for an unknown trip where you will train in an unknown way and stay an unknown amount of time? Yeah, I have no idea. So, just the essentials it is. I lay my sword across the seat as well and closed the door. I open the front passenger side door and there he is. The one and only Logan Lewis who seems to have an unknown key to my heart. Another mystery.

"Good morning," he smiles and sounds way too cheery. "I got you coffee," he points to a Starbucks cup in the center console cup holder.

Seriously? I mean, how can I stay upset with him? How can I stay strong in my defences when one second in his presence and my walls come crashing down without a fight? It's like he's a sharp knife and all I am is butter waiting to be sliced through.

I look at him and can't help but smile back, "good morning. Thank you, that was sweet of you."

I set my daggers down on the floorboard. My sword is in the back, but I want quick access to the daggers, just in case. I don't think I'll not need them, especially not with Logan around, but again, better safe than sorry.

"I just need to say goodbye to Griffin and lock up. I'll be right back."

It takes me longer than it should but I just don't want to leave Griffin! He's my baby, my Angel, and I'm already missing him. This is by far the hardest thing I've had to do with all this Unseen nonsense.

When I finally say my goodbyes and give all the hugs and kisses I have time for, I lock the door and jump into the truck. This is not ok. I feel like a terrible mom. I'm abandoning him and he's going to think I don't love him anymore. What a horrible feeling it is leaving him.

"Awe man, I was looking forward to seeing the little guy. At least *he* would have seemed happy to see me," Logan teases, but I can't help but feel like a part of him is serious.

Had it been just as hard for him to leave me as it had been for me telling him to? I need to know more about this connection we have and why we have it. What it means.

I'm not about to start this trip off by telling him I know about him and Hallana. I sure as hell refuse to tell him I'm jealous! I don't even want to think about any of it, honestly. Easier said than done, but I have to try. This is going to be a hell of a trip, locked inside this truck together, if I start our day off with that bomb of information. Besides, we're both adults and there's no reason we can't be mature about the situation. We could get along and be friendly with no strings attached. We're going to be around each other for the foreseeable future. We don't have a choice.

"Hey, that's not fair. I'm happy to see you...brought me coffee," I tease back.

"Oh, ouch!" He dramatically grabs his chest as if it hurt his heart. "Using me for coffee benefits! The truth comes out," we both laugh together and I feel more relaxed. I can do this.

We pull out of the driveway and Logan turns up the volume on the radio a little bit just as *Lightning Crashed* by Live comes on.

"Oh, what a great song," I say out loud.

"Yeah? You like this?"

"I do. It reminds me of my sister. She's eleven years older than me so I grew up listening to this, a lot of eighties music," I laugh, "but honestly, there's not much music I don't like. I feel like music is a part of my soul."

He nods his head, "exactly! I love music too. There's a song for literally every feeling and every moment. Music speaks when we can't find the words."

"Exactly!" I agree excitedly.

We both grin at each other as he merges onto the highway. I realize I have no idea where we're going or how long it'll take us to get there.

"So, where are we headed?" I ask, as I sip my cup of coffee.

"We're headed down south. It should take us about two hours driving plus a good seven or eight hours of hiking to get to the

Fire Fey's home. I'm glad you're wearing sneakers for that part, but you should put on some jeans, so you don't scrape up your legs."

"It's going to be way too hot out for jeans. I'll survive some scrapes. So, down south two-ish hours...that's like by T or C?"

"No, more southeast, we're going to be right outside of a small town called Carrizozo."

"I know where that is. I grew up in another, even smaller town, called, Hondo. I still have family out there, my mom. Although, I guess she isn't really my mom, is she?" I sound lost, even to myself. So much for small talk.

"She raised you for thirty-four years, Amarah, she will always be a mother to you. Just because she isn't your blood, doesn't make her not family. Family is so much more than just Bloodlines. Your life in the human world is just as important as starting your new life in The Unseen. Don't let anyone take that away from you."

"It's just...I don't know what to say. How am I going to explain to them when it's evident I'm no longer aging and they are? Am I even allowed to let them know? Won't that put them in danger? Wouldn't it be better if I left now and never looked back? Let them mourn me and move on." I have so many questions.

"Unfortunately, I don't have these answers for you, but the decision is one hundred percent yours to make. They are your family. This is your life. You have the choice of how you live in both worlds. You may not have a clear path yet, but you will. Just give it time. I know that you'll make the right choice."

Well, this is fun. Way to start a two-hour road trip with depressing and morbid talk about faking my death for my human family's sake. I'm on a journey that seems to have a million different roads that I need to cross. Even half Angel, I'm still just *one* person. I can't be in more than one place at a time. I need to focus on the task at hand and let everything else unfold in due time. It's only been a few days. I have a few years before I need to address anything. So, focus on the here and now. All I can do is cross one bridge at a time, and right now, that has to be enough.

I can't afford to be distracted by things I can't control. Things I have no clue how to handle. So, I force myself out of my head and out of my thoughts and just focus on the next thing in front of me. Easy peasy, lemon squeezy. More like messy stressy, lemon zesty.

"Amarah, wake up," I hear Logan's deep voice, barely above a whisper. I feel him brush the hair out of my face and I have déjà vu of the morning he woke me up the same way.

I open my eyes and he's leaning over the center console, his green eyes watching me closely.

"You're beautiful when you sleep." His words send my heart into overdrive, his body consuming my oxygen and it's suddenly too hot in this truck. I feel my body betray me yet again as the heat sneaks into my cheeks without my permission.

He leans back and gives me that cocky smirk I know so well. "We're here,"

"Oh, shit. I never fall asleep in vehicles. I must have been more tired than I realized," I reach my hand up to my mouth to check for drool. None. Thank God for small miracles! I just hope I didn't snore.

"It's ok. I'm glad you got some sleep. C'mon, we've got a long hike ahead of us, so we better get going."

I hop out of the truck. We're in an underground parking garage. I grew up in this area and I had never seen a parking garage anywhere. Maybe we're not where I thought we were going to be after all?

"Where are we? I thought you said we were going by Carrizozo?"

"We are. We're about five miles outside of Carrizozo."

"I've never seen a parking garage out here. There is nothing out here. Well, except the Valley of Fires and the tourist viewing areas."

The Valley of Fires is the Carrizozo Malpaís, Spanish for *badlands*. The Valley of Fires was created by a vent near a volcano known as Little Black Peak. The Valley of Fires stretches for about ten miles but is a part of a bigger lava flow connecting to others that total over forty-five miles.

Of course, that was thousands of years ago and the volcanos were long since dormant. How did I know so much about this? We had several school field trips to the Valley of Fires. A bunch of old, black lava rock for miles and miles. Soooo much fun for a kid.

Logan laughs, "it's called, glamour. The Fey use it everywhere to hide what's there from humans. A human will only see what the Fey want them to see." Logan is checking his backpack, which is huge compared to mine, for supplies.

"I see. Glamour like they use for their appearance? Will I be able to create glamour? That seems like it would be very useful." I strap on my daggers and sword. My backpack can then go over the scabbard, leaving my hands free.

"Yes, you will eventually be able to use glamour. Are you ready?"

"I'm as ready as I am going to get," I shrug.

"Let's go."

He heads towards the end of the garage which turns into a tunnel. The tunnel isn't very long, maybe half of a football field, and it narrows down the further we go. Once we're out of the tunnel, Logan shows me where we're headed.

"We're going to be hiking northwest from here, toward that mountain range," he points in the direction we would be heading. We're in a valley but there are mountain ranges all around us. The one he points at doesn't seem too far away, but distance is usually very deceiving. I know it's a hell of a lot further than it seems.

"We'll go around this first set of mountains you see and into the middle of the mountain range. It's far and well-hidden as it is, but the Fey also use glamour there too, to hide from unwanted eyes," he explains.

"Can't be too careful," I say matter-of-factly. "You know, the Fire Fey living in a volcano valley is a bit *nail on the head* don't you think?"

"Oh, it gets better than that. They don't just live in a volcano valley they live inside of the volcano itself."

I watch his face for any signs that he's making a joke but his face gives nothing away.

"Wait...What?" I ask, confused. "You're joking, right?"

"You'll just have to wait and see I guess," he smirks. "You ready for this hike?" He asks again.

"About as ready as I'm gonna get. Hiking has never been my jam, and this one is going to take an entire day. Yippie."

"I can usually make it in about four hours but with you, yes, it'll take all day. It might not be fun, but I promise you, it *is* worth it."

Logan heads out and I follow behind him. I just buckle down and try not to think of the long hours ahead. I should have brought headphones to listen to music. Hindsight is always 20/20. At least the terrain isn't tough to hike for now. I know it will be once we got into the mountain range, so I take my wins where I can get them. Not to mention the scenery is not bad at all. And I'm not talking about the landscape if you know what I mean. I just put my eyes on the prize in front of me and one foot in front of the other.

Straight on until morning.

Camping

You and Me by Lifehouse

I'm so thankful that I'm used to working out. If I didn't have decent strength in my legs, I'm sure that they would've been Jell-O by now. We've been hiking for about five hours, but are currently taking a water break, and snacking on some beef jerky.

"I'm so glad that you came prepared for today. I had no idea what to expect and would have been poorly prepared if I had to do this on my own," I admit.

"There's no way you could have known what to expect. That's why the Queen sent me with you. That, and of course, to help keep you safe."

"Well, whatever the reason, thank you. How much further is it?" I ask.

"Not too far. We're actually about two hours from where we'll camp for the night."

"Wait, what? We have to camp out here? Why aren't we going the entire way tonight?"

"The last hour hike is through a forest-like area and the sun will be too far set in the sky behind the mountains. We need light from midday to see where we're going. I can use my Werewolf vision and senses to pass through just fine, but it would be extremely hard for you. Trust me on this."

"Well, shit!" I throw my arms up in frustration, "again, something I'm not prepared for." I cross my arms and can't help feeling useless and inadequate, which in turn, makes me grouchy. I might as well stomp my foot and pout like a child because I sound childish, even to myself.

"No need to worry. I've got everything covered. I know the area well and it is perfectly safe. It'll be fine."

You know the area well, huh? Is it because you've come through here a thousand times to see your precious Hallana? See? Grouchy. At least I'm smart enough to keep the thought to myself. Kudos to me.

What I say out loud is, "fine. Let's just keep going."

We're climbing up a rocky mountainside, Logan climbs it easily and is waiting for me at the top. I'm almost there when Logan reaches back to help pull me to the top.

"Remember when I said the hike would be worth it?" He asks as he pulls me up to stand next to him.

"Oh. My. God!" Is all I can say. I'm breathless. Partly from the climb and partly from what I'm seeing. There's a crystal-clear lake beneath us and the mountainside we're standing on surrounds half of the lake and luscious green trees surround the far side. The trees are so thick, you can't see anything between them. Now I understand why we need the sun above us when we travel through them.

Behind the trees, a mountain rises up, alone and majestic. It's like it has been centered perfectly in the middle of a stage, displaying all of its glory for me to see. The sun is setting behind us, and it throws vibrant colors across the mountain. The mountain is alight with shades of red, pink, and orange, giving the illusion that it's on fire. The subtle movement of the water in the mountain's reflection only exaggerated the illusion of flames.

"I think this is the most beautiful thing I've ever seen! It doesn't even look real!" I'm in awe.

"Yes. Beautiful," Logan says, but his eyes are on me.

I glance at him and that's a mistake. I feel his desire to touch me, to kiss me, as much as I see it in his eyes. His eyes look at my lips and his tongue slides out to wet his full lips before he meets my eyes again. My chest is rising and falling heavily and now it has absolutely nothing to do with the hike. Logan reaches out and pulls my bottom lip out from under my teeth. Before I even know what I'm doing, my body is leaning towards him, and then I slip on a lose rock and slam my head into his chest.

"Owwww," I say reflexively, even though it didn't hurt, as I rub my head. The embarrassment shows immediately in my cheeks and he chuckles as he steadies me on my feet again.

"You alright?" His voice is filled with quiet laughter.

"Fine," I quickly look away and back to the view in front of me. I'm thankful the scenery gives me a reason to change the subject. "I could stay here and look at this all day."

I decide that isn't a bad idea and sit down. No way to fall into Logan if I'm already sitting on my ass. Logan sits down next to me and we admire the beauty of the nature surrounding us until the sun drops lower and the colors fade along with the illusion of fire. It's still a beautiful place, but it's lost some of its magic and seems more natural, more normal, without the colors to bring life to it. As my wonderment fades, the exhaustion from the long day and hike hit me hard.

"I'm suddenly thrilled that we're camping and not finishing up the hike tonight. I'm not sure my body can do it even if I wanted to," I sound tired too.

"Let's make our way down. You can rest while I get things set up. You also need actual food and not just snacks," he lectures. "We both do."

I had been stubborn when I didn't want to stop and eat earlier. I had been fine with the protein from jerky and water, but after the hike, my body needs carbs. It needs fuel.

We slowly make our way down the mountainside. Logan probably could have gone quickly, but he helped me down, making sure I didn't *slip* again. I make it to the bottom in one piece. So far, I've kept up and hadn't fallen, not even once! I feel pretty proud of myself for that but I'm beat. There's no way I'm going to make it much further. Logan, on the other hand, looks like he's completely fresh and hasn't just hiked a million miles. That's annoying.

I follow Logan to a clearing off to one side. The forest trees surround it on one side with an open view of the lake on the other. There's a hole dug into the ground ready for a fire and tree trunks arranged around it for seating. It looks like this area gets used for camping often, which is strange considering it's literally in the middle of nowhere. It makes me wonder if this is where Logan often camps when he comes to see Hallana. Ugh. Seriously. I have *got* to stop thinking of that.

"We'll camp here for the night. I'm going to gather some firewood so we can start a fire later. It gets chilly here at night and we need a fire to cook on too."

"Well, aren't you the perfect boy scout," I tease.

"As long as I've been alive, I better be useful."

I sigh, "I still can't wrap my head around you being over three hundred years old."

"Give it about a century yourself, and then you'll understand the magnitude of being immortal. Well, almost immortal anyway. We can still die, but not by old age."

I just stare at him and don't know what else to say. I'm still in shock about all of this being real. I wonder if I'll ever *not* be in shock about all of this? Doesn't seem likely.

"You stay here and rest. I'm going to get the firewood. I'll be back shortly," he starts walking towards the tree line. "Don't forget to drink your water," he yells back.

"I know, I know," I mutter to myself, annoyed. I don't like people telling me what to do or making me feel like I'm a helpless child. But, for once, I don't argue back. The hike kicked my ass, and I know he's right. I need to rest, and I need to drink water. I don't like the fact that I'm still feeling rather...*human*, and can't keep up with Logan or be of more help.

I desperately want to learn how to use my power to be stronger, faster, harder to hurt. I know I have to learn about my power to fight demons and save the world. Or would that be two worlds? I know that my power is worth so much more than just petty personal gains, but I can't help it. The thought of being a total badass is thrilling, and I want it badly! Especially when I'm up against other women like Hallana, who doesn't like me and is in direct competition with me for Logan's attention.

I want to be confident.

I want to be powerful.

I want to be noticed.

Selfish, but true.

It's getting dark when Logan returns and I can feel the heat from the day slipping away and the dark, cold shadows of the night sneaking in. He held an armload of firewood, which I'm suddenly extremely grateful for, and I notice something else dangling at his side. As he gets closer, I can see that it's a rabbit.

A dead rabbit.

"Well, you've been busy. Firewood and dinner. Although, I'm not sure I'll be able to eat a rabbit."

"Why wouldn't you be able to eat the rabbit?" He asks as he tosses the firewood down, off to one side, and lays the rabbit across one of the logs.

"Because it's a cute bunny rabbit, that's why!"

Logan laughs, "oh, Amarah. A rabbit is no different than eating chicken or beef."

"It's way different! Rabbits are closer to being pets than food!"

Now he's really laughing at me, "your thinking is still so human. I know it will take you some time to get past that mental block. We are more in tune with nature and how things were before fast food and technology. We know how to live and survive off of the land and what's naturally provided. Rabbits, along with all other animals, all have their place and purpose. Rabbits were never meant to be locked up as pets. They're food."

Great, now I'm being lectured *and* laughed at. It's not a fun combination, and it makes me grouchy. Well, grouchier. I cross my arms and scowl at him. He laughs some more at my attempt to be grouchy.

"I'll get the fire started and then get dinner ready," he says as he piles up some firewood in the pit. "Would you like to see a small demonstration of what your power might be like?"

I still want to be grouchy, but I'm more interested in learning about my power. I have to let my mood go or it's going to be a long night.

"Yes, of course. I want to learn everything I can," I get up from leaning against a log and kneel beside him.

He starts a fire with a lighter, which surprises me.

"A lighter, huh? Why not rub two sticks together or some other old school way?"

"I can do that too, but no need to work that hard when I have the use of a lighter. Just because we know more about living without today's advances doesn't mean we don't use them. Stop being so damn difficult, Amarah."

I sigh, "you're right. I'm sorry. I'm just tired, grouchy, and hangry. Now, show me what you wanted to show me. I want to know."

"Good. Well, as you know, I have some Fey power. I'm the only one outside of the Fey Bloodlines that has ever had their power. At least that I know of. One of the things I can do is this..." he concentrates on the small flame that he started and it suddenly flared to life!

"Whoa! You can control the flames," I say eagerly. "The Queen mentioned that we can control fire when I asked her how they could have a fireplace underground without a vent for the smoke."

"Yes. The Müstik Family, the very first Fey, your mother's Bloodline, can control all the elements. Each other Fey Family can only control their specific element. But they are Masters of their element. They can not only just control that element they can create it. For example, Hallana and her Family can create fire from within and control it completely. I cannot create it, but I can somewhat control it once it has been started. Although once started, all I can do is control it. I cannot extinguish it with power."

"So, I'll be able to control each element because of my Bloodline but I won't be a Master of anything. I see how that's useful but, not being a Master of anything, can also be a disadvantage."

"The Queen seems to think you're special somehow. I'm not sure why, but she said that you may be capable of more than we know. Did she tell you why she thinks this?" He's searching my face for a reaction. I turn and stare at the fire.

As a matter of fact, the Queen did tell me. I'm half Angel. She also said that no one else can know this about me. It surprises me that this includes Logan. He seems to be her right-hand man for everything. I realize that this is a secret the Queen has been keeping for thirt-four years, and now it's also mine to keep.

"Amarah, what is it? I can see all the different thoughts play across your face. She told you something, didn't she?"

Damn! I have to do a better job of hiding my thoughts and emotions. "She told me a lot. She told me about my grandmother, Analise. How she's the one responsible for the rip that now allows the demons access to this realm. She told me that my mother..." I swallow hard and start to tear up again at the thought of never being able to know my real mother. I gather myself and lift my head, looking at Logan, "she told me that my mother, Alexandria, died giving birth to me and never told her who my father is."

Logan reaches out and wipes away the tear that was determined to fall from my eye. "Amarah, I am so sorry. I didn't mean to bring those thoughts back up," he says softly.

I wipe at my eyes, "it's ok. I need to address my past and come to terms with it all. But that's all she told me, Logan. I don't know why she thinks I'm special. Maybe because I'm the closest thing to her sister she has. Maybe just because I'm her family."

"You're probably right. Let's forget about it for tonight. You must be hungry. Let's get dinner ready," he smiles at me and I nod my head in agreement.

That last emotional reminder takes all the fight out of me. I feel like I have no energy for anything, not even attempting to argue about eating rabbit. It's food, and I desperately need it. I also feel tired and empty and void of feeling one way or another about it now. Logan also cooked up some potatoes he had brought with him. I eat everything he hands my way. Surprisingly, the meat tastes good. It isn't gamey or wild tasting like some elk or deer can taste. It tastes somewhat like chicken. Why is it that we compare everything to chicken?

We eat in silence, I'm too tired for anything other than the task of eating and I think Logan senses that. He has the uncanny ability to read me. I can read him somewhat too, but it seems easier for him than it is for me. Still, I try, and what I'm feeling from him right now, as I stuff my face with food, is satisfaction and, oddly…*turned on*.

I'm thankful for the faint firelight that hopefully hides the blush on my cheeks, yet again. I'm surprised my head hasn't exploded with all the blood rushing to it all the time. This man may very well be the death of me.

28

Reckless Passion

Bad Habits by Nerv

It's late in the night and the darkness is full out now. The only light is from the fire and the moon above us. Logan had pulled out some blankets and warmer clothes from his bag and I had changed into some sweatpants and a long sleeve t-shirt that were way too big for me. We're sitting on a blanket side by side, backs against a log, and I have another blanket thrown over my legs.

Logan sits to my left, the forest behind us, and the lake in front of us. He's lounging in only a pair of sweatpants he changed into and I had to wipe at my mouth and make sure I wasn't drooling when I saw him. Why are grey sweatpants one of the sexiest things a man can wear?

And that's *all* he's wearing.

He never wears any damn clothes! And it's not easy to keep ignoring this pull I have towards him. Not that I even need some phantom connection to be attracted to him. The man is unrealistically gorgeous. Like Brad Pitt in Troy, gorgeous.

Only bigger.

More muscle.

All consuming.

Impossible to fucking resist.

"Aren't you cold?" I ask.

"I'm a Werewolf."

He says it like that's the entire answer. Like it's common knowledge and I should understand what it means.

"Okayyyy," I drag out the word so he knows I'm totally confused.

"I always run hot. The Wolf side of me is made to be outside in the elements. This is natural to me and my Wolf ensures by body is safe."

"Oh, I guess that makes sense. Explains why you're always half-naked," I grumble. I'm not happy about it because I want him, can't have him, and it isn't fair to be so blatantly taunted.

"I can put on a shirt if you want me to."

I'm about to vehemently agree that he do just that when he turns his body so he's facing me and his chest is in full view. I manage to drag my eyes up his chest and he's wearing that infuriating cocky half-smile that says he knows exactly how he affects me.

My heart races just looking at him and I take a minute to fully appreciate every inch of him. My eyes stop over his scar and before I can even think about it and change my mind, I reach out and touch it. Logan closes his eyes and inhales deeply at my light touch. I trace it with my fingertips. It's a perfect circle, over his heart, and a smaller scar in the shape of a star off to the side.

"What's this scar from and how did you get it? You don't have any other scars that I can see."

"This circle is my birthmark. It represents the full moon and my Werewolf Bloodline. I'm from the Täiskuu pack, which means Full Moon. I was born a Werewolf and not turned. There's a difference between those of us born in the Bloodlines vs those who were born human and turned by us."

"What's the difference? How do you tell each other apart?"

"Natural Werewolves are stronger and dominate over the others. You will always be able to tell a natural Werewolf and their pack or Bloodline by their birthmarks. However, since I was given a Fey life-force, I became something different. Something more than just a Werewolf. I'm stronger, faster, and now have some abilities to control elements, as you've seen. I'm the only one of my kind and therefore, I no longer have a place within my pack. This scar represents one lone star in the night sky. It scarred my skin because it was made with a silver brand. Silver is dangerous and one of the only things that can be deadly to a Werewolf. The star represents what I am. A Lone Wolf." He explains this all matter-of-factly, but underneath the fact spilling, I sense that he's sad even though he hides it well. Unlike me, he has complete control over his emotions, but even though his face is a blank slate, I can *feel* his sadness.

"I am so sorry, Logan. I can't imagine what that must have been like for you to lose your pack. Your family. I don't understand why they wouldn't want you with them if you're stronger. Wouldn't you be a benefit to them?"

"Yes, but packs are strict. They have pack laws and everyone has their place within the pack. Before I was given the life-force, I was Beeta Libahunt of my pack, Beta Werewolf. I was the next in line to be Alpha. I had never challenged the Alpha to take his place. He was an excellent Leader, my mentor, and I respected him.

After the life-force changed me, it was no longer an option for me to challenge the Alpha because it would no longer be a fair fight. And since I was not Alpha, only Beta of my pack but now too powerful, I no longer had a place with them. Pack law forced me out."

"That's so unfair. It's not like you asked for the life-force, right? It sounds cruel to kick you out of your family just because you became something better than them. They're stupid to force you out and lose you."

He pulls away and stands up, walking a few steps away from me, and runs his hand through his hair. He's physically present but I feel him pull far away, deep in his thoughts. Even though he isn't expressing any emotion, I sense his longing as if it was my own. Longing for family.

"Werewolves have to have law and rules, Amarah. There has to be punishment and consequences or else the animal side will take over and Werewolves would be more dangerous to everyone. They have to be kept in line. It's just the way it is. So, they had to follow pack law and remove me. Had I been Alpha already, it wouldn't have mattered. But, because I was only Beta with an advantage to become Alpha, they had no choice."

It's my turn to stand up and I walk towards him. He has his back to me and I want to reach out to him, but I let him be. "Everyone has a choice. I mean, I understand the rules and why it happened, but everyone has a choice, Logan. Your Alpha could have kept you. He could have fought for you. It sounds to me like this Alpha cared more about being in power than he did about the members of his pack. He forced you out because he feared you. He feared you would take the spot of Alpha and that fear made him turn his back on you."

"Perhaps you're right, but what's done is done, and that was a *very* long time ago," he turns around to face me and, like always, his face is unreadable. "When Anaxo became the Fey Queen, she took me in, gave me a place and a purpose. I've been by her side ever since. I haven't been alone."

I take the last step so I'm standing right in front of him. "No, not alone, but not whole either. You hide your emotions well, but I don't know how or why, but I *feel* your sadness," I place my hand flat over his heart. He closes his eyes and lets out a heavy sigh.

"I feel your heartache."

He places his hand over mine and laces our fingers together. He opens his eyes and looks at me from inches away. His eyes are so captivating and I feel myself falling.

Falling into them.

Falling into him.

Falling *for* him.

I'm like a train off the rails, uncontrollable and bound for destruction, but there's no way to stop.

I can feel his heart change speed, pumping faster beneath my hand. I look at his big hand engulfing mine, everything about him engulfs and over powers me, but the contrast of his caramel skin against my lighter skin is beautiful.

Big and small.

Hard and soft.

Dark and light.

Yin and yang.

His deep voice pulls me out of my thoughts, "that's because we're connected."

"But how? And why," I meet his eyes, barely able to handle the intensity I see and feel. He leans down towards me, his heart pounding against our hands as he holds mine tightly to his chest.

"Does it matter?" he asks.

His lips are inches away from mine, and my heart is pounding now too, matching his. I'm staring at his full lips, starving for a taste and I tiptoe, stretching to reach them. I normally have better self-control than this. Yeah, me and Janet Jackson.

"Yes," I whisper.

It *does* matter to me, but this close to him all I can think about is kissing him again. The pull is too strong to fight. The need feels vital to my existence and sanity. All other thoughts, everything else, slips away.

Our lips meet, and this time, there's no testing each other's willingness. We both want this. *Need* this. My tongue finds his and we open completely to each other. Logan's hand slides into my hair and gently turns my head so he can kiss me deeper. It's hungry and passionate and sets my skin on fire.

His hands grip my sides helping to hold me in place on my tiptoes. The tightness in my chest opens up and my power is swirling around us without a thought. It *is* me. He follows my lead and his power meets mine. It's like he's touching me physically, but also inside my body, setting my soul on fire to match the fire on my skin. The intense pleasure is almost painful. I'm burning alive and I never want to be put out.

He moans into my mouth and the sound hits me low in my gut, I feel the desire slick between my legs, and my knees buckle, breaking our kiss. I cry out, part in pleasure from the overwhelming sensations and partly in desperation to have his lips back on mine.

He moves his hands down my body like a trail of fire, grabs me from under my ass, and lifts me off my feet. I wrap my legs around his waist and my arms around his neck. He walks us a few steps and then I feel rough bark of a tree digging into my back.

I have no time to register any discomfort or pain before his lips crash back into mine in a fierce kiss. Like my mouth is water in the desert and he is determined to drink up every ounce of me. I tighten my legs around his waist and he pushes his hard body into mine. I gasp as I feel his large erection press against me making me throb with need. I've never felt passion and heat like this. The power surrounding us and pushing against us is almost too much riding the thin line between pleasure and pain.

I gently bite his lip, and he groans, as he pumps his hips into me. He breaks the kiss and trailed his searing lips down my neck. I shiver at the sensation and am thankful I'm no longer standing. I run my hands through his hair and gently pulled him back. I kiss him deep and then followed his lead, trailing my lips and tongue down his neck, tasting his skin. Salt, soap and wet Earth. Masculine. Logan.

I suddenly have the urge to bite him, to mark him, to *claim* him, and I don't think it's my urge I'm feeling, but I don't care. I don't think. I just close my eyes and let my teeth pull his skin into my mouth. I bite down with force and Logan calls out my name, "Amarah," as he falls to his knees.

My back slides down the tree and I can feel the roughness of the bark tearing at my skin. I cry out, partly in pain and partly still wrapped up in the pleasure. The next thing I know, Logan wraps his strong arms around me, pulling me away from the tree. He lays me down on my back, my legs still wrapped around him, as he holds himself above me, breathing hard. His eyes are a deep, dark green in this light, but the look in them is still the same. Desire.

He holds my gaze as he moves his hips, rubbing his hard length over me, only sweatpants separating us and doing nothing to hide his size. He moves over the most sensitive parts of me, back and forth, long slow strokes, and it's not enough. I want to feel his body on mine, skin to skin. I grab his ass and move my body in rhythm to his strokes, adding more pressure. I throw my head back and try to moan my pleasure to the sky but Logan's mouth drinks it down instead.

I can feel how hard he is and my core is throbbing with the need to feel him inside of me. To take me completely and consume me. I move my hands to grip his arms and feel the strength under my hands.

"God, you're perfect. How can you be so perfect?" I ask breathlessly.

He smiles and I swear my body melts into the ground. "Amarah, I lose all control with you. You're so...*unexpected*. I never...I don't..." he shakes his head. "You drive me fucking crazy." He grinds his hard length against me. "You're all I think about. You're intoxicating and I want you so badly. I want to touch you, and kiss you and feel you underneath me as I push myself inside of you," a growl rumbles deep in his chest. "I want to claim you. *All* of you."

"Can't you tell the feeling is mutual?"

"This doesn't feel like anything else. I don't want to go too fast, I don't want to scare you away, but...fuck," he starts to move his hips, stroking me again.

"I don't want to stop. I don't ever want to stop feeling this. Whatever this is. I don't want to stop feeling you take over every inch of my being. Please, Logan, claim me."

I kiss him again, but this time, more softly and not with as much recklessness. I put in this kiss everything I feel. Everything I feel but have no right to, and yet, I can't deny that I do.

Logan's hand dips beneath the band of my sweatpants and I'm not wearing anything underneath. His thick fingers part my lips and spread my wetness across my clit. Our lips brush against each other as I gasp and he exhales. I don't know where I stop and where he begins.

"Damn, you're soaking, Amarah," he speaks with his lips still against mine.

His finger is stroking up and down across my clit, slick with my desire, and building up the fire inside of me. He moves his body to the side of me, holding himself up on his forearm as his free hand lifts up my shirt until he reveals my bare breast.

Another grown rumbles through his chest as his mouth descends on me and I fell a finger push inside of me causing me to gasp and moan to the open night sky.

There are too many sensations fighting for attention. I grab onto his hair as I arch my back and push my hips further onto his hand. He slides in another finger, pumping them into me, while his thumb rubs over my clit with each thrust of his fingers inside of me.

I can feel the orgasm building quickly and I rock my hips, chasing the pleasure he's giving me.

"Oh, fuck, Logan. You're going to make me cum," I pant through my heavy breaths.

His growl vibrates through me as he bites down on my nipple causing me to cry out right before the orgasm breaks. Then, he stops.

He.

Stops!

His fingers slide out of me and he pushes my shirt back down, covering me. I have no idea what's wrong. Did I do something? Or say something? Did he change his mind about doing this with me?

"Logan, please…"

"Shhhh…." he put his fingers on my mouth, and I can smell my desire on them. I have the urge to suck his fingers into my mouth and bring his attention back to me, but his focus is out into the woods.

"Did you hear that?"

He moves his body off of mine and I sit up, straining to hear anything other than my heart pounding in my chest and blood rushing in my veins as I come down from my high.

"Logan, what is it?"

"Demon. I smell demon."

"Shit! It has to be my power. I let my power out, and it drew them to us, like you said. I let down my guard. I'm so stupid."

"No. It wasn't you, Amarah. I wouldn't have let you do that if it wasn't safe. There should be no demons out this far in the middle of nothing," he lets out a growl that's way more vicious than the ones that purred through his chest a minute ago. This one is a warning and a sound that's no longer human.

"Logan, what are you talking about?"

"Stay here. Get your sword and don't stay too close to the fire," he grabs my shoulders and makes me look at him. "Whatever you do, stay here. No matter what you see or hear, ok?"

"But…"

"Amarah, promise me," he pleads.

"I will," I say. Which isn't exactly a promise but seems to ease him.

He touches my cheek with one hand, "I'll be right back."

He doesn't wait for me to say anything else. He runs off into the woods, barefoot and with no shirt, faster than anyone should be able to run. I have a split second to see him disappear into the darkness of the trees and then there's nothing. I can't see him. I can't hear him. The only sound is the pop and crackle from the fire. I stand still, staring off into the forest, in shock. My eyes are glued to the place where Logan disappeared and I feel utterly alone and helpless.

Trust Your Instincts

Game Of Survival by Ruelle

I don't know how long I stand here, frozen, but it feels like forever. Reality comes back to me slowly along with Logan's words.

Grab your sword and don't stay too close to the fire.

I race to where my stuff is and grab one of my dagger harnesses and strap it to my right thigh. Then I reach for my scabbard, pull my sword free, and walk to the edge of the clearing where Logan disappeared. I scan the forest but I can't see anything through the darkness. I strain to hear what's happening out there but all I can hear is my erratic heartbeat.

"Calm down, Amarah. You need to calm down and focus or you're going to end up like you did last time. That will *not* happen again," I breath in through my nose and slowly blow it out through my mouth, steadying my heart rate. I try again to hear any signs of Logan out there or returning. Nothing. Why can't I hear anything?

"Come on, Amarah. Use your power. You can do this," I close my eyes, which is probably a terrible idea, but I need to focus.

I remember the feeling I felt when Logan helped me call me power.

Logan!

He's alone out there with demons right now trying to keep me safe. The thought that he's in danger distracts me.

"Focus, Amarah!"

I concentrate on my breathing. I feel my chest rise and fall with each breath. I think about Logan again, but this time, I think about his lips on mine. The feeling it gives me and how easy it is to use my power once I have a handle on it. I don't want to think about what will happen if I can't do this. I'm focusing on the task at hand. I'm trying to open up to my power.

Nothing.

Nothing is happening.

"God, please! I need to help him," I pray out loud. I look up at the night sky, as if I'm going to see God in the clouds like Simba saw Mufasa, but the image that he's *somewhere*, up there, helps me.

"Please, help me," I whisper as I stare at the sky.

I see a falling star shoot across the sky and suddenly feel that familiar spark inside of my chest. My power is there, ready for me to use. I pull it all around me and will myself to hear out into the forest. I close my eyes and send my power out searching. I feel it moving like fog across the ground, smoothly moving around trees and up and down over roots and rocks. Further and further into the forest it searches.

There.

Logan.

I can't see him but I can sense him, his energy. I can also feel the evil energy surrounding him. There's too much evil! He's fighting but he's being overwhelmed. I need to do something. I use my power to sense around us and I don't sense any other energy beyond what's surrounding Logan.

Before I can talk myself out of it, I run into the forest, in the energy's direction, following the path my power carved out. I open my eyes but it does nothing to help me see where I'm going. I'm using and relying on my power to guide me safely through the forest.

I run, as fast as I can, in the blinding dark, and I don't fall. I don't trip on anything and I don't run into any trees. I trust my power to lead me, and miraculously, it does. I'm close to them now. I can hear the fighting, the growling, and the howl of a Wolf in pain.

"Logan!" I yell out.

I come crashing into a small clearing and I see a large Wolf struggling to keep the demons off him. I count five demons and I don't feel any other energy beyond this clearing. I don't think about the danger and I don't have time to be scared. Logan needs me.

"Hey!" I scream at the demons. "It's me you want, assholes! Come and get me," I pull my power all around me and push it down into my sword.

The crosses etched into the blade flare to life, illuminating the clearing in a glowing white light. I have the same feeling now as I had in my dream. I focus on securing the Heavenly white light around me, except, it's coming from *within* me. I feel powerful. I feel protected. I feel at peace. All I know is that I have to fight.

Two of the five demons turn their glowing red eyes to me and snarl. They leave the fight with Logan and come charging at me. I grip my sword tightly in my right hand, and with my left hand, I push my power out as hard as I can toward one of the demons. It falls back as if it ran into a brick wall. That leaves me with one demon to handle. More my speed but still way out of my depth. I grip my sword with both hands and when the demon is almost on me, I jump to the side, drop to one knee and swing the sword upward towards the demon's body.

I feel the sword connect as it sliced through the demon's mid-section and it doubles over with a roar. I don't wait for the demon to regain its fight.

I stand up and swing the sword over my head, "Ahhhhh!" I yell out as I bring it down and across with everything I have. The demon's head falls to the ground and a few moments later, the body follows. The fallen demon burst into flames and I have to jump back away from the body to avoid getting burned.

My feet are suddenly pulled out from under me and I land on my back, hard, knocking the breath from my lungs. Glowing red eyes aappear above me and I have déjà vu. So much for not ending up like the first time.

I had been distracted by killing the first demon that I completely lost focus on the other demon. Not smart, Amarah! I keep my eyes on the demon above me as I try to crawl backwards and feel for my lost sword at the same time. It's no use. There's no way I'm getting away from it like this.

The demon opens its mouth and shrieks. The sound pierces my ears and I cringe, quickly covering my ears. I get a splendid view of all the sharp teeth about to descend on me. I remember I have one dagger and reach for it. I pull it out of the harness and hold it out in front of me. Yeah, déjà vu.

The demon moves with blinding speed and I feel its claws tear into my arm as it knocks my dagger out of my hand. Blood pours down my arm, too much, too fast. The calm resolve I felt a moment ago is nowhere to be found and I start to panic. The demon rears his head back ready to strike and I swear time slows to a crawl. I feel like I have all the time in the world to do...*something*! Anything! But what?

This is it. There's no way I'm going to survive this demon ripping me to shreds. A thought comes to me, as if it's being placed in my mind for me.

Use your power.

My power.

I pull it around me and imagine it's a shield. I hold my arms outstretched and push it out towards the demon. I see him strain against the force but he stays on top of me. His red eyes drill into me from just feet away.

Evil.

Angry.

Empty.

I can see the frustration in them and the determination to kill me as if nothing else matters. One goal. One job. He keeps pushing against my power, my body shaking with the strain of holding my power with such force. The blood from the gashes on my arm is streaming faster with my effort, the blood pumping too quickly in my veins. I won't be able to hold him back much longer.

"Logan!" I cry out.

The demon is pushing through my energy shield and his teeth are now inches away from my face. My hands are pressed directly against its chest. I push with all my might, but it's like trying to move a mountain. There's no way I can keep him from getting to me. I see white spots and my vision starts to blur. Too much blood loss. Too much exertion. Too much adrenaline seeping away and fatigue taking its place. I cry out in desperation when suddenly the demon stops moving towards me. It snarls and turns its attention over its shoulder.

When it turns, I see an arrow sticking out of its shoulder. It moves off of me in a blur of speed. My arms collapse and I try to hang on to consciousness. I try to get up and can't. It's like my mind is trying but my body doesn't respond. I feel heavy and numb. I'm looking up at the stars and remember this is exactly what happened to me the first time a demon attacked me and I swore it wouldn't happen again. I try to laugh at the irony of the situation but only a strangled sound manages to erupt from my scratchy throat. My vision is fading around the edges when a face I don't recognize comes into view above me, blocking out the stars.

"She's alive," he says.

Oh, he's handsome, I think, right before the world goes black and cold.

30

Who's The Enemy?

White Flag by Bishop Briggs

I hear people talking, but it sounds far away, and I can't make out what they're saying. The voices gradually get louder and clearer as I surface back into consciousness. I open my eyes and I'm greeted by a waking summer sky. The darkness that swallowed me whole is being pushed aside along with the darkness of the night.

I try to sit up and wince in pain. My back is sore and tight, my body is stiff, and my entire right arm is throbbing. It feels like my heart is going to beat right out of it. I look down and see that it's been bandaged. I force my aching body into a sitting position, but the effort is slow and painful.

"She lives," says an unfamiliar voice.

I turn my head toward the voice and I immediately see Logan. I always sense him and find him no matter who else is around. Logan is sitting on one of the logs around the firepit next to a guy I don't know, but I recognize him as the one I saw last night before I passed out. There's also another man sitting on the log next to them.

Logan gets and walks over to where I'm sitting by the dying fire. He drops to one knee, reaches his hand out to touch me, and then hesitates.

He put his hand back down and asks, "how are you feeling?"

"Is that a serious question? I fought demons last night. I didn't spend the night at a spa. I feel like fucking shit," I say with feeling. I don't know why I'm being snarky but I feel like shit and I don't like that there are men I don't know staring at me.

"You should have stayed here like I told you, Amarah. You could have died last night! What were you thinking," he scolds me.

"But I didn't die, did I. You could have died too. I saw that they outnumbered you and I couldn't just stand by and do *nothing*. A *thank you* would be nice instead of a lecture."

"Thank you," he gives me small smile. It immediately warms my frozen heart and I smile back, but he continues his lecture before I can say you're welcome.

"But I could have handled it. I've survived worse and you're not trained yet, Amarah."

And just like that, the warmth is gone, "wow! Ego much? The big, bad Logan doesn't need help from anyone, is that it?"

"No, that's not what I'm saying. You can't just throw yourself in front of danger like that. You're too important. We need you and you can't be careless. It could have been a lot worse than this," he gently touches my bandaged arm. He looks at me then, really looks at me, and I see the emotion in his eyes. He was genuinely worried about me and I just can't stay mad at him when the look in those beautiful green eyes is full of relief that I'm ok.

My entire body feels like it took a beating, not just my bandaged arm. I think back on the night and remember sliding down the tree and feeling it tear into my skin.

"Not all the bruises are from the demons you know," I blush as I gesture towards my back.

Logan blushes for the first time, *ever*, "I lost myself last night. I'm so sorry I hurt you, Amarah."

"Oh, I'm not complaining about that, trust me. But you're right. I wasn't thinking it through. I just couldn't stand by and do nothing."

"Awe, well isn't this just too sweet," the man who spoke earlier interrupts.

He looks amused and smirks in my direction, which shows off a very defined dimple in his left cheek. He's clean-shaven and has a baby-face but doesn't look young. He's still masculine, even with the baby-face. His dark brown eyes are too deep and full of life for him to be young, even though they dance with amusement at the moment. I can't help but stare at them a little longer than is appropriate. They tilt up at in a completely unique angle. I don't think I've ever seen eyes quite like them.

His hair is cut short on the sides and about an inch on top, straight, and styled to messy perfection. He's leaning forward with his elbows resting on each knee, twirling a knife in his hands, and I take in all the ink that covers both muscular arms and disappears under the black tank top. Black jeans tucked into black boots top off the outfit. My hot, bad boy alarm is going off in my head. He's definitely attractive.

"Like what you see, love?" He smirks bigger.

And trouble.

I scoff.

Logan interrupts before the stranger can say anything else, "Amarah, let me introduce some of our hosts. This is Andre Sanchez and Nicholas Gonzales of the Tulekahju Family. Hallana sent them to check on us since we didn't arrive last night."

"It was you who showed up and helped us fight the demons last night," I say plainly.

"Yep, that was us. Come to save the day! Or rather, the night. I do enjoy saving a beautiful damsel in distress," Andre jokes and winks at me.

I haven't known him for more than thirty seconds, but I already know he's always angling to be the center of attention, He's the guy that always has something to say.

Nicholas just nods his head in my direction. He's quiet compared to Andre, but his dark brown eyes are focused and observant. I would bet money that he doesn't miss much that happens around him. It's usually the quiet, observant ones that you need to watch out for. My guess is, he's quite a bit older than Andre. You can't tell their age by looking at them, but something in his demeaner says he's seen it all, done it all.

His face is narrow with a nice defined jawline, and his hair is kept short, all around, in a very no-nonsense style. He's also wearing all black, but nothing about him stands out. Nothing to draw unwanted attention. It's like he can blend in anywhere and I bet he uses that to his advantage. One word comes to mind. Dangerous.

They both have similar skin tone as Hallana. They both have jet black hair and dark brown eyes. There's no denying the Latin spark that seems to be the Bloodline of the Fire Fey. I can see Andre being a loud, hot-head, like his Princess, but Nicholas seems to have absolute control. I can't imagine him letting his emotions get the best of him. Then again, what the Hell do I know?

I nod back at Nicholas, "thank you. Both of you. I don't want to think about what would have happened if you hadn't shown up when you did," I shudder.

"It was my *pleasure*, love. Hallana seems very...*heated* over you. I couldn't resist the offer to be one of the first to see what all the fuss is about," Andre says as he rakes his eyes over me.

"I'm *not* your love," I say defensively. "And I'll just bet she's *thrilled* to have me in her home," I glance at Logan as I say it. "I'm sure she'll be overjoyed that you saved me and didn't let the demons kill me," I add sarcastically.

"Ooh, is she always this feisty?" Andre asks Logan as if I'm not sitting right here.

Before Logan can say anything, "I can speak for my damn self, Andre."

"I can see that. My apologies, love. It won't happen again," he places his hand over his heart in a very serious and sincere manner. The cocky smile is gone, but his eyes sparkle with humor. He obviously is fucking with me and doesn't mean the apology. I have a feeling he's going to continue to be a pain in my ass.

I roll my eyes at him in response which just makes him smile wider.

"So, what happened last night?" I ask. "Last night, you said that demons should not have been out here. I thought my power was like a beacon to them. Isn't that what led them here?"

Logan shakes his head, "demons don't just magically appear. Yes, your power draws them but they have to travel to you. There is only one rip that we know of and all demons come to Earth from that rip. There is no way they could have sensed your power and been way out here in minutes. They had to have already been close by to find you. Someone had to tell them you would be here."

"What do you mean someone told them? The only people who knew we were traveling are the Fey Leaders, Ethan, and the Queen, right?"

Logan just nods.

"So, you're saying someone *betrayed* us? A Fey, or Ethan, betrayed us to the demons?"

"Yes," Logan says seriously. "It doesn't make any sense. No one from the Fey would have done this, and Ethan is also on our side and our greatest ally. We've all lost so many in this war and we all want the same thing. To save our people. To save the humans and get back to winning this war on the demons. You're the key to making this all happen. I don't know who would jeopardize that."

"I have an idea." I look at Andre, "you said Hallana is heated about me. What exactly do you mean?"

His eyes widened a bit, "nothing crazy! Hallana is a hot-head, yes, but she wouldn't do anything to defy the Queen. She wants this war to end as much as anyone. What reason would she have to betray you?"

"I can think of one," I look at Logan.

Logan has the audacity to look confused, "what do you mean?"

I scoff, "Seriously? You saw the way she came at me in the meeting. She's no fan of mine and she doesn't think I'll be of any help. You heard her say it yourself. Also, I know your history with her and our little display at the meeting didn't help my cause."

Logan looks embarrassed and shocked that I know about him and Hallana. Leave it to a man to be totally oblivious and then try and remain innocent of any wrong doing or deception. It pisses me off.

"No, she wouldn't go this far. Hallana is loyal to the Queen and the Fey. She wouldn't do this."

"Are you sure? Women do crazy things when they are hurt, jealous, or...*heartbroken*. Men bring out the worst in us. Whose idea was it for me to come here and start my training with the Fire Fey?"

He stares at me and doesn't answer, and he doesn't have to. His silence is answer enough.

"So, I'll ask again. Are you absolutely sure she doesn't want me out of the way?"

I look at the two men who also know Hallana well. They meet my gaze but no one defends her further.

"That's what I thought. None of you are sure that it *wasn't* her. I don't even know her and I know she has a temper. Now I'm expected to spend time in her home, and trust her to protect me through my training?!" I laugh sarcastically, "yeah, that's not going to fucking happen."

Nicholas finally speaks, "I have known Hallana for centuries. I know she has a temper, everyone does, that's not a secret. She's strong, determined, and will do difficult things that need to be done. She's abrupt, headstrong and speaks her truth. That doesn't always make her a lot of friends. However, as Logan and Andre have said, I don't believe she would betray the Queen or the cause. I can't say for certain because love makes people do...*terrible* things, but before we condemn her for this betrayal, we need to simply ask her."

I laugh again, "yeah, ok. Like that's going to go over well. You think she's going to just admit to betraying her Queen if it is her?"

"There is only one way to find out," Nicholas states plainly.

"Great. Let's go see the Wicked Witch of the West then, shall we? Should I bring a bucket of water?"

Andre busts out laughing, but Logan and Nicholas don't seem to get the reference to the Wizard of Oz, or they just don't find my sarcasm funny. I happen to agree with Andre and think it's hilarious and a spot-on reference. I don't want to finish the rest of this journey and face off with someone who hates me and wants me dead. Yet, what choice do I have? This is my life now and I can't run and hide.

We've come this far only to discover someone has betrayed us. We need to know who it is and what their ultimate end goal is. Is it purely targeted towards me? Or is it a bigger betrayal that we don't know of? There are too many questions that need answers. I need to know if I'm being targeted not only by demons but by my own people.

So, off we go to confront the Wicked Witch. Time to find out who our true enemies are.

31

On My Own

No Time To Die by Billie Eilish

The sun is a beautiful warm, round glow climbing the sky by the time we finish arguing and are ready to head out. My back is stiff and hurts with every movement I make. It's amazing how much you use every muscle in your body daily, yet you don't realize it until you're hurt. It's going to be a slow, painful hour traipsing through the forest for me. I have both daggers strapped to my thighs, but I'm carrying the sword and Logan is carrying my small backpack. My back is too scratched up to have anything rubbing against it.

Last night, my power had guided me through these trees effortlessly. I had run, physically blind, through this mess of forest without getting even one scratch. Now, I'm stumbling on every rock and root, and getting caught on every single branch. It's frustrating, annoying, and painful. I'm no longer a happy camper, and as much as I don't want to see Hallana, I want out of this awful forest, badly.

"You're from the Müstik Family, right?" Andre asks as he walks slowly and gracefully a few steps ahead of me. "The very First Fey Bloodline."

"Yeah, that's what I've been told," I respond shortly.

"They can not only control all the elements they're known to be skilled healers. Why don't you use your power to heal yourself? We could move faster if you weren't in pain."

"Well, gee thanks for your obvious concern about my well-being," I say coldly. "I barely know anything about my power at all much less how to *heal* with it."

"You seemed to know a decent amount last night."

I laugh sarcastically, "oh, you mean like how I was about to get killed right before you guys showed up?"

"Well, you held off two demons on your own before we got there. That's impressive given the fact that you know absolutely nothing about...well, *anything*. But don't worry love, we'll change that," he glances back at me with a wink and another teasing smile. I knew it, he's going to be a pain in my ass.

"Are you done mocking me, Andre? This is going to be an unpleasant enough trip already without you being a pain in my ass."

"I'm not mocking. I will help you learn and nothing is going to happen to you here," he stops walking and looks directly at me.

I looked him in the eyes and glimpse something else in him. Something in his eyes that's more serious and observant than he initially led on. That lasts for a quick second before his cocky smile is back in full-force. But I had seen it. The joker isn't the only card up his sleeve and it makes me think better of him, but also to take him more seriously.

"I am a pain in the ass, love. It's just in my nature. In time, I'll grow on you. Until then, I'll leave you to your thoughts," he gives one last dazzling smile and wink my way before he struts on ahead of me.

"I am not your love," I hiss under my breath as I watch his backside disappear into the forest. It's not a bad backside to look at come to think of it. I shake my head and smile.

Nicholas is now the one leading the way, slow and steady, in front of me. He's being very considerate of my slow pace, and I'm grateful to him for that, and also for his ability to walk in silence. Logan is bringing up the rear, but staying close to me, making sure I stay safe.

"Don't let him get to you, Amarah. Andre is just Andre. He's a perpetual flirt and enjoys getting a rise out of others. He's a child."

"Well, that's good to know," I mutter.

Although, a part of me is enjoying the attention and the flirting. It's a tad disappointing to hear that he's like this with *every* girl. I don't know why it bothers me. I have Logan's attention, but I can't forget that so does Hallana. I guess that's why a part of me welcomes Andre's flirting. I'm not looking to add more drama to my already overflowing plate but it's a nice distraction. Every girl likes to feel noticed.

"And he didn't get to me. This entire past week has gotten to me. So, forgive me if being targeted and attacked by my own people is a blow I didn't see coming and wasn't prepared for. I think I've earned the right to be grouchy."

"You're right. You have had a tremendously tough week and you have every right to be upset. We all are. But we need to make sure we're being upset at the *right* person. We can't just accuse Hallana of this betrayal based solely on suspicion."

"So, what? You're defending her? You're defending her actions at the meeting? Is it because you believe she's innocent of betrayal or because you're sleeping with her and that blinded you to it?" I ask angrily.

"Amarah, I..." he sighs heavily.

I wait for him to say more but he doesn't. He has no argument. He has nothing to say in his defense. I wasn't sure if he was still sleeping with Hallana before but he just confirmed it. My heart constricts in my chest and my eyes start to water. I blink to hold them back and let the anger wash away the tears instead. The things I let him do to me last night. We almost had sex. And he's sleeping with another woman! A woman whose territory we almost had sex in!

No. Tears won't do for this situation. I have every right to be angry. I *refused* to be the other woman in the human world and being here amongst the preternatural, uncommonly and ridiculously gorgeous men, doesn't change that. It's not who I am, and the fact that Logan put me in that situation, makes me hate him a little. Yes, that's probably a bit harsh, but it hits too close to home, too soon after the same type of heartbreak.

"Yea, that's what I thought, Logan," I say coldly.

Why can't I ever find a decent guy? Princess Aralyn had been right. They're all the same. In this world or the human world. I pick up my pace to distance myself from him, gritting my teeth and welcoming the pain. I want to get as far away from him as I can.

Unfortunately, I'm stuck with him out here in this damned forest.

On this damned journey.

To this damned bitch's home.

Is it too late to turn back and choose the blue pill instead of the red pill? Neo couldn't take back his choice in the Matrix and neither can I.

We continue walking in silence for another twenty minutes before Nicholas and Andre stop in a small clearing. We're almost to the base of the mountain.

"Why are we stopping?" I ask. "I'm ok to keep going."

"This is where we head underground. We'll travel the rest of the way in the caves and tunnels," Nicholas explains.

"I don't see anything. Where is the entrance?"

"It is hidden by glamour. Can you not detect it?" Nicholas asks but not in a condescending tone, just genuine curiosity.

I shake my head, "no, I already told you guys. I don't know how to use my power at will yet." I'm getting a little irritated at constantly having to admit I don't know shit. It doesn't exactly make me feel good.

"It's ok, Amarah," Nicholas reassures. "You'll just have to trust us and follow us through."

"Or I can lead you," Andre says with a smile and holds out his arm, offering to escort me.

I contemplate slipping my arm through his, and leaning into his body, just so Logan can feel a small bit of the pain I feel. Hell, that's if he even cares! But I'm tired and drained. I'm not in the mood to be petty.

"No, thanks," I say dryly. "I'm sure I'll manage." I give Nicholas my attention, "lead the way."

He nods and walks straight towards the line of trees on the other side of the clearing. "Make sure you enter exactly where I do," Nicolas orders. He walks right through the trees and disappears.

"Ok, now that is cool," I say excitedly. "I feel like Harry Potter at Platform 9 ¾!" I have the biggest cheeser, and I want to run at the trees like he does his first time through. But I manage to contain my excitement and calmly walk towards the trees.

"Amarah, let me help you," Logan insists.

"I don't need your help," I say harshly. Andre snickers. "I don't need anyone's help," I glare at Andre.

"After you, love," Andre says with a sweeping bow.

"God, you're insufferable," I say with a sigh.

He fake-pouts as I walk by, pushing out his bottom lip as far as it'll go. I just shake my head and keep walking. I'm at the tree line and use my right hand to push through the glamour. Once my hand touches it, I can feel the air tingling. I suddenly realize that touch seems to be a connection to my power. I feel my power react to the glamour and I use my power to push the glamour aside. It's hard to explain what you can't see or describe but that's what it feels like I do.

With the glamour now gone, I see a rocky hillside in front of me. Not quite a mountainside, we're still pretty from the main mountain, but smaller ones are surrounding it. The trees had just been a mask to hide the entrance. It's like a cave entrance, but it's extremely narrow. That's why Nicholas had told me to follow in exactly where he did. If I hadn't, I would have run right into the side of the rocky hill. The opening doesn't look big enough for Logan but I know it has to be. Maybe he changes into his Wolf to pass through? I don't wait to find out.

I walk into the entrance and continue until I've walked completely out of the light and have to stop and let my eyes adjust to the darkness.

"Are you ok, Amarah?" Nicholas asks from somewhere down the tunnel.

"Yes, I'm fine. Just can't see a damn thing."

Up ahead, a flame of light illuminates the darkness, guiding me further into the tunnel. I don't wait or look back to see if Logan and Andre are behind me. They know where they're going and I'd rather not be around either of them at the moment. So, I walk towards the flame. I thought Nicholas had lit the end of a torch to light our way, but as I walk up to him, I realize he holds the burning flame in his open palm.

"You are a Master of Fire," I say in awe. I reach my hand out towards it and it's real, heat-producing, skin burning, scorching fire. "How does it not burn you?"

"It's just a part of me. It's in our blood. It's within us. Just like your power is a part of you and does not hurt you. Some things just are and don't need nor have an explanation."

He turns around and continues to lead the way down the tunnel. The further we go, the more room there is. The tunnel is slowly opening up, so I move to walk beside Nicholas instead of behind him. I still don't know where the other two are, and I don't care.

"How much further until we're there?" I ask.

"It's not too much longer. Maybe about ten minutes."

I sigh, "great. I'm not looking forward to this next part."

"Princess Hallana is...*uninhibited*, I'll say that. She can come off very harsh, hateful even, I know. Yes, her approach may be tactless, but she's always honest. I've never known her to lie, and I've known her for a *very* long time."

"That is the nicest way I've ever heard the term, bitch, described," I laugh. "You don't think she's the one who betrayed us."

"I do not. You don't have to believe me or take my word for it, but I ask that you have an open mind. It seems to me, you have already decided you dislike and distrust her, based on very little."

"Well, you weren't there when she came in hot, shooting shots at me without a reason. So, she seems to dislike me, also based on very little. I'm just returning the favor."

He sighs loudly, "I will never understand the unspoken rivalry between women."

I snort, "that makes two of us!"

"Look, Amarah, all I'm saying is you need to go in there with the ability to see her as innocent just as much as you can see her as guilty."

I sigh, "I know you're right it's just easier said than done. But I promise I'll try."

"Think about this, Amarah. If she wanted you dead, would she have sent Andre and I out last night to find you? If she did truly betray us and consort with demons, why would she send us out to ruin her own plan?"

"Maybe she sent you as her defense, her alibi. Maybe she sent you for that reason exactly, to feign innocence. Maybe she was betting on you guys being too late to save us. Maybe her plan backfired."

Nicholas shakes his head, "there are too many what-ifs and maybes. You could be right. However, my gut instinct tells me otherwise."

"Well, I do hope you are right. Although, if you are, that just means it's someone else."

Nicholas stops walking, and I follow suit. We just stare at each other, and at this moment, we have complete understanding.

We know *someone* betrayed us. Someone we trust. There's no way around that cold, hard fact. And as hard as it is for me to swallow that truth, I can't imagine what he must be feeling, considering he's known these people for *centuries*.

"We're here. Are you ready?" Nicholas asks.

I look ahead of us and only see more darkness, more tunnel. "More glamour?"

"Yes," he nods, as he walks forward and disappears, leaving me in utter blackness. I like the fact that Nicholas doesn't hold my hand through all of this shit. He just tells me what needs to be done and trusts that I can do it. He seems to be the only one who believes in me, even just a little.

The nerves suddenly hit me. This next part is going to be crucial to our next steps. I've been so distracted with it all that I had forgotten all about my aches and pains. Thinking of them brings them all back but the nerves and adrenaline are pushing them back down again. There's no time for pain.

I take a deep breath, "you can do this, Amarah."

I reach my hand out and feel when it passes through the glamour. I can feel the heaviness of the blackness as it tingles against my skin. I use my power to push the glamour away, and I see steps heading upwards, and an opening with light flooding in above. I sure wish I had Dorothy's magical shoes right about now, I think as I start climbing the stairs.

There really is no place like home.

32

Princess Hallana

Do We Have A Problem? By Nicki Minaj

I hesitate at the top of the stairs. My next step will take me to the landing and the world beyond. I have a million thoughts and a million emotions tearing at my mind but there's only one that screams louder than all the others.

Uncertainty.

Whatever awaits beyond, Hallana is one or the other, a friend or a foe. This could be an uncomfortable conversation or a knock-down, drag-out fight. I'm ready to bet my money on Hallana being the traitor, but Logan and Nicholas seem certain I'm wrong. Although Logan's opinion is biased, Nicholas's is not. At least not intimately. I don't think? After all, she did send them to find us. Gah! I just am not a hundred percent sure.

I'm uncertain.

And, if I'm being honest...

I'm scared.

I take a deep breath and try to settle my loud thoughts. I strap on my sword, and even though it hurts, it isn't the kind of hurt that's debilitating. It doesn't impair me, it just...well, *hurts*, but I'd rather have my weapons ready if I need them than the alternative. No need to take unnecessary chances. Plus, the pain helps keep my brain from spinning and helps me focus. I can do this.

Taking the last step, out into the light, I have to blink and let my eyes adjust to the light after being in the darkness of the tunnel for so long. When I can see again, I'm in more shock than I think I've ever been in my entire life. I'm standing inside of an old, hollowed-out volcano, just like Logan said. There's a gigantic castle, like...legit *castle*, in the middle. It has towers all around, the tallest one stands straight in the middle, and goes up, up, up to the very top of the mountain.

There's a large opening at the top of the mountain that lets the sunlight in, but it's too far away for the light to make its way down here to the bottom. I mean, this hollowed-out mountain is enormous! Once again, I feel like just a tiny speck in a big ole unnatural world. There are flames all around the sides of the mountain and the castle, which seem to glow way more than normal, to produce the light.

The castle and grounds are surrounded and filled with nothing but greenery. The ground is almost covered in plants and trees. It looks like this is their garden and primary source of food. I can see apples, cherries, and pears on some trees, and tomatoes, zucchini, chiles, huge sunflowers, herbs, and who knows what else in the gardens. It's spectacular and beautiful and unlike anything I've ever seen.

"We're definitely not in Kansas anymore," I whisper to myself.

I finally notice that there are people scattered around the grounds, tending to the gardens, and the joyous sound of children laughing and running around. They all have similar tan skin tone and dark hair that I recognize as they Fire Fey Bloodline.

I head towards the castle casually, still trying to take it all in. As I get closer to the Fey in the gardens, I notice some of them are in their true Fey form. Their skin is adorned with scales, the same kind I saw on Hallana at the meeting. I know it's rude to stare but I'm so taken aback by all the beauty, that I can't help but gape.

As I walk past the others, I realize they're doing the same thing to me, staring. Only the children don't seem interested in my presence. They continue running around and playing as if nothing's changed. As if a stranger isn't walking amongst them. In their home.

"Welcome to the home of the Tulekahju Fey," Andre says from behind me. "What do you think, love?" He spreads his arms out wide and I can't tell if he's asking what I think about *him* or everything *around* him. So,,I ignore his flirting.

"I think it's stunning and unreal," I say in awe as I look up and around. "I can't believe I'm standing *inside* of a mountain, next to a fairy-tale castle."

"Amarah, is everything ok?" Logan asks as he joins us.

"Fine. What took you guys so long?" I ask the two men standing in front of me. They glance at each other, but I can't read the look.

Andre throws on a cocky smile that seems to be his go-to for flirting and lying, "male bonding, love."

"Uh-huh," I cross my arms and look from Andre and his nonchalant demeaner over to Logan and his blank, unreadable face.

Logan gives nothing away physically, but I can feel his tension. I know he's not happy although, I can't tell why. I don't know what happened between them but I do know that we're about to be in a *very* uncomfortable situation. Even if we weren't planning to ask Hallana if she betrayed us, which we are, I would still have to be here knowing her and Logan are a…*thing*.

Have history.

Hooking up.

Bumping uglies.

Whatever you want to call it. That alone is going to be uncomfortable. So that makes two of us that are unhappy, and honestly, I could give a shit if Logan is happy or not. This is all his fault. He should suffer.

"Princess Hallana is expecting us," Nicholas says, as he walks back to us from the castle.

I turn around and look at Nicholas, hoping to see something in his expression, some kind of clue for what to expect from Hallana. We make eye contact and he just nods, giving nothing away.

I nod back, "lead the way."

I don't look back at Andre or Logan, even though I really want to look at Logan for some kind of clue or encouragement. I want him to tell me everything is going to be fine, like he's done before. I want to run to him for comfort but he lied to me. Led me on. This is not the time or place to depend on Logan. I need to stand on my own when I face Hallana.

Lord, help me, I pray silently as we enter the castle.

The castle is immense and exactly like what you see in movies. There's a huge entryway with a massive, wide staircase directly in front of us. The stairs then part and continue up to each side of the room and the hallways and rooms beyond. I follow Nicholas into a large hallway to the right. We walk about halfway down and then he stops in front of two white doors. If you can call them doors. I've never seen doors this big anywhere. They're at least three times the size of a normal house door and they have flames engraved in them from the bottom to the top. They're massive and, I reluctantly admit, impressive.

"We're here. Are you ready?" Nicholas asks.

I'm tired of people asking me for my opinion when it truly doesn't matter.

I can't say, *no, actually, I'm not ready, and I never will be.*

How does anyone prepare for any of this? And it's not like I can just turn around and go back home to my mundane existence knowing that I'm half Angel, half Fey, and that demons and preternatural people exist.

I sigh, "Everyone keeps asking me if I'm ready like I have a choice. Ready or not, I have to do this so, let's get on with it."

Nicholas nods and pushes on the doors. They part inward, and I follow him through. I feel like I'm walking into a cage with a wild animal at the zoo. Why can't I just observe from a safe distance? I take a deep breath, hold my head high, and walk into yet another, enormous room. Although, it's not nearly the size of the throne room at the Fey Headquarters, it's still impressive.

We walk straight towards the dais in front of us. You can hear our footsteps on the polished white floor. I don't know what it's made of, but it's spotless, and as I look at it closer, I can see very subtle flames engraved in it. I glance around the room as we walk, it's all white and immaculate. I can't see the dais or Princess Hallana because I'm directly behind Nicholas and he frame, although much smaller than Logan's, still eclipses me.

When we finally reach the dais, Nicholas steps off to the side and kneel before the dais. I stop next to him, but I don't know if I should kneel, or bow, or what? All I know is that I don't *want* to. I don't want to give Hallana any authority over me. Andre moves up to my left side and kneels, like Nicholas. Logan is next and stands to the left of Andre but he doesn't kneel. I glance at him and he slightly shakes his head, as if he knows the question I'm asking, without me having to say a word. I stay standing, shoulders back and I finally look up to the dais.

Princess Hallana stands out like a red-hot flame in all the white. Even the throne she sits in is pure white stone. The back of the throne is tall and ends in the shape of flames. Like everything else in The Unsee, it's unique and stunning.

Hallana sits completely still and elegant on her throne, and yet, she has a buzzing energy about her. It's like she can ignite at any second. Her black hair is combed behind her ears and lays, straight as a razor, down her back, leaving her face fully bare. It's the same face I saw at the meeting, so I know she's using glamour to hide her true Fey form.

She's wearing another skin-tight red dress, but this one isn't made of leather and looks more comfortable. Oddly, she's barefoot. I hate to admit it, but she's striking, and I can see why anyone would be attracted to her.

"I expected you last night. What happened?" She has eyes only for Logan.

"The traveling took longer than expected, so we had to make camp at the lake," Logan responds plainly. No emotion or inflection in his voice.

Hallana laughs harshly, "well, that doesn't surprise me. Look at her." She finally looks at me and sneers. "She even got hurt from a little hike. Pathetic."

I hold her eye contact and glared at her. All that unprovoked hate makes her ugly and I take back what I thought a second before. I don't know how Logan could want to be with someone so hateful.

I want to tell her to go to Hell. I want to turn around and walk out of here and leave Logan to deal with her hate and jealousy. I don't trust myself to say anything friendly, so I keep my mouth shut, which is difficult. I stand still, under the weight of her gaze, and don't flinch. I send as much heat and strength of my own, through my eyes back at her, as I can.

"She didn't get hurt from the hike. That is from a demon attack last night," Logan says in my defense.

I don't need or want him defending me but he knows more about her and this type of politics than I do. So, I let it be for now.

"A what?!" Princess Hallana stands up aggressively and looks shocked. It's either spectacular acting or she's genuinely shocked.

"Nicholas, report."

Nicholas and Andre both stand up, but it's Nicholas who speaks, as requested.

"Yes, Princess, Logan speaks the truth. We arrived just in time to help them fight a demon attack. There were five soldier demons when we arrived. Logan was fighting three and Amarah was fighting two. Logan said there had been seven soldier demons total. Andre and I helped them defeat the remaining demons. Amarah was hurt in the process and lost a lot of blood. We could not continue traveling last night."

"You fought two demons?" Hallana asks me directly.

There's something other than pure hatred in her eyes when she looks at me this time. Maybe curiosity. Maybe disbelief. Who knows what goes on in that crazy brain of hers.

I hold up my bandaged arm, "not very successfully."

"Actually," Logan interrupts, "something...*different* happened when Amarah killed a demon."

Something different? Why hadn't they told me this before?

"What do you mean something different happened? What happened?" She asks in frustration. At least I'm not the only one confused.

"The demon didn't dissipate into the normal black fog. The body burned," Logan explains.

Hallana looks at me with so many questions in her eyes. Questions I don't have answers to. I had no idea demons didn't burn when others killed them. I have no fucking clue what this means or if it will happen again. Why hadn't anyone told me about this until now?

Hallana is pacing the dais now and seems to talk more to herself than to us, "what the fuck does that mean? How did these soldier demons end up in *my* forest on the same night you were traveling? A pack of seven?! That isn't normal. The attack had to be organized."

She stops pacing and faces us, "somebody tell me what the Hell is going on?"

No one speaks for what seems like forever. Hallana finally, impatiently, throws her hands I the air. "Logan? What is going on?" She demands.

"Someone has betrayed us. We thought you might have some answers."

"You what?" She looks confused, "how in the Hell would *I* have answers to any of this?"

"Few people knew we were traveling here, and this is your kingdom. You also made it very clear that you had no desire to accept Amarah as our Võitleja."

"You think *I* did this?" She looks at Logan, and all the fiery energy fades. The look in her eyes is no longer anger and confusion. I no longer see a Princess, just a woman, and her feelings are hurt at Logan's accusation.

Logan shifts a little in his stance, the only thing that betrays his discomfort for the situation, "someone close to us did. We just need to know who and why. You understand that we have to ask you."

"She didn't do it," I say.

Everyone looks at me in shock but it's Logan who speaks again, "you said..."

"I *know* what I said," I cut him off. "But here and now, in front of her..." I shake my head. "I can't explain it, but I just *know* she's telling the truth. I can *feel* it."

I look at Hallana, "I'm sorry that I accused you. I had my reasons and your actions at the meeting did *not* help your case, but I know it wasn't you and I'll admit when I'm wrong."

Hallana looks at me and I think she might be finally seeing me for me, another independent woman, and not as competition for Logan. Although, I don't know how long that will last considering what happened between Logan and me last night. I don't know what's going to happen with this love triangle. I know it isn't over this easily, but at this moment, we're just two strong women on the same side.

"I assure you it was *not* me," she glares at Logan and then returns to her seat on the throne. She's regained control of herself and her emotions. A*, thank you for defending me*, would have been a friendly gesture, but I'm also not burnt to a crisp. I guess I'll take the win.

"So, you didn't betray us and try to have me killed, but *someone* did," I look at the others in the room, but no one has any more answers now than they did when we first found out.

"Yes. Someone did. We will find them and we will make them pay, Amarah," Hallana says defiantly.

She's fierce and I'm thankful to no longer be on her nasty side. At the moment at least. I also have no intention of getting back on her radar. Logan is our contention, and his actions put me in the fighting ring, without my permission. I'm not happy about it and I have no intention of fighting for him or *any* man. Just thinking about it tears at my heart and I hate it, but I'm officially stepping out of that fighting ring and into another.

I'm going to put all my attention and energy into my training and finding our traitor. Nothing else matters. Not Logan. Not Hallana. Only my life and the person trying to end it.

I will find them.

They will pay.

33

Pleasantly Surprised

The Other Girl by Kelsea Ballerini, Halsey

I'm lying on my back, sweating and breathing hard, looking up into Andre's eyes. His eyes really are beautiful, with their slight upward tilt, and thick, dark lashes. He's looking down at me, perfect and not a drop of sweat to be seen.

I can smell his deodorant, but underneath that, I can smell *him*. His skin. He smells like a campfire, like the smell of hickory burning in a fireplace, giving off warmth and comfort. The scent is intoxicating. I want to nuzzle his neck.

Nuzzle him?

The thought of doing that brings me back to reality. What is wrong with me?

Andre has been staring at me and I don't know how long we've been laying like this. "Not that I'm complaining about this position, love," he gives that cocky, flirting smile, "but you're distracted. And as much as I'd like to think it's because of me, I know better."

He sits back on his heels and reaches an arm down to help me up. "You're fighting is better than this. You need to focus. Where is your head at?"

I take his offered hand and we stand on the mat together. Andre has been training me to fight over the past couple of days. I'm learning quickly, and seem to be a natural with the physical training part, which surprises me. What I'm having a hard time with is meditating and mentally controlling myself and my power.

"I know, I know," I say frustrated. "Trust me, you do *not* want to know where my head is at. I just feel so anxious and on edge. It feels like my body is pulsing and my heart feels like it is going to jump out of my chest." I start pacing, "I don't know what's going on. I've never felt like this before."

"You're feeling my Wolf," Logan says as he walks out onto the fighting mats. I hadn't even heard him come in and I wonder how long he's been watching us.

I've been trying to avoid Logan as much as possible since I found out he's still been sleeping with Hallana. It had worked, for the most part, but you can't completely avoid someone being locked up in a castle with them. God, he looks so good. I want to ravage him.

Ravage him?

These thoughts are so animalistic. I shake my head and try to focus on what he just said.

"What do you mean I'm feeling your Wolf?" I ask.

"I've been able to block our connection to each other until now. There's a full moon tonight and I don't have as much control. My Wolf is feeling the moon's energy and is very close to the surface.

He wants out. I'm concentrating on keeping him in check which has opened our connection again."

"Well, that makes sense. It explains why I had the urge to nuzzle Andre's neck a minute ago."

Yes, I admit this out loud on purpose. I want to get a reaction out of Logan. I want him to be jealous. I know, it's immature and childish, but I want it regardless, and it works. I'm betting on Andre to take the comment and run with it. He doesn't disappoint.

"Oooo, don't tease me with a good time, love," he stalks towards me and walks behind me letting his chest touch my back, in the exact same way Hallana had done with Logan at the meeting.

He whispers in my ear, "you have my permission to nuzzle me *anytime*." He looks at Logan as he says it. I'm not sure why he likes to taunt Logan so much but I know he does and I just used it to my advantage.

Even looking at Logan, I can't help but react to Andre's body against mine. As much as he annoys me, I am attracted to him, and the animal senses only heightened the feelings. I close my eyes and I can smell his smoky scent. I lean into his body, feeling his hard chest against my back. I know that Logan will also feel my attraction through our link.

I take a deep breath and step away from Andre so that our bodies are no longer touching. Logan's physical appearance hasn't changed but I feel his energy from our connection. He's beyond angry. His Wolf wants to jump on Andre and tear his throat out. The sensation of teeth piercing skin is overwhelming.

"That's enough! Both of you," I say with force. "Logan, if you can't control your Wolf and get this connection under control then you need to get as far away from me as possible before I do something I'll regret."

"I promise you won't regret a thing," Andre says confidently behind me.

"And you," I turn to Andre, "you're not making this situation any better. Training is not going to work right now, so let's just call it quits for today. I need some fresh air."

I walk out of the training room without looking back but I can feel Logan down an invisible rope that seems to anchor us to each other. I know once I get far enough away from him I'll no longer feel the connection. I didn't realize that I had been relying on Logan to keep our connection blocked. I seriously need to figure out how to protect my damn self.

I want fresh air but I also want to be alone. So, instead of heading outside to the grounds, I make my way upstairs to my room where I've been spending most of my free time lately.

Once I'm alone in my room alone, I feel better. I take a deep breath and head out to the balcony. My room is up high in one of the many towers. I'm guessing it's about five stories high, which makes it very private and quiet up here.

I trained longer than I thought and the abuse and tiredness start sinking into my body. I'm sore and bruised every day and very much look forward to the day my body gets used to the abuse. One of the Fey Healers, usually Helena, visit me every night to heal my body, so I can turn around and hurt it all over again the next day.

It's already late afternoon and I can feel the sun and warmth slipping away from the day. There's a knock on my door and I sigh. I don't want company, and I don't want to fight with Logan or flirt with Andre. I know I started the measuring contest between them a minute ago, but I soon realized that the back and forth just exhausts me, and I'm too exhausted to deal with either of their egos.

There's another knock on the door, and I want to ignore it, but I hear, "Amarah, are you in there? We need to talk," Hallana speaks loud enough for me to hear her.

I'm not sure this particular visitor is any better. I've avoided her as much as possible as well since I've been here. I finally concede.

"It's open! Come in!" I yell from the balcony.

Hallana comes in and shuts the door behind her. She joins me on the balcony ad my mind is racing, trying to figure out why she's here and what she needs to talk about. I've voided Logan like the plague, so she should be happy about that. I have no idea what's been happening between them and I *don't* want to know.

"I just spoke with the Queen," Hallana starts.

"And?" I ask hopefully. "Any news?"

"No, none," she sounds tired. "The Queen has questioned everyone, personally, from our meeting, and she could not uncover the traitor. There were only a few of us who knew where you would be and when. I just can't imagine one of the other Leaders betraying us."

"But someone did," I say frankly. "What other options are there? What else explains the attack?"

Hallana shakes her head, "I don't know. If the Queen couldn't find the traitor, then...how will we?" She's being more vulnerable than I've ever seen her. So, I decide to return the gesture.

"I don't know. What I do know is that their first attempt to kill me failed. They *will* try again, and to be honest, I'm scared," I say truthfully.

"I know we started on the wrong foot, Amarah, but I am on your side. You're not alone and we will protect you," she seems sincere when she says it.

I just nod my head and lean out over the rail, looking at everything and nothing. We stand silently for a few minutes and I decide to really offer the olive branch.

"Hallana, I'm sorry about Logan. I didn't know you two were…" I hesitate, "seeing each other. Had I known I would have *never* kissed him. I haven't spoken to him much since I found out. I'm not that type of girl. I just wanted you to know."

Hallana looks at me then. It's a moment when you have complete understanding and respect for another person without having to say anything.

"Thank you, Amarah, I know it's not your fault," she sighs. "It's mine."

"I don't understand. If it is anyone's fault, it's Logan's, for putting us both in this situation."

She shakes her head, "no. Logan has always been honest with me. It's never been more than just sex for him. He's never opened up to me emotionally. I kept holding out hope that he would. It was always a possibility because there was never anyone else. Until you."

"I never meant to…"

"It's ok," she cuts me off. "I have a temper and it got the better of me. Hell, it often does. Jealousy is *not* a pretty thing and I'm extremely embarrassed at how I've acted. It's just hard when you love someone who doesn't love you back."

"I know *exactly* how you feel, trust me," I laugh coldly. "Men are the actual demons." We look at each other and all the tension completely fades as we bust out laughing together.

"Yes," she says in between laughter. "Yes, they are!"

When we finally stop laughing, we're silent for a moment again before she breaks the silence.

"Logan hasn't been with me since the night he found you. He is not mine and never has been. I don't think his heart has belonged to anyone in hundreds of years. If he is opening up to you and there's a possibility for him to find love again, I cannot deny him that. As much as it will kill me inside, the pain is no one's fault but my own. I knew the rules when we started playing and I broke them."

"Wow."

"What?"

"You are leaps and bounds ahead of me in the self-reflection department. I did the same thing with my ex and I think I was just too embarrassed to admit that *I* was the fool," I say honestly. "With Logan..." I shake my head, "I don't even know how to explain it. We're connected by something powerful. It was instant and almost like I don't have a choice. Honestly, that scares me too."

"Trust me, I'm far from perfect. I wanted to hate you, Amarah. I *really* did but I just can't. You've shown that you have great character and...there's just something *good* about you. Although, I may slightly hate you for that part," she chuckles. "Logan hasn't told you about his past, has he?"

I shake my head.

"I think that will explain the connection. At least, that's my theory. Ask him about it, Amarah, and don't worry about me. I want him to be happy, that's it. I'm sorry for how I've treated you, but I'm happy that you're here, and I'm happy that we had this talk."

"Me too! You have no idea," I laugh, relieved that, once again, I'm not burnt to a crisp.

"I do think we'll make a great team. You have a lot to learn but your character is strong and honest. Hell, we may even be friends," she smiles and nudges me with her elbow.

"I would like that," I smile back. "And I promise, I'm going to do everything I can to win this war. I may not be what everyone wanted or expected but I am ready to learn how to be."

"I know," Hallana says definitively. She places her hand on my shoulder, smiles again, and the leaves.

I stand on the balcony, staring at the closed door, in shock, for a solid five minutes. I can't help but think about Logan and what she said. She's just given me her Blessing to be with him. She admitted that he hadn't been with her physically since he met me.

I had been wrong about her, in so many ways.

I had been wrong in assuming Logan was playing us both.

God, why are men so bad at communicating?! But what was in his past that would explain our connection? That piece doesn't make sense. I have to talk to him and find out. My heart is racing and I can't help but smile. Not only is Logan *not* a player, Hallana and I might become friends! Maybe all of this won't be so bad after all. With my newfound energy, I head out of my room.

I need to find Logan.

34

Playing With Fire

A Little Fire by Two Way Crossing

I look everywhere for Logan but he isn't in the castle or on the grounds. Since it's a full moon tonight, it makes sense that he would go out into the forest where he can change into his Wolf form, safely. I assume he'll have to hunt? I hadn't talked to Logan much about his Wolf, his power, or the transition. Come to think of it, I've learned very little about him at all. I don't know who he is and he doesn't know me.

Why am I so affected by a guy I don't even know? Is it purely physical? I've felt just physical attraction before and this feels deeper than just surface level attraction. Although, obviously that's there too. Is it because of this mysterious connection? Do we truly not even have a choice? Is it this connection making us want each other? Would we feel the same way about each other without this magical connection?

I have too much on my mind and find that I've wandered into the herb garden. I don't know why but I love it here. I love the smell of all the natural herbs growing. It's quiet and peaceful. This is where I come to practice my meditating and attend sessions with Nicholas on how to control fire. It's been a slow process for me compared to the fight training. Nicholas says I'm still holding back mentally, and that I don't fully believe in all of this, and that's why I'm struggling. He says my life up to this point, growing up as a human, is hindering my mind.

He's not wrong.

But still, I try.

Since I'm here, and have nothing better to do, I sit down on the ground, cross-legged, and try to meditate. I've figured out that touch helps me hone my power. So, I place my palms down, flat on the ground, and concentrate.

There's natural power in pretty much everything around me, but the Earth has power that I can use. It's one of the four elements that the Fey, me, can control. When I concentrate hard enough, I can feel the power vibrating in the Earth, so I used that as a link to my power. It isn't as easy as sensing actual magic, like glamour, but it works.

I close my eyes and focus on my hands feeling the ground beneath me. I can feel life all around me. I can sense the roots of the herb plants. I can sense the other living creepy crawlies that live under the surface. The power calls to me and I open up to meet it.

I don't know how I know, but I just *know* that I can control the Earth, and everything else that's a part of it. It's like my basic internal instinct that's connected to my Fey Blood. I know that I can push my power into the roots of the plants to make them grow and bloom just as easily as I can take their life away.

I send my power out, out wider and deeper, traveling through the Earth. If Logan is close enough, perhaps I can sense him like I had when the demons attacked. I'm sensing all the natural power of the surrounding ground, but something else tingles against my power. Something that's not a part of the Earth.

Magic.

It feels like glamour but stronger. I push my power further, deeper, following the trail that this magic has left behind. What on Earth is down there?

The hairs on the back of my neck stand on end. I quickly reign in my power and open my eyes, looking around. I'm shocked to find the sun long gone and the darkness of the night surrounding me. There are some torches lit throughout the grounds but mainly on the paths outside of the gardens. I feel a sudden gust of wind, the hair on my arms stands up and a chill runs down my back. There's no wind down here. I'm not alone.

"Who's there?" I shout.

My heart is beating faster now, and I have to calm myself, so I can hear movement around me, and not just my heart beating in my ears.

"It's probably just someone tending the grounds or making rounds for the night," I say to myself.

I sit silently and listen for another minute and then I hear footsteps and spot a light headed my way. I quickly get to my feet. It's better to be standing and ready to fight instead of being a sitting duck, just in case. Paranoid? Who me?

"Amarah, is that you?" Nicholas's voice travels towards me right before I see him. He's holding a glowing flame in his hand.

"Shit, Nicholas!" I say with feeling. "You scared the shit out of me."

"My apologies. I didn't see you at dinner, and someone said they saw you coming into the herb garden earlier, so thought I'd come check on you. Is everything ok?"

"Yea, I lost track of time, I guess. I came in here to meditate and practice using my power. I thought someone was watching me. Did you feel a gust of wind a minute ago?"

"No. There isn't any wind down here, Amarah."

"It was probably just in my head. Apparently, I was in there for longer than I thought."

"And? How did it go?"

"Good! I think," I say excitedly. "I mean, it felt good. It felt easier."

"Show me."

He came to stand in front of me and then we both sit down on the ground, facing each other. This is what we do during our lessons.

"Tell me when you are ready." He holds his palm with the flame open and waits patiently.

I nod my head and close my eyes. I place my palms back down and feel the Earth beneath me. I focus on feeling the living power underneath my hands and further below as I had done earlier. The power comes to me easily and my power reacts to it. I pull my power out and around me like a shield. I open my eyes and I can see the white glow of my power radiating all around me. My skin resembles a big, bright glow stick.

"I'm ready," I say as I reach my palm up and out towards his palm with the fire. I push my power down and out of my hand around the fire with my mind. You can't see anything happening but I'm willing the fire to move into my palm. The flame moves in a steady line from his palm into mine.

"Very good, Amarah. You've been practicing. It's becoming easier for you," Nicholas says proudly. "Now, make the flame grow larger, stronger."

I nod and focus all my efforts on the flame in my palm. I imagine it burning larger and brighter. As I will it, the flame grows in my hand.

I smile, "it's working!"

Just then, the full moon reveals itself from behind a cloud and a Wolf's howl pierces through the night. I look up at the moon and whisper, "Logan."

"Amarah, look!" Nicholas practically shouts. I've never heard anything other than calm wisdom in his tone before. It brings my attention back to what we're doing. The flame is burning hot and bright in my palm but my power has faded. Logan's howl distracted me and my power is no longer protecting me. The second I realize what's happened, I feel the flame burn into my palm.

"Nicholas, take it!" I scream in pain. "It's burning me!"

He immediately pulls the flame back into his hand, and we both stare at my red hand, blistering in front of our eyes.

"Son of a bitch! It fucking hurts!"

"C'mon. Let's get you to Helena right away," Nicholas is back to being calm and all-knowing, but he's looking at me differently. A look that I've never seen in his eyes before. It's a mix of awe, surprise and curiosity. He's looking at me like I've done something spectacular. Like I've just grown a third eye in the middle of my forehead or something.

"Why are you looking at me like that? Like I just did something surprising?"

"Because you did," he says camly.

"All I did was burn the fuck out of my hand."

"We'll talk about it after you see the Healer. And don't argue," he says automatically. Psh! It's like he knows me and my argumentative, stubborn ways. But fine, he can win this time. I'm in too much pain to argue.

We're in the Healer's chamber and she's coating my palm with some kind of salve. Helena is unlike the other Fey here. She doesn't waste any of her power on glamour, ever. She's always in her natural Fey form. Her skin resembles dragon scales but her touch is soft. I'm told that the scales react to fire, and will protect them against it, but not until they Master their power. So, unless she's around fire, the scales on her skin are soft and smooth.

Her black hair is pulled away from her face and out of her way but hangs in beautiful waves down her back. Her face is soft but determined as she leans over me, not a drop of makeup on it. She's naturally beautiful and the exact opposite of her fiery twin sister. Helena and Hallana Chavez. Yin and Yang.

If there's one good thing about being burned, and trust me, there's not, but if there was, it would be getting burned while at the Fire Fey's home. It's the most common in injury here, for obvious reasons, and they're exceptionally prepared for it and know how to heal it.

The second the salve touches my hand, the pain stops. She lets the salve sit on my hand for a few minutes and when she wipes my hand clean, she reveals perfectly healed skin, as if the burn never happened.

"There," she smiles. "All better." Her voice is soft yet firm, like her.

"Thank you, Helena. Again," I sigh. She healed my back and arms the day I arrived and has been healing me up every day since. "I'll get the hang of all of this eventually. I hope."

"Oh, I'm sure you will. You have some of the best teachers," she smiles sweetly at Nicholas. "Just have Faith and belief in yourself. You'll get there," she pats my hand in a very motherly manner. Helena always makes me feel so comfortable. I guess that's a trait of a great Healer.

Nicholas escorts me back to my room for the night, after I make a pit stop in the kitchen for a snack. Having missed dinner unintentionally, I'm was starving.

"Alright, so, spill," I stop outside of my bedroom door.

"When you got distracted, and your power receded, the flame didn't burn you," he explains.

"Ummmm, what are you talking about? You were there. You *saw* it burn me and you just spent five minutes watching Helena heal me."

"Yes, I know, but the flame didn't burn you until you *let it* burn you," he holds up his hand to stop me from interrupting with another, *you were there,* redundant statement.

"You got distracted when you heard Logan's howl. Your power receded immediately once the howl broke your concentration. You held the flame in your hand freely. No power. It didn't burn you until you looked at it and realized what was happening. Again, your human thoughts betray you. You thought it should burn, and so, it did. But until you *thought it*, it would not have harmed you, Amarah. These powers are tied to us, they are a part of us, and our thoughts have power."

"What does that mean? I shouldn't be able to hold fire like you. Not without my power."

"You know what it means, Amarah. You can become a Master of Fire. I don't know how or why, but I saw it plain as day."

"I don't understand…" I shake my head in confusion.

"I don't fully understand either. It looks like the Queen is right. You're special. Maybe in ways we don't even know yet. I need to report to Princess Hallana. Have a good night, Amarah," Nicholas dips his chin and departs as if his ass is on fire, leaving me standing in front of my bedroom door, gaping after him.

I walk into my room and shut the door behind me. I head straight to the bed, kicked off my shoes, and lay down. I'm physically exhausted and now my brain is mush. How is any of this real? Can I become a Master of Fire? Create it from nothing? From *within* me?

Am I holding myself back as much as everyone says I am? I'm not doing it on purpose. What else am I capable of? And is it a good thing? I desperately wanted to talk to Logan. I hear another howl far off in the night.

"Logan," his name falls like a prayer from my lips as I fall into an exhausted asleep.

35

Valmont Sinclair

Animals by Maroon 5

There's a chill in the air and a shiver runs down my exposed arms and legs. I open my eyes and realize I fell asleep on top of my comforter, still wearing my workout clothes. I also didn't close the balcony door from earlier. Shit, I must have been more exhausted than I thought.

It's late August and the summer nights are still warm, we haven't crossed over into fall just yet, so there shouldn't be a chill in the air. I feel around the bed next to me until my hand finds my cell, I blink against the light as I turn it on, 1:12 a.m., I groan.

A gust of wind flutters across my body and I jerk up, instantly alert. The adrenaline pumping through my veins is insisting that I get up and defend myself, but I force myself to sit quietly, listening.

Nothing.

Not a peep.

Not a cricket or a cicada.

Too quiet.

Maybe I imagined it? Maybe I'm so in my head from the day's events that I'm making shit up. That, and constantly pushing my body to exhaustion, it's entirely possible.

Still, I need to make sure.

I start to reach for the bedside lamp but stop. If I turn the light on, it will give whoever is out there the advantage of seeing me clearly, while I'll be unable to see into the darkness. I mean, *if* someone is out there. But who would be? I'm at least five stories off the ground. Logan or any of the Fey would just come to my bedroom door if they need me. I'm safe here. The Fey are protecting me.

Then again, there *was* an attack when I thought I was safe. That's all it took for my mind to take my fear and run with it. What if it's a demon out there? Can they get inside the grounds? Can they scale walls? Or is it the traitor themselves, coming in the middle of the night, to catch me in my most vulnerable state? Lured into a false sense of confidence, of *protection*. My heart is starting to race with panic. Shit. Shit. Shit.

Still no noise. Think, Amarah!

I close my eyes, take a deep breath and concentrate on the spark of my power inside my chest. I say a silent prayer, asking for help and guidance. It takes a minute for me to grab a hold of it, I send up a silent *thank you* to whoever is listening, it is getting easier.

I send my power out, searching for other energy. It doesn't have to go far when I feel it. It's not demon or Fey. I can't tell if it's good energy or bad. It's something...*cold*. I shiver again. I don't know how or why, but here is definitely someone or *something*, right outside the door, on my balcony. I slide off the bed as quietly as possible.

I find my sword, propped up next to the bed, and unsheathe it slowly. Once it's in my hand, I feel it's Heavenly energy hum against my skin. It matches mine and calls to mine eagerly. I push my power effortlessly into the blade and the crosses glow to life. I'm prepared for whatever is out there and finally turn on the bedside lamp. I'm not Logan, I have no Wolf vision. I can't see in the dark. So even though it will allow my enemy to see me, it will allow me to see my enemy too.

I stay on the far side of the bed, keeping it between me and whatever is on my balcony. The light from the lamp is a soft glow and barely reaches to the balcony door. I keep my eyes on the darkness beyond, sword at the ready.

"I know you're out there," I shout. "I can sense you. Come into the light, *slowly*," I demand. "Or I won't hesitate to kill you."

A man saunters into the light with his hands held up in front of him to show he isn't armed. My immediate thought is, damn, he's tall. Taller than Logan and Logan is six feet, *at least*. My second thought is, damn, he's beautiful.

Long, white hair frames his face and falls to his chest. His skin is the palest I've ever seen, almost matching his hair. He's swagger personified, in a slate grey suit, tailored to perfection. He's wearing a stark-white button-up shirt, that you think would wash out his skin, but it actually provides a contrast and highlights the very subtle tan in his skin tone. The turquoise tie and pocket square provide a stunning pop of color. He's the perfect mix of feminine and masculine, oozing sex appeal with no effort at all, and I immediately know what he is.

"You're a Vampire," the words barely escape my lips.

He smiles seductively, and wide enough for me to glimpse his fangs. My heart starts beating faster in my chest and my hands are sweating, making the grip on my sword weak.

"Very good, Amarah Rey, very good," he's says, in a smooth British accent.

As if he isn't sexy enough, he has to have an accent? Of course, he does. Of course.

"How do you know my name and what do you want," my voice is still steady, but it comes out rushed. He has to know I'm afraid. I'm sure he has special Vamp hearing and senses, right? Shit, I'm totally screwed and way out of my league. Again! I suddenly feel silly holding my sword, as he stands there with his hands in the air, but I guess it beats the alternative of *not* being armed.

He slowly lowers his hands and slides them into his pockets. The look is disarming, relaxed and completely tantalizing.

"Everyone's heard of you, Amarah Rey. You're quite the buzz amongst the preternatural world. I must say, you *are* very lush, but the way people have been talking about you, you're more petite than I imagined," he studies me very hard and it makes me extremely uncomfortable.

"Well, sorry to disappoint. Now, what do you want?" I say with more force.

"Disappoint?" He shakes his head, "rubish. I quite like being surprised." He smiles at me again but this time not wide enough to show his fangs. It still sets my skin crawling, and I'm not sure if it's a good crawling or a bad one?

"Forgive my bad manners. I'm Valmont Sinclair, Leader of the Vampires in this region," he gives me a sweeping bow. "I mean you no harm, I swear this to you. I could have killed you in your home, while you meditated in the garden, or while you slept. Please, put the sword away."

I ignore his request to give up the sword. "The gust of wind. It was you," I say more to myself than to him. "I knew I hadn't imagined it. You've been watching me!"

"I have," he inclines his head.

"Why?" I ask suspiciously.

He sighs heavily, and in the blink of an eye, he's towering in front of me. I'm staring directly at his chest, which is almost pushed into my face. His energy is powerful. Suffocating. My breath gets stuck in my throat and I don't know if it's from his energy suffocating me or the fear.

I'm terrified.

I can't move.

I'm frozen in shock and disbelief.

He has his hand on my hand that's holding the sword. He leans down and whispers into my ear, sweetly, as if he's telling me sweet nothings.

"You're untrained and entirely unprepared to protect yourself against me. I've come in good faith, to speak with you, and I've sworn not to harm you. My word is *everything* to me, Amarah Rey, and you keeping a hold of this sword is utterly rude and shows a lack of trust."

He takes a step back from me, gently grabbing my chin, and raises my head to look at him. "What do we have if we do not have trust, hmmm?

All I can do is stare at this man's exquisite features. Strong, determined jaw and eyes that match his turquoise tie perfectly. His full lips are just the slightest shade of pink and I have the urge to trace my finger over his exaggerated cupid's bow. What is it with these preternatural men being gorgeous and having the perfect, kissable lips? This isn't fair.

"Amarah Rey," his breath caresses my face as he speaks, the scent of mint and...*something* else I can't quite make out, full my nostrils.

"Look at me," just a whisper but I want to look at him. I drag my eyes back up his face until I'm staring into their deadly depths. "I'll ask you one more time," his eyes began to churn. A vortex, leading to the deepest, darkest parts of the ocean, threatening to pull me under and drown me.

"Put the sword away," he demands.

I'm still in shock. Still terrified. All I can manage is a harsh swallow and the slightest shake of my head. No.

"Interesting. Very interesting, Amarah Rey," he pulls the sword easily out of my hand, reaches for the scabbard, sheathes it and throws it onto the bed.

And I let him take it. I can't fight it. I can't move a muscle. I'm too scared to make any movement that might alert the predator to my position. My body is on the verge of flight or fight mode, but is paralyzed in reactive immobility. I'm aware of it but I can't release myself from it.

Valmont is standing right in front of me and his scent is subtle and yet, overwhelming. Black salt sea, bergamot and honey. It's intoxicating, just like he is. I want to bury my face in his neck and memorize his smell just as much as I want to run, screaming in the opposite direction.

"Bloody Hell," he rubs his forehead. "My apologies. I did not mean to frighten you, Amarah Rey. Come," he reaches out and grabs my hand, "let's have a seat and a proper introduction." He leads me over to the bench at the foot of the bed, my body moving willingly, in a dream-like state.

He pulls me to sit down on the bench next to him, "I believe I have quite terrified you. I didn't realize how...*human*, you still are. Are you alright?" He asks sincerely.

"I...I...ummmm..." I can't seem to think much less speak. "You...how...I mean...you were standing across the room and then..." I shake my head. If he *is* here to kill me, I'm not putting up much of a fight. I'm in shock down to my bones and feel helpless and pathetic.

"Yes. I am a Virtuoso Vampire. Let me try to explain it in terms you will understand. I'm not only a Leader of my kind, but I am a Master Vampire. Just as the Fey can Master their power, so too, can Vampires. Except, it's harder, and takes *much* longer to do, and most never quite become Virtuoso. In plain words, I'm tremendously powerful and very rare among my kind. One of my many strengths is speed, which can often look like magic. Well, to humans, mostly."

"So, basically, you're a badass," I reply. My mind is slowly swimming up to the surface after being drowned in shock.

Valmont chuckles, "I haven't heard it put so crudely and...*humanly* before, but yes, I'm a badass."

"Great. So now that I've completely made a fool out of myself, what are you doing here? I've given you a million opportunities to kill me, or at least hurt me, and you haven't. So, I trust that you're not here to do me harm. What do you want?"

"Oh, I wouldn't say you've made a *complete* fool of yourself. I wanted to see for myself what kind of person you are. I needed to see for myself what all the fuss is about and to make my own decision about you. You know," he shrugs, and even that looks graceful, "gossip can be quite dodgy. I have to admit, you have proved to be very interesting indeed," he smirks but doesn't show his fangs. "I have felt your power several times now, and you could be dangerously powerful, but...will you allow yourself to be?"

I sigh, "great. You think I'm holding myself back too."

"Yes. You're still playing human, Amarah Rey, and human you are most definitely not."

You have no idea I think to myself. It's still my secret to keep about being half Angel. "You can call me Amarah. Just Amarah, and I'm not doing it on purpose. It's only been a couple of weeks since my entire life has been turned upside down. I just need some time." I stand up and pace in frustration, "I can't just stop thinking like a human because I'm told I'm not one, but everyone keeps rushing me!"

"Time is of the essence. The demons are growing stronger and harder to fight, and they are not the only enemy you will face."

"Why do you care?" I ask defensively. "The Queen told me that the Vampires don't fight. So why do you care, Valmont?"

"It's true," he nods his head. "I've kept the Vampires out of preternatural dealings, both good and bad. I respect your Fey Queen and would never deliberately cross her path. However, I see no gain in aligning with her. What could the Fey offer me? The way I see it, the Fey would gain a powerful ally, and the Vampires would gain a burden." He's so nonchalant about it all.

"Wow, you are so arrogant! Is power all that matters to you?"

His eyes turn hard as he looks at me, "arrogance has *nothing* to do with making the right decisions for my people," he says defensively. "And to answer your question, yes, power is essential to survival. Power from within and power from allies. It's the way of The

Unseen, Amarah Rey, and the sooner you realize that the better off you will be."

I shake my head, "there is more to having allies than just power. What about trust? You just mentioned how important trust is to you, did you not? What is the point of having a powerful ally you can't trust? If all power seeks is more power, then your powerful allies will betray you in a second. And from what I see, you'll deserve it," I cross my arms over my stomach.

Valmont throws his head back and lets out a deep, throaty laugh that seems to slide across my skin, "you speak so daringly to me! You are either very brave or very stupid." He stops laughing, leveling his gaze on me, but there's still humor in his eyes.

"I don't think I'm either of those things. I just say what's on my mind. It is not bravery or stupidity to speak the truth. It just is," I shrug.

"In The Unseen, it is always one of the two, but because you're new to this World, I'll not take offense to our idle banter. It's quite refreshing to have someone speak to me directly and unafraid. Oh, Amarah Rey, what fun you are going to be!" He grins widely, flashing his fangs and my heart skips a few beats. I'm not entirely sure it's all fear he inspires in me and that crazy thought *is* frightening.

"Now, I'm not so naïve to think that power is all I will require of my allies, but it is a priority. Thus, this is why I'm here, speaking with you."

"You lost me. I don't understand? You just said the Fey are not powerful enough to have as allies."

"But *you* are. Therefore, I wanted a chance to speak with you, Amarah Rey. You intrigue me already, and you *will be* powerful, there's no doubt about that. I believe we would make better allies than enemies. But I need to know who you are. Who are you at your core? What will you do with your power? Can I trust you?" Valmont asks, skeptically.

"I'm terrified," I admit. "I'm terrified of you and of this world I know absolutely nothing about. But just because I'm scared doesn't mean I won't stand up for myself. I believe in honesty and will always speak my truth. Betrayal has never been in my character. Not as a human and not now. What about you, Valmont? How can I trust someone who has been so solitary and selfish?"

"You're right. I don't have a glorious history with the Fey to give as an example, but I don't have a terrible history either. This, we have in common. So, I propose we start our history now, you and I. I'll go first, to show you I'm sincere in my intentions. If you'll allow me?"

"Go on."

"I know there was an attempt on your life, which obviously, failed. Since that plan failed, this person approached me, with the proposal of an alliance. My part, to secure the alliance and show my allegiance, is simple. Kill you."

"What?" I ask, suddenly nervous and fearful again.

He continues as if he didn't hear me, "Easy enough for me to do if I wished, as you saw tonight. Although I admire this person's grab for power, again, the betrayal does not sit well with me. You and I, again, have this in common."

He leans back against the bed, arms wide, causing his dress shirt to pull tight across his muscular chest, and props his ankle on his knee in a casual posture.

"Amarah Rey, you have a traitor amongst you and *I* know who it is," he smiles deviously.

36

A Traitor and A Proposal

Bring Me To Life by Evanescence

"You know who tried to kill me?" I stare at Valmont, trying to read his expression, but I can't.

His eyes are sparkling with arrogant humor. He's probably enjoying the fact that he knows who the traitor is dangling the information right in front of me, taunting me.

"I do," he says with a smirk.

"And I'm assuming this vital information *doesn't* come freely."

He smiles wider.

I roll my eyes.

"I don't like playing games, especially, not when my life is at stake. Tell me what you want, Valmont." I'm tired of all the cat and mouse games I've been forced to play over the past few weeks.

"Do you know why we Vampires hesitate to join in the war against the demons?" He's searching my face, my reactions, as if to see how much I know. He's going to be disappointed to find out I know absolutely nothing about the Vampires or much else for that matter.

"No, but I assume you're going to tell me."

"Fire," he says plainly, but I see something slide behind his eyes when he said it. Is that fear? Is Mr. Badass, Valmont Sinclair, scared of something? I wait for him to say more but he doesn't. He's still sitting on the bench physically, but he's else in his mind, as if he forgot I'm standing here for the time being. Is he meaning to show me this vulnerability? I doubt it.

When it's clear he's not going to explain, I probe for more info, "ok, fire. I don't understand? Does this have something to do with the Fire Fey?"

Valmont looks at me and I see his mind re-focusing and joining me back in the present. He shakes his head, "yes and no, we have no issues with the Fire Fey, although, we try to steer clear of them as well. Demons are from Hell. What is the one thing Hell is known for, Amarah Rey?"

I shrug, "ummmm, never-ending torment and fire."

"Yes," he breathes out sharply.

"What does an eternal pit of fire have to do with the Vampires fighting demons? I still don't follow."

"Seriously, Amarah Rey?" He looks disappointed, "what are they teaching you here? Or rather, what are they *not* teaching you?" He stands up and walks towards the balcony but doesn't leave the room. He continues speaking with his back to me.

"The Fire Fey are not the only ones that can control fire. Demons can as well. General demons can create it and soldier demons can manipulate it. Did you not know?" He turns around to face me.

I just shake my head. I didn't know, and I'm mad that I didn't know. You would think this would have been a vital piece of information for me to know, considering I've already faced *two* demon attacks.

I know Valmont sees the frustration on my face. He nods in agreement, "and what is one thing that can kill a Vampire?"

"Fire," I whisper.

"The slightest touch from fire and we go up in flames, forever. No healing. No coming back. Now, you understand."

"Yes, I understand why you hesitate to put your people in that position, but I'm still confused. The Fey and the Werewolves have both lost people to this war. They've sacrificed where you will not. You're not the only ones susceptible to fire. Forgive me, but I think that's cowardly of you to cower away in your solitary darkness."

"Again, you speak so brazenly to me. If anyone else were to call me a coward to my face…" he's instantly standing in front of me again with his hand around my neck, lifting my feet off the ground.

"I would rip their throats out," he says through gritted teeth.

I'm betting on the fact that he wants me and my future power *alive* more than he wants me dead. I'm playing chicken with a Vampire. Not a great idea, Amarah! I can feel my heart beating like a drum in my throat against his hand. He isn't squeezing, just holding, so I'm able to speak. Again, I'm terrified, but my voice comes out steadily. A bit strangled but steady.

"Then why don't you?" I'm looking directly into his turquoise eyes. He looks conflicted and I don't understand why.

He slowly lowers me back to the floor, removes his hand, and whispers, "I don't know."

He walks away from me again. "Perhaps because you're unbiased and unmotivated to any cause but your own. You're not playing games with me. You don't say things I want to hear nor do you say them to provoke me. You are so...*pure.*"

He turns to face me again, "I can *feel* it. You're like a mirror, and when I look at you, I cannot hide from myself. From the truth. And the truth is, I'm afraid to die." He slowly heads out to the balcony, and I lose sight of him in the darkness.

I follow him out and stand next to him, staring out into the blackness and the spots of light down below on the grounds. He stands so completely still and doesn't make a sound. I have to look at him to make sure he's still here and I haven't imagined all of this.

I place my hand on top of his arm, "we're all afraid to die, Valmont. You're not alone in that fear. But death isn't what defines us. What defines us is how we live. What people will remember is what we did while we were alive. How we affected their lives. Not how we die." I shrug, "maybe that's a *human* thing to say, but I believe it."

We stand in silence for a while before he inhales and seems to come back to life. "The person who approached me about the alliance, your traitor, said that something is being protected here, in the Fire Fey's home. Something that the Vampires can use in defense of fire. This is what the traitor offered me as their part of the alliance. This is what I want for information about your traitor."

I remember the feeling of strong magic deep in the Earth, under the castle. Can that magic be protecting something valuable? This... *thing...* that can protect against fire? I don't have the answers Valmont wants to hear, but I want to find out what the Hell the magic is regardless. It's not natural and it means *something.*

"I've only been here a few days, Valmont. I don't know of anything here like that," I say truthfully.

"Fair enough. Based on our conversation, I believe you." He looks at me now, with his beautiful eyes, lost to the shadows. Still, I can feel their intelligent gaze reading my face, "but do you swear to find this item and will you share it with the Vampires?"

"Valmont, what if this was a ruse by this person? What if this person lied to you and there isn't such a thing? I mean, they are betraying their own kind, can you trust them?"

"Not for a second, but I trust you, Amarah Rey. Will you find this truth for me?"

I hesitate, "I want to know this truth as well but, Valmont, this item, if it exists, is not mine to give. I cannot promise you something that I don't control. I won't lie to you and say yes, just for the traitor's name."

"Again, your honesty astonishes me. So naïve in our ways, so delicate, and yet still so determined," he reaches his hand out and gently caresses my cheek.

I'm not expecting the touch and I gasp. His hand is warm on my cheek and sends a shiver down my spine. He holds my chin lightly and leans down closer to me. I can see his eyes now, but they look deep blue in the shadows of the balcony.

"I believe that you will do your best to find this truth and do what is right for your people and our future alliance. If this item exists, speak to your Queen. Persuade her to give us this gift and in return," he moves even closer, his lips inches away from mine as he whispers, "I will be your *fiercest* ally, Amarah Rey."

He's beautiful. Dangerous and terrifying, but beautiful. His energy calls to something deep inside of me. Something foreign. And although he scares the living shit out of me, I want to lean in and taste the peppermint on his breath. I want to find out how sharp his fangs are. I bite my bottom lip and lean further into him as a heavy sigh escapes me.

He starts to move his head closer to mine and I close my eyes, my lips part, waiting for his lips to land on mine. Instead, I feel his silky hair shift across my bare shoulder as he runs his nose along my neck, inhaling deeply, causing goosebumps to erupt across my skin.

"Gods, you smell delicious."

His lips lightly brush against my skin right before I feel the warmth of his tongue as he tastes me. A small moan escapes me and he groans deep in his throat. He pulls away, taking a step away from me, the air instantly cooling in the absence of his warm body next to me. Something deep inside of me cries out at the loss and wants to reach out to him.

Damn it, Amarah! Not another complicated attraction! I scream in my head.

"Your traitor is Princess Aralyn. She wishes to be Queen," Valmont says. He looks at me one more time, so much hope and need in his eyes, and then in a gust of wind, he's gone.

Time to Act

Had Enough by Breaking Benjamin

"Princess Hallana!" I'm frantically banging on her bedroom door, "we need to talk! Now!" I'm still banging on her door when she opens it and I push my way into her room, "shut the door."

Hallana has a annoyed and puzzled look on her face but she does as I ask. "Jesus, Amarah! It's the middle of the damn night. What's going on?"

"Princess Aralyn. It's her. We need to contact the Queen, now!" I'm still reeling, and terrified, from the information Valmont gave me. "Her life is in danger."

"Whoa, Amarah, calm down. You're not making any sense." She grabs my hands and leads me to the bench in front of her enormous bed, "sit down. Ok, now take a deep breath. Calm down. Good." She's no longer annoyed and just looks concerned. "Now, what on Earth are you talking about."

"Princess Aralyn. She's the traitor who tried to have me killed."

Just thinking about it sends me into a fury and I'm up on my feet, pacing, again. She had been one of the only ones who was nice to me when I first met everyone. She seemed so sweet and like she wanted to befriend me.

"I don't understand. How do you know its Aralyn? Why on Earth would she want to have you killed?"

"She wishes to be Queen, and in the process, she's been trying to form an alliance with the Vampires. God! Who knows what else she's been up to! If she had succeeded in making that alliance, she would be *very* powerful, or at least have a powerful ally. She wouldn't need me, the Võitleja, and she knows I'll never go along with her plan if she kills the only family I have left. It makes perfect sense now." I'm still pacing, "don't you see it?"

"Amarah, where did you get this information?" She's still calm, which surprises me, knowing she's so quick temper. But she's gathering all the information she can before making a decision or jumping to conclusions. It makes me think better of her as a Leader.

I stop pacing and stand in front of her, "I had a visitor tonight. Valmont Sinclair."

She scoffs, "Valmont Sinclair? Was here? And he gave this information to *you*?" She looks shocked.

"Yes."

"And you believe him?"

"Yes."

"Why would he give you this information? Why does he want to be involved all of a sudden?"

"He wants an alliance."

"After all of this time? Now he wants an alliance with the Fey?!"

"No," I shake my head. "He wants an alliance...with *me*," I say softly.

She snorts, "With you?!"

"Trust me, I'm just as shocked as you are, believe me."

"Ok. This is all madness," she's shaking her head, but behind all of her questioning and doubt, I can see the wheels spinning in her mind.

"Why do you believe he was telling you the truth?"

"He knew about the demon attack on my way here. He said it was Aralyn's doing, and since it failed, she approached him. She asked him to kill me! Can you believe it?" I look at Hallana's calm demeanour and try to reign in my emotions.

I sit back down next to her, "I know he was telling the truth, Hallana. Don't ask me how, I just do. It's just like a gut instinct, but stronger. Just like I knew it wasn't you who had betrayed us. I don't know how I know, I can just...*sense it*. You have to believe me," I plead.

"I believe you, Amarah. What about the Queen?" She asks. "What information did Valmont have on the Queen?"

I shake my head, "nothing. He doesn't know what the attempt on the Queen will be. He just said that Aralyn wishes to *be* Queen. How else can she become Queen except by killing Anaxo?"

We look at each other and I can see the fire in her eyes. She might be holding back her temper but she's angry.

"That fucking bitch," she finally says. "I knew something was off about her lately. She's always too perfect, too accepting. She's been hiding in plain sight behind feigned allegiance. No one is that fucking perfect! I should have seen it," she seethes.

"Come to think of it, she was the one who told me about you and Logan. She was trying to put a wedge between us all along. She wanted me to be alienated and vulnerable. What I took as befriending, was a strategy. Fucking bitch," I agree.

"I need to call the Queen right away. There's nothing more we can do tonight, Amarah. Try to get some sleep. You're safe here. We need to tell Logan as soon as he comes back in the morning. He's the Queen's right hand and he needs to protect her."

"I won't be able to sleep," I shake my head. "Ugh. I hate feeling so helpless!" I sigh in frustration as I head to the door, "I'll tell Logan as soon as he returns. Besides, we have other things to discuss too." Even though she gave me her Blessing to pursue Logan, it's still awkward talking about him with her.

"Good," is all she says. "I'll keep you updated on this situation once I speak to the Queen."

I just nod my head and open the door.

"Amarah," Hallana stops me before I walk through the door, "we will make this right. We will make her pay."

"I know," I say solemnly. For all our differences, Hallana and I appear to be the same when it comes to betrayal, and protecting our family.

I'm happy we're on the same side. When it comes to fighting an enemy, I know we'll make a great team, just like she said earlier. And although I'm grateful for the breakthrough we've had, I still don't know her well enough to trust her completely. I didn't lie to her about Valmont's visit and information, but I also didn't tell her everything either.

I hadn't mentioned what Valmont wants in return. We may be sisters in war but I don't know how she'll take to me asking her if there's a secret item she's protecting. Oh, and by the way can I have this secret item you have protected for centuries to give away to the Vampires? Ha! Yeah, I don't see that going over very well, so, one hurdle at a time.

Eliminate the current threat and focus on the alliance later. With Hallana distracted by this Aralyn business, it will give me time to do some snooping on my own. I had sensed *something* hidden deep in the Earth and my gut told me it has to be what Aralyn mentioned. What else could it be?

Time to do some metaphorical digging.

38

The Connection

Earned It by The Weeknd

I'm sitting on the stairway, in the entryway, when Logan walks in. It's still very early in the morning, but the sun is on its way up and the moon is headed to rest, which means, so is his Wolf. He's barefoot and only wearing a pair of workout shorts hung dangerously low on his hips. His muscular chest and arms are on full display, and I'm the on-looker admiring the goods. My chest restricts at just the sight of him. My heart picks up its pace, as if wanted to jump into his hands, as he walks towards me.

God, it hurts just to look at him and I have to fight for control not throw myself at him.

"Amarah, what are you doing sitting out here? Is everything ok," his steps quicken until he stops and stands in front of me at the bottom of the steps.

I've been sitting here waiting for Logan to tell him something important, but now that he's here, I'm having trouble remembering what that is. Now that I know the truth about him and Hallana, that he hasn't been with her, I'm not locking myself behind Fort Knox, and I'm not denying the possibility of what this might be. Whatever this is.

I want to go to him. To jump into his arms. To kiss him. I remember what it felt like to be engulfed by him, his hands and lips on my body, and I shiver from the memory. Great. I'm acting like a damn addict, feening for another hit. The accuracy of that thought hits me hard. Am I already addicted to this man? What will happen when I finally give him everything?

"Amarah!"

I shake my head to clear away the daydream, "uh, yeah, sorry. We need to talk but I'm going to need you to put a shirt on. Please."

Logan gives me his sexy, half-smile that says he knows *exactly* what I'm thinking and feeling. He runs his hand through his hair, "ok. Come on, you can wait for me while I shower, and then we can talk."

I nod my head and follow him up to his room. His room is exactly like mine except it's on the other side of the castle. Our rooms are as far apart as they can possibly be. Coincidence? Or had Hallana done that purposefully? I'm betting on the latter but that's all water under the bridge now.

"I'll be quick," Logan says as he heads into the bathroom with a pile of clean clothes in his hands.

He leaves the bathroom door open and I hear the shower turn on and the click of the glass shower door when it closes. That is, if his room is identical to mine, which I think it is. I'm standing in the middle of the room, staring at the open door, and I swear he did that on purpose. It's an invitation.

My heart is pounding in my chest as I take small, slow steps towards the door. I have no intention of taking things further until I get answers, but a little eye candy can't hurt, right?

Steam is rising into the air from the hot water, already fogging up the mirror, as I take a tentative step inside. The glass on the shower fogging as well but I can still make out the shape of Logan's massive body. He seems to take up every inch of space, no matter where he is, but he definitely overwhelms the small shower. And my senses.

I smell the scent of soap as he lathers it on the loofah and I continue to watch as he moves it over his body. He turns away from the spraying water and I'm looking at his profile as he continues to lather up his body. His hand moves down his stomach and reaches between his legs. Then it stays there. I see his hand moving up and down, up and down.

Oh God.

My mouth waters and I have to swallow my desire down. Unfortunately, it sinks lower and settles right between my legs. I feel myself getting slick as I stand here watching him pleasure himself.

"I'd love to have another hand in here," his deep voice echoes off the tiled shower walls.

I jump at the sound of his voice and take a hurried step back, slamming into the door jam.

"Owwww," I mutter, rubbing my shoulder.

He chuckles and I'm mortified. I can't believe he caught me watching him! If I thought it was hot in here before, now it's scorching, as the blush rushes up to my cheeks faster than a strike of lightning. I can't escape the bathroom quick enough as I run out onto the balcony.

I suck in the fresh morning air into my lungs, desperately trying to cool off my overheating body. I breathe in and out deeply, trying to slow my racing heart, and steady myself. That was one of the sexiest things I think I've ever seen or done. Something about only seeing the outline of his body and the image of soap and water running over his muscled, caramel skin while he jacked himself off.

"Jesus," I laugh to myself. "What the Hell were you thinking, Amarah, you fucking pervert."

I just shake my head at my own brazenness. How the Hell am I going to face him when he gets out of the shower? Just focus on what's important. We have a lot of important things to discuss, and none of them are his soaped up, slick body.

It's so easy to let the important things slip through my fingers when I'm around Logan. It's like nothing else matters but that's not true. It *all* matters. Our connection, why we have it, and what it means. Most importantly, the traitor information we have, and what we're going to do about it.

"So, what did you want to talk about?" Logan asks from inside of the room. I turn around and he's walking towards me in a pair of dark blue jeans, still barefoot, and still displaying his gorgeous upper body.

"A couple of things. *Really* important things. So, again, I'm going to need you to put a shirt on." I'm trying to be stern and serious, but it's hard to accomplish when my voice comes out soft and breathy, and I can still feel the desire between my legs.

I blush again.

"I don't understand why you try to fight this, Amarah. I know you want me. I don't need any *connection* to know that." He's now standing inches in front of me and we're looking in each other's eyes, but neither of us touches the other.

"I don't want to fight it anymore, Logan, it's impossible and exhausting, but I *do* need to understand it. Once I touch you, I know all talking and intelligent thoughts will be out the window. There is also a new development you need to be made aware of, but I *need* to understand our connection first."

Logan leans in and places his hands on either side of me, on the balcony rail, effectively blocking me. His eyes are dazzling, polished peridot, stripping me bare and looking into my soul. His wet hair is leaving water trails down his face. His lips are calling to me and I know what it's like to fall into them.

And oh God, he smells amazing. He smells like clean soap, and fuck, I'm never going to react to the smell of soap the same way ever again, but he also just smells like Logan. He smells like outside. Like a crisp morning mixed with the woods and wet Earth. A warm, rainy, summer day.

I want to rub my cheek against his. I want to feel his naked chest on mine. Skin against skin. I want his scent all over my body. I know it's his Wolf I'm feeling. The thoughts are about claiming what's mine. I feel his cheek against mine. I'm doing exactly what I thought about doing.

I snap my eyes open and pull back. I hadn't even realized I closed them to begin with. Fuck, this is not good. He affects me like a drug affects an addict.

"Shit," I breathe out and close my eyes. I don't just close them I squeeze them shut. I can't afford to look at him and get distracted again.

I feel his warm breath against my ear, "I know you were watching me in the shower. But do you know that I was imagining slipping inside of you as I touched myself?"

He trails one single finger down my arm and I swear it's as if he touched me right between the legs instead.

"I imagined your sexy, naked body underneath me, slick and shaking with the need to have me fill you up completely and claim you as mine."

He pulls away and grabs my chin in his fingers, forcing my head back. Forcing me to look at him. "Because you're mine, Amarah, whether you believe it yet or not."

His breath is warm on my lips, his lips so achingly close to mine, testing me, teasing me, but waiting for my approval. It feels like all of my nerve endings have been laid bare and there's a torch being passed over them.

Igniting my skin.

Igniting my heart.

Igniting my power within.

Igniting my desire.

Igniting my *need*.

"I…" I try to think of something to say, *anything* to say!

But no words come to me. I want him to claim me just as much as I want to claim him. I want him to be mine and only mine. I've never felt the need to possess anyone so deeply. And something in my mind clicks. Possession is not love. I need to understand this connection. I need to know that I have a *choice*. And I need to know *him*.

I feel his warm breath on my lips, almost touching as he whispers, "what does it matter when it feels like this?"

I let out a frustrated groan and duck under his arm, escaping seconds before I explode. I regret my decision as soon as I make it. I want to be in his arms more than anything. But the truth matters. I need to know it's *my choice* when I decide to give myself to him.

"It matters to me, Logan. That should be enough," I say as I hug myself, trying to replace the warmth of his body against mine.

He sighs heavily and hangs his head, "fine. You're right. It's only fair that you know as much as I do." He walks back into the room, into the closet, and comes back out with a black, v-neck t-shirt on. It looks like the same shirt I had first seen him in that night outside of the club. It fits him like a second skin, and does nothing to hide his body or temper my attraction, but what else can I do? Other than making him sit on the opposite side of a door so I can't see him, not much.

"Thank you."

Logan sits down on the bench in front of his bed, which appears to be the style in every room, and I sit on the bed putting little bit of distance between us.

"How much did the Queen tell you about your family?" Logan asks.

I shrug, "not a whole lot."

I think back on the memory with Ana, and it's still painful, "she told me how my mother, Alexandria, died, and about my grandmother, Analise, causing the rip. I know that's why the Fey now fight the war because it was my grandmother's doing to begin with." I look at him now, "what does this have to do with our connection?"

"Did she also tell you how Analise died?"

"She did. She told me they thought she was a Witch and burned her at the stake."

261

"Yes." He's sitting a few feet away from me but I can tell his mind is far, far away. I try to sense what he's feeling but he must be blocking our connection, because I can't feel a thing. "But she didn't die at the stake. Thank God, she did not burn alive."

"Logan, I don't understand. What does my grandmother have to do with you and me?"

"I was there, Amarah," he looks at me now and his eyes are haunted by the memory still. All this time later. "I was the one fighting to get to her. I was a young Werewolf and not strong enough to save her. She managed to get free and..." he shakes his head and looks away.

I remember Ana telling me about my grandmother. She had a lover, a Werewolf, who fought to save her and almost died. She used her power to kill everyone, causing the rip, but she was set free. She crawled to her lover and gave him her life-force, and saved his life. It was all coming together now.

"It was you," I say in shock. "My grandmother gave you her life-force to save you. We have the same Fey power running through our veins. Our power recognizes each other." I look at Logan now, "why don't I feel the same type of connection with the Queen? She also has the same power."

Logan shakes his head, "I don't know. I don't have the same connection to the Queen either. I don't know exactly why you and I have this connection, but this is the only thing I can think of, that connects us. Your grandmother's life-force. That's all I know, Amarah."

"My grandmother..." My thoughts are running in circles in my mind, "you...and my grandmother..." I rub my eyes, trying to clear my thoughts, "you were...*lovers.*" I'm talking to myself more than to Logan now.

I had to hear it out loud. Logan and my grandmother were lovers! Logan slept with my grandmother and could have potentially become my grandfather if she had lived! This is freaking me out!

"You slept with my grandmother," I say out loud, still in shock.

"Amarah, that was *hundreds* of years ago."

I shake my head too much, too fast, I'm freaking out, "no, no, no, no." I get up and start pacing.

Logan stands and tries to take a hold my hands, "Amarah..."

I move out of his reach, "Don't touch me!"

"I don't understand why you're so upset. Amarah, this was a lifetime, no, three lifetimes ago. It's actual ancient history. Amarah, please," he pleads.

I know he's right. He has a point. It was over three hundred years ago, but in my mind, all I can think about is the fact that he loved my grandmother. He had *sex* with my grandmother. Maybe it's still my human brain thinking this way, but it disturbed me, *greatly*. I feel dizzy and sick to my stomach with the news.

"And after three lifetimes you're still haunted by her. I can see it in your eyes when you talk about her. A part of you still loves her even now. That's why you blocked our connection. You didn't want me to feel your feelings. Do I remind you of her? Are you trying to fill a void by using me to feel closer to her?"

"What? Amarah, no. That's not..."

"I'm sorry, Logan. I can't do this. I just need some time," I head towards the door.

I'm walking through the door when I remember I still have to tell him about Aralyn. I speak with my back to him, "you need to go see Hallana right away. The traitor is Princess Aralyn, and the Queen's life is in danger. You need to protect her." I don't wait to hear what he's thinking or get his reaction to the news. I need space. I need to get out of here.

"Amarah..." Logan calls after me. I slam the door behind me as the tears starts to fall.

And I run.

Distractions

Lovely by Billie Eilish, Khalid

There aren't any more tears left to cry as I lay on my bed, in the fetal position, feeling numb. Up and down, up and down on this rollercoaster of emotions that's way out of control. I'm so emotionally drained when it comes to figuring out what will happen with Logan. At the peak, I'm full of hope that we'll be together, and then I come crashing down with yet another truth bomb. It's like the universe is putting up these roadblocks to keep us apart. Maybe they're signs. Maybe I'm being ridiculous. I wish I knew.

I sigh, "oh Amarah, when will you learn?"

Maybe I'm just meant to be alone. Besides, there's so much more going on that I need to focus on.

A war.

A traitor.

My training.

Oh yeah, a hidden secret and a Vampire on the edge of being an ally or an enemy. I force myself out of bed and head into the bathroom. I stand in the middle of the room and stare at the shower.

The same looking shower I just watched Logan in. My heart sinks in my chest as I turn away, not wanting to relive the memory. I splash cold water on my face and look at myself in the mirror.

"You're being so selfish and childish. Get it together and handle your shit," my reflection is so disappointed in me and I don't blame her.

I decide to change into some workout clothes and see if Andre is willing to start my training early. I need the distraction and the release, but first, some coffee for comfort and food for energy. Even though food is the last thing I want to stomach, I know I need it, fuel and all that. Detour to the kitchen it is.

I sit down at the table and pull my feet up onto the chair with me. My legs tucked in close, and both hands on the coffee mug, I let that warmth and familiarity sink into me. I miss home, my couch, my space, and my little Angel, Griffin. The last time I was home feels like a lifetime ago. I need to go back soon.

"You're up early, love," Andre says as he walks into the dining room area.

"Technically no, I'm not. I haven't even been to bed yet," I sigh heavily. I completely forgot about having zero sleep. All of the shocking events, adrenaline, and emotional madness has kept me moving. Now that I think about it, I do feel a bit tired, but the coffee will get me going again. I hope.

Andre raises his eyebrows and studies me, but all he asks is, "what's keeping you up, love?"

"What's *not* keeping me up is more like it. I'm hoping you'll be up for some early training? I desperately need to hit something."

"Then allow me to be your punching bag. If you think you can actually hit me today," he smirks, dimple on full display.

Fat chance of that happening. He's the Fire Fey's best fighter and I'm a thirty-four-year-old woman, raised to be human, who has never thrown a punch in her life before this.

"You know damn well I'll try my hardest."

"Now that's the truth, love. We can get started after breakfast. I'm starving," he says as he heads into the kitchen.

"You're always starving," I call after him. I smile and shake my head. He may be an annoying flirt but he's easy to be around. It's just what I need today. No drama.

One thing I enjoy about learning how to fight is that it takes *all* of my attention and focus. All I can hear in my mind is my ragged breathing, random grunts and groans, the loud crack of our wooden weapons attacking each other, and the occasional scream of pain. Always from me, of course.

We both hold two training sticks, one in each hand. They're about two feet long and resemble a cop's baton. Fighting is *not* easy. You have to be a million percent present and think on your feet. Any small distraction can be used against you in the blink of an eye. You have to take account of your opponent quickly and mentally examine their style for weaknesses all while trying not to lose a limb or die. Not to mention, also being aware of your surroundings.

Andre is coming at me *hard* today. I can't complain though, I asked for it. He's on the attack and I'm just reacting to his movements, defending myself as best I can. I'm pretty good at defense though and just started learning how to fight offensively.

Andre is attacking with combo after combo and I'm slowly being backed up. I don't want to be cornered, so without thinking, I drop down to one knee and extend my left arm out so my baton connects with his knee on the back-end of my knee spin. His knee buckles, but he doesn't fall.

I'm smiling as I get back to my feet, "Hey, I..."

That's all I get out before my feet are swept out from under me and my back slams into the mat. The fall forces all the air out of my lungs and I'm temporarily paralyzed, lying here, trying to breathe. Andre is on top of me in a second and holds one of his batons to my throat. Killing blow.

When I can finally breathe again, I manage to cough out, "son of a bitch!"

Andre is smiling down at me, "you did good, love, for a second, until you wanted to celebrate. You never celebrate in a fight until your opponent is dead. Do you hear me? Not injured, dead."

"Yeah, yeah, I hear you," I say from my back, still trying to breathe normally. "But I *did* get you," I grin up at him.

"And what is it they say?" He rolls off of me and sits down on the mat, "pride always comes before a fall?"

I pull myself into a sitting position opposite of him, "that is what they say. I've never experienced it quite so literally before." I'm still grinning like an idiot, with the thought of my small, inconsequential victory.

He smiles back at me and we both start laughing. He shakes his head, "alright, alright, you did good. That was a nice maneuver, but next time, think of the next steps. How is your opponent going to respond to your movement? You need to know their attack style so you can always be a step ahead of them. You can't just use your eyes you have to use *all* of your senses." Andre is a jokester ninety-nine percent of the time, but here on the mats, he takes training very seriously. "Oh, and don't get distracted."

"Yes, Captain Obvious," I mockingly salute him.

"You can joke all you want, as long as you take everything I teach you to heart. It *will* save your life, Amarah," he says seriously.

"I know you're being serious when you use my name," I chuckle. "I promise, I do take it to heart. I'm trying my best with…all of this."

"I know you are, love," he smirks at me.

"Ahhhh, there he is!"

"I told you I would grow on you," he winks at me.

I shake my head and laugh, "I guess you did."

We sit in silence for a few minutes and my mind starts racing again with all of last night's news. "Did Hallana tell you about the traitor?" I look up at him.

"She did. She's working with the Queen to come up with a plan on how to handle Princess Aralyn." He's studying me now, "but that's not what's bothering you."

I scoff, "and you know me so well?"

"Better than you think, love." He doesn't use my name, but there's no teasing in him now. "This war and traitor stuff is crazy, sure, but there is only one person who affects your emotions. He did something to hurt you. Again."

Wow. I guess I *am* pretty easy to read. Logan is my kryptonite and apparently, Andre knows it all too well. But does he genuinely care? Is he just the perpetual flirt Logan said he is? Is it just some kind of competition between him and Logan?

I drop my eyes so Andre can't see them, "he didn't do anything new, or even anything *wrong* really. I just can't get past my own hang-ups," I shrug. "I thought I was doing a better job at hiding my emotions but I guess not." I gather myself and look up at Andre again, "there are more important things to deal with right now besides my cursed love-life."

Andre's eyes are sincere, no sign of their regular humor. I've seen this in his eyes once before. When he let me glimpse it in the forest on the way here. There's so much more to Andre than he lets anyone believe. He's also smarter than I initially gave him credit for because he listens to me and changes the subject.

"Hallana told me about Valmont coming to see you. Is it true he wants an alliance with you?"

"Yes, but I don't know if I can come through on my end for this so-called alliance to happen."

"What do you mean? What does the bloodsucker want?"

"He said that Aralyn offered him something if he was to pledge his allegiance to her."

I contemplate my next words carefully. Should I ask Andre about this mysterious *something* that Aaralyn says is hidden here? It's not like I can ask Hallana, and I'm not about to ask Nicholas. He's all about loyalty to his Princess. Andre is the only other person I feel comfortable asking, and somewhat trust that he will keep my secret. Fuck it.

"She told him that the Fire Fey are hiding something that could protect the Vampires from fire."

"Shhhhh," Andre looks around in a panic. "We can't talk about this here."

"So, it is true!"

"Amarah, if the Vampires find out this is true, it would be a war between them and us. This is dangerous. Did you tell Hallana about this," he whispers.

"No," I whisper back. "You're the only one I've told."

"Good. Keep it that way. I'll come and get you tonight and take you somewhere where we can talk in private. Until then, go about your day as if nothing has changed. Do *not* talk to anyone about this. Do you understand?" He's practically begging me.

"Yes, I promise."

"Stay in your room all night. I'll come to get you." He stands up and leaves me sitting alone on the training mat wondering what in the actual fuck is going on.

It must be true. Andre all but confirmed the rumor. The Fire Fey are hiding something powerful. What is it? Will it assuredly be war with the Vampires if they know this item exists? Shit. Aralyn has undoubtedly betrayed her people by revealing this information to Valmont. Whether it's true or not, Valmont will find out, one way or another. It's either going to be by me, peacefully and in the form of an alliance, or slaughter as Valmont brings the Vampires here to search for himself.

I'm eager for night to come. What is Andre going to share with me? Can I trust him? What if he goes to Hallana? Shit, shit, shit, Amarah! Even if I can trust him, what's going to happen? How am I going to get my hands on this...thing? How am I going to get the Fire Fey to hand it over to the Vampires?

One step at a time, Amarah. Find out all the information you can and then figure out the rest. I'm in way over my head, but then again, what's new? How am I even still alive and not drowned yet?

Oh yeah, I'm half Angel. It's all a damn miracle!

40

TMI

Mad World by Demi Lovato

It's only one o'clock in the afternoon. I have half a day before night falls and I have no idea how I'm going to distract myself while I wait. The anticipation of wanting to know what Andre is up to and what he's going to tell me tonight is killing me. I decide to try some more meditating, by myself, so I can explore tis foreign magic I felt. Maybe I can get my own answers? Or at least, gather an idea of what it is or why it's there. I head to the herb garden with a determined, yet easy, stride. No need to look suspicious.

"Amarah! Wait up," Nicholas shouts from across the grounds as he starts to jog toward me.

"Shit," I whisper to myself as I wait for him. I wasn't planning on practicing with Nicholas and was hoping I could avoid him. If Nicholas is with me, I won't be able to do what I want. I can't be nosey.

"You're early today. It isn't our usual training time," Nicholas says as he reaches me.

"Yeah, I know. I finished my fight training with Andre early and had a little bit of time to kill. I was hoping to just have some alone time to clear my thoughts and practice if that's ok?"

"Of course. Shall I come and meet you at our normal time then?

I smile, "that would be great!" I force a joyful smile. No need to make him question me if I say no to our normal routine. "Thank you for understanding."

Nicholas dips his chin in reply before jogging off just as quickly as he had arrived, off to do whatever it is he was doing before. He's not one for unnecessary talk most of the time and I appreciate it, especially today, and I hope he wouldn't pry in our training session later. As long as I focus and am not distracted, I'll be ok.

I have to take advantage of what little time I have and try to find out what I can on my own and then wait until tonight for the rest. I can't let Nicholas start asking questions. The only problem is, not much gets past him.

I take my regular seat in the garden and place my palms on the ground. It takes longer than I'd like to admit for me to quiet my mind and focus on the vibrating magic in the Earth. Why is it that matters of the heart are so consuming? All I want is to think about Logan. It takes a lot of effort to push him, and all of my problems with him, out of my thoughts.

Once my mind is quiet, I pull the vibrating energy into my body and open my power to meet it. I immediately push my power into the ground and send it searching. I search and search and I can't find a thing. Maybe I had imagined it last time? Maybe I'm making shit up in my mind? I take a deep breath, focus my thoughts, and keep my power pushing down and out, going deeper and wider, casting my net. It takes a while but I eventually feel the magic. It's deep, deep within the Earth. The fact that I found it last time is sheer luck.

Now that I've located it, I reign my power back in and concentrate it solely on the magical area. This magic deposit is huge and extremely powerful. It doesn't feel like Fey power. Fey energy has a very natural feel to it. It almost blends in the nature. This is a completely different energy that seems to sit on top of the Earth instead of mesh with it. Like it doesn't belong. I've never felt this energy signature before. At least, my power doesn't recognize it. It screams, *danger,* along my skin and in my mind. I know that whatever this is, it's nothing to be messed with.

Where did the Fey get magic like this? It's hard to gauge exactly where the magic is, but there's no denying, it's here. There must be access to it from somewhere on the grounds or from inside of the castle.

This discovery just opens up more questions. There are still so many things I have no clue about. It doesn't surprise me but it does frustrate me. I'm so ignorant when it comes to The Unseen. The problem is, you don't know what you don't know, until it is staring you in the face with glowing red eyes trying to kill you.

Ignorance can be bliss, yes, but I can't not afford to be blissful. My life and the lives of everyone around me, is at stake. I need someone to take the training wheels off and tell me *everything.* Valmont seems to think they're not doing a great job of educating me. Maybe he's the one I need to talk to in order to get more answers and information? But can I trust him? Maybe it's Andre I can turn to? Sigh. I just don't know.

There's nothing more I can find out about the magic on my own, but at least now I know for certain, that it *is* there. They're hiding *something*. I pull my power back inside of me and open my eyes.

I jumped, "Holy shit! You scared the shit out of me!" Nicholas is sitting in his spot in front of me. I hadn't heard him or sensed him. How long has he been sitting here? Does he know I'm up to something sneaky? Damn him and his unreadable face! Damn everyone and their control!

"My apologies," he says, cooly. "You were so peaceful and focused I didn't want to disturb you. Did you find what you were looking for?"

Did I find what I was looking for? Does he know I was searching for something? Or am I being paranoid and reading into a simple, harmless question? Or is he suspicious and fishing for confirmation? Fuck.

"Yeah, I cleared my head for a bit, which was nice and *much* needed," I put my hand over my heart. "Damn you really scared me though," I laugh nervously.

He's studying me with shrewd eyes but his face gives absolutely nothing away "You must be concerned about the recent news about Princess Aralyn."

He's prying. Is he prying?

I let out a heavy sigh, "I can't believe it. How could she betray everyone like that?" It's a rhetorical question and I don't expect a response, so I keep going. "I'm worried about the Queen. At least here, I'm more protected, but she's more vulnerable."

Do I mention Valmont? If I don't, will he think it's suspicious? There's no way he knows that Valmont wants what's hidden here. I have to talk to him like I would if I wasn't conspiring.

"And I don't know if I should trust Valmont," I shake my head, "I don't know where to focus my energy first, or who to trust, and that's an unsettling feeling," I say honestly.

"The Vampires look out for themselves. Always have. The fact that Valmont wants an alliance now is suspicious. Do not let your guard down with him. Did he tell you anything else?"

I shake my head, "nothing else. Thank you for the advice. I won't let me guard down."

He's still studying me and it makes me uncomfortable. I want to squirm and look away but I hold my ground.

"There's something else bothering you. Something you're not saying. If it's important information, we need to know, Amarah."

Fuck, Nicholas! Back off! I knew he was dangerously observant. He's been reading people for centuries, of course he knows when someone is hiding something or not being completely truthful. Andre warned me that what I know is dangerous and told me not to talk to anyone about it. I trust that Andre is looking out for me. I have to put my trust somewhere and I have to tell Nicholas something to get him off my ass.

"Logan slept with my grandmother," I blurt out. I mentally cringe and face palm myself.

Nicholas's eyes widen and he looks genuinely shocked. I don't think that's the answer he was expecting but it's the truth nonetheless. It's so much harder to lie and maintain a lie than it is to talk about the truth. So uncomfortable and embarrassing as it is, truth it is.

Nicholas is the one who looks nervous now. One thing he doesn't handle that well, other people's intimate problems. Especially when those problems included sex.

He's the one who looks away first, "yes, I know about Logan's history with Analise. He's the only Werewolf with a Fey life-force. Everyone knows the history."

I scoff, "everyone but me apparently. Well, I mean, *now* I know." I shake my head, "I can't believe no one told me."

"It's not our story to tell."

"No, I guess not. Still…" I rub my hands down my face, "I can't get over it. I know for everyone who's lived hundreds of years, I'm probably being ridiculous, but…" I don't have any more words so I just shrug. Thinking about losing Logan again makes my throat tight and tears swell behind my eyes. This makes Nicholas even *more* uncomfortable.

"Let's call it a day for training, huh? It looks like you did a good job on your own today," he says softly. He's trying to be careful with my delicate, girly emotions. Considering the fact that he's the one struggling with them, I appreciate his effort.

And the truth shall set you free! At least I got the bloodhound off my scent. For now. But that was a close call. I need to be more discreet and careful.

"Ok, thank you," I sniffle for dramatic effect and let a tear slide down my cheek. Ok, the tear is real but I'm not denying I'm exaggerating the emotion for my benefit.

Nicholas smiles nervously and can't stand up quick enough. He's off without another look or word in my direction. Once he's out of sight, I relax and let out a sigh of relief.

That was close, Amarah. No more unnecessary encounters. I scold myself. I decide to call it a day. I'll grab some food from the kitchen and eat a quiet dinner in my room as I wait for Andre. It's a boring but safe plan.

Waiting, waiting, waiting...I pace my room and it's driving me crazy. I *need* to do something. Anything. I pull out my cell phone and decided to call the Queen.

She answers on the second ring, "Amarah, what's wrong?" She asks hurriedly.

"Nothing's wrong. Well, I mean, isn't everything wrong? But I'm ok. I'm more concerned about you being there alone."

"Oh, thank goodness you're ok. Yes, everything is wrong and I'm so unbelievably shocked that Princess Aaralyn could do this, but don't worry about me, Amarah. Logan is here now and we're taking precautions here at Headquarters. We won't be caught unaware."

My heart skips a beat just hearing his damn name. Knowing that he's gone and I won't see him or be able to talk to him, weighs on me. It's as if my heart now weighs a thousand pounds and it's crushing my ribs, making it hard to breathe.

Yes, I'm the one who ran away but there was always the possibility to run *back* to him. Now, I don't have that option and I'm pissed we left things the way we did. All he did was be honest with me and I ran away. Turned my back on him. On his history. On his loss and heartache. I feel like an idiot. A child. A bitch. And yet, he was in love with my grandmother! Ugh, why are emotions so fucking complicated?!

"Amarah, are you still there?"

"Yeah, I'm here, just thinking. I'm glad that Logan is with you. I know I don't know you well yet, but if anything were to happen to you, I don't know what I would do. You're my only family."

"Don't worry about me, Amarah. I'm not going anywhere. Aralyn can try her best, but I've been Queen for two hundred and fifty years for a reason. She's out of her damn mind if she thinks she can take the Crown and rule our people." Her sweet voice doesn't change but I can hear the defiance in her tone. The fight. She's pissed and ready to protect herself and her people.

"We need to be careful who we trust. There's no way she's doing this alone and we don't know who else is helping her. Do you have a plan on how to handle this?"

"We will find them all. Hallana, Logan, and I, are working on a plan. Hallana will be joining us here shortly along with Prince Emrick and Prince Vadin. We're going to question them again to see if they're working with Aralyn or not. Then, we will decide how to proceed."

"I wish I could do more to help. I feel so useless," I sigh in frustration.

"Are you kidding? We would have never found out about the traitor if it wasn't for you. I'm not surprised that Valmont wants an alliance with you. He's always been drawn to power and you *will be* powerful, Amarah, but be careful. Don't let anyone know about your birth. That needs to stay hidden, at least for now. Do you understand?"

"Yes, I'll be careful. I promise." I sigh again, "I wish we could call a time-out because I have so many questions."

"Life is very rarely pretty or perfect. We just have to keep moving forward because life continues with or without us. You adapt and overcome or you get left behind. I wish I could answer all of your questions, but I'm confident you will find your way. I have to go now, Amarah. Focus on your training and watch your back, ok?"

"I will. Will you keep me posted on everything?"

"I will."

"Thank you, Ana. Watch your back too."

"Don't worry about me. Talk to you soon." She hangs up.

I let out a groan as I throw myself onto the bed. I don't feel better after talking with her. I mean, yes, she has way more experience with all of this than I do, and she doesn't sound too concerned, but she could be protecting me from the worst of it. No. No, she would be honest with me. I have to trust her to always be honest and real with me if she expects me to be the Warrior they need.

She's powerful on her own plus, she has Logan. Soon the other Leaders will be joining her and she'll have a small army. She's fine, for now. I need to focus on myself and my tasks. First things first. Tackle my hunger.

I finish a sandwich as I stand out on the balcony. I can't see the sun from inside the mountain but I can feel the warmth seeping away. Night is coming. Andre said he would come and get me, but he didn't say exactly when. Great. Patiently waiting is not one of my strong suits.

I sigh and head back inside. My phone pings, notifying me that I have a new message. I scoop it up as I sit on the bed and unlock it. The name on the screen has my heart racing immediately.

Logan.

I open the text message.

Logan: Don't worry about Ana, I won't let anything happen to her. I promise. And just so you know. You're mine.

Spotify link: You're mine by Disturbed

I click on the link and play the song, listening to the lyrics closely. They're powerful and hit me square in the chest. As much as I want to just give in, I can't. I don't know why, but I can't. I still don't understand out connection and I don't like feeling like I'm not in control of myself or my feelings. The annoying control freak in me.

Still, I hot repeat on the song, wanting to devour every word and feel what he's feeling through the song. As soon as I lie down, I feel the mental exhaustion and lack of sleep from the night before crash into me. I hadn't planned on falling asleep but I'm no longer in control. I'm a passenger and sleep is the driver. It takes the steering wheel and slams on the gas. Wide awake to deep, dreamless sleep in 4.5 seconds flat.

Neglected sleep is a powerful machine and I'm too weak to fight it. I fall asleep hearing Logan's voice in my head.

Because you're mine, Amarah, whether you believe it yet or not.

Andre

For Tonight by Giveon

"Amarah. Amarah, hey, wake up."

I feel someone brush the hair out of my face. Déjà vu has me remembering the morning Logan woke me up. I could really get used to this. To having him here. Waking up to him every morning. But Logan's not here? Am I dreaming? Or had Logan come back?

"Logan," I whisper as I blink my eyes open.

"Sorry to disappoint, love. Just me," Andre sits on the side of my bed and something like hurt passes over his features. His smile fades as he stands. I can't imagine any guy likes being called another guy's name.

"Andre, hey," I say quickly. "I'm sorry I didn't mean to…" I shake my head. "I just had déjà vu is all."

"No worries," He puts on his usual smirk but the humor doesn't quite make it to his eyes.

I'll be damned! He's genuinely hurt, and I feel bad, but it's not *that* big a deal. I know they have this rivalry thing going on but it's not like I did something bad. All I did was call him Logan and it wasn't even o purpose. I was half asleep. I hope I don't have to deal with a hurt ego all night now. Great, just what I need, more balls to juggle. Pun intended.

"Are you ready?" He asks.

"Yes. What time is it?" I ask as I get out of bed and stretch. I feel good. I must have slept quite a bit and my body is thankful for it.

"It's almost 3:00 a.m."

"Oooo, the Witching hour," I joke.

The humor finally makes its way back into his eyes. It's a mask he wears constantly and he's good at it. It makes me wonder what exactly he wanted me to see? Did he want me to see that he was hurt? Is he trying to open up to me in new ways? Or was it a simple mistake that he let me see behind the mask?

"It's the perfect time of night, when most people are deep asleep, and too close to dawn for the Vampires to be out. It's the best time for privacy."

"Makes sense."

We head to the door. Andre whispers, "follow me, and don't make a sound."

I nod and out the door we go like a couple of ghosts.

Andre leads me down the hallway to the main set of stairs and then heads up. I've never gone up further than this floor that my room is on. I'd make a terrible spy since I've been here for weeks and haven't once gone snooping around.

We stop on the next landing and walk back down a similar hallway. Andre stops half-way down the hallway and presses against the wall where a hidden doorway opens. Hidden passageways in a castle? Who'd of thunk? It's literally just like the movies. I smile to myself and follow Andre through. He points at the door behind us and

I close it obediently, causing instant darkness to surround us, and I can't see shit. My heart naturally picks up its pace and I have a split second to wonder if I really can trust Andre. Maybe I made a mistake coming here, alone, with him.

"Andre," I whisper, trying to hide the uncertainty in my voice.

I'm about to reach for the hidden door again when there's a spark of light a few steps ahead of me. Andre holds a flame in his palm like Nicholas dis when he led me through the dark tunnel.

"You're a Master of Fire!" I whisper yell with excitement.

Andre is so much more than he appears, and I shouldn't be surprised, and yet, I am. I didn't know Andre was a Master of Fire because I only did fight training with him and practiced the other stuff with Nicholas. I just assumed he hadn't Mastered it yet. Here is a lesson in never assuming or underestimating people.

Andre smiles and winks at me, then turns around and continues leading us down a narrow hallway. At the end of the hallway, we come to a spiral staircase, and we start to climb. I can't see anything other than a few feet around us that the flame illuminates. Round and round we go, climbing until I'm sure we're going to reach the sky. I feel Jack climbing the beanstalk, up, up, and up. I just hope I don't find a giant ready to grind my bones into bread or whatever. Hey! Maybe it's magic beans they're hiding?

Finally, Andre steps off the stairs onto a landing I would have completely missed had he not moved onto it. It makes me wonder what else I missed? Andre opens a door, again, one I couldn't see until it was being opened. Andre closes his hand around the flame and out it goes as I follow him out onto the moonlit balcony.

The balcony is about three feet wide and circles the tower we just climbed up. As long as we climbed, it's not surprise that we're standing outside of the highest tower of the castle. We're so far up that we're able to get the moonlight from the opening at the peak of the mountain. I lean over the rail to look down at the grounds below but all I can see are tiny orange dots that I know are the flames lighting the grounds far, far below.

"Holy shit," I'm still whisper yelling, not wanting to make any noise but not able to contain my excitement either. "I guess this is one place to get privacy."

"You don't have to whisper up here. No one can hear us or see us for that matter."

"I can see that," I laugh a little nervously. "This is either where you tell me all of your deepest darkest secrets or send me falling to my death." I'm joking, mostly, but I can't help but be a little bit nervous at this new setting.

"You don't trust me, love?" Andre is leaning back against the rail, arms crossed, studying my face.

"I don't know," I say honestly. "Mostly, I do. I mean, I followed you here, didn't I? But trust with my life…" I shrug. "Trust like that doesn't just happen."

"Yet, here you are, with me. *Alone*. At the top of the highest tower in the castle."

I let out a sigh, "yeah, here I am."

"Why? If you don't trust me?"

"I think subconsciously I trust you more than I realize. My gut says I can trust you. It's hard to explain, but I get this feeling around people. When I focus and listen it's like I can *feel* their intentions. But it's not always full-proof and I'm still trying to figure it out. I wish I would have been listening when I met Princess Aralyn," I shake my head. "And I don't exactly have other options than to trust you now do I?"

"I guess you don't." He's still studying me and I'm starting to feel more nervous. Did I offend him? Hurt his feelings again? He uncrosses his arms and relaxes, "you can trust me, Amarah."

He says my name. I always know he's being serious when he uses my name.

"I know," I say and take a step closer to him. I reach out and touch his arm tentatively. "Thank you," I smile.

We watch each other for a moment, in silence, until he finally gives me his cocky smirk, "you're welcome, love." He turns around to lean over the rail and I follow suit.

"So, Valmont has asked you about something being protected here."

Right to business, here we go. "Yes. He said that Aralyn told him there is something here that could protect him and his people from fire. He is aware that Aralyn may have been lying to him and just wanted him to kill me. He asked that I find out the truth about the rumor, and since we're way the hell up here talking, I'm assuming it is true." I glance at Andre but he's still looking out over the rail.

"It's true. Our people have been protecting it for centuries. It's a very rare part of our ancestors and belongs to the Fire Fey by birthright. If there is even the smallest chance Valmont believes this rumor, he *will* come to search on his own. He's giving you the chance to bring it to him peacefully, but if you fail, I have no doubt he will come forcefully."

"That's my thought exactly. He'll do anything to become more powerful and to protect his people. Andre, I know I don't know much about the Vampires or this world, but Valmont terrifies me. He's dangerous, and if he comes here by force, I'm not sure the Fire Fey would stand a chance against him."

"We control fire, love, the Vampires fear us for that reason. We have the means to kill Vampires literally at our fingertips," he produces a flame out of each of his fingertips and looks at me with such defiance in his eyes. He's a warrior through and through. No fear.

"Dramatic effect. I get it. It would be a Hell of a fight, but there's one thing I know for sure," I look into those fierce eyes, the ones that refuse to back down from a fight, and make sure he sees the fear in mine, "too many Fey would die in the process."

I see him clench his jaw in frustration and defiance but he doesn't argue. He knows I'm right and he doesn't like it. He sighs heavily, "you're right. One Fey dying by the hands of the Vampires is one too many. Especially since we have the means for a peaceful alliance."

"Exactly! So, what's the problem?"

"I don't know if Hallana will agree to just hand over something to the Vampires that would make them even more powerful to stand against us. It makes me nervous too. We're feared by the Vampires and we want to keep it that way. They have never gotten into Fey dealings one way or another, but there's always been that equal respect and fear when it comes to standing against each other. If we give them this protection against fire, we lose all of our strength against them. We knowingly and willingly weaken ourselves. Hallana would not do that to her people or ask them to make that choice."

"I know and I understand, I do. It's a risk for sure, but if Valmont is being honest, the Fey would gain a powerful ally against the demons and anyone else who decides to show up. The alliance would be worth the sacrifice. It's either barter for an alliance or die fighting. He *will* come, Andre."

"And you trust him?" Andre studies me.

"Trust him?" I sigh, "I don't know, but I believe he's telling the truth when he offered an alliance. I don't believe he want to make any enemies, especially the Fire Fey. I can't speak on more than that."

"Your gut instinct," he smirks.

I smile, "yes. Still, it's a hard decision to make and I don't take it lightly."

"I think we only have one option from here."

"We have to tell Hallana.". He nods his head in agreement. "And the Queen," I add.

We stand in silence for a while. I think we're both going over the pros and cons in our minds, trying to convince ourselves that giving Valmont this power is the right move. At the end of the day, I'm glad I'm not the Queen and I don't have to make this impossible choice.

"Andre," I break the silence and wait until he looks at me. "What is it? What is this special thing that can protect the Vampires from fire?"

"Dragon scales, from the very last dragon that existed centuries ago. The dragon scales, with the help of some magic, can be turned into a magical shield for the Vampires, or anyone for that matter, as long as they have it on them."

"Wow! You're serious? Actual dragon scales?" Just when I think I can't be shocked anymore, boom!

Andre chuckles, "yes, love. Dragons were real and true at one point."

"Holy shit! That's insane." I shake my head, "man, I would have loved to see one."

"You and me both, love."

"You are a Master of Fire, so you have scales, like a dragon, that protect you from fire." I sound like I'm rattling off facts from Google.

"Yes, I do."

I've never seen Andre without his glamour. "Will you show me?"

He hesitates, "it's not something you're used to seeing, love. It's not...*normal*, for you, like it is for us."

Why is he hesitant to show me? Is he insecure about his scales? Does he think I'll run away, screaming? Does he always have his glamour on around me because he wants to appear human? Maybe he does care what I think about him more than I realize.

"I've seen them before, on others. Helena never uses glamour but I think it's rude to stare or ask to touch them." I chuckle, "I want to see them and feel them. You're not going to scare me away, Andre."

He sighs, as if he's contemplating it, but still hesitates.

"Please?" I ask sincerely.

"Alright," he finally agrees. His eyes never once leave my face as he releases his glamour. I think he's watching for *any* sign of fear or disgust.

"Whoa," I say in awe. I slowly move my eyes along his body, taking it all in, really looking at every inch of exposed skin that I can see. His skin is covered in scales in shades of grey, silver and white.

His tattoos are still there, still a part of him, adorning each scale in a beautiful design. I reach my hand out to feel them but hesitate.

"May I?" I look into his eyes and he's so guarded. His block wall has turned to steel, the muscle in his jaw twitching, his hands in fists at his sides.

I can't tell what he's thinking or feeling other than he seems to be preparing to protect himself. There's no humor in his eyes, there's nothing except hardness and, underneath that, a sense of pain. The look makes my heart ache for him. I don't like seeing those beautiful eyes filled with anything other than his normal sparkle of humor.

"Yes," he finally grits out. I know his decision to say yes is beyond difficult. I see it in the tension of his body. The rigid line of his spine. This is costing him something to do this.

I smile and look at his arms, which are always exposed in the tank tops he wears. I reach both of my hands out to each of his arms and start at the shoulders. I lightly touch his skin with fingertips at first and then allowed my palms to run down his arms. Andre closes his eyes and lets out a strangled breath that he seems to have been holding and shudders as I caress his arms.

"They're so soft," I look at his face but his eyes are still closed. "Andre, are you ok?" I drop my hands. "I'm sorry. I didn't mean to…"

He opens his eyes, "no, it's ok. I'm ok," he reassures me.

There's a look of relief in his eyes. He's clearly relieved that I hadn't turned away in disgust, or run screaming, which makes me wonder if someone had?

I reach my hand up to feel the scales on his cheek. "I've never felt anything so soft," I whisper. I look into his eyes and hope that mine show him the truth of the words I speak next, "they're beautiful."

Andre closes the gap between us leaving our bodies almost touching. He hesitates, but then he slowly brings his hand up, and very gently caresses my cheek with the back of his fingers, "not more beautiful than you." His voice is so low I almost don't hear it.

The pain in my ass, confident, in your face, flirting Andre that I'm used to is nowhere to be found. Instead, standing in front of me is an unsure, guarded man that has been hurt badly by someone. I recognize the look in his eyes because I'v seen it in the mirror too many times. I desperately want to take that look away because I know what it means. I know what he's feeling.

A small voice in the back of my mind whispers, *Logan,* but I quickly silence it. There are too many questions about the sincerity of what Logan and I have. Would I feel the same way if it weren't for a magical connection? Is he using me to fill a void left by Analise? The answer is, I don't know. What I do know, is that here and now, I want to take Andre's pain away.

When I don't back away or look away, Andre brings up his other hand and holds my face gently, as if he's worried he might break me or I might disappear if he tries too hard. His eyes are darting between mine, searching my face, my eyes, for *any* sign of rejection, but there isn't anything to be found. I move my hand from his face and place both of my hands to his chest. I can feel his heart beating fast and hard, betraying his otherwise steady appearance.

"Amarah, I..." he hesitates again and licks his lips. "Can I kiss you?" His eyes tighten with tension, waiting for me to stop this. Waiting for me to say no. Waiting for rejection.

"Yes," I slide my hands up his chest and around his neck in invitation. I close the gap between our bodies, letting my chest pus into his, as I meet him for a kiss.

I don't need to tiptoe to make the kiss easier. I follow his lead and the kiss is just a soft brush of our lips at first. His lips, like his scales, are extremely soft and smooth.

He pulls away, "are you sure about this?"

"Andre, stop teasing me and kiss me," I pull on his neck, and this time I take the lead. I kiss him softly, but solidly, letting him know I'm not going to change my mind. He moves his hands from my face and down to my sides, gripping them, and lifting me easily onto the rail.

I gasp and wrap my legs around his waist and hold tighter onto him. I know he's not going to let me fall, but I can't help but feel that slight fear of falling. The risk sends a rush of adrenaline through my body. And as much I know it shouldn't turn me on. It does.

Our faces are almost even now and I smile at him, "you better not let me fall. I'll come back and haunt your ass."

"I'm not letting you go," he smiles and leans in for another kiss. All his hesitation and fear, gone. His tongue touches my lips, asking for entry, and I eagerly obeye. Andre kisses me deeply and I kiss him back just as deep, but it's still soft. It isn't reckless with passion but it *is* passionate. It isn't setting my body ablaze with fire but it's full of emotion and need.

Need to be seen.

Need to be felt.

Need to be chosen.

Need to be loved.

Need to be healed.

And to be honest, I need it too. We hold onto each other like our lives depend on it.

When he finally breaks the kiss, he drops his forehead to rest against my left shoulder, and let's out a heavy sigh. I hold onto him tightly and run my fingers through his hair. I can smell his smoky scent, reminding me of sitting in front of the fire at home on a cold night. It's comforting and wonderful.

"Damn," I say, with my cheek resting against his head.

He lifts his head to look at me, "what is it?" His eyes still hold a bit of the hurt I saw earlier. He's still not sure I'm not going to run away.

"You're one hell of a kisser!" I smile as I watch the last bit of hurt and fear lave his eyes and I'm rewarded with a dazzling smile I've never seen from him before. It makes me happy and I giggle. Straight up, giggle, like a schoolgirl.

Andre throws his head back and laughs. Not a chuckle. A full-on, heart-felt, belly laugh. It's the first time I've ever seen him so candid. So unguarded. So *free*. In this moment, he's truly *happy,* and that makes me happy. I didn't realize how sad he is and how well he hides it until now.

The mask of humor and flirting is to keep everyone at arm's length away. If everything is a joke, then nothing matters, and he won't be hurt again. It makes so much sense now that I'm seeing the *real* Andre.

"I like the real you," I say smiling. "All of the real you. Your true Fey form and your true character underneath all the teasing."

He smiles brightly, dimple on full display. I lean in and lay a kiss on his dimple, then trail my lips along his jaw and down his neck.

His scales are the softest thing I've ever felt. Softer than silk. Softer than cashmere.

Andre's hands snaked under my shirt and the feeling of his hands on my skin sends goosebumps flying across my skin. His grip tightens on my waist as I graze my teeth against his neck. He lets out a moan before taking my mouth with his again.

When he starts to pull away again, I grab his face, "don't," I breathe out before I pull his lips back onto mine. The way he kisses me, the way he touches me, makes me feel special. It doesn't consume me or make me lose control, like being with Logan does, but it's special. I feel it, and I selfishly want more.

He groans against my mouth and pulls me closer to his body. I can feel his chest rising and falling against mine. He starts pulling away from me again.

"Andre..." I beg.

"Please, let me say something," he breathes against my lips. I nod and he pulls away so he can look at me.

"Thank you," he says softly. "Thank you for seeing the real me. I haven't felt this way in a *very* long time. Happy and..." he hesitates, searching for the right word, "free. More like myself, the *real* me. You're special, Amarah. I knew that the moment I saw you."

I scoff, "I don't know about special. I'm just me, doing the best I can. Honestly, most of the time I feel so lost and useless."

"Considering where you came from and how long you've known your true self, I think you're doing beyond amazing, and don't argue," he says before I can make my usual smartass retort. "You *are* special, love, don't let anyone tell you differently."

"Andre, I..." I let out a heavy sigh. "I don't want to hurt you." Thinking about that look in his eyes makes my chest tight. "That's the last thing I ever want to do to you. I don't want you to think of me and think of pain."

"But?"

"But you know there's something between me and Logan. I don't know if it's real, but there *is* something there, and I don't know what's going to happen. I don't want to lead you on or make promises I can't keep."

"I know, and I understand. Just let me have tonight. I haven't felt this peaceful in a long time and I have you to thank for that," he brushes my hair behind my ear and kisses my cheek. The next kiss falls on my neck, "so thank you," he whispers against my skin and kisses my neck again. It sends chills through my body and I melt into him.

"So, can I have tonight?" He asks with his lips hovering above mine.

I feel like I can barely speak but manage to get out a breathy, "yes," before his lips claim mine again and I'm lost in his need.

42

Feelings and Fighting

Battlefield by SVRCINA

Straddling Andre, looking down into his beautiful eyes, I can't help but let my gaze linger on his lips. My lips remembering how they felt on mine. How soft they are and how good they felt on my skin. My heart is racing and my breathing is heavy. Damn, this is going to be harder than I thought.

I pull my baton away from his neck, "you're not even trying to fight back. Who's the one distracted now?"

Before I know it, he grabs me, rolling me over. I let out a little yip of surprise. He's straddling me now, "I'm not the only one distracted."

He has my wrists pinned above my head and I can't move. Not that I'm *trying* to fight him back. No, I'm fighting myself. I fight the urge to kiss him, but it's *hard.* Especially with Logan gone. What is it they say? Out of sight, out of mind? Ok, that isn't completely true. I never get Logan out of my mind, but with him not being here physically, it's harder to keep Andre at bay. Part of me doesn't want to, because he's a good distraction, but I know I have to. I don't want to hurt him. He knows the truth and the consequences are on him just as much as they're on me. We're two consenting adults who know the risks.

Andre finally breaks the silence, "or maybe I'm teaching you how to fight offensively and what it feels like to take down your enemy." His words say one thing, the smile on his face and mischief in his eyes says another.

I smile back at him, "Andre, we agreed to let what happened between us be a one-night thing."

"And it has been," he says, truthfully.

We spent the whole night together. Talking and kissing and touching. No, we didn't sleep together. I mean, yes, we did. I fell asleep in his arms but we didn't have sex. Still, what happened that night was very emotionally intimate. Pillow talk is dangerous. I had thought about it, a lot, and I'm betting that he had too.

We're frozen, laying here, staring at each other. The air is crackling with tension and chemistry I can't deny. Why is this so hard? Why is everything so damn complicated? Hallana had left for Headquarters, so I'm not worried about her seeing anything and telling Logan. Although, so what if she had? Logan and I are not together, never have been. So why do I feel guilty?

"Don't make this harder than it has to be," I whisper.

"Why should we fight it? You can't tell me you don't feel anything," he's searching my face.

What do I feel? I'm honestly not sure. I'm confused about *everything*. I'm not sure if I feel more for Andre or if I just like feeling special when I'm with him. I know it's real and he's choosing me because he *wants* to, not because of a connection, and that feels good. It's so easy to be around him. We had shared a very intimate moment and that does lead to feelings. I am attracted to him too, so what do I feel?

"I'm not sure what I feel and you know I have feelings for Logan too."

He hangs his head, lets go of my wrists, and rolls off of me. Bring up another guy and that's sure to be a mood killer. Ugh! Why does it feel like I got punched in the gut? If being with Andre feels right, why am I fighting it?

"Fuck, this sucks," I say with feeling.

"No, you're right. You told me what it was in the beginning. I agreed to it. I shouldn't be putting you in this situation. I'm sorry," he says sincerely.

I look at him and I know he's doing his best to control his emotions. He's been more open and relaxed with me, letting me see everything, and it kills me to see him putting up the mask because of me. He's not quite fast enough, I see the hurt in his eyes, and it breaks a piece of my heart. I'm used to being the victim not the one who causes the pain.

"It's hard for me too. I didn't expect any of this. I'm sorry too," I'm now fighting back tears and losing. I have no idea where they even came from?

Andre leans closer to me and wipes his thumbs across my wet cheeks, "Amarah, don't. Please don't. The fact that you know the real me and accept me means more than you'll ever know. I feel alive again and that is the gift you've given me. To know that you care for me, even a little, even if it has to stay hidden, is enough. I can't ask for more."

"Then why do I feel so bad? Why does it hurt?" I'm fighting to keep my voice from cracking. If my voice goes, the tears will be uncontrollable, and I'll become a blubbering mess.

"Because it's real," he smiles sadly, kisses my forehead, and leaves me alone on the training mat once again.

It's real, I repeat in my head. Have I developed feelings for Andre over the past few weeks we've spent together? Not because of some mystical connection shit. Had this happened naturally, over time? I do care for him and that won't change ever, Logan or no Logan, but is it deeper than that? A part of me is scared to say it is. What would that mean for me and Logan?

I sit here, alone, feeling sorry for myself for a while. I take time to pull myself together before I meet with Nicholas for my power training. I finally join him in the herb garden for our lesson, but I'm not mentally present. My body is here, I listen to him and I'm going through the motions, but I'm not really here. I know he can tell, but after he tried questioning me last time when I blurted out my issues with Logan, he's stopped asking questions. At least there's one small victory.

"Despite you being *very* distracted today, you are getting better, Amarah."

I just nod my head.

"I wish you would trust yourself enough to control the fire within you. I know you're still having a hard time believing that you can be a Master of Fire, but I know what I saw. I wouldn't ask you to do it if I truly thought it would hurt you or you couldn't do it."

"I know, it's just getting burnt isn't the easiest thing to get over. Even if Helena can heal me, it still hurts like a bitch in the process."

"That's your fear of pain. Fear has no room in what we do and becoming a Master. Your mind isn't ready." He sighs, "we'll continue training and one day, you'll be ready to try again." He gets up and leaves without saying another word. People love leaving me alone lately. Why do I feel like I'm letting everyone around me down?

I sulk back to my room. A few weeks ago, when I thought Logan and Hallana were sleeping together, I came here to be by myself so I wouldn't have to see them together. I had felt truly alone, but I was ok with it. I hadn't made any friends or connections yet.

Now, I come to my room and I *feel* the loneliness of being alone. Now, it's hard to be alone when there are people I want to see and be around. Still, this is the safest option, not the easiest by far, but I have to put Andre's feelings before mine. It's cruel to be in his presence and tell him not to act on his feelings. How do I know it's cruel? Because I have to tell myself the same thing.

I stay in my room for the rest of the day. I don't even venture out for dinner. Hell, I have no appetite anyway. Tossing and turning and haven't been able to fall asleep. I'm so restless. My mind just won't stop spinning.

Logan.

Our connection.

Andre.

My feelings.

My power.

My fear.

My weakness.

Traitor and alliances.

Demons and war.

Round and round and round it goes. I pick up my cell phone to see the time, 2:36 a.m., almost the Witching hour I think, and that immediately send my mind back to the night with Andre. I think about sneaking up to the tower again tonight but Andre might have the same thought. Too risky. I toss the covers off and walk out onto the balcony for some fresh air.

I try to think of something else besides Andre. Who else is there to think of? Logan. I wonder what he's doing? I miss him. I miss his presence and his energy. I miss his deep voice. I miss his scent. I miss seeing him. I just miss him. I wonder if he would run back to Hallana for comfort since I had run away from him. Would she take him back? Just the thought guts me. It feels like someone takes a blender to mu insides.

"No, Amarah, don't even go there. You're just driving yourself even crazier."

The last thing I need is to be distracted by guy problems and not be aware of someone coming to kill me. I need to focus! Why is life so difficult? Why can't I just know which path is the right path? I decide to sit on my balcony and meditate. I can at least try to quiet my mind so I can have a moment of peace.

Before I know it, my power is out, searching. I didn't consciously do it, but my power *is* me, it's intuitive and knows my subconscious. Hell, I think my power knows me better than I do. My power is searching the grounds and castle for a certain type of energy, and eventually, I find it.

"Andre," I whisper to myself.

I can feel his energy. He's out patrolling the grounds, but honestly, he probably just can't sleep, like me. I'm about to pull my power back when I sense something else. A chill runs down my spine and I send all of my focus to the new energy I feel. I've felt this energy before.

Evil.

Demons.

I don't have time to think or question why or how demons are here. I spring up and run into my room. I put on my shoes as fast as I can and reach for my weapons. I strap on the daggers and sword in seconds and run as fast as I can to the grounds. I'm winded from five flights of stairs by the time I reach the grounds, but that's not what makes me stop in my tracks when I emerge onto the grounds.

The grounds are catching on fire and it lights up the scene in front of me. Demons are everywhere! They're climbing down the side of the mountain. It's another planned attack, and this time there are enough demons to fight the entire Fire Fey family. I stand here, paralyzed in shock. It doesn't seem real. This can't be happening.

Someone slams into my shoulder as they run past me to join the fight. I stagger and snap back to reality as all the noise comes rushing to my ears. There's a loud horn blaring, the warning alarm for an attack. People are running, screaming, scared all around me. I have déjà vu from my dream, and I know it's a sign. I have to join the fight.

I remember Andre had been out patrolling and must be in the middle of it all. "Andre," I yell and start running.

I pull out my sword as I run, feeling the thrum of power against my palm, and open up to my power. I pull it out and around me like a shield and push it down into the blade. The crosses flare to life with their white light and I join the fight.

A Fey woman is kneeling on the ground over a body I can't see. A demon is heading right towards her, an easy kill. I run to the woman and put myself in between her and the demon right at the last second. My sword takes the demon across the chest and he falls to his knees. I pull the sword back and stab the demon through the heart. His body burst into flames and then is nothing but a pile of ash.

"Are you ok," I turn to the woman.

"Yes. Thank you, Amarah. Go help the others fight. I'll continue to heal. I'll be ok," Helena says.

I hesitate to leave her alone, unprotected.

"I know how to fight too, now go," she orders.

I nod my head and run into the fight. Everything is happening so fast! It's all a blur of bodies colliding on the grounds surrounded by angry flames, smoke, black mist, and ember sparks flying in the air. I keep moving and swinging my blade at anything that isn't Fey in my path.

"Amarah," I hear Andre calling my name. I'm so relieved! He's alive! He's ok!

"Andre," I yell back. I can't see him. There are too many bodies, too much fire. "Andre!"

"I'm here," he says from behind me.

I turned around and as he jogs towards me. His arms and face are covered in black soot and something darker and thicker. Demon blood.

"Oh my God! Are you ok," I reach out to him as he reaches for me. I touch his arm and it's hard as a rock. His scales are activated and protecting him against the fire.

"I'm fine. Amarah, you shouldn't be out here. It's too dangerous."

"I can fight too. I can help. I can't just sit aside and do nothing while my people die! We don't have time to argue."

"Stay close to me. I'll keep you safe."

We return our attention to the battle surrounding us. It seems like the fighting is starting to gather around us. My power is drawing them to me. I'm the beacon. I'm the target. Shit.

"Everyone! Circle around Amarah! She's the target and we will keep her safe by order of the Queen!" Nicholas is shouting orders. Before I know it, there's a protective circle around Andre and me. They're all fighting to protect *me*. To keep *me* safe. Fey are being injured or dying to keep *me* safe.

"Andre, this isn't right! I can fight too. I don't want anyone dying just to protect me!"

"You're going to be the savior of our people, Amarah. You're special and we must protect you."

"No," I argue. "This isn't right!" I look at the fight surrounding me.

There are too many demons. They're not going to be able to keep them all at bay. Too many people are going to die! I drop to my knees and set my sword down beside me.

"Amarah! What's wrong? Are you ok?" Andre kneels beside me.

"Lord, please help me. You made me to help my people and they are dying! I can't do this alone! Please, guide me. Please help me," I pray out loud on my knees. I can feel the heat in the Earth from the fires burning all around us.

"Fire," I whisper.

There's no time to hesitate. No time to doubt. I've held fire in my hand with no protection, and Nicholas swore I could do it again. The Earth is pushing heat into my hands. It's like it's telling me I can do it too.

I let out a heavy breath and settle my thoughts. I let the fighting and shouting die away and I focus on myself. I focus on the heat under my hands. I feel my power responding to me, to my thoughts and my intentions. It's burning inside of me and I know I can turn that burn into a flame.

Into fire.

My power is already around me, protecting me, all I have to do is make it burn. I feel my power wavering, shaking, growing. I put all my thoughts into it and think one word.

Burn.

"Amarah…," Andre takes a step back from me.

I didn't even realize I'm now standing. I look down at my hands and they're holding two blazing flames. I remember in my dream, I was surrounded by a Heavenly, white light, and I knew that nothing evil could harm me in that light.

I know what I have to do.

I channel my power, not the fire that's inside of me, but the Angel part of me. The power that is unique to *me*. The orange and red flames in my palms turn a brilliant white.

"Amarah, your eyes! What is this?" Andre exclaims.

"Don't worry. It won't hurt you."

I close my eyes and focus on the fire burning within me. I focus on the Heavenly light surrounding me and I know I need to send this protection out to the Fey. I push the burning fire out of me as hard and as far as I can. My vision is lost to blinding white light. I throw my head back and scream with the effort. I physically feel my power explode out of me and it takes all my strength to remain standing. It takes only a few seconds but my body feels as if it just ran a full marathon at record breaking speed.

The blinding white light in my vision slowly recedes and I'm left with nothing but darkness as I collapse to the ground.

Master of Fire

Awake & Alive by Skillet

I wake up slowly. I feel groggy, as if I took sleeping pills or I'm hungover. I drag my eyes open and immediately recognize my surrounding. Thank God. I didn't need to add disoriented to my list of ailments. My head is pounding and I groan as I look around. I'm lying on the bed in my room, and Andre's slumped over the side of the bed, where he must have fallen asleep as he sat by me. His head is resting on the bed and he's clutching my right hand in both of his. A wave of relief washes over me. He's alive. I don't want to wake him up but I need to see and *hear* that he's ok.

I reach my left hand over and run my fingers through his hair. "Andre," I whisper.

He lifts his head up, quickly, "Amarah, you're awake. Thank God! No one knew what happened or what to do. Let me go get Helena." He starts to get up, but I hold onto his hand, not letting him leave.

He's wearing the same clothes from last night. They're filthy and torn and he's covered in ash, dirt, dried blood and who knows what else. He looks as exhausted as I feel.

"Andre, I'm fine. Just a little weak but I'm ok. Please stay," I pull him down to sit next to me on the side of the bed.

He caresses the side of my face, "I was so worried about you. You passed out and no one could wake you. I didn't know what to do and I felt so helpless."

"I'm ok," I smile up at him, trying to reassure him. "I was worried about you, too. Well, I was worried about everyone, but mostly you. Don't tell anyone I said that though," I manage a little chuckle.

"It'll be our secret," he smiles down at me, dimple on full display. His eyes hold so much relief that I'm ok and I'm sure mine mirror his. I use my left hand to push myself up. My body is a little tight and sore, but mostly I just feel really drained.

"Amarah, don't push yourself. You need to rest and relax."

"I'm stronger than I look, I promise." Nothing wrog with a little white lie here and there.

I reach my left hand up and cup his face as I lean in and kiss him. He hesitates for a brief second before he scoots in closer and kisses me back.

Just like before it's soft, passionate and full of need. I let the relief wash over me. Feeling Andre, physically, knowing he's ok, releases some of the heaviness in my chest.

We break the kiss and lean our foreheads together. "Not that I'm complaining, but what was that for?" Andre asks.

"You could have *died* last night. Seeing you here, next to me this morning..." I pull my head back so I can see him. "I just needed to know this is real and not a dream. I needed to feel you. I don't know what I would do if…" I start to shake my head but stop as the thumping increases with the movement.

"I'm here. I'm real. This is real. We're both ok," he says reassuringly. "Come here." He opens his arms and I wrap mine around him, laying my head on his chest. I can hear his heart beating strong and steady. I close my eyes and listen to the beat of his heart. His heart pumping life into his body. We sit, hugging each other, for a long time. I don't want to let go. I don't want to face the reality of what happened last night but I know I have to. There's no turning a blind eye to the attack and the tragedy that happened here. It would be weak and disrespectful to the Fire Fey.

I mentally prepare myself the best I can, steeling my mind and my heart, for the truth about to rain down on me like a hurricane. I finally pull away and make myself sit up taller.

"What happened last night. Did anyone die? Oh my God, Andre, what about the children?" Dread rises up from the depth of my and pulls my heart down into my stomach.

"All the children are fine. They were taken to the cellar," he reassured me. I know the cellar is well hidden with an underground tunnel that can be used for escape if needed. I saw it once when I first arrived, as a precaution, in case I needed to use it.

I sigh in relief, "and the others? Tell me what happened."

"We weren't prepared for an attack. No demon has ever set foot in our territory much less *inside* our home, until now, and we were vastly outnumbered. Still, we're fierce fighters and we held our own but…" he looks at me with such awe, "we wouldn't have survived if it wasn't for you. The Fire Fey would be all but extinct if it weren't for you. I've never seen anything like what you did."

I try to remember what happened before I passed out. I close my eyes and images start flashing across my mind.

Fire.

Smoke.

Bodies on the ground.

Screaming and shouting.

Demons surround us. Surrounding me. A horde of demons. Way too many.

Praying.

Fire.

"I remember seeing my hands on fire," I lift my hands up, examining them. They're just as dirty as Andre is, but other than that, they're fine. No burn marks or blisters of any kind.

"And I remember just thinking one word..." I look and Andre, "*burn*. Oh my God! Did I hurt anyone?"

"No, Amarah," he grabs my hands and squeezes them. "You didn't hurt anyone, I promise. You *saved* us. All of us. It was..." he shakes his head, "I don't know. It's indescribable."

"Please," I beg. "Try to explain it to me. What happened? What did I do?"

"You were upset that the Fey were surrounding you and protecting you from the demons. You said that you didn't want people to die for you. You dropped to your knees and I heard you praying. The next thing I know, you're standing up, but your eyes..." he's staring intently at me now, at my eyes, as if he's seeing them in the same way he saw them last night. "Your eyes were lost to a glowing white light and your hands were on fire. Pure. White. Fire," he says each word purposefully.

I nod, "I remember the fire. Then what happened?"

"You told me not to worry. You said that it wouldn't hurt me. I didn't know what you meant until your power, that pure white fire, hit me like a hurricane wind. Your fire erupted out of you like a bomb had been set off. Your fire engulfed everything and everyone on the grounds. The Fey were stunned but unharmed. The demons all started to burn," he's looking over my shoulder now, as if he's seeing it again in his mind.

He refocuses and makes eye contact with me again, "just like the demon burned when you killed him with your sword. Something about your power kills them, Amarah. Not just dissipates their form, but *kills* them."

"I don't know how or why."

I honestly don't know, but I do suspect, that it has something to do with me being half Angel.

Heaven vs. Hell.

Good vs. evil.

Angel vs. demon.

It would make sense that my power can kill them, and although this is what I suspect, I can't tell Andre. I can't tell a single soul.

"I told you. You're special, in so many ways," he smiles at me. "Last night proves you're special and who knows what you're capable of. It was like magic. Like a miracle. You are our miracle. Our Võitleja. I don't know how you can be a Master of Fire, but I saw it. Hell, *everyone* saw it! You're all everyone can talk about."

"Oh great. The freak, Amarah. Just what I need."

"No. Not a freak at all. A *hero*. Everyone is in awe of you and what you did for us. Let me remind you…you *saved* us."

"Maybe. But you can't tell me that no one is scared of what I did last night."

He shrugs, "maybe, but it doesn't matter. A little fear is a good thing to have, Amarah."

I sigh. I need to get out of this bed and walk around. I'm starting to feel adrenaline again and I need to stretch out my body. I throw the covers back and slowly slide my legs off the side of the bed. I stand up cautiously, testing out the strength in my legs and the pounding in my head. When my knees don't buckle and I don't immediately fall down, I take a few shaky steps, and walk out to the balcony.

"Amarah, you really should stay in bed. You need to rest," Andre scolds as he follows me.

I ignore him, pulling fresh air deep into my lungs, but there's still bit of smoke polluting the air. Still, the air helps and I feel my head clearing a little. My strength slowly coming back.

I don't want to see the grounds and the damage that was caused but I have to. I have to see it. I have to confront the reality of what happened.

I look down and there are patches of green and black all mixed together. Not everything burned, thankfully, but a lot of damage has been done. It's going to take time, and a lot of work, for the Fire Fey to get their home back to where it was. At least they still have a home. At least there are still Fey in need of a home.

"You never told me how many died," I say, without looking at him.

"Six," he whispers. "Many more injured, but Helena and the other healers have been able to heal them all."

I stare out at the damage and think about the six who died. Six people who will be missed. Six people who will leave families behind. Six families that will never be whole again. The grounds start to get blurry as my eyes water and tears roll down my cheek. I rub my chest, desperately trying to massage my aching heart, with no luck.

"How? How did this happen?" I want answers and I want, no *need*, someone to blame. Someone needs to pay for what's been done here.

"A traitor led them here. Someone who could see past our glamour. Someone who knew how to infiltrate us without being detected until the last minute. A Fey. We found him trying to escape and locked him up."

"What?!" I snap my eyes to Andre, "you caught the traitor who led them here? Is he working with Princess Aralyn?"

"That's my best guess, but he isn't talking. No one knows who he is. Not even Nicholas."

"I want to talk to him. Now," I demand.

Andre looks at me and I don't know what he sees in my eyes, but he doesn't argue. He doesn't tell me that I need to lay down and rest. I care for him so much more in this moment. The fact that he *sees* me, and understands me, understands that I need this. And he doesn't treat me like I'm fragile or can't handle it.

"He's in a cell, down below in our dungeon, I can take you to him."

I walk back into the room with purpose. No slow or shaky steps anywhere to be seen. The pounding in my head, gone. Nothing but sheer determination to get answers driving me forward.

I slip my shoes on, "let's go."

I refuse to let this go unanswered. This traitor *will* talk to me. I'll *make* him talk to me. I don't know how I will but I'm determined. He will pay for what he's done here.

I'm sad.

I'm hurt.

I'm livid.

He betrayed his own kind, *killed* his own kind, and I will find out why, so help me God.

44

No More Hiding

Rewrite The Stars by Zac Efron & Zendaya

He's hanging by his hands, toes barely touching the floor, head hanging to his chest with strands of blonde hair that escaped the top knot on his head, framing his face. He's average height, and his shirtless body shows his slim, but solid build. He's just as dirty as Andre is and also has dried blood on his face, chest and stomach. Battered and torn black jeans hug his hips and show the results of battle. He fought last night. Against his own people. Seeing this traitor and knowing what he caused here has my blood boiling in my veins.

"Open it," I say through clenched teeth as I stare at the limp, hanging body before me.

Andre doesn't argue. He takes a key from his pocket and opens the cell door. I walk in with Andre right behind me. I walk up close to the traitor but I can't quite see his face.

"Watch his legs. He can grab a hold of you and hurt you with them."

"I'll burn them off if he dares touch me," I threaten. "Who are you?"

He doesn't answer. He doesn't move a muscle. Great. He's going to be difficult. Fine. I didn't want to do this the easy way anyway.

I want to hurt him.

"Do you know who I am?"

He slowly raises his head, stray strands of hair hanging in his eyes. God, he looks unbelievably young. Then again, you never can tell with mystical beings. His face is delicate. His chin is narrow, thin lips turned slightly downward, and cold, solid brown eyes meet mine.

"You're going to be the downfall of the Fey," he says in a voice that also sounds young.

Too young to be involved in something so dangerous. I can't help but wonder why he's here? Why he chose to do this? Is he being forced? Being young and naive can sometimes lead us into making really stupid mistakes we often regret later. Will this be one of his? I don't have any answers about this traitor's state of mind but I *will* find out who's using him.

I scoff, "says the boy working with demons to kill his own people."

There's no hiding my anger and disgust. My power is scratching just below the surface and I want so badly to let it out. To hurt him. To destroy him. Instead, I used my power to sense his energy, his aura, and as soon as I feel it, I know who he's working for. I've felt this energy signature before.

"You're Air Fey," I say as fact, not a question. "I bet if I take your glamour away, I'll see you for what you really are. Won't I?"

He laughs then, "you can't do that, and you'll never know who I am. Good luck trying." He smirks at me. Cocky, this one. What's new? All these mystical beings seem to be cocky. Well, he's gonna learn today.

I don't need help from Andre this time, like I needed help before, at the meeting with Logan. No, I've been practicing and my power is just as eager to make this traitor pay as I am. It's not hiding but practically throwing itself at me.

I pull my eager power out and all around me. I wiggle my fingers, feeling the energy like a living thing in the air around me. I walk behind the boy and place my hand solidly in the middle of his back. He starts to jerk and flail in the chains, but he can't get to me back here. I push my power onto him and willed it to reveal the truth.

The boy gasps as his wings emerged from his back, his skin shimmering, even in the dim light of the cell. I walk back around to face him and violet eyes look down at me. They're almost the same shade as Aralyn's, but lighter. Violet eyes must also be a sign of the Air Fey Bloodline. Good to know. His eyes meet mine, but this time, they hold a bit of fear. Andre is right, fear is good, and I want him to fear me.

It's my turn to smirk, "you were saying."

"Now, we know for sure you're Air Fey. I don't care what your name is, that's irrelevant. You're nothing more than a pawn and I know who you're working for. Princess Aralyn."

His eyes widen but he doesn't say anything. He doesn't need to. The fact that I know about Aralyn is clearly a shock to him. Good. Maybe she still believes her treachery goes unnoticed. Maybe we have the upper hand after all.

"Oh yes, we know all about Aralyn and her attempts on my life and her ambition for the crown. As you can see, both of her attempts have failed, and if I were you, I would reconsider whose side you want to be on, because I promise you one thing," I walk up close to him and look in his eyes, "I will kill her and *anyone* who follows her," it comes out a hard, cold whisper.

He doesn't break eye contact but I know he's scared. There's hesitation and doubt in his eyes now. He believes that I'll do it. The question is, is he willing to die for his Princess? We'll find out.

I turn to Andre, "I need to take him to the Queen. I need to let everyone know what happened. I'm done hiding away here. I think I've learned everything I can from the Fire Fey for now. I can continue my training at Headquarters, but I need to be a part of the planning, and the mission to take down Aralyn."

"You can't go alone, Amarah. It's too dangerous."

I put my hand on his chest and meet his eyes. "Then come with me."

"Amarah, I don't know if that's a good idea. Logan will be there, and…" he sighs, "maybe distance will be good for us."

He can't, or chooses not to, hide the sadness in his eyes, and honestly, the thought of leaving him here makes me sad too. Maybe he's right though. It would only complicate things and make things harder.

I touch his cheek, "I understand. Perhaps you're right and I'm just being selfish. Either way, I have to go." I lower my hand, "I can go with Nicholas. He's just as capable of protecting me," I smile sadly. "I'll be in my room, packing my things. We have a long day ahead of us to get back to Headquarters. We need to leave as soon as possible. Send Nicholas to get me when everything is ready to go."

I look into his eyes one last time, and I don't want to go. I don't want to say goodbye. Why is this so damn hard? I feel my throat tightening and my eyes watering. I turn my head and walk out of the cell while I still have the courage.

I'm pacing in front of my bed waiting for Nicholas to come and get me. I'm anxious to get back to Albuquerque. I want to know the Queen is safe, get answers out of this prisoner, and go back home to my simple comforts for a while. I miss home and I miss Griffin. Am I leaving anyone out? Duh. Logan. I still haven't processed all the info he told me, and I'm not sure how I'll feel seeing him. Especially now, since things have changed between Andre and me.

There's a knock on my door. "Come in," I yell. I'm strapping my daggers on my thighs, my sword and backpack lying on the bed, ready to go. I just need to grab water and a bit of food on the way out and I'm good to go.

"Almost done," I say with my back still to the door. When I'm done with the last buckle I stand up and turn around, "ok, ready."

It isn't Nicholas.

"Andre, I can't say goodbye again, please don't make me. It's hard enough as it is."

"I know. That's why I'm coming with you."

"What?" I can't help but smile but it also makes me nervous. I don't know what's going to happen when I see Logan and I don't want Andre hurt in the process. "Are you sure this is a good idea? Andre, I don't want to hurt you. I truly don't, but I have to be honest, I don't know what's going to happen with..."

"I know. I know this isn't going to be easy for either of us, but it's going to be just as hard to let you leave while I stay behind. I won't know if you're safe. I won't be able to see you." He steps close to me and cups my cheek, "I've spent way too long feeling empty and numb. You've brought me back to life, Amarah. I would rather feel pain and heartbreak than nothing at all. At least the pain lets me know I'm alive. It gives me hope. You give me hope."

"Hope is one thing, but I don't want to give you pain, Andre," my eyes were starting to water just thinking about it. I *will* have to choose between him and Logan, and I don't want to. Either way, someone gets hurt. Either way, I lose someone I don't want to lose.

"Amarah, we've had this talk. You've already given me so much more than I ever expected. I know what going with you has in store for me and it's my burden to bear. It's my choice, and I choose to go with you."

"That's not fair! None of this is fair!" I'm so upset at the situation, and I have no one to blame but my damn self. *I* put myself in this situation.

"Life's not fair, love," he says with a sad smile.

I reach up and touched his dimple, "your smile has always made me happy. I hate to see it this way, sad." I look into his eyes and I hope he can see how much I truly care for him. I hope he knows I don't want to hurt him, but want or not has nothing to do with it. It is a possibility.

"We may never be here again. Is it extremely wrong and selfish to ask you for one last kiss?" He asks hopefully.

"Yes, it probably is, but it's just as wrong and selfish that I'm happy you asked."

He steps in close, our bodies touching. My heart is racing and the tears are drying on my cheeks. I put my hand on his chest and feel his heart beating just as fast as mine. How can this be wrong if we both feel this way? Is it just lust? Physical attraction? Or is it deeper? Could it turn into more?

"My body feels heavy," I whisper. "I feel like…"

"Like you're drowning in the best possible way, struggling to breathe," Andre finishes.

"Yes," I whisper so low I barely hear myself.

"I'm yours, Amarah. For good or bad, I'm completely yours."

His lips meet mine in that strong, passionate way they had before. It's pure emotion and pure need.

Like our lips are the only thing saving us from drowning.

Like our lips, our kiss is the lifeline.

I know he feels the same way as he moans into the kiss, sending my knees buckling. He catches me, easily picks me up and lays me down on the bed. I'm lost in the moment and don't even think twice as I pull him down on top of me. I wrap my legs around his waist and hold on for dear life. I want to hold on to this lifeline and never let go.

Andre is kissing down my neck, his hand glides under my shirt and he grips my side. His bare hands, his grip, his need, feels like fire and brings my power out in a hot rush, so I wrap us in it.

Andre gasps, "what's happening?" He asks in a shaky breath.

"I'm sorry," I say breathlessly. "It's' my power out. Did I hurt you?"

"No. It feels amazing. It's like fire, like home," he smiles and there's no traces of sadness now. Except this time, instead of being the usual casual flirtatious smile, it's filled with a deeper passion. It's that smile that a guy gives you when he knows exactly how he affects you and that you want him.

And he isn't wrong.

The power and the passion are consuming me. I want him. I want to pull his tank top off and see his body underneath. I want him to see me, all of me. I want to take it to the next level, but not just physically. I want him in every way. His body, his heart, his laughter. I want it all to be mine. I'm drowning in my need and I want to grab a hold of him and swim to safety.

I move my hands to his shirt and start pulling it over his head. He grabs the back of it, pulling it over his head, and tossing it to the side. He's kneeling between my legs and I have the perfect view of him. His tattoos extended on to his chest and down his sternum. My hands move to touch his solid chest and down his rippling stomach. His abs flexed under my touch and he closes his eyes as I trail my hands over his skin.

I need his lips on mine. I pull him back down to me, and this time, the kiss is more reckless. More passion. More force. More heat. And my power pushing in around us. I hold on tighter with my legs and he takes that as a sign and pushes his hips into me. He grinds his erection between my legs causing me moan my pleasure into his mouth.

I push against his chest and he lets me roll on top of him. I want to feel the ripples of his defined abs under my tongue. I kiss his chest and circled his nipple with the tip of my tongue. Andre let out a sigh of pleasure as I continue making my way lower. I'm at the top of his jeans and I can see his large cock straining against the confines of the jeans. I run my hand over him and he groans loudly. I desperately want to free him.

Andre's hands clasp over my upper arms and he pulls me aggressively back on top of him. My legs straddle his hips and I rub myself on him, frustrated that we have clothes in the way. Andre pulls me down and kisses me, his hands trail down my body and grip my ass, pulling me harder onto his erection. We're both ready and eager for more. I want to let go. I want to lose control. I want to give myself, every part of me over to Andre, but I know that's not possible. Not right now.

I yell at myself, knowing the decision I'm going to make, as I break the kiss, "Andre, we can't. I can't."

I slowly pull my power back and immediately feel cold without it. The passion is there, some feelings are there too, I can't deny that, but what about love? Do I love Andre? Do I love the thought of loving Andre? Or do I love the way he loves me? Freely.

"Yes, we can. It feels so right. Can't you feel it?"

"You know I feel it. I want you, all of you. Not just this, but everything. I want you to give me everything." I laugh harshly, "God, that sounds like possession, doesn't it?"

"You have me. I'm yours. I *want* to be yours. You can have it all." He's looking in my eyes and I know he's telling me the truth.

"I know, but that's the problem. *I* can't give you everything. I don't want to do this unless I know I can give you everything you're willing to give me. I need to know exactly where my heart lies before we cross this line. It's not just sex to me, Andre. It's so much more than that and it needs to be right." I sigh, "I don't know how else to explain it."

"You aren't like anyone I've ever met, love. You feel everything so completely, and you don't do anything just to do it. You always do what's right to you. I don't like it, especially not right now," he groans as he palms his erection. "But I understand what this would mean for you. I'll wait patiently because I know once you've made up your mind, it'll be worth it."

He raises up on his arms and kisses me again. This time, back in control. It's a full and deep kiss and sends my heart fluttering again. The feeling is similar to the butterflies Logan makes me feel, but different. How in the Hell am I ever going to pick between these two men? I have royally fucked myself this time and I haven't even had their dick yet. Nice one, Amarah.

I finish putting my sword and backpack on and we head down to the kitchen. We grab water and snacks for the trip and head to the front entryway. Nicholas is waiting there for us with the prisoner.

"Well, that took long enough," he lifts an eyebrow in suspicion. I blush, Andre smirks, but Nicholas doesn't comment further. Thank God.

Andre picks up his backpack from the floor and throws it on, then takes the rope binding the prisoner's hands from Nicholas. It's going to be one Hell of a hike out of here with a prisoner whose hands are bound but what choice do we have? The sooner we get back to Headquarters the sooner we will have more answers. More answers to *everything*.

Never in my life did I imagine I would say I'm ready to deal with war, traitors and Vampires, but I *am* ready to deal with Princess Aralyn and her accomplice and to speak with the Queen about Valmont's alliance. One thing I'm *not* ready for? I'm so not ready to deal with my personal male dilemma. Again, what choice do I have? The answer.

Absofuckinglutely none.

Time To Man Up...Literally

The Right Kind Of Wrong by LeAnn Rimes

We're driving north on I-25 approaching Albuquerque. The sun is starting to set leaving behind vibrant shades of pinks and purples. The sunset on the Sandia Mountain Range makes the tops of the mountains look like a watermelon, hence, how they got their name. Sandia, in Spanish, means watermelon. The sunsets in New Mexico are some of the most beautiful I've ever seen and they never cease to amaze me. Sometimes, you just have to stop and appreciate the small things in life. Harder to remember when your life is a hot mess like mine is.

It's been an extremely long twenty-four hours and I'm exhausted. I honestly don't even know how I made the hike. I'm still weak and drained from the demon attack. I think pure aggression and determination are the only things keeping me going.

I'm so thankful Andre is driving because I've already zoned out a couple of times. He's making great time by hauling ass in his fire red Dodge Charger SRT Hellcat. Yeah...it suits him perfectly. We haven't said much in the last hour of driving, and surprisingly, my mind isn't racing. I think there's too much in there to process, so instead of trying to make sense of it all, my brain is just ignoring it for the time being. Fine with me. I'm content with music playing low in the background, the soft hum of the tires on the freeway, and the scenery zipping by.

I sigh, "I'm *so* tired. I wish I could just go home."

"If that's what you want to do, then let's do it," Andre says without hesitation.

"You know I love that you'll support me no matter what," I look over at him and can't help but smile. He glances at me and it's hard to meet his gaze knowing what's waiting for us shortly. Logan. I look back out my window, "We have to take this piece of shit traitor to the Queen. I need to know what's been happening and what the plan is. Then, maybe, I'll be able to relax."

"Whatever you want, love."

Whatever I want? Shit, I wish. If only Andre had the power to give me whatever I want. A life with no war, no traitor, and no heartbreak. Yeah...that life is called a dream, and as good as that dream might sound, it would just hurt me too. It would crush me the moment I awoke to realize this is my life and the perfect life is only a dream. It would be a reminder of what I can never have. What's worse? To have it all for a short time in a dream, knowing you'll never *actually* have it? Or...never dreaming of it at all?

We're exiting Rio Grande and will be at Headquarters within minutes. The five o'clock rush hour has already passed, so there isn't much traffic. Most of the businesses in Old Town have closed for the day, just a few lingering shops and restaurants remain open, which means we find a parking spot right away. Shit. I'm not ready for what comes next, and I'm not talking about the evil treachery. I can handle that no problem. How am I going to handle seeing Logan, a man I'm literally drawn to and attracted to, as I waltz in with Andre, another man I'm attracted to?

"Amarah?" Andre reaches over and touches my arm.

It makes me jump as I come back to reality, "sorry." I don't want to look at him. I don't want to face him, but I have to. I can't be a coward.

He half smiles, "it's ok."

He's the one trying to reassure me when I should be the one reassuring him, but it would be a lie. I know it, he knows it, and I don't want to face him because of it.

I just need to focus on the matter at hand. We've been attacked. Betrayed. Six Fey died. We have the traitor and we will make everyone behind this pay. This isn't about *my* problems. I'll deal with them another time. Now is not the time or the place. Get your shit together, Amarah.

I take a deep breath, "let's go."

I get out of the car, strap my daggers back onto my thighs, and put the sword on, tightening the strap across my chest.

"You won't need those here, love."

"Need? Probably not. But I'm Võitleja," I say as I glare at the traitor. "*Everyone* will be reminded of that."

Last time I was here, I was scared and timid. I had no idea what I was even portraying as Võitleja. I've changed so much in a matter of weeks. I'll walk in there with my head held high, my power ready just below the surface, and my weapons on display. There will be no guessing who I am or why I've come.

I remember what Andre said about a little fear being a good thing. If any of the other Leaders have thoughts about joining Aralyn, or trying anything similar, I'm going to give them a reason to change their mind. I want everyone to know that *any* thought of aggression or betrayal against the Queen is a grave mistake. I want the power. I want the fear. Why? I have zero control over my heart and I hate it, so I'll be damned if I don't control *this* narrative.

We're walking into the Church and there's no one around to question why we have someone tied up. I lead the way down the hallway to the back storage entrance with Andre bringing up the rear. I had held onto my nerve until now, but walking down the stairs to the throne room, my heart starts to race. I stop with my hand on the doorknob. Am I ready for what's on the other side? I have to be.

"They're waiting for us, love."

Fuck. I let out a shaky breath, open the door, and walk through. I immediately feel Logan's energy and can pin point exactly where he is in the giant room. He's in his seat as Kaitsja on the dais next to the Queen. I can always feel him except when he's blocking our connection. I feel relief flooding towards me, quickly followed by desire, and then irritation.

Why is he not closing the link down now? I realize I'm watching my feet take one step in front of the other and immediately snap my head up. I won't cower away from this but I also don't have to make it quite so hard.

I've gotten leaps and bounds better at controlling and using my power, so I use that control now, to protect myself. Not from a demon or a blade but from myself. I imagine putting a wall around my heart. I cut off the connection to Logan. Logan has been the one in control, cutting off the link when *he* wanted too, and I refuse to let that be a one-sided advantage.

With the link blocked, I immediately feel better, more in control. Still, it feels like the longest walk to the dais with everyone watching my every move. Are they watching me? Probably not. We are parading in a traitor after all. Guaranteed their eyes are all trained on him. Still. I feel exposed.

We walk past the table where the other Fey Leaders and the Leader of the Werewolves are sitting. I feel their eyes following us but I don't lose focus. We finally reach the dais and I have eyes only for the Queen. I bend down on one knee and see Andre out of the corner of my eye do the same, pulling the traitor down with him.

"You may rise, Võitleja," the Queen's soft, yet demanding voice echoes through the room.

I stand up and the Queen does the same. She walks down the dais stairs and stops right in front of me. The look in her eyes is too much to decipher. Hurt, anger, determination, relief. I'm not expecting what comes next.

The Queen hugs me. "Oh, Amarah! I'm so glad you're safe," she moves back but her hands gently hold my arms. "Come. You must tell us everything," she says as she leads me to the table where the others are eagerly waiting. They're all here, Princess Hallana, Prince Vadin of the Water Fey, Prince Emrick of the Earth Fey, and Alfa Libahunt, Ethan.

She takes the seat at the head of the table and motions for me to take the seat to her right. Andre comes around and takes the seat next to me on my right, still holding the rope that binds our prisoner's hands. Logan walks down the dais and sits to the Queen's immediate left, directly across from me.

Our eyes meet and my heart drops into my shoes. Having the link blocked helps me keep my head above water, but I've already slipped into the pool with just a look. Those green eyes have the ability to strip me bare. As if he can see into the very heart of me.

See what I've done with Andre.

Even with the link blocked, stopping me from feeling his emotions, his eyes have plenty to say.

Pride.

Relief.

Attraction.

Heat.

Curiosity.

His eyes quickly flick to where Andre sits next to me and then back to me. I look away and focus all of my attention on the Queen. Now is not the time or place. Later, I'll deal with it all later. For now, we have bigger issues we need to discuss.

Don't Kill the Messenger

Redemption by Zayde Wolf

"Amarah, tell us everything. Tell me about the attack on my family, and who the Hell is this," Hallana sneers at the traitor, her lip curling in disgust.

I meet her eyes, "yes, unfortunately, there was an attack inside the grounds. This is the traitor who led the attack. He's from the Õhk Family, and working with Aralyn although, he hasn't admitted it yet. As you know, we weren't prepared for this type of attack," I shake my head and re-live the memory of people running, screaming, the smoke and fire, the noise of a battle.

"There were too many demons, *way* too many. There was no warning, they were just all of a sudden, on us. There was fire and smoke and chaos." I look back up at Hallana now with tears in my eyes, "I couldn't save them. I'm so sorry. I couldn't save them." My voice remains solid but my lip quivers as I face her and the memory at the same time.

Hallana sits straighter in her chair, preparing for the news, "how many?"

All I can do is shake my head, tears threatening to fall, and I can't find my voice. I can't speak or I'll lose all my control. So much for being the fierce Warrior after all. Fuck.

"Six," Andre answers for me. "Six died. We were overrun. There had to be close to a hundred demons. It was an attack that had to be planned out for weeks. We would have all died if it wasn't for Amarah."

"Motherfucker!" Hallana stands up with such force she sends her chair crashing to the floor. She storms over to the traitor with her hands in fists, filled with fire, at her sides.

I stand up quickly and put myself in front of the traitor, "Hallana, trust me, I know how you feel. I was there, I saw it all. I want to hurt him as much as you do, but we need to question him. We need to find out everything he knows."

"He killed my family! He killed his own people! He deserves nothing but pain and I will happily give it to him," she raises her hands burning with her powerful flames.

I place my hands on top of hers and command the flames out, suffocated them. After what happened during the attack, I no longer question that I'm a Master of Fire. I know I can put out her flames and so, I do.

Her eyes widen, "that's impossible. Nicholas said he thought you could be..." she stutters, in shock, "but that's impossible."

There's a sudden murmur of whispers back and forth with the Leaders at the table. It's like I've just spurted a tail or something.

Although that probably would have been easier for everyone to accept.

"I told you," Andre says with a confident smile on his face. "We would have *all died* if it wasn't for Amarah."

The Queen comes to stand with us. "Amarah, what is this?"

"Apparently, I'm a Master of Fire," I shrug.

"Not just a Master of Fire. Amarah is so much more than that," Andre says from his seat at the table, but he has eyes only for me, and I see everything his eyes are saying.

Adoration.

Gratitude.

Pride.

Love.

The old Andre would have been taunting Logan, but he isn't. He just means what he says. I glance at Logan but his eyes are studying Andre, who seem oblivious.

"What do you mean, Andre?" The Queen asks.

"We were surrounded by demons and it was just a matter of time before we all fell. Amarah turned into pure, white fire. It's like it came from *inside* of her. Her eyes were filled with it, and it just...*exploded* out of her, and *killed* all of the demons. I'm not talking about just temporarily taking away their physical forms. They *burned*. Amarah killed them all. I've never seen anything like it."

"I've never seen a demon die. How is this possible?" The question comes from Prince Emrick.

"I've never seen this happen either," Prince Vadin agrees. "I'm not sure I can believe it without seeing it. No offense."

"I've seen it too," Logan says. "On our way to Hallana's we were also attacked." He looks at me, "Amarah killed a demon with her sword and the body burned. Now, she's a Master of Fire, but not of the Tulekahju Family. We all saw her extinguish Hallana's flames, we can't deny it, but I don't know what it means."

All eyes are on me and I have no fucking clue what to say. Luckily, the Queen steps in and saves me.

"Come, everyone, sit. I think I can explain." She waits for me and Hallana to take our seats. Now, all eyes are on her, eagerly waiting for an explanation.

"Amarah is very special. I've told you all this before. I told you to trust me and now you see why. We do not know what she's capable of, but I *know* she is going to be very powerful."

"But that doesn't explain anything, My Queen," Prince Vadin argues. "*Why* is she so special? Who is she?"

"She is who I've told you she is. She is the daughter of my sister, Alexandria."

"Then it must be her father. Was her father Tulekahju?" Prince Vadin questions the Queen.

The Queen and I know the truth. I'm half Angel. I'm half Divine. Angels can kill demons. It makes sense to us because we know the truth but I understand why everyone else is confused. It doesn't make sense to them. The Queen says this has to be our secret to keep. For how long? And why?

"Amarah's past is not what is important here. The only thing that matters is that she is one of us. She is *family*, and she is our Võitleja. She is the first of her kind and we are all in unfamiliar territory. Do any of you still question that, after hearing what she did, and seeing her control Hallana's fire today?"

Everyone is shaking their heads and there is a resounding, "no," around the table.

I look at Ethan, "You've been awfully quiet throughout all of this. What's on your mind?"

He shrugs his big shoulders, "this is more Fey business than it is Werewolf business. We're allies, but I don't try to understand the powers of the Fey, just as the Fey don't always understand the ways of the Wolves. As long as you're a powerful ally to the Wolves, I don't care much about how or why."

"Fair enough," I dip my chin. "Now that you all have heard about what's happened on our end, what has happened here? What's the plan for Aralyn?"

"Maybe we should ask him," Logan says, looking at the traitor.

"Good luck, he hasn't said more than a few sentences since we captured him," Andre explains.

"Well, are you ready to talk to us?" the Queen asks. "How about we start with a name?"

All eyes are on the traitor and I can see the unease and fear in his eyes. He's young, has to be. Most of the older, more experienced Fey I've met would never have shown fear, even if they were consumed with it.

"My name is Caleb Thomas, and yes, I'm from the Õhk Family. Aralyn did send me to lead the attack."

"He speaks," Andre says sarcastically.

"You wouldn't say a word all day. Not that I'm complaining, but why talk to us now?" I ask.

"I didn't believe you were as powerful as you said. Now, I do. Now I see that Aralyn is wrong to come against you. I don't want to make the same mistake."

I can sense that he's telling the truth. "You're young, but you learn fast. I can see why she chose you." I turn to the Queen, "he's telling the truth."

"Good. So, tell us what you know Caleb," the Queen demands.

"I don't know much. Aralyn came back from the meeting last month with all this talk about how you had made a fool of yourself by showing off and backing Amarah as Võitleja. She said Amarah was weak and would be the downfall of the Fey. She said that anyone who put their trust in her, and you, were fools. She said that she couldn't stand by and watch you lead the Fey into death and extinction. She said that you had lost sight of what it meant to be Queen and that the Fey needed a new leader. That's when she started sneaking around and making plans."

"Did she announce this to the entire Õhk Family? Is everyone standing behind her?" The Queen asks.

He shakes his head, "no. She knew that not everyone would just follow her. The Fey are loyal to you, my Queen, so she was very careful and only trusted a few completely."

"You are not loyal to me."

"I believed what she said about Amarah. A Fey raised as a human was meant to be our Warrior and change the course of the war? I didn't see how that could be true. Also, Aralyn has her ways of persuasion," he looks away, as a blush creeps up his cheeks. "She also promised positions of power given to those who helped her become Queen. I made a mistake. A grave mistake, that I regret, and cannot take back."

"You love her," I say plainly. I know the signs. I know what he so plainly expresses with his eyes but tries so hard to hide.

"Yes," he admits in a low voice.

"What do you know of her plans," the Queen continues.

"I only know that I was meant to lead the attack on the Tulekahju Family. I was to get the demons past their glamour and defenses. She kept me in the dark about everything else. She was very good at distracting me, and I let her. I'm sorry, I honestly don't know more."

"So, you're totally useless," Hallana dismisses him. "I say we go get her and question her ourselves. She needs to pay for everything she's done!"

"I was supposed to check in with her after the attack. The fact that I didn't is a warning. She either thinks I'm dead or caught, and she will assume the worst. That I'm caught and talking. I doubt you'll be able to just walk in and grab her. She's too smart and too prepared for that. I don't know her plans, but I can give you the names of those I know to be working with her."

"That's a great start," the Queen says. "I agree with Hallana. We need to bring Aralyn here and question her. We don't know what else she has in the works. Everyone needs to stay alert and cautious. No one is to be alone. We stay together until this threat is over."

Hallana snorts, "I'm the threat Arayln needs to worry about now."

"She will pay for what she's done," I look at Hallana. We have a deep understanding of each other now, we're on the same side. "I promise you she *will* pay."

"We'll send people to bring her and her accomplices back here right away," the Queen says.

"I'll go," Prince Emrick volunteers.

"As will I," Prince Vadin agrees.

"Good, but you won't be going alone. We'll send a small army to bring her back. We *must* show force and make her allies hesitate. I think we're done here for now?" She makes it a question.

Everyone nods and starts to get up out of their chairs but I need to talk about the alliance with the Vampires. I'm not sure this is something the others need to be a part of. I don't know what they know and don't know about the dragon scales hidden away in the Fire Fey's home. So, it's better to err on the side of caution.

"Actually," I speak up. "There is one more thing I need to discuss with you and Princess Hallana my Queen."

Here we go. This is not going to be a fun conversation. I'm not sure I'll be able to convince Hallana to give up her power over the Vampires, but I might be able to get the Queen to see the benefits of the alliance. I know one thing for sure, one enemy, plus the demons, are more than enough to handle. We sure as Hell don't need the very powerful, Valmont Sinclair, also coming for us, and I know that he will if we don't agree to the alliance. Even if we told him that Aralyn had lied to him, and there was nothing to protect his Vampires, he wouldn't just take our word for it. It would be another attack on the Fire Fey and I don't want that to happen. I'm hoping it's enough to make Hallana realize that too.

Pros Vs. Cons

New Divide by Linkin Park

Ethan left us to gather some Werewolves to go with Vadin and Emrick. The two Princes took Caleb, to get the names of the accomplices, as they get ready to head to the Õhk Family in hopes of bringing Aralyn back. That leaves me with Andre, Hallana, Logan, and the Queen. Logan seems to know everything the Queen does, well except for me being half Angel, but everyone else at the table knows about the dragon scales.

I sigh, "as much as I wish we only had Aralyn to worry about, I'm afraid we need to discuss Valmont's request for an alliance."

Hallana speaks first, "considering we have more enemies than we realize, and he gave us Aralyn, I don't see why we don't honor this alliance. Treading carefully, of course."

"I agree," Logan says. "Why would we *not* want to keep them close? I see it only as a benefit."

The Queen echoes my sigh, "I've known Valmont for a long time. We've never worked together, but I know him as a Leader, and I'm afraid it's not going to be that simple. Is it Amarah?"

I glance at Hallana and then Andre, and back to Hallana, "no, it's not. Valmont wants something in return."

"Well, what is it?" Hallana asks, she's frustrated and impatient. I don't blame her.

"As you all know, Aralyn went to Valmont with the terms for an alliance of her own. All he had to do was kill me. What you don't know is what Aralyn promised him in return. She promised him something that is not hers to give, something that can protect him and his Vampires from fire." I ready myself for the inferno that my next words are bound to ignite. "Your dragon scales."

"What?!" Hallana shoots up, sending her chair flying again. "No way! This is not an option. How in the Hell did Aralyn even know about them? They've been protected and hidden for *generations*. And you," she turns to Andre, "you just gave this information up to Amarah?

"Not exactly," he shakes his head.

"What the fuck do you mean, not exactly?"

"I accidentally stumbled upon the magic keeping them hidden when I was meditating and practicing with my power. I knew you were hiding something, and after Valmont brought this to my attention, I figured it all had to be connected. So, *I* asked Andre. It's not his fault. I would have kept searching on my own if he hadn't been honest with me. Don't be mad at him. Be mad at Aralyn for putting this all into play."

She's pacing now, "no way. There is no way we are giving the Vampires any advantage against fire. Against *us*. It's completely out of the question."

Andre leans in and whispers, "told you."

I sigh again, "I understand your hesitation to hand over something so powerful to the Vampires, but can we discuss how this alliance would benefit us? My Queen, what do you think?"

"It's a lot to consider. I need to keep my people safe, and one of the advantages we have against Vampires, is fire. We don't have much else when it comes to fighting or defeating them," the Queen explains.

"I know, but what choice do we have?" I argue, "Valmont has it in his head that there is *something* out there. He doesn't know the details, he doesn't know how it all works, but if I don't tell him the truth, I'm afraid he will go looking on his own and you know what that would entail."

"Another attack," Logan finishes my thought.

"Yes, and even with the upper hand of using fire against them, they are extremely powerful, and fucking fast! More Fey would die, and I know none of us want that."

"Motherfucker! I hate this day!" Hallana huffs as she retrieves her chair and sits back down, "what other options do we have?"

We all looked around the table at each other, but no one has anything better to suggest.

"For what it's worth, I *do* believe Valmont is sincere in his offer to be an ally," I say optimistically.

"I don't see how that's true," Logan argues. "Valmont doesn't do anything for anyone without a reason. Yes, he would get protection against fire, but they've survived as long as we have without it. There has to be something else."

I look at the Queen and then at Logan, "me, the something else, is me."

"What do you mean he wants *you*?" He leans forward across the table, his serious eyes not wavering from mine, "you mean like physically?"

I can't help but laugh out loud, "no Logan, he doesn't want to *sleep* with me, my God. He's only interested in my *power*, not my body. He wants me to be his ally because he wants my power on his side."

"Oh." Logan looks a little embarrassed.

I feel bad for him, but it's nice to know he's jealous. He hasn't even looked at Hallana the entire night. Maybe he hadn't run back into her arms after all. Great. That just adds to my guilt for my actions with Andre. Way to be a hypocrite, Amarah.

"I know it seems unlikely, but Valmont gave his word and I believe him. He'll be our ally and an immense help with not only the demons but with Aralyn and any enemy that decides to surface. I know it's a big advantage the Fire Fey are giving up, but the pros heavily outweigh the cons on this one. In my opinion," I quickly add.

"I still say no," Hallana says defiantly. "We've survived without the help of the Vampires this long. We don't need them now."

I look at the Queen, "my Queen. What are your thoughts?"

"I don't know, Amarah. Hallana is right, but we also have been slowly losing more and more Fey to the war. Now we're also facing an internal war."

"One that you wouldn't have even known about without Valmont. He may have saved your life." I'm getting frustrated, "look, I know I'm new to all of this. I know that you have your reasons for not trusting the Vampires, but all I know is what I know *now*. I believe

Valmont is being honest. I believe it's in our best interests to ally with the Vampires. If you don't trust Valmont, then trust me."

"I do trust you, Amarah," the Queen says. "If you put your neck out for Valmont, you know you will be blamed the second something goes wrong. And if something does go wrong, if Valmont betrays us, it will be up to you to take care of it, Amarah. Do you understand?"

"I do."

"Well, then, it looks like we'll be gaining another ally."

"You can't be serious? My Queen…" Hallana starts to protest.

The Queen raises her hand to stop Hallana, "I've made my decision and it is final. I won't risk the Vampires attacking your family to only take by force what we can give them peacefully."

Hallana turns her glare on me. "You better be right," she says through gritted teeth, then turns on her heel and storms off. I swear she has steam coming out of her ears.

I look at Andre and he gives me a nod and a reassuring smile. Just seeing his smile and having him beside me gives me comfort. Not long ago, it would have been Logan sitting next to me, comforting me.

"It's gonna be ok. She'll get over it," Andre says as he grabs my hand and squeezes it.

"Yeah," I sigh and give him a weak smile.

Logan catches my eye. He glances back and forth between me and Andre. Shit. Is it obvious that something has happened between me and Andre? Is Logan going to bring it up? I hope he's smart enough not to bring up our personal drama, here, in front of the Queen.

I look away from his suspecting gaze and back to the Queen, "thank you, my Queen, for trusting me. I do truly believe it is the right choice."

"I hope you're right. Now, is that all for tonight? I'm not sure I can handle any more surprises," she smiles softly, but she looks as tired as I feel.

"You and me both," I laugh nervously. "I guess I have a Vampire to visit before I can go home and relax." I realize I have no idea where to find Valmont. "Ummmm, speaking of, I have no idea where to go."

"Logan can take you. He knows where to find Valmont, and I don't want you alone, Amarah. You're just as much in danger as I am, if not more."

The thought of being alone with Logan makes me nervous for many reasons. What will we talk about considering how we last left each other? I'm still attracted and connected to him, that hasn't just disappeared. It's going to be awkward. Not to mention, what will Andre think? Will he be worried something will happen between me and Logan? Of course, he will! I would be if I were in his shoes. I don't want to hurt him and put him in that situation. I have to do something.

"My Queen, what about you? Logan needs to protect you more than me. I can handle myself."

"Nonsense, Amarah. Stop trying to be the tough hero. You're the most important thing to the Fey and I do *not* take that burden lightly. Logan will be with you to protect you, end of story. It's not up for debate. It's an order from your Queen." She stands up and walks over to me and hugs me again, "I'm so happy to have you back and I will not chance it by having you go off alone into Vampire territory. I'm doing this for you."

"I know," I smile up at her.

She smiles back at me, "keep me in the loop."

I nod my head and watch her walk away, leaving me sitting at this table, between Andre and Logan. I'd rather been sitting between demons and Aralyn. This is so uncomfortable and I have no idea what to do or say. Focus on the task at hand.

I make myself sit up straighter in my chair, "looks like I don't have a choice." I look at Logan, "are you ready to leave now? I want to get this over with so I can go home. It's been a long day and I don't want to make it any longer than it needs to be."

"We can leave now," he says plainly.

"Good," I stand up and the two men stand up with me. I look at Logan, "give me a minute. I'll meet you at the door."

He glances at Andre again and then back to me. He looks curious, a hint of anger passes through his eyes, but he turns around and leaves without a word.

"I'm so sorry," I start to plead.

"No, Amarah, don't. We've been over this and we both knew this would happen. It's ok. I promise," he cups my face in both hands. "I'll be ok."

"Nothing is going to happen. I promise. He just has to be with me to protect me."

"Amarah, don't start lying to me now, and don't make promises you can't keep. I know what's between you and Logan is something you can't completely control. You can control how you feel about me, though, and that means so much more to me. I know you care about me, *genuinely*. I will hold that thought with me. I'll be ok," he repeats.

"Now who is lying," I chuckle sadly.

"I'm not," he smiles, showing off his dimple. "No lies between us, ok?"

"Ok," I whisper.

"Now go," he kisses me on the cheek. "Logan is waiting and you can finally get home once you see Valmont. You can call me later. I'll be here. I'm not going anywhere."

I nod but can't speak. I have the urge to kiss him goodbye, but I also don't want Logan to see me kissing him. If I kiss Andre, Logan will be hurt. If I don't kiss Andre, Andre will be hurt. It's a no-win situation. How is it possible to be so torn?

I reluctantly turn around and leave Andre standing there alone. I know he's right. I can't promise that nothing will happen with Logan, and I don't want there to be lies between us. How has my life become so damn complicated? I'm thankful to still be cutting off the link to Logan. I don't want to know what he's feeling and I sure as Hell don't want him to know what I'm feeling. First things first, deal with a Vampire. Then, I can go home to Griffin and relax. I'll deal with my love triangle later. Will Logan let the change between Andre and I slide without bringing it up? Probably not.

Fuck me.

48

Proposing An Alliance

Queen by Loren Gray

I'm back in Logan's truck and we're headed north on I-25. I'm trying to focus on what I'm going to say to Valmont, but it's hard to focus with Logan only a few feet away. Even when I close my eyes or look away, I can *feel* him, I can *smell* him. Everything about this damn man is intoxicating. I'm concentrating *very* hard at keeping my heart closed off to the connection.

"Amarah, are you ok," Logan's voice breaks the silence.

"Fine. Why?" I ask through gritted teeth.

"You're squeezing your eyes shut, and I think you're going to break my arm rest. It looks like you're in pain."

I didn't realize how tense I am. I let out a long, slow breath, release my death grip on the door, and open my eyes, "I'm fine. Just tired. It's been a rough couple of days."

"I'm sorry I wasn't there to protect you."

"You're not the only one who can protect me," I snap. I immediately regret saying it. I don't know why I'm being like this with him. He hasn't done anything wrong, other than completely invade me, and turn my life upside down. But, not his fault.

"No, I guess not. Andre seems to protect you just fine," he snaps back.

Is that jealousy I hear in his voice?

"That's not what…" I sigh, I don't want to fight with him. Not now. I finally look over at him, "I don't need *anyone* to protect me. I can protect my damn self."

A part of me is pleased that Logan is jealous and another part of me just doesn't want to deal with the macho shit. "I saved everyone else, not the other way around. In case you missed that part," I say sarcastically.

"You're still upset about our last conversation."

I sigh heavily and slump down in my seat, "I don't want to talk about this right now. Can we just focus on one thing at a time? I need to have my head clear when I see Valmont."

He doesn't argue and leaves us to deal with the silence on our terms. I have no idea where we're going, but I don't ask. No sense is asking when I'll know soon enough. I'm too tired for small talk, much less anything deeper and more important. I need to save my energy for my meeting with Valmont. He's powerful and intelligent. Not to mention his supernatural senses. I need to be on my toes.

We exit on Tramway and head East. There isn't much out here except the Sandia Casino and a road that leads towards the mountain and turns back south towards I-40. It's one of the ways that will also lead to my house, eventually.

So where do Vampires hide? Are we heading out to some dark, lone, scary cave in the mountain?

I'm shocked as Hell when we pull into the casino.

I snort, "a casino? Really? That's where the Vampires stay?"

"Valmont owns all of the casinos in the Albuquerque area. Casinos are open 24-7, so Vampires can come out at night without it being odd. Plus, everyone knows casinos make bank. No one questions his lavish lifestyle."

"Yeah, I mean it makes perfect sense, but no one questions that he's only ever seen at night?"

"Humans don't believe in the preternatural world. Like we talked about before, they're blissfully ignorant. They just take him for a rich, casino owner who likes to manage at night when he's the busiest and sleeps during the day when it's slower."

Logan pulls into the valet lane.

"Will my weapons be safe in here?" I ask.

"Yes."

An attendant comes over and opens my door courteously. They do work hard for those tips and I feel bad that I have zero cash on me.

I hop out of the truck. "Thank you," I smile politely to the attendant. He bows his head, closes the truck door, and meets Logan on the driver's side. They exchange a few words that I can't hear and then Logan joins me.

"You ready?" he asks.

"Ready or not. Everyone always asks me that as if I have a choice. How are you so calm?"

"We're here to agree to an alliance. Is there a reason I should be worried?"

"No, but they're Vampires. The way everyone else talks about them, there's always something to be worried about." I shrug, "let's go and get this over with. Lead the way."

We start walking towards the entryway doors. As soon as I step inside my senses are bombarded. First, it's the noise you hear. The ping and chimes of the machines and then the loud rumble of all the voices talking over each other. Then the smell hits you. That's harder to explain. It's a mix of different perfumes, colognes, body odor, old people, and above all of that, smoke. I've never understood why anyone would ever take up smoking to begin with. It's such a disgusting habit and it sticks to your hair and clothes. I cleaned up a bit at Headquarters, but I'm still filthy from my last twenty-four hours, but if I wasn't, I'd need a shower after being in here for even a second. I can already feel the smoke clinging to me.

I'm also not a fan of gambling, at all. I'm a sore loser. I lose twenty bucks and I can't help but think of what I could have used that money for instead. A new book, definitely. Gambling may not be for everyone, but the casino also has restaurants, a bar, and a night club. I've been here for those things a few times before. Something for everyone.

We're about half-way through the casino, heading towards the back where the nightclub is when two guys approach us. They 're both tall, one being a little shorter than Logan, and the other a good four inches taller. The shorter one has pale skin, blonde hair slicked back on top, shaved on the sides, and a clean, but strong face with artic blue eyes.

The other guy has very dark skin, hair buzzed short with a matching beard and mustache, and not just dark, but black eyes.

Idris Elba comes to mind, but not quite as…charismatic. No, his demeanor is about as approachable as a rock wall.

They're both wearing black suits that fit them perfectly and reveal they're both very muscular and solid. Nothing left to the imagination here. They're definitely security.

The one with the dark skin speaks as he nears us. His voice is deep and rumbling as if he has rocks tumbling around in his throat, "Amarah Rey, Valmont is waiting for you, follow me."

He doesn't wait for any type of reaction or response. He just turns and heads back in the direction he had just come from. The other guy positions himself behind us.

I glance at Logan and he shrugs. Great. A lot of help he is. As we wind our way towards Valmont, I decide to drop my wall and re-establish the link I have to Logan. If he can't talk to me with words, maybe being able to feel his emotions will come in handy. I imagine the walls crumbling down and as soon as I do, I'm flooded with emotions.

Caution.

Alert and awareness.

Adrenaline.

Protectiveness.

Logan is definitely preparing for anything. His calm, bored demeanor is just for show. He's alert and seeing everything and everyone. Ready for any threat. I immediately feel better.

Safe.

We're in the back corner of the casino and head up some stairs. The security guard stops at the top of the stairs, just outside a closed-door that reads, *Private Do Not Enter*.

"Only Amarah Rey enters. Logan stays here with us," he instructs.

I'm tired and cranky. I'm fine with going in to see Valmont alone, but there's no way Logan is going to agree to that. So, I speak up before the testosterone has a chance to, "yeah, I don't think so sparky. Logan is with me and we're both going in."

"I'm afraid I must insist."

"Look, I've had a long ass day and I'm not in the mood to play games. Either Logan comes with me in there or I turn my ass around and change my mind about this whole alliance thing." I raise my voice, "I know you can hear me Valmont. No games or I walk out of here and don't come back!"

The door opens and Valmont stands in the doorway. His silky silver-white hair lying smoothly on a light grey suit. He has on another white shirt, and a silver tie with turquoise design in it. The cuff links are the same matching turquoise and he finishes off the look with black dress shoes that I could have used for a mirror. One thing's for sure. The man knows how to dress and compliment his features. Damn him for being so elegant and alluring.

"Amarah Rey," he looks amused. "It's good to see you haven't lost your feisty spirit, although, you do look a bit worse for wear." He turns his attention to Logan, "Logan, always a pleasure, mate."

"Valmont," Logan nods his head, but I notice he doesn't look at the Vampire.

Valmont steps aside and motions for us to come inside, "do come in, both of you. I've been eagerly awaiting an update from our last conversation." His British accent makes everything seem so easy and non-threatening. I know that's a damn lie, but thankfully, we aren't here for threats.

I walk in and realize this must be his office. It isn't overly large, but it's a nice size, and surprisingly, cozy. It isn't lit too bright, but also not too dim. The lighting is perfect. The walls are painted a soft blue-grey with decorative art and paintings hung on the walls. There's a desk with two matching chairs off to the right. To the left is a minibar, of course. Why did that not surprise me? Further, into the room, there's a seating area, a couch, and two more chairs, but lounging chairs, surrounding a glass coffee table. The far wall is nothing but windows. They must overlook the nightclub, if I remember its location correctly.

"Can I offer either of you a proper beverage?"

"No, thank you. We didn't come here to drink with you Valmont," I say harshly.

"No need to be rude, Amarah Rey. I'm just being polite. It seems you've left all of your manners elsewhere tonight."

I sigh, "I mean no offense. I've had a rough couple of days and I just want to get business over with so I can go home, if you don't mind."

"Very well. Come, let's have a seat and discuss business."

Logan and I follow him over to the couch and chairs. Valmont takes a seat on the far side of the couch. Logan and I opt for each of the chairs. I had been right. The windows overlook the nightclub. I feel like I'm in a movie.

"Well, isn't this snazzy," I say, looking out the windows.

"Amarah Rey, the way you compliment me, I might blush," he says with a mocking smile. "Now, I'm sure you did not come to see my *snazzy* office. Have you discovered the truth of what we discussed?"

"Yes, I have, but before we discuss the details, I want you to know that I fought hard in your defense. Honestly, I'm not quite sure *why*, but I believe you're sincere with this proposed alliance. If anything goes wrong, I'm going to be the one to blame and I won't take the betrayal lightly. I've had more than enough of that to deal with. Do you understand my position?"

"I understand, and I have no plans to betray you. I could have killed you many times if I wished, as you well know. I've put my trust in you just as you have in me. We're starting to pave a new path, you and I, and I am deeply excited to see where this new path takes us together, Amarah Rey."

Logan shifts a little uneasy in his chair. He doesn't say anything but I feel more protectiveness coming through our bond, and a little jealousy. I don't like the way Valmont worded that either, but I'm not going to backtrack on the progress of the conversation.

"Good. I'm to be your direct contact with everything moving forward."

"Amarah," Logan protests. "What are you doing? It should be the Queen who handles all of the decisions."

"The Queen has agreed to this alliance. She made the final choice for the Fey, but this alliance is *my* responsibility. The alliance is between me and Valmont. Isn't that what you wanted, Valmont?"

"Indeed," he smiles but doesn't show his fangs.

"But..." Logan tries to argue.

"No, Logan. If you aren't going to support this choice, support me, then leave," I glare at him. I don't have time to argue with him and I don't need anyone undermining me and making me look weak.

He meets my eyes and clenches his jaw. He runs his hand through his hair, in his nervous gesture, but he doesn't say anything. He dips his chin in agreement but I'm sure I'll get a mouthful later, but right now he's following my lead, and it feels good to know he believes in me.

Valmont lets out a light-hearted laugh, "oh Amarah Rey, you have so much confidence. Either that or you're just *that* stubborn. Maybe both. Either way, I do enjoy having you around. You constantly intrigue me, and not many can say that."

"How lucky of me," I say sarcastically.

"Now, what are the details," he leans forward, resting his elbows on his knees. He gives me direct eye contact, eager to hear the rest. I can't say I blamed him. This is a huge benefit for the Vampires.

"The Fire Fey do have something that can protect the Vampires from fire," I watch his face closely when I admit it. He doesn't show much expression but something glints in his eyes.

Excitement?

Mischief?

A devious thought or plan?

Who knows?

"What is it? How does it work?"

"It's dragon scales, from the last dragon that lived with the Fire Fey. As long as you wear the scale on your person, it will act as a shield against fire, but they need to be infused with magic for them to work. We'll need to find a Witch that is willing to help us. The Fire Fey have been protecting this secret for generations. It's part of who they are. It's their history and they do not give this up to you lightly.

Because it's something so rare, there isn't a lot of it to be given. Not all of your Vampires can be protected. Do you understand?"

"So, you're saying that there *is* something that can protect my people, but not enough of it to protect my people."

"Yes. You will only be able to give this protection to some. How you choose who gets the protection is up to you."

"This is not what we agreed to. I want an alliance that will protect all of my people from fire, not just some of them," he says angrily.

"To be clear, we didn't *agree* to *anything*. You asked me to find out the truth about what Aralyn told you. Well, this is the truth. We can't change the circumstances. You either choose this alliance with what we have or you don't."

Valmont is suddenly standing over me with his hands on either side of the chair. My heart is back in my throat, but I'm not as terrified as I was the first time. I'm ready for his theatrics, and I have better control of my power this time. I feel it right below the surface and decide to pull it out and shield myself. I can also feel Logan's Wolf, his haunches raised, lips pulled back in a snarl.

Valmont's face is inches away from mine. I can smell his clean cologne, his hair is gently brushing my face, and it feels like silk against my skin. His eyes are studying mine but I don't back down. Instead, I lean in closer and put our lips almost touching. I smell the peppermint on his breath and that other scent I couldn't make out last time. Logan's Wolf senses are stronger than mine and I'm picking up on them through our bond.

Metallic.

"You smell like blood," I whisper.

I feel Logan next to me, "if you touch her, you die." His voice is a low growl that isn't exactly human.

Valmont ignores him as if he's not even here, and keeps his eyes locked on mine, "you *are* something special, aren't you?" He trails one fingertip gently along my jaw. "You better not be lying to me, Amarah Rey."

"Why would I lie to you about this? You get protection for your people. For yourself. We're giving you the only power we have over you."

"If only that were true, Amarah Rey, but I can see that you believe it," he slowly backs away from me and finally looks at Logan.

"There's no need to fight, mate, we're allies after all. You can put those away," he glances down to Logan's hands and I follow his gaze.

Logan's hands have transformed, instead of his normal, yet large, hands, he now has elongated fingers ending in even larger, Wolf claws. I watch them slowly shrink as his hands morph back to normal, and I look up just in time to see his eyes melt back into green from amber.

"Holy shit," I whisper.

I can feel his Wolf's desire to rip into Valmont's neck. I can feel how hard Logan has to fight to maintain control, but he does, and I feel it as his Wolf retreats and settles. Now that the alliance is in place, I concentrate on putting the block back up. Part of me feels better once I'm back in my own feelings, but another part of me, misses the bond terribly. It feels like I'm cutting off one of my own limbs.

"So, just to be clear, you *are* agreeing to the alliance?" I ask Valmont.

"I would be a fool not to align with you, Amarah Rey," he's still looking at me curiously. "We have a deal."

"Good. Like I said, you and I will work together to find someone to help us with magic. In the meantime, we can use some extra manpower to bring in Aralyn and her accomplices. Some Fey and Werewolves are traveling there tonight to bring her in before she tries something else."

"I will talk to my people and let them know of this new alliance. I will contribute to this hunt for Aralyn. Although, without her treachery, we may never have been here and now, working together. Ironic, isn't it?"

"Every decision has an outcome. An action and a reaction. All we can do is hope we're making the right decisions. Some are easier than others," I glance at Logan.

"Only time will tell," Valmont leads the way towards the door. "Pierce and Emerson will escort you back to your vehicle," he says as he opens the door to reveal the two security guards still standing at attention outside the door. "I eagerly await our next meeting to get the ball rolling. Pierce will provide you with my direct contact information as well as his and Emerson's." He reaches for my hand, slowly brings it up to his mouth, and gently brushes his lips on my knuckles, "it's always a pleasure, Amarah Rey."

He still gets my skin crawling and I still don't know if it's in a good or creepy way. I pull my hand back. I don't want him touching me, because I don't know how it makes me feel, but I don't want to insult him either. "I'll be in touch," I say calmly, even though I don't feel calm. I want out of here.

Back in the safety of Logan's truck, I finally relax. "Well, that went...well," I sigh.

Logan starts the truck but he doesn't start driving. He's staring at me like I have a third eye on my forehead.

His face is gorgeous and his eyes are piercing my soul, but the look he's giving me, *isn't* sexy. It's making me uncomfortable, "what are you looking at? Do I have something on my face?" I scrub at my face, trying to feel for something that shouldn't be there.

"You were looking in his eyes," he says in awe.

"Ummmm, yeah, that's a pretty normal thing to do when you're talking to someone."

"How were you able to do it?"

"I'm so confused. What do you mean?"

"Vampires can *hypnotize* you with their gaze. That's one thing that makes them so dangerous. And you straight up *lied* to him about the dragon scales. Amarah, if he finds out you lied..." he shakes his head, "I don't have to tell you how bad that would be."

I shift in my seat, "can we not talk about this here? I would feel more comfortable having this conversation where no one can overhear it."

Logan stays staring at me for a few more seconds then nods, "you're right." He puts the truck into drive and slowly pulls out of the valet lane.

Once we're safely away from the casino, and on our way to my house, I feel a bit more at ease. Still, nothing in my new life ever made me feel completely safe and at ease, but I guess I'll take what I can get.

I turn to Logan, "alright, so what do you mean Vampires can hypnotize you with their gaze?"

"Exactly what it sounds like. They can influence you to do things and feel things you normally wouldn't. The more powerful the Vampire the more powerful the effects. Valmont is the most powerful Vampire I've ever met, and yet, you looked in his eyes like they were normal. How?"

"I don't know. I didn't even know Vampires could do that. You would think I would be educated in this type of shit, especially when I'm going to confront the most powerful one."

"First, you're a Master of Fire and now you're immune to a Vampire's gaze, and you honestly want me to believe you don't know how or why?"

I don't know why, but according to Ana, I *can't* tell him. I can't tell anyone. I just have to deal with people looking at me like this. With suspicion. It's not that they're suspicious about my intent, they know they can trust me, but they don't understand *why* I can do the things I do, and I don't blame them. I would be suspicious if the tables were turned. It frustrates me that I have to deal with the suspicion, the looks of uncertainty, from everyone, the constant asked, and unasked questions.

I sigh and cross my arms with the frustration I feel, "Logan, you're the one who found me. I had no idea who I was or what any of this other world shit was. You've been there with me every step of the way. You know as much as I do, Hell, more than I do! I'm literally flying by the seat of my pants, figuring this all out as I go. I don't know why I can do the things I can, and who knows what else will happen in the future, but I don't know."

He keeps looking at me as if he's trying to decide if he believes me or not. I'm not sure he fully does believe me, but he decides to let this particular battle go. For now, at least.

"Why did you lie to him about the dragon scales? You don't know how many there are, but I'm betting there's more than you insinuated."

I sigh, "I convinced everyone to give up their power against the Vampires. The least I could do is limit the number of Vampires who have protection. It seemed like the right thing to do for our people."

"Yes, I agree. It's a smart move, but Amarah, you know how dangerous that lie is. If Valmont ever finds out…"

"He won't," I interrupt him. We look at each other and I can see the worry in his eyes. "He won't."

"I hope you're right," he turns his attention back to driving.

I hoped I'm right too. We drive the rest of the way to my house in silence and I welcome it. Sitting in the comfort of Logan's truck, the exhaustion starts to pull at me. Every piece of my body is tired. Hell, the hair on my head feels tired.

I'm relieved when we finally pull into my driveway, but I hesitate in getting out of the truck. There's a pink Jeep parked on the side of my driveway. Yup. A pink one. I've never been that girlie but some girls love it. It must belong to the girl who's been house and dog sitting.

"It feels like it's been forever since I left home."

"It's only been a month, Amarah. Not long at all."

"I know, but so much has happened in this past month. It definitely feels like longer. So much has changed. *I've* changed. What if it doesn't feel like home anymore?"

"Only one way to find out," he says plainly.

49

Three Little Words

My Drug by Anthony Mossburg

The driveway is lit up nice and bright with a motion sensor light that came on when we pulled up. The front door opens right as I'm reaching for the doorknob and I'm greeted with bubbly energy I'm not prepared for.

"Oh, my goodness! You must be, Amarah!"

This young girl throws her arms around me and gives me the biggest, tightest hug, as if she's known me forever and desperately missed me. She looks like she's late teens, maybe early 20's, and she's *tiny*, only about five-two, but her energy is ten feet tall.

"It is so nice to finally meet you!"

I'm awkwardly patting her back, "and you must be, Mariah."

She finally pulls away and is beaming at me, "yep, that's me!"

She's a ball of positive energy, I can feel it coming off of her in waves, and I recognize the energy signature as Müstik Fey. Her naturally curly blonde hair suites her. It's bouncy, just like she is. It's cut just above her shoulders and brings out the hints of gold in her brown eyes.

"It is nice to finally meet you too. I can't thank you enough for staying here and watching the house and Griffin while I've been gone."

"Oh, it was no problem at all! I've enjoyed it here and Griffin is soooo cute! He's been no trouble at all. He has missed you though. I've tried to keep him distracted but sometimes he just sits and stares at the door waiting for you. Breaks my heart!"

We're all still standing in the doorway. "Do you mind if we come in?" Her energy is contagious and I can't help but smile at her.

"Oh, my goodness! Yes, of course. I'm so sorry. I was just so excited to meet you."

"It's ok," I laugh as I step inside. "Griffin," I yell wondering where he is. He comes charging through the doggy door, runs straight for me, and I bend down to pick him up. He's barking and yelling at me in a high-pitched whine. His entire body is moving and jumping and I can barely hold him. I sit down on the floor so he can jump around safely.

"Oh, my sweet boy, Mama missed you too!" I'm home.

"Awe, look how happy he is. He's missed you so much," Mariah says sweetly.

"That makes two of us."

"Well, I'll just get my things and be on my way so you can relax."

"You're more than welcome to keep what you want here, in the guest room. I have a feeling you'll be house-sitting often. I mean, if you don't mind continuing to do it."

"Really? That's so sweet! I don't mind at all. I love your house and Griffin. Ok, I'll just get what I need for now and I'll remember to bring some extras over next time that can stay. Thank you so much for letting me do that."

This girl is as sweet as pie and I can't help but love her already. "It's the least I can do. I do appreciate all your help, more than you know," I smile at her.

"Oh, this is going to be perfect," she says as she disappears into the hallway.

"You seem happy after all," Logan says from where he still stands in the doorway. His arms are crossed and he's leaning against the door, watching me with a smile on his lips. We haven't made it very far inside.

"Yeah, it still feels like home. I'm happy to be back, and how can anyone not be happy around little miss sunshine," I laugh.

Logan laughs too, "she is a little ball of energy, that one. I'll go grab our bags and your weapons."

"Thank you. I'm tired and smell like sweat, dirt and...smoke." I smell my hair, "ugh, I'm gonna go take a shower."

I get up and head to my bedroom. I say my goodbyes to Mariah and get another massive bear hug in the process. Leaving my bedroom door cracked, so Griffin can go and come as he pleases, I grab some pajama shorts, a tank top, and add a bra to the pile. I don't like wearing bras when I'm home and trying to relax, but Logan is staying. I know, it makes no sense considering he's seen me in underwear, pretty much, but I just don't want to give the wrong impression. I told Andre nothing would happen, so I might as well take some steps to make that more likely to be true, even if deep down I know it's a lie. I take the pile of clothes with me into the bathroom and close the door.

I stand under the hot water letting it rinse away the past two days. I've just been in a battle with demons, hiked seven hours, argued with the Fey for an alliance with the Vampires, and met with the most powerful one to solidify it. To say I'm tired mentally and physically is an understatement. All I'm missing is being emotionally tired and I have a feeling that's about to happen. I do *not* want to get out of the shower. I do *not* want to face everything I've tried to bury when it comes to Logan.

It terrifies me.

I sigh and turn off the water. I towel off, then wrap my hair up, and get dressed. I put some lotion on, brush my teeth, and finally brush out my hair at the end. I stand there, leaning against the counter, and look at myself in the mirror. I've changed so much in the past month. I'm stronger, more in control of my power, and more confident. I still have a lot to learn, and I still recognize the lost look in my eyes, when it comes to love. I have no idea what I'm going to do, but I can't hide in the bathroom forever.

"Oh, Amarah, the mess you've gotten yourself into," I say to my reflection.

I walk out of the hallway and Logan is sitting on the couch with Griffin. He's wearing nothing but basketball shorts and my heart immediately starts to race. I can feel my resolve crumbling just by him sitting there, without a shirt on. Shit.

"How do you feel?" He asks carefully.

"I'm fine. I'll feel better once Aralyn is caught and this dragon scale business is done," I say as I walk into the kitchen. I grab a glass from the cabinet and pour myself some water. I take the glass and head to the couch to relax. Not sure if it's a great idea, but this is *my* house and I'm not going to let Logan being here make me uncomfortable.

The pull-out ottomans are pushed in, but the right side has a built-in chaise. I sit down on it, put my feet up, and try to relax, but it's hard to do with Logan shirtless three feet away from me. He has my attention. How can he not? The man fills up the entire couch, Hell, the entire room. The butterflies are back in my stomach and he hasn't even done or said anything. He's just…him.

"I know you're tired, but I've been wanting to talk to you. I've had a lot of time to think about this connection we have. I know I'm not great at talking about my feelings. I haven't had much practice. I've been alone for a long time, Amarah. This isn't easy for me," he admits, "but I'm willing to try if you'll let me."

Fuck me. I knew it. I knew this wasn't going to be easy and that he wouldn't leave it alone. "Logan, I don't know what you can say. Nothing is going to change the fact that we have this connection that neither of us can control. How you think you feel about me isn't real. You don't have a choice."

"That's where you're wrong. The connection only works when we're close, right? And even then, we can both block it, like you have been doing since you've been back, by the way. Even without the influence of the connection, I still *feel* the same way about you, Amarah."

"Logan…"

"No, let me finish. I've thought about you every second I've been away from you, ever since that first night. You're like a drug to me, Amarah, I *crave* you. I *need* you. And it's a feeling that comes from deep inside of me. The one thing in my life I have no control over, the one thing I can't, and don't want to, refuse. You. When I'm near you, it takes all of my control not to touch you. I want to be next to you, I want to feel you, I want to talk to you, learn everything about you, and laugh with you. I want to protect you. God, it sounds so silly when I say it out loud," he runs his hand through his hair, "I just want to be with you, connection or not."

"It's the same for me, but I'm sorry, I can't trust that it's real," I watch him. He's utterly serious and I can see the wheels spinning in his mind. He's determined to make his point and get me to understand.

"You say this connection we have is the issue. You say that we have no choice in how we feel because we're drawn to each other, but I disagree. The connection *is* real. It's our reality, and honestly, I think it's a benefit to have it compared to not having it."

"What do you mean?"

"Think about it. This connection we have allows us to *feel* each other's emotions and energy. We have the advantage of calling out the BS. You might be able to lie with words, but you can't fake your emotions. You get a front-row seat to my truest self, Amarah. How is that not a benefit?"

"I guess I've never thought about it that way before."

"We haven't even tried to learn how to use or control this connection we have. Who knows what possibilities there are with it. You say that it's not real, what's between me and you, but that's not true. I don't think it can get more real than this. Let go of your block, Amarah. Feel that I'm telling you the truth."

I hesitate, "I don't think taking it down is a good idea."

"Why?" He asks as he moves closer to me.

He's right in front of me and I want to reach out and touch his chest. I can't look at his body, so I look up into his eyes. That's a mistake too. His eyes are so intense. He's looking at me as if he's trying to memorizing every detail. My heart is racing and I'm having trouble breathing.

"I know how you're feeling, Amarah, because I feel the same way. This is *real*. You're blocking our connection and yet you're still feeling everything. No connection. Right now, we're just like anyone else in the world. How you feel about me is *real*, Amarah. How I feel about you is real. The connection only intensifies what's already there. Please, stop blocking me so you can *feel* the truth and not just listen to my words."

I'm staring at this gorgeous man, pouring his heart to me. To *me*! For me! And I feel frozen. I'm scared.

I'm scared to *feel* his emotions.

I'm scared for him to feel mine.

I'm scared that he's right, and this is real.

Because if it *is* real, and not forced by this connection, I'm doomed. Because I already feel more for Logan than I've ever felt for any other soul. Ever. What's going to happen if I acknowledge it and let myself fall?

I've always craved all-consuming love.

I've always feared all-consuming love.

How will I remain me? How will I stay true to myself if my feelings for Logan swallow me whole? What if I let them?

Logan reaches out and gently touches my cheek, "Amarah, please, trust me."

Just like that, one-touch and my willpower fails. The protection walls around my heart come crashing down. I'm flooded with such intense emotion it takes my breath away. I have to catch my breath and focus on what I'm feeling. I can feel Logan's attraction to me. I know he wants to touch me, kiss me, be next to me. There's so much emotion to sift through. It's coming at me all at once and I can't concentrate.

I finally look at him, "I know you're attracted to me, I can feel it, but I also feel your hesitation. Why?"

"I'm afraid you've made up your mind about us. You've run away from me once and I'm afraid you'll turn away from me forever. I'm afraid of jumping and falling. And crashing. I'm afraid of how I feel. I'm afraid of how *you* make me feel, Amarah."

"How do I make you feel?" I ask breathlessly.

He leans in even closer to me and I can't help but look at his lips, wanting to fall into them.

"You can feel it, can't you? That's more real than any words will ever be. Must I say it?"

"Yes," I whisper against his lips.

He pulls back so he can look me in the eyes. He holds my face softly in his hands. His eyes dart back and forth between mine, "I love you, Amarah."

My heart sinks like an anchor in my chest. Anchoring me to this moment, to his words, to him. The butterflies in my stomach flutter uncontrollably. I can feel the truth of his words through the connection.

He loves me.

Holy shit.

Logan loves me!

And it's *real*. Lord, help me, but I know it's real. Those three words hit me hard and obliterated all of my defenses.

No more walls.
No more lies.
No more pretending.
No more hiding.

Done Fighting

I Want It All by Kat & Alex

I'm in shock at the reality of it all. I'm just sitting here, on the couch, next to this perfect man, and I know I can't run from it anymore. I can't run from him.

"Amarah, say something, please."

"I'm done running," I say with sudden realization. I let go of the uncertainty and fear and immediately feel free and alive.

"What does that mean exactly?"

I pull my legs under me and sit up on my knees, completely facing Logan. I grab his face with both hands and looked into the beautiful green eyes. I put all of my emotion, all of my truth into our connection and hope he feels it all. He takes a deep shaky breath and I know he feels it. He understands it.

"I love you too," I whisper.

He smiles a big, genuine Logan smile and my body melts, like it does every time. He leans in and kisses me. It isn't the reckless passion we had before. It's soft and gentle, full of *love*, causing my heart to pound in my chest. He pulls me towards him and I throw one leg over him, so I'm straddling his lap, his strong arms hugging me close to him, as if he'll never let me go.

He pulls away from my lips and starts kissing down my neck. It sends chills down my body and I shiver under his touch. I feel his strong hands slip under my shirt, and the second his hand touches my sensitive skin, the power is there. It's hot and feels like my skin will burn with it, but it isn't painful, just intense. We both cry out from the sensation of it and then Logan lets out his cool breeze.

Hot and cold.

Yin and Yang.

We balance each other perfectly.

Logan slowly moves his hands upward bringing my shirt with them. There's no hesitation. I put my arms up above my head and he pulls my shirt off and throws it aside. He leans in and kisses me again but this time it's more forceful. More passion. More need. His hands trail the line of my bra on my back but he hesitates.

He pulls back so he can see me, "are you sure?"

I put my hands on his chest and I can feel his heart pounding. Is he still scared I'm going to say no and run away?

"I've never been more sure about anything," I say looking into his eyes.

He keeps intense eye contact as he unhooks my bra and gently traces his fingertips up my back, to my shoulders. His hands are rough and the calluses gently scratch against my skin. I close my eyes and shiver again. He slips the straps down and gravity does the rest. I throw it off to the side somewhere along with my shirt.

He hugs me close to him and all of a sudden stands up. I'm not ready for it and let out a little yip of surprise, and we both laugh. He's carrying me to my bedroom and I turn on the light as we pass the switch. There's no way I'm not watching every second I'm with this perfect man. He puts a knee on the bed, leans down, and gently lays me down. It's effortless and his immense strength turns me on even more. He's half kneeling and half standing in front of me. I raise up on my elbows and just soak it all in.

"God, you're beautiful," he says as he takes in every inch of my body.

"I was just about to say the same thing about you. You're perfect."

He smiles that same confident smile he had before. His confidence is back in full force now. He knows *exactly* how he affects me. Not that I can hide it with our connection. He crawls on the bed, wraps a strong arm under me and lifts me further onto the bed. I wrap my legs around his waist and pull him down to kiss me. His body is huge and covers mine easily. I feel so small next to him. Next to so much strength. His power pushes through the kiss and I feel like he's caressing me inside. Touching places no one can ever touch.

I moan into his mouth and he pushes his hips against me and I feel his erection. He's hard and ready and I'm already slick with desire just from kissing him. He breaks the kiss and trails small kisses down my neck. My heart is racing as I watch him work his way lower. He keeps eye contact and the heat in his eyes is just as intense to see as it is to feel his lips gently hovering over my breast. He finally takes it in his mouth and cups the other one with his hand. The power caressing me, the sensation of his warm mouth on me, it's almost too much. It makes me close my eyes, arch my back, and moan with the pleasure of it all.

All of a sudden, he bites down and I hiss with the instant pinch of pain, but it's gone quickly, swallowed up by the pleasure. He continues kissing lower until he reached my shorts. He trails his tongue along the top of them.

I giggle, "that tickles!"

He looks up at me and smiles as his fingers slipped inside the top of the shorts and he gently pulls them down. The giggling stops immediately and I lift myself, so the shorts can slide off, and he tosses them on the floor. I bite my bottom lip as I watch him lower his head down towards me.

I feel his cool breeze caressing my skin and meeting my power inside my chest. I know that isn't exactly possible but I feel it stirring inside my body. It' like he's touching me on the inside while he's physically touching me on the outside. I close my eyes and focus on what he's doing.

His hands are holding my hips tightly and his lips are trailing soft kisses up my inner thigh. I feel the warmth of his mouth moment before I felt the first lick of his tongue.

"Oh, God," I moan.

The warmth of his mouth on me and the slippery softness of his tongue sliding over my clit, back and forth, back and forth, is building up what feels like a tornado inside me. I look down and his hair falls over his forehead, almost in his eyes, but not quite. His eyes lock with mine and I see the possession in them. He reaches one hand out towards my mouth and I suck in his finger. He growls deep in his chest and it makes me even more slick, I moan as I let my head fall back on the bed.

He flicks my clit with the tip of his tongue making my body jerk involuntarily with the pleasure before he flattens his tongue and caresses it in slow, steady circles. Then he pushes in the finger I just sucked and that tornado starts building, building, building and I feel like I'm going to be blown away.

I reach down and grab a hold of his hair. "Don't stop," I manage to get out between heavy breaths. I'm moving my hips in motion to match as his finger slides in and out of me, all the while his tongue never leaves my clit.

Then it feels like the tornado lands inside of me and the power comes rushing out of me. My body jerks with the intensity of the orgasm and I scream Logan's name as I cum on his finger and tongue. The after-shocks seem to last forever, wave after wave, and I can't help but squeeze my thighs together, suffocating Logan between my legs. He doesn't stop and never falters. When the last intense wave finally passes, I let my legs fall open, my body is left languid and weak. I open my eyes to see Logan above me. He leans down and kisses me, I can taste myself on his lips, and it calls to something deep inside of me. My scent on him. I'm claiming him as mine, and his kiss is bringing me back to life.

I break the kiss, breathless, "holy shit! That was amazing, but now it's my turn," I smile as I push my hands against his chest.

There's no way I can move him if he didn't want me to, but he concedes. He lays down on his back and it's my turn to grab a hold of his shorts and pull them off. He helps me and I gasp once I finally see him. I knew he'd be big from what I felt before but he's bigger than I expected. His cock lays thick and hard against his stomach, up to his belly button.

I pull my hair up but then Logan reaches out to hold it up. I want to watch him as I take him in my mouth for the first time. I hold his gaze as I grab him in my hands first. He's so big, both of my hands can't cover him. And he's heavy. Jesus, if I wasn't soaked already, I would be now.

I lower my mouth and lick around the tip, tasting the pre-cum that leaked out. He twitches and lets out a hiss, then I let mouth fall on the velvety softness of him. I start stroking him up and down in time with my mouth, gathering saliva and working it all the way down to the base of him so my hands can glide smoothly as I squeeze and suck him. He watches me for a minute and then closes his eyes, moaning to the ceiling. I explore every inch of him, balls and all, as I send my power out to caress his body too. He groans and I swear it's the sexiest thing I've ever heard. I echo it and moan with my mouth around him.

His hand tightens in my hair as his body tenses underneath me. He lifts my head, "Amarah, stop. No more, please. I want you. All of you."

I sit back on my heels and stare at him. He's perfect, from head to toe. I can't believe this gorgeous man is in *my* bed. This gorgeous man that I can't resist. The gorgeous man that I'm in love with, and he's in love with me.

I crawl towards him and kiss my way up his stomach and chest. Something I've been dying to do since I saw him in the towel a month ago. I reach his soft lips and slowly licked across the bottom lip and then kisses him long and deep. I'm straddling him and I rub my clit along his hard erection, up and down, I can feel him getting slick with how wet I am. The feeling of him against me and his tongue on my tongue…God, I can kiss him for the rest of my life, but I want more. I want to feel him inside of me for real, not just the power.

"Do you have a condom?" I ask?

"Do we need one?"

"I'm on the pill, and I'm clean but..."

"I'm a Werewolf, Amarah, we can't get any kind of human disease, and neither can the Fey by the way."

"Well, ok then."

I reach back and positioned him at my opening. I'm looking in his eyes and I see the raw need. Men are physical and sexual beings, but I also see the emotional need. I can feel it too, deep in my bones. This is going to be healing for both of us, but he holds me still, right above him. Not letting me sink onto him.

"I want you to be *mine*, Amarah. Mine in every way. No one else's."

"I've always been yours, Logan. From the first time I laid eyes on you, you had me completely. I'm yours."

He eases up on his grip and I slowly lower myself onto him. He's huge and I'm forced to take him slowly, inch by glorious inch, letting my body open up to him.

"Fuck, you're so tight and wet," he girts out.

Just working myself on to him is building up another orgasm. When I finally take it all, it feels like he fills up every inch inside of me.

I start to slide off him and back down the length of him, "Oh my God," I throw my head back, close my eyes, and just moved my body on top of him. His big hands move to grip my ass and he starts controlling the movement with his hips, driving up into me.

"Fuccckkk...." Logan says through gritted teeth.

He slides his length almost all the way out before pumping into me in long, hard strokes. I can feel another orgasm approaching rapidly.

"Logan, you're going to make me cum again," I manage to warn him right before I explode around him. I can feel myself pulsing and coating him as he drives into me, ruthlessly, drawing out the orgasm. My legs are shaking and cry out as I fall onto his chest.

He flips me over and I'm laying on my stomach, sideways across the bed. He lifts my hips up, ass in the air, chest still on the bed, as he kneels behind me.

"I want you to watch, Amarah," Logan gestures to the floor to ceiling mirror doors on my closet. I roll my eyes up and watch him through the mirror as he positions himself to enter me.

"I want you to watch us, as I claim you. I want you to see how beautiful you are when I make you cum and you come undone."

I watch as he slowly pushes his massive cock inside of me. His body is huge behind me. His chest and stomach muscles are glistening with a sheen of sweat. The veins on his forearms are popped out even more, pumping blood faster through his body as he hangs on tightly to me and pumps into me.

"Oh, my God," is all I can manage to say.

He's gorgeous and I swear I'll cum just having him sheathed inside of me, stretching me and filling me up so completely, and seeing his sexy body behind me. But he's moving in and out of me at a steady pace, hitting that sensitive spot inside of me, over and over, building me up again.

"Don't close your eyes," Logan commands.

I'm struggling to keep them open and not get lost in the pleasure that's threatening to break me. The orgasm erupts from deep inside of me and my eyes flutter but I manage to keep them open, and I'm glad I do, because I get to watch Logan follow me over the edge.

He's moaning and cussing, his rhythm speeds up and I feel him get even harder right before he slams himself into me, as far as he can go. His grip is bruising on my hips, his eyes are lost to the pleasure, mouth slack as I feel him pulse and empty himself inside of me.

He slides out of me and collapses on his side next to me. His chest is heaving, breaths coming fast. He moves my hair out of my eyes and leans in for a kiss, just a press of his lips on mine, but it fills my heart up with everything I feel form the simple gesture.

"You're so beautiful, Amarah. It felt like I was struck with lightning the first time I ever saw you. On that rooftop bar, the breeze blowing your hair around you, your eyes were closed and you looked like an Angel."

I gasp at his mention of the word, *Angel*.

He smiles that cocky smile, "I told you so."

"Told me so, what?" I ask, confused.

"You were always mine. From the moment I saw you. Now, I think you finally believe it too."

He wraps his arms around m and pulls me in close to his chest. I breathe him in, sex, sweat and a sunny summer, rainy day. My body feels like liquid, relaxed and utterly spent and drained. This is the start of something powerful, Logan and I. I can feel it deep in my soul. A flicker of fear tries to rise up but I silence it.

I focus on Logan's arms around me, his large, solid body next to me, his scent all around me, completely engulfing me, and for right now, in this moment, I let myself fall.

Will I fly?

Will I fall?

I guess I'll find out in the morning.

Better Than Any Dream

Safe by Katie Armiger

I wake up to Logan's big body laying behind me, hugging me close to his chest. Last night's memories come flooding back and I can't help but smile. I close my eyes and focus on how Logan's body feels against mine. I fit into his arms perfectly, as if he was made just for me. I had dreamed of what it would be like to wake up next to him too many times to count, but none of the dreams even came close to how perfect and wonderful it feels.

I feel his chest rising and falling against my back, his breathing is deep and heavy, and I can feel the steady thump of his heart. His strong arm is wrapped around me, and even though he's completely relaxed with sleep, he still manages to hold me tightly. I think this is Heaven. I sigh in contentment.

Logan must sense my slight movements and is pulled from his sleep. "Mmmm, good morning, beautiful," he says as he snuggles the back of my neck.

I giggle, "good morning indeed. I could wake up like this every day for the rest of my life. Are you sure I'm awake and not just dreaming?"

"It feels too real to be a dream," he pushes his hips towards me.

I felt his erection growing between us and it makes me catch my breath.

It's pitch black in my room, thanks to the blackout curtains, so I can't see him, but damn…I *feel* him. I feel every inch of his massive body lying next to me. It wakes up the butterflies in my stomach and my heart picks up its pace, wide awake.

"What do you say we take this good morning and make it fucking amazing?" I ask as I position myself where he can enter me.

"You're reading my mind," he whispers, his voice husky with sleep and desire.

I feel his fingers slip between my legs, but no foreplay is needed. I'm ready for him. I'll always be ready for him.

"Damn, you're already wet," his voice rumbles through his chest in a slight growl.

He positions himself to enter me but stops. "Amarah?"

"Yes?" I manage to breathe out.

"You're mine, and only mine," he slowly starts to push his way inside of me.

He claims me with his words and then claims me with his body. I gasp with the feeling of how big he is and can't help but groan out loud with pleasure. No dream would ever compare to the real thing, it's better than I ever imagined, and I never want to fall asleep and dream again.

His hand grips my hip and covers half of my stomach too. I love how small he makes me feel. He holds me tightly as he pumps his hips behind me. He slides almost all the way out, just the tip inside of me, before he pushes again, filling me all the way up. Again, and again with these massive, long strokes. His hand moves from my hip and snakes around my waist and grabs my breast. He pulls me against his hard chest and holds me tightly against him as his rhythm starts to increase.

I reach my arm back and grab as much of his leg as I can, pulling him into me. Our breathing is heavy, I moan with every push as he enters my body. With every stroke he brings me closer and closer to the edge.

"Damn, you feel so good," I breathe. "I'm close."

"Cum for me, Amarah."

Hearing him say those words, with my name on his lips, sends a bolt of lightning straight between my legs.

"Oh, God...Logan..." I groan. A growl sounds deep in his chest and reverberates through my back, he kisses my shoulder and sends chills down my spine just as my body releases its pleasure around him.

His rhythm changes again, as he pumps shorter, faster and harder strokes into me, and lets out a groan as he meets his release right after mine.

We're wrapped up in each other, tangled limbs, and out of breath. Normally, I would have died to know what someone was feeling in a moment like this, but with Logan, I don't have to wonder. I can feel all of his emotions. Pride, of course, and pleasure, but I can also feel the contentment. He's happy. Genuinely happy, and overshadowing all of that, is love. I still can't believe Logan loves me! I hope I never lose this feeling.

He rolls onto his back and brings me with him, my head is resting on his shoulder, and I snuggle into his neck. I love the way he smells. Just him. Just Logan. His natural scent is both intoxicating and comforting. He feels like home to me. My hand is on his chest and I close my eyes, concentrating on his heartbeat, slowly going back to normal, and the rise and fall of his chest as his breathing slows too. His every sound and every word are my new favorite song, and I want to play it over and over and over, again. He's gently caressing my arm with his left hand and holding me tight against him with his right.

I can feel his muscles, his strength, in such a small action. I feel small and weak next to all his strength. When I stop to think about what Logan is, because it's easy to forget he's not human, it's a little terrifying. He's a powerful and dangerous Werewolf, and maybe I should feel scared, but I feel utterly relaxed and completely safe wrapped up in his arms. Like nothing bad will ever affect me again, as long as I'm right here, in his arms.

"Logan…" I break the silence.

"What is it?" He asks calmly, but I feel a slight hesitation through our link, as if he's still unsure of us, of me choosing him. I don't want him to be, but I had run away from him so many times, I can't blame him. But I will do everything in my power to reassure him that this is what I want.

He is what I want.

"Can I play you a song? Remember when we talked about songs being able to say things better than we can?"

I feel him nod.

"Well, there's one I'd like to play for you now. To say how I'm feeling."

"Ok," he kisses my forehead and I reach over to the night stand for my phone. I find the song on YouTube, hit play, and snuggle back into my spot against his neck.

Safe by Katie Armiger starts playing. Logan is aimlessly running his fingertips over my skin as we both listen to the lyrics.

"This how you feel?"

I answer by softly singing the chorus. "Can't you feel what I'm feeling, right now?"

"Yes."

"You do, you know... make me feel safe," I whisper against his neck.

I feel him release a small sigh of relief. He kisses my forehead and hugs me tighter to him, "you *are* safe with me, Amarah. I will never let anything or anyone hurt you."

Logan's phone rings on the nightstand next to the bed and we both grumble at the disruption.

"Let it ring," Logan says as he holds on to me.

"What if it's something important? Something about Aralyn."

He sighs, "you're right." I let him up so he could lean over and get his phone.

"Hello," he grumbles into the phone.

He sits up higher, giving more attention and focus to whoever is on the other side of the call, and I feel his energy change. I hate that I can only hear one side of the conversation. I get up and open the curtain on my side of the room so I can see him. I sit back down and pull the blankets around me.

"Yes. Ok. We'll be there as soon as we can," he hangs up.

"What's wrong? I can feel your tension."

"That was the Queen. She said there's an update with Aralyn and she wants to see us in person."

"Something she didn't want to say over the phone. That can't be good, right?"

"Only one way to find out."

We're showered, separately, and dressed in record time. Although I wanted to shower with Logan for the first time, I know that it would distract us and delay us. So, it's something to explore another day. Something to look forward to.

I'm in the bathroom finishing blow-drying my hair and putting a little makeup on. Logan comes in with two cups of coffee in his hands.

"Here you go," he places a cup on the counter.

He's wearing a pair of blue jeans, a v-neck forest green t-shirt that hugs his arms and chest just right. It's a great color on him and brings out the darker green in his eyes. His hair is still slightly wet from his shower, the weight of the water pulling his hair down a bit in the way of his right eye. I know once it's dry and the slight curl kicks in, it will fall perfectly right above his eyebrow.

I reach up and gently pushed his hair to the side and out of his eye. I still can't believe this is all real. I still can't believe that this gorgeous man is in love with me. The thought is like a broken record in my mind but I can't help. It all seems too good to be true and I'm waiting for the other shoe to drop.

No, Amarah. Get those negative thoughts out of your head!

"What's wrong?" Logan asks.

I shake my head, "nothing. Absolutely nothing." I smile, "thank you for the coffee." I grab it and take a sip, "Oooo, that's sweet! Did you add creamer and sugar?"

"Yeah," he rubs the back of his neck, I feel his insecurity through our connection, "I wasn't sure how you liked it."

"Normally, just creamer. I try to stay away from the added sugar."

Ok, so he doesn't know how I like my coffee, that doesn't make him any less perfect. Hell, I don't know how he likes his coffee either. We don't know much about each other, but this is exactly how new relationships start, you learn little things every single day, as you go. I'm looking forward to getting closer to Logan and learning everything there is to know about him and vice versa.

"I should have asked, I'm sorry. I'll get you another cup," he reaches for my cup.

"I pull away, "no, no! It's delicious! I'm just not used to it. I'm going to enjoy the extra sugar. Besides, I think I burnt enough calories in the past seven hours or so," I say as I bite my lip and thoroughly check him out.

He laughs and ducks his head as if he's a little embarrassed. I've never really seen Logan embarrassed except one time when he blushed. "I told you, I can't completely control myself when I'm around you, Amarah."

"I love when you say my name, and who says I'm complaining? It was fucking mind-blowing and I wish we could stay in bed all day today."

He smiles, eyes sparkling, and I melt all over again. "That makes two of us, but duty calls. Speaking of, are you almost ready? We need to get going."

I sit my coffee cup down on the counter. "Well, if you continue to stand here looking scrumptious, we won't make it out of this bedroom."

I run my hands up his chest, tip-toe, and tilt my head, inviting a kiss. He leans his head down and obliges without a second of hesitation. It was meant to be a quick kiss, but he steps into the bathroom, backing me up. I hear his coffee cup clink on the counter as he set it down, and then he's gently lifting me to sit on the counter too. I wrap my legs around him, hands in his hair. His tongue is searching for mine. I tilt my head more so I can open up to him and make the kiss deeper. I didn't mean to moan but Logan echoes it.

Logan is the one who finally pulls himself together and breaks the kiss. "Damn, this is going to be difficult."

"What's going to be difficult?" I ask, breathlessly.

"Keeping my hands off you when all I want to do is touch and explore every inch of your body until I know you better than I know myself. Staying in control and staying alert. I told you, I lose all control with you. This could be dangerous for us, Amarah."

"I know," I agree. "But we're safe in my house right now. We'll both be more careful when we're out, deal?"

He nods his head and gives me a half-smile, "deal. Now hurry up and finish getting ready so we can leave." His says hurry, but he doesn't move a muscle. He's still standing in front of me even though I'm no longer holding him captive with my legs. He's looking at me like he wants to start that exploring right this second.

"Ummmm, I'm gonna need to get down so I can finish getting ready, and if you keep looking at me like that, we're *never* leaving this bathroom," I laugh.

"Ok, ok," he steps back and grabs his coffee as he heads out the door. I watch him walk out with the biggest smile on my face, damn, it's a good view coming *and* going. I hop off the counter and finish getting ready.

Arriving at Headquarters, we find parking easily. It's early, and only employees are here, getting ready for the day, or the early bird customer grabbing breakfast. I have déjà vu as we walk into the church, but this time there's zero leather. I'm wearing jean shorts, a green, *talk to me goose*, tank top, and tennis shoes. I look over at Logan and laugh.

"What are you thinking that's so funny," Logan watches me with a smile on his face. Energy is contagious and we're both beaming. I think it's blatantly obvious what we've been up to.

I shake my head, "I just realized we're matching and we didn't even plan it."

"Oh yeah. Look at that," he laughs, stops walking, and pulls me close to him. "I know we haven't had a chance to talk about last night..." he smirks, "*and* this morning, but I want you to know that it meant something to me. *This*, you and me, means something to me. I know how impossible it is to find this type of connection with someone. I know how rare it is to truly love and care about someone. I'm not going to take this or you for granted, Amarah. I'm in this a hundred percent."

I place my hand on his chest, over his heart, "I know. I can feel what you feel, remember? Still, thank you for being vulnerable and talking about it. Thank you for *telling* me how you feel. It means a lot to me too and I'm looking forward to every second I get to spend with you."

He leans down to kiss me and I tip-toe to meet him for it. This time, it is a quick kiss, but still makes my stomach do somersaults in the best possible way.

"C'mon, we better hurry," he leads the rest of the way, never letting go of my hand.

We're officially holding hands! In public! It makes me stupid giddy and I'm grinning like a damn idiot, but I can't help it.

Oh fuck.

I just remembered Andre is still here.

Fuck, fuck, fuck!

The fact that I have been so completely consumed by being with Logan and hadn't even *thought* of Andre, makes me realize, I made the right choice. I *do* care for Andre, and I don't want to hurt him, but I don't love him like I love Logan. There's no comparison and never has been. I had only been distracting myself. I had only been fooling myself in thinking there was anyone else in the universe that could compare to Logan. Still, I don't want to see him hurt.

I stop Logan just outside of the final door into the throne room. "Ummmm, there's something I need to tell you before we go in."

"What is it?"

"Ummmm, well, after we had our last talk and you came back here to be with the Queen, I was *really* upset. I got closer to Andre, and I've come to care for him." I try to down-play it and then feel guilty about that too.

I can't lie to Logan. What kind of relationship starts based on lies? And I don't want to take what I feel about Andre away either.

"What exactly do you mean by *close?* Did you sleep with him?" His voice s steady and calm, but I can see the fire in his eyes, I can feel the anger blazing through our connection. He's trying to fight it, but I feel it.

"No! I didn't sleep with him, but we did kiss...and after the attack, when I thought I could have lost everything and everyone, we did come close, but I promise we didn't cross that line. We didn't cross any line other than kissing."

"Do you love him?" His jaw clenches as he waits for my answer.

"I do care about him. I know you don't see him the way that I do, but he's not just the jokester everyone sees. He's different around me. He's been hurt and I really don't want to hurt him again."

"We've all been hurt, Amarah. You didn't answer the question. Do you love him?" I can feel his Wolf stirring now. Maybe he's angrier than I thought. Shit.

I think about it long and hard before I answer him. Do I love Andre? Or did I use him for comfort in my time of need? Am I that selfish? I don't want to answer, because then the truth of the situation and *myself*, will be real.

I meet Logan's fierce green gaze, "no, I don't love him. You have *all* of my heart, all of *me*. I don't want anyone else. I just want you, all of you, every day, for the rest of my life, and that scares me a bit if I'm being honest. I think part of why I got close to Andre is because I'm scared of how I feel about you. We don't even *know* each other and I'm completely head over heels for you. I love you, Logan." I send all of my truth down the connection and hope he feels it.

He sighs, "good." He moves the hair from my face, pacing it behind my ears, and then holds my face in his hands, "because I love you too and I *won't* share you. You. Are. Mine. Amarah."

His words should scare me.

The possessiveness.

The control.

But I like that he's claiming me. I feel it too. He's mine, no one else's and I'll be damned if I let anyone else touch him.

"Ditto," I agree.

"Well, then, let's make it clear to everyone then, shall we?"

He pushes the door open, grabs my hand, and we walk through the door.

Together.

52

What's Next

Rise Up by Andra Day

We approach the table and the Queen, Princess Hallana, Prince Vadin, Prince Emrick, and Ethan, are all in attendance. I'm shocked and confused to see Emerson also sitting at the table. Isn't he a Vampire? How is he out in the daytime? I don't want to ask and risk looking naive and vulnerable in front of him and the others, so I sit down and listen, and hopefully I'll gain some answers. If I don't, then I'll ask later.

Logan and I sit down next to each other, he pulls his chair closer to mine, and he put his arm around me. Ok, I guess we're doing this. All in. I'm not the only one who doesn't keep the shock off my face. Everyone notices Logan and I are...*together, together*. Some eyebrows raise, a small smirk here and there, but no one says a word about it.

Someone clears their throat trying to hide a chuckle. I'm relieved when the Queen starts talking.

"Thank you all for getting here so quickly. We have some updates on our traitor situation," the Queen say firmly. The atmosphere immediately changes. Logan and me no longer important as everyone's focus is intently on the Queen.

"I want to take this time to thank you, Emerson, personally, for joining the others on their mission so quickly last night. I'm happy to be in alliance with Valmont and the Vampires."

Emerson nods his head to the Queen, "as are we, Queen Anaxo."

"As you know, Vadin, Emrick, Ethan, and Emerson travelled to the Air Fey's home last night. Unfortunately, Aralyn was gone. She's disappeared, along with the handful of Fey that were helping her."

"What?!" Hallana and I echo each other, but it's Hallana who stands up angrily, "you have got to be fucking kidding me!"

I'm used to Hallana's reactions now. I would have been a bit scared and intimidated before, but I know now that's just who she is. Considering her people have been attacked because of Aralyn's betrayal, I don't blame her for being pissed that she's gone.

"No, this isn't right. She *has* to pay for what she's done! She can't just get away with it!" Hallana is close to bursting into flames, I can feel her energy crackling around her.

"I agree," I say. "Where could she have gone? We have to find her. Until we find her, no one is safe."

"I don't know where she could have gone, but we will continue searching for her. We will find her and she *will pay*, but yes, you're right, Amarah. No one is safe while she's out there with her followers, no matter how few, she has nothing to lose now. She knows that we know what she's done. She'll be more dangerous than ever."

Hallana is pacing now, but everyone else at the table is silent. We're all going over the thoughts and possibilities of what this means. Aralyn betrayed her own people, she had ambitions to become the Queen, she had led an attack that *killed* Fey. What else is she capable of? I don't want to find out. We have to find her sooner than later.

"Unfortunately, that's all the news I have for now. Everyone is to keep their ears to the streets and eyes everywhere. Any rumors or whispers you hear come directly to me, and be on guard. No one is safe, understood?"

Nods and agreement all around.

"Gentleman, I need to speak with Princess Hallana and Amarah alone. Would you please excuse us? Logan, you can stay as well."

Once everyone files out of the throne room, the Queen continues, "there's one more thing. Caleb also told us that Aralyn knew about the dragon scales. Chances are, more of her followers know too. I think it was a smart move to be truthful and make the alliance with Valmont. I think with that many people knowing, he would have gone searching on his own."

"About that," I clear my throat. "I may have told a tiny, little white lie to Valmont. I told him the dragon scales were limited and that he was only going to be able to protect some of his people, not all. So, Hallana, when you get back, move most of your scales to another location. Keep them hidden and keep them protected. Tell only who you must and who you absolutely trust."

Hallana looks at me with such relief and gratitude in her eyes, "Amarah, I don't know what to say. That was extremely dangerous to lie to him. If he finds out there are more than enough, he'll probably kill you."

"Yes, I know, but he won't find out unless someone tells him. That's why you need to be careful when you move them. It needs to be kept a secret. I know it is your Family's legacy, but you need to keep this quiet, even the Fire Fey must believe there's only a limited supply and that it's all going to the Vampires."

"I thought for sure we were screwed giving the Vampires our only advantage against them. This is the best possible outcome. Thank you, Amarah."

"It's the least I could do."

"I still don't know how Aralyn even knew about them in the first place. Only the Fire Fey know of their existence."

"I can help with that," the Queen sighs. "I'm afraid that it is one of your own who let the information slip to Aralyn. Caleb said that Aralyn often met discretely with several others. He was jealous, so he often spied on them, without their knowledge. He said Aralyn was sleeping with, and using, several Fey from the Fey families. It would appear that she has been at this for a while now. She just used the meeting and Amarah as the last straw. One of the men she was sleeping with and using was Andre. Hallana, I'm so sorry. I know he's one of your Leaders."

"That motherfucker!" She slams her fists on the table. They're covered in flames, "where is he?"

"In the dungeon," the Queen says, softly.

Hallana doesn't wait for anything else. She storms off so fast her hair is flying behind her. One of her very own, closest to her, betrayed her too. This is not a good time for the Fire Fey. They've been through so much. I don't envy what's coming to Andre shortly. I want to confront him too. To make him tell me why he did it, to my face, but this is Hallana's fight more than mine.

I sink back in my chair. I can't believe it. I didn't see Andre being a traitor to his people. Is he working with Aralyn? Had he fooled me that completely? Had he played me this whole time? What was his end goal? Was he trying to get close to me and find out everything I knew? Was he supposed to get close to me and then kill me? Or bring me to Aralyn? Looks like I made the right choice in men after all. Perhaps the connection with Logan is a benefit after all. He can never hide his true intentions from me. I'm thankful for that now more than ever.

Am I ever going to get off the rollercoaster that is now my life? I was literally on cloud nine mere hours ago. I have everything I've ever wanted.

I got the guy.

He chose me.

He loves me.

I allied the Fey and the Vampires for the first time in *history*.

I'm a Master of Fire.

I'm immune to a Vampire's gaze and who knows what else.

Yet, I couldn't see betrayal literally staring me in the face.

Andre betrayed Hallana, his people, and *me*. He played us all. Am I that bad at judging people? How can I help the Fey, or anyone, if I let the traitor almost seduce me? Aralyn has disappeared with her followers. She's out there, plotting her next move. I'll have to live my life looking over my shoulder, constantly questioning everything and everyone around me. I need to solidify the alliance with Valmont and find a Witch to help us.

Hell, I still have my human life I need to tend to. What am I going to tell everyone in my life about who I really am? Ok, so, there's a lot I don't know.

What I do know though, is that what comes next is *my* choice, and I'm not alone. I look across the table to the Queen, my aunt, and at Logan, a Werewolf with a Fey life-force. I'm not alone.

I've been awakened to my *true self*, and I know this is my purpose in life.

I am Amarah Rey Andrews, half Angel, Võitleja of the Fey, Master of Fire.

This is my destiny and I will rise to the challenge.

AUTHOR'S NOTE

This is my first author note, and honestly, I don't even know where to begin. I guess I want to first remind you to please (insert praying hands emoji here) don't forget to leave your review for Awaken. Any and all social media platforms are appreciated, Instagram, Goodreads, Facebook, YouTube, TikTok, but most importantly, Amazon! Amazon reviews are one of the most supportive things you can do for us Indie authors. So, thank you in advance for taking the time to leave your thoughts!

Now, where to start with Awaken. I suppose starting at the beginning is always a good idea. I wrote Awaken in four months. And when I say I had no idea what I was doing I'm not lying! The writing in my first edition was…beginner status to say the least! I also could not afford an editor and did all of the designing myself. The layout, the formatting, the cover…everything. And let me tell you, it is NOT easy! I've taken no classes on writing, and honestly, I don't have a desire to. Writing has absolutely become a passion and I feel like I've finally found what truly makes me happy! However, I don't ever want this to feel like a chore. I don't ever want it to feel like work. So, for now at least, I am going to continue to do it my way. For me. What does that mean for you, the reader? Well, a more raw and unpolished book.

Awaken has been rewritten and updated a year later. The third edition is the rewritten edition and I added about nineteen thousand new words and changed a lot withing the writing. I hope that everyone who has been with me from the start can see the amazing progress I see! And for those of you new to me and Amarah, I hope that you enjoy what you've experienced and I hope that you'll be around to see the next milestone of growth.

As far as production today, I still do everything for myself for the most part, with the tech help of my wonderful husband. I have also been paying for character art and the character art on the covers is NOT mine, however, all the other designing and fitting is all me. So, I ask you to please keep that in mind when reading and reviewing. Not all of us have the means to pay professionals.

Now, back to Awaken! Awaken is my COVID baby. Like so many others, I struggled during this time, and Awaken became my outlet. I started writing it on the notes app in my phone, on my lunch break at work. I was in a miserable job, that drained me and I absolutely HATED having to get up everyday and go to. It got me thinking, is this is? Is this life? There's got to be more, right? Well, ladies and gentleman, the MORE became the Amarah Rey, Fey Warrior Series!

Needless to say, there is a lot of me in Amarah and a lot of my life in Awaken. At least in the beginning. Once the story started progressing, Amarah quickly became her own character and in charge of her own life! As all my characters are.

I know I'm not the only that wishes, so desperately, that there was a hidden magical world out there! I know I'm not the only one that wishes *I* was a part of that magical world. So, one of my goals was to make Amarah real and relatable. I want anyone who reads this book, to feel like they can be Amarah. That they can escape into this magical world with her. I also didn't want to make Amarah perfect. She struggles, she makes mistakes, sometimes she's immature and petty, because aren't we all at times? But she's good, she works hard and she's determined to do what's right, even when it's hard.

Another goal I had when writing this book, was to showcase strong, powerful women who support each other. Hence, why I have a Queen and a woman Warrior. Unfortunately, we live in the real world where this isn't always the case. In fact, more often than not, it's the opposite. I wish so badly for this to change, and so, I just had to have this dynamic in my book. However, woman are capable of evil too, and this is why I also have female villains. Two sides to every coin! Now, I know that some people have said, or you may think, too many people like Amarah. Issues get resolved too easily. You have to keep in mind, she's NOT human! She's half Angel and could you imagine what it would be like to know an Angel? Even half of one? I would imagine they're magnetic! They would have something good, positive and light, that you would want to get close to. That's my thought behind it anyway.

I'm not sure what else to say at this point other than THANK YOU. Thank you to everyone who has gone on this journey with me and Amarah and who are still sticking around to see what happens! All of the amazing support I've received along the way has been astounding! All of the posts on social media I've seen of Awaken, all of the reviews and all of the private messages, have all meant more than I can even say! Thank you doesn't come close to portraying the gratitude I feel in my heart to each and every one of you.

My door is always open and I would love to hear from you! Come and find me on Instagram @harmonya.haun_author and let's chat!

Enjoy a sneak peek

into

Book 2 in the Amarah

Rey, Fey Warrior

Series

Dangerous Love

Dangerously In Love by Beyonce

It's only been two months since my entire life has been turned upside down. Only two short months since I learned about the hidden, magical, mystical preternatural world that exists right in front of my eyes. A world full of beauty and magic, but in the blink of an eye can turn evil and dangerous. My world. Then again, the regular human world isn't so different. The stakes are just a bit higher in The Unseen. If we fail, if we let evil win, we're not the only ones who will perish. Evil won't stop at the human world just because they're oblivious to it. If we fail, no one will survive.

I had been thrown in… no, aggressively pushed, into the deep, turbulent end of the pool. I've barely been able to keep my head above water. I still struggle to believe I have power and am capable of...only God knows what. Literally. I grew up believing I was human, and being human comes with a lot of limitations. I'm still having a hard time getting out of my head and out of my human thoughts. They hold me back and everyone is frustrated, myself included. Even if they don't say anything to my face, they don't have to, I can feel the frustration. I can see it.

I have come a long way in only two months, but demons and betrayal are unrelenting. They don't care that I still need training wheels. They aren't going to take a break and wait until I'm ready for them. Unfortunately, that's just not how the world works. Either of them. So, I work hard. I push hard in all of my training. I'm getting very good at fight training, which is weird because I've never considered myself to be a fighter. Now I'm the official Võitleja, Fey Warrior. Oh, how life throws you curveballs! I'm getting better at accessing my power, but it has so much more potential. *I* have so much more potential. That part of my training is all mental, and well...we've discussed that. So...

Some people have already played on my naivety and ignorance. Someone I let myself get vulnerable with, someone I thought I could trust with no hesitation, is now being held in a cell at Headquarters. Also, someone I thought was trying to befriend me early on, was just trying to alienate me from those that would help me the most. Turns out, she's unhappy with the Queen and wants to be the one calling the shots. Her betrayal led to several attempts on my life and the death of six Fey from the Tulekahju Family, the Fire Fey. Princess Aralyn of the Õhk Family, Air Fey, is still out there, somewhere. She's still scheming and plotting her grab at the throne and who knows what else. Yeah, I've been way too gullible and am beating myself up for it.

In all of the madness, I did manage to finally get one thing right. I've finally accepted the unnatural, magnetic connection I have with Logan instead of running away from it. I still don't understand it, he doesn't either, but it's our reality. It's our normal, and it has been one mind-blowing, glorious month since I finally got out of my head and followed my heart. We all know how foolish and reckless the heart can be, and considering my previous character misreads, my caution was necessary.

Yet with Logan, it's the complete opposite of judging a book by its cover. The connection we have lets me know the whole story, down to his core. He can't hide from me and I can't hide from him. We can literally feel each other's feelings completely.

No guessing.

No wondering.

No BS.

It's honest and pure, but can also be extremely distracting. We both have the power to block the connection when we need to. We still don't know the full possibilities of our connection, but just like everything else in my life, I'm figuring it out as I go.

I'm sitting at the kitchen island, coffee in hand, eyes only for the six-foot, muscular and flawless man standing at the stove, making us breakfast. My little dog, Griffin, also has eyes only for him, but for *very* different reasons. Logan is wearing a pair of basketball shorts, low on his hips, hugging a nice, firm ass. I know what that ass feels like under my hands when his gorgeous, naked body is on top of me. Just thinking about it sends the butterflies flying in my stomach and throbbing between my legs.

Logan turns around and catches my eye. He gives me that half-smile that means he knows exactly how he affects me, and then he slowly walks toward me. A circle birthmark and small scar on his chest, over his heart, are the only things marking his otherwise flawless body. My eyes slide lower, tracing that v until it vanished under the shorts sending my heart into fits. He spins the stool around, places one hand on each armrest, and leans that perfect body into me. His dark brown hair is tousled from sleep, but his green eyes are alert and utterly serious as he looks at me.

"You keep thinking those thoughts and I'll burn breakfast," his voice is deep and seductive and his words caress my skin. He really is perfect.

I place my coffee cup down on the counter and take my time running my hands up his arms, appreciating the muscles he works hard for. "Who needs food for breakfast anyway? I can just have *you*," I bite my lip as I look up at him.

He gently pulls my lip out from under my teeth. "You already did," he chuckles as he leans in closer.

"What about dessert?" I find his soft lips with mine.

He slips his big hands under my thighs and lifts me easily onto the island counter. The feeling of his fingers digging into my skin quickens my breaths. I wrap my legs around his trim waist, run my hands through his hair at the back of his neck, and lose myself in the kiss.

This has been my life over the past month and my only regret is that I fought it for so long. I'm entirely consumed by my feelings for Logan, and not just the physical ones, though they are always a look or word away. When we're together, nothing else matters.

Nothing.

And that's dangerous because the reality is, too much matters. There's too much at stake, too many threats, and a million responsibilities. We can't afford to be distracted. It could be way worse than a burnt breakfast. It could be fatal.

Logan is the one to pull away. He always has way more control and willpower than I do. Then again, he has had *centuries* of practice. How can a girl compete with that?

"As I was saying," he gives me that teasing half-smile and chucks my chin, "breakfast is the most important meal of the day."

He walks back over to the stove, giving me his muscled back for my viewing pleasure, and busies himself with cooking.

"Breakfast isn't the most important meal. If it was, then people wouldn't have success with intermittent fasting. Every meal is important," I sigh. Breakfast is a moot point. I'm just trying to think of anything else besides what I have planned for the day.

Logan senses my mood change, as always. "Are you sure you still want to do this? You don't have to, you know. You don't owe him anything, Amarah."

I sigh again, "I know, but I need to see him. I need to see his face and ask him why. It doesn't make sense to me. I know you don't get it, but I need to understand. I want the truth and I want closure. I can't get that if I don't go see him in person."

Logan walks over to the island with two plates, "c'mon, you need to eat."

I hop off the counter and go back to my seat. "I'm not even hungry," I grumble. I'm feeling grouchy now and it isn't fair to Logan. Then again, life's very rarely fair.

"You need your strength."

He's right. He's usually right, and I hate to admit it. He made us veggie omelets and sweet potato hash browns. It looks and smells delicious. I love that we we're both into fitness and staying healthy, most of the time. The second I take the first bite, my hunger emerges from my grumpy cave. I *am* hungry and my body needs the fuel. Damn the mind for being so stubborn sometimes.

We finish eating breakfast and cleaning up the kitchen and I head to the bedroom to get ready to leave the house. While we're home, I'm usually in a tank top and boy short style underwear. I'd switch to the unattractive, oversized sweats and long-sleeve tees for winter. We'll see how much Logan loves me then. It's late September, and it's still warm. One of the things I love about Albuquerque is that we get all four seasons, very distinctly, and we're still at the tail-end of summer.

I put on a pair of black jean shorts, a black t-shirt with white Harry Potter glasses and lightning scar, black sneakers and I'm good to go. Once upon a time, I thought I wore black to mourn my broken heart, but turns out that's just what I buy more of. As the Fey Warrior, black is the best thing to wear anyway. You can blend in and hide with the shadows at night. I even dyed my hair back to my natural dark brown. The fire red had been fierce, and I miss it, but it isn't practical.

I walk out into the living room and Logan is sitting on the couch with Griffin, waiting for me. He's wearing dark blue jeans, a red v-neck t-shirt, and black and red sneakers. The man makes t-shirts the sexiest damn thing I've ever seen. They hug his chest and arms like a second skin. The red of his shirt is the perfect contrast to his caramel skin but I don't think he could look bad in anything. His hair is combed to messy perfection. It's grown out since I met him and is longer all around. His hair has a natural curl to it and it comes down longer in the front, just above his right eyebrow.

I walk over to the couch, sit down on the arm, and lean into him. I run my fingers through his hair, "I love your hair like this."

"Really? I was thinking it needs a trim."

"No way! It's perfect." I still can't believe this gorgeous man is here with me. And it isn't just that. He *loves* me. I still have to pinch myself sometimes to make sure I'm not dreaming.

"You're perfect," he whispers as he lays a gentle kiss right below my ear. "So perfect I could *eat* you." His teeth graze against my skin causing me to sink further into him. The memory of his face between my legs earlier that morning brings a moan from my throat. Then he pulls away. "Are you ready?"

"Oh, you evil, evil, man. You're going to pay for that later." The gleam in his eyes and his devious smile says he's looking forward to it. I sigh, "I suppose. I just want to get it over with."

Logan usually drives us around, but today, I want to drive. I open the garage door and it's the perfect picture of his and hers. His black Chevy Silverado 1500 and my Black Camaro SS. We complement each other in literally every area of our lives. It's more than just our connection, it's our style, our taste in music, our personalities. It's almost like fate. We are meant to be together. Considering my background, the truth about my conception, perhaps I'm not far off in thinking that we were destined to find each other.

I pull onto I-40 heading West at a quick 70 mph. I signal over to the far-left lane and keep it at a steady 80 mph. I drive a Camaro for a reason. I love the speed but keep it safe. Again...*most* of the time. I'm not in the mood for talking, so I turn up the stereo, and Three Days Grace's song, *Right Left Wrong*, blares through the speakers. It's the perfect song for how I'm feeling about getting close to the wrong person. Music always has the words and the feel. Always.

I finally exit on Rio Grande and head towards Old Town. I find a parking spot easily, which is a miracle, and put the car in park. I'm not looking forward to confronting Andre, but I have to. I shouldn't have even waited this long. The truth is, a part of me feels guilty about using him. I didn't do it intentionally, but I did it nonetheless. I had been running away from Logan and Andre was there to comfort me and give me what I craved at the time. Someone choosing me for me, not because of some crazy connection.

It isn't fair to lead Andre on, although, in my defense, I was always upfront about my feelings for Logan. Still, feelings got involved, on both ends. I've definitely come to care for Andre. The *real* Andre, that he never showed to anyone. He hides behind jokes and flirting as a way to keep everyone at arm's length. Why? Why else? He's been hurt badly before and doesn't want it to happen again. Hence, why I'm feeling so damn guilty about being that person, but that's not the only reason why I'm here, and that's not the reason he's locked up.

Andre has been accused of being the one to tell the traitor, Aralyn, about the dragon scales. They're the Fire Fey's...*family heirloom* if you will, and they've been hiding them in secret for generations upon generations. What Andre did is a huge betrayal to his people. He's locked up for working with the traitor. The traitor who tried to have me killed! And I had let him get *very* up close and personal. He violated my trust. Hell, he lost everyone's trust, and the Andre I know, or thought I knew, would never have done that. That's why I need to talk to him. I need to know why.

"Amarah, hey, come back to me," Logan is gently shaking me.

Reality slowly comes back into focus. "Sorry. I was just thinking about everything that's happened. You know, I'm not blameless in all of this. I think that's why it's taken me so long to do this."

"What do you mean?"

"Andre fell for me and I let him. I let things go too far. I knew what he was feeling and I didn't stop it. Hell, I was confused about what I was feeling too, with our connection, Hallana and your past. I just...I wanted something *normal* and simple. I wanted to believe that's what I wanted." I shake my head and finally meet his unwavering, patient gaze, "but...the second I saw you again, I couldn't deny it. I tried," I snort. "Lord knows I *tried* to fight my feelings for you. But the second I saw you again, I turned my back on him and I let him *fall*. That wasn't fair to him."

"Are you regretting your choice to be with me?" His eyes watch my reaction closely.

I know he's asking because of all the complicated emotions he must be feeling from our connection. We're still figuring it out and emotions aren't always easy to decipher. Especially mixed and complicated ones. Still, how can men be so dumb sometimes? So insecure?

I scoff, "you're joking right? You can't *seriously* be asking me if I regret being with you."

"I can feel your regret. No BS, remember?" His eyes are guarded as he waits for my answer.

"My regret is for *hurting* Andre. For leading him on in the first place when I could have, *should* have, stopped it. I may have been confused about our link and your history but..." I lean over and reach for his face, "Logan, there was never any other option. Connection or not, I know I was always meant to be with you. You're like the sun in my sky, or in your case, the moon," I smile. "Just one look from you, one smile, and I melt. The way I feel about you, honestly, scares me sometimes. I feel like I'll never be able to get enough of you, and with all the danger in our lives, the only thing that scares me is the thought of losing you. I love you Logan Lewis, and I need you to know that."

"You're not going to lose me." He brushes my hair out of my face, his gaze heavy and heated, "Amarah Rey Andrews, I am so in love with you."

We both lean in for the kiss and my heart feels like a stone in my chest. It's so full of love, and need, and emotion, it's almost painful. This man is everything to me, and I barely know him. It scares me how much I loved him, need him, want him. I'm scared of not only losing him but also losing myself. Love is a dangerous, dangerous thing, and I'm dangerously in love with him. I get it, Queen Bey, I get.

www.ingramcontent.com/pod-product-compliance
Lightning Source LLC
Chambersburg PA
CBHW030541260626
47157CB00006B/2144